BEWARE, KZIN,
OF MONKEY-BOY WRATH . . .

Sylvia was watching the holo walls, the three that showed the face of Mercury: rocks blazing like coals in fading twilight. The fourth holo wall we kept changing. Just then it showed a view up the trunk into the waving branches of the tremendous redwood they've been growing for three hundred years, in Hovestraydt City on the Moon.

Suddenly, Sylvia was shaking my shoulder. I heard it as soon as I stopped talking. *"Tombaugh Station relayed this picture, the last broadcast from the* Fantasy Prince. *Once again, the* Fantasy Prince *has apparently been—"*

Starscape glowed within the fourth holo wall. Something came out of nowhere, moving hellishly fast, and stopped so quickly that it might have been a toy. It was egg-shaped, studded with weapons.

Later, I decided that the warcats would have to be deep in the Solar System before the asteroid mining setup can be any deterrent. Then one or another warcat ship will find streams of slag sprayed across its path, impacting at comet speeds.

For my part, I worked on the computer. We kept the program relatively simple. Until and unless the warcats destroy something that's being pushed by a lifting laser from Mercury, nothing will happen. The warcats must condemn themselves. Then the affected laser will lock onto the warcat ship . . . and so will every Mercury laser that's getting sunlight.

If the warcats can be persuaded that Sol system is defended, maybe they'll give us time t‑ ‑ ‑ ‑ ‑ ‑ ‑

We might get one‑ ‑ ‑ ‑ ‑

It might be worth‑ ‑ ‑ ‑ ‑

—from ' ‑ ‑ ‑ ‑ ‑ ‑ ven

THE MAN-KZIN WARS SERIES
Created by Larry Niven

THE BEST OF ALL POSSIBLE WARS

THE BEST OF THE
MAN-KZIN WARS

CREATED BY
LARRY NIVEN

THE BEST OF ALL POSSIBLE WARS

Copyright © 1998 by Larry Niven. "Introduction" copyright ©1986 by Larry Niven. "The Warriors" copyright ©1990. Published in *The Man-Kzin Wars*. "Madness Has Its Place" copyright ©1990 by Larry Niven. Published in *Man-Kzin Wars III*. "The Man Who Would Be Kzin" copyright ©1991 by Greg Bear and S.M. Stirling. Published in *Man-Kzin Wars IV*. "In the Hall of the Mountain King" copyright ©1992 by Jerry Pournelle and S.M. Stirling. Published in *Man-Kzin Wars V*.

A Baen Books Original

Baen Publishing Enterprises
P.O. Box 1403
Riverdale, NY 10471

ISBN: 0-671-87879-4

Cover art by Stephen Hickman

First printing, June 1998

Distributed by Simon & Schuster
1230 Avenue of the Americas
New York, NY 10020

Printed in the United States of America

CONTENTS

CONTENTS

Introduction

Larry Niven

"The Warriors" wasn't just the first tale of the kzinti. It was the first story I ever offered for sale. I was daydreaming in math class, as usual, and I realized that I'd shaped a complete story. So I wrote it down, and bought some magazines to get the editorial addresses, and started it circulating.

It was years before anyone bought it. By then I'd rewritten it countless times, trying out what I was learning from my correspondence writing course. Fred Pohl (editor of *Galaxy* and *Worlds of If* in those days) saw it often enough that he eventually wrote, "I think this can be improved . . . but maybe you're tired of reworking it, so I'll buy it as is . . ." It was probably his title, too.

The kzinti look a little blurred here, don't they? I mean, if you've known them elsewhere. Subsequently they changed in several ways.

I learned to answer John W. Campbell's challenge: "Show me something that thinks as well as a man, or better, but not like a man." The kzinti took on more detail, gained greater consistency and lost some of their resemblance to humanity. They were born as one of a thousand catlike aliens in science fiction. As I learned how to make an alien from basic principles, body and mind and soul, the kzinti became more themselves.

At the same time they were changing in another way, evolving over several centuries. The Man-Kzin Wars changed them far more than they changed mankind, because the wars killed off the least intelligent and most aggressive.

This book was conceived in a casual encounter. Marilyn and I were driving to a Nebula Awards banquet with Jim Baen in the back seat. She drove, we talked . . .

I knew about franchise universes. Jim and I had edited *The Magic May Return* and *More Magic*, tales set in the *Magic Goes Away* universe but written by friends whom we had invited in. I had played in neighbors' playgrounds, too. "A Snowflake Falls" used Saberhagen's "Berserkers," by invitation. I'd written a tale set at Lord Dunsany's "edge of the world," and a report on the year the Necronomicon hit the college campuses in paperback, and a study of Superman's fertility problems.

I've never been in a war, nor in any of the armed forces. Wars have happened and may happen again in most of my series universes, including Known Space, but you'll never *see* them. I lack the experience. Here are a couple of centuries of Known Space that are dark to me.

By the time we parked, Jim and I had agreed to open up the Man-Kzin Wars period of Known Space.

Any writer good enough to be invited to play in my universe will have demonstrated that he can make his own. Would anyone accept my offer? I worried also that intruders might mess up the playground, by violating my background assumptions.

But I did want to read more tales of Known Space . . . and I hadn't written any in years.

For the Warlock's era I had written a "bible," a set of assumptions, list of available characters, backgrounds, a few story ideas. For the Man-Kzin Wars the "bible" was already written, by John Hewitt for the Chaosium role-playing game, "Ringworld." I photocopied the appropriate pages, with his permission and Chaosium's.

I did not anticipate what happened.

I had to turn down one story outline and one completed story. It didn't matter. Poul and Dean both turned in 40,000-word novellas! And now they're talking about sequels.

It's as if you can't say anything *short* in the Known Space universe.

I guess I'm flattered. And I surely got my wish. These stories read like good Poul Anderson, and good Dean Ing, and good Niven; and Niven couldn't have written them.

from *Man-Kzin Wars*, Vol. I

THE WARRIORS

•

Larry Niven

"I'm sure they saw us coming," the Alien-Technologies Officer persisted. "Do you see that ring, sir?"

The silvery image of the enemy ship almost tilled the viewer. It showed as a broad, wide ring encircling a cylindrical axis, like a mechanical pencil floating inside a platinum bracelet. A tinned craft projected from the pointed end of the axial section. Angular letters ran down the axis, totally unlike the dots-and-commas of kzinti script.

"Of course I see it," said the Captain.

"It was rotating when we first picked them up. It stopped when we got within two hundred thousand miles, and it hasn't moved since."

The Captain flicked his tail back and forth, gently, thoughtfully, like a pink lash. "You worry me," he commented. "If they know we're here, why haven't they tried to get away? Are they so sure they can beat us?" He whirled to face the A-T Officer. "Should we be running?"

"No, sir! I don't know why they're still here, but they can't have anything to be confident about. That's one of the most primitive spacecraft I've ever seen." He moved his claw about on the screen, pointing as he talked.

"The outer shell is an iron alloy. The rotating ring is a method of imitating gravity by using centripetal force.

So they don't have the gravity planer. In fact they're probably using a reaction drive."

The Captain's catlike ears went up. "But we're lightyears from the nearest star!"

"They must have a better reaction drive than we ever developed. We had the gravity planer before we needed one that good."

There was a buzzing sound from the big control board. "Enter," said the Captain.

The Weapons Officer fell up through the entrance hatch and came to attention, "Sir, we have all weapons trained on the enemy."

"Good." The Captain swung around. "A-T, how sure are you that they aren't a threat to us?"

The A-T Officer bared sharply pointed teeth. "I don't see how they could be, sir."

"Good. Weapons, keep all your guns ready to fire, but don't use them unless I give the order. I'll have the ears of the man who destroys that ship without orders. I want to take it intact."

"Yes, sir."

"Where's the Telepath?"

"He's on his way, sir. He was asleep."

"He's always asleep. Tell him to get his tail up here."

The Weapons Officer saluted, turned, and dropped through the exit hole.

"Captain?"

The A-T Officer was standing by the viewer, which now showed the ringed end of the alien ship. He pointed to the mirror-bright end of the axial cylinder. "It looks like that end was designed to project light. That would make it a photon drive, sir."

The Captain considered. "Could it be a signal device?"

"Urrrrr . . . Yes, sir."

'Then don't jump to conclusions."

Like a piece of toast, the Telepath popped up through

the entrance hatch. He came to exaggerated attention. "Reporting as ordered, sir."

"You omitted to buzz for entrance."

"Sorry, sir." The lighted viewscreen caught the Telepath's eye and he padded over for a better look, forgetting that he was at attention. The A-T Officer winced, wishing he were somewhere else.

The Telepath's eyes were violet around the edges. His pink tail hung limp. As usual, he looked as if he were dying for lack of sleep. His fur was flattened along the side he slept on; he hadn't even bothered to brush it. The effect was far from the ideal of a Conquest Warrior as one can get and still be a member of the kzin species. The wonder was that the Captain had not yet murdered him.

He never would, of course. Telepaths were too rare, too valuable, and—understandably—too emotionally unstable. The Captain always kept his temper with the Telepath. At times like this it was the innocent bystander who stood to lose his rank or his ears at the clank of a falling molecule.

"That's an enemy ship we've tracked down," the Captain was saying. "We'd like to get some information from them. Would you read their minds for us?"

"Yes, sir." The Telepath's voice showed his instant misery, but he knew better than to protest. He left the screen and sank into a chair. Slowly his ears folded into tight knots, his pupils contracted, and his ratlike tail went limp as flannel.

The world of the eleventh sense pushed in on him.

He caught the Captain's thought: ". . . sloppy civilian get of a sthondat . . ." and frantically tuned it out. He hated the Captain's mind. He found other minds aboard ship, isolated and blanked them out one by one. Now there were none left. There was only unconsciousness and chaos.

Chaos was not empty. Something was thinking strange and disturbing thoughts.

The Telepath forced himself to listen.

Steve Weaver floated bonelessly near a wall of the radio room. He was blond, blue-eyed, and big, and he could often be seen as he was now, relaxed but completely motionless, as if there were some very good reason why he shouldn't even blink. A streamer of smoke drifted from his left hand and crossed the room to bury itself in the air vent.

"That's that," Ann Harrison said wearily. She flicked four switches in the bank of radio controls. At each click a small light went out.

"You can't get them?"

"Right. I'll bet they don't even have a radio." Ann released her chair net and stretched out into a five-pointed star. "I've left the receiver on, with the volume up, in case they try to get us later. Man, that feels good!" Abruptly she curled into a tight ball. She had been crouched at the communications bank for more than an hour. Ann might have been Steve's twin; she was almost as tall as he was, had the same color hair and eyes, and the flat muscles of conscientious exercise showed beneath her blue falling jumper as she flexed.

Steve snapped his cigarette butt at the air conditioner, moving only his fingers. "Okay. What have they got?"

Ann looked startled. "*I* don't know."

"Think of it as a puzzle. They don't have a radio. How might they talk to each other? How can we check on our guesses? We assume they're trying to reach us, of course.

"Yes, of course."

"Think about it, Ann. Get Jim thinking about it, too." Jim Davis was her husband that year, and the ship's doctor full time. "You're the girl most likely to succeed. Have a smog stick?"

"Please."

Steve pushed his cigarette ration across the room. "Take a few. I've got to go.

The depleted package came whizzing back. "Thanks," said Ann.

"Let me know if anything happens, will you? Or if you think of anything."

"I will. And fear not, Steve, something's bound to turn up. They must be trying just as hard as we are."

Every compartment in the personnel ring opened into the narrow doughnut-shaped hall which ran around the ring's forward rim. Steve pushed himself into the hall, jockeyed to contact the floor, and pushed. From there it was easy going. The floor curved up to meet him, and he proceeded down the hall like a swimming frog. Of the twelve men and women on the *Angel's Pencil*, Steve was best at this; for Steve was a Belter, and the others were all flatlanders, Earthborn.

Ann probably wouldn't think of anything, he guessed. It wasn't that she wasn't intelligent. She didn't have the curiosity, the sheer love of solving puzzles. Only he and Jim Davis—

He was going too fast, and not concentrating. He almost crashed into Sue Bhang as she appeared below the curve of the ceiling.

They managed to stop themselves against the walls. "Hi, jaywalker," said Sue.

"Hi, Sue. Where you headed?"

"Radio room. You?"

"I thought I'd check the drive systems again. Not that we're likely to need the drive, but it can't hurt to be certain."

"You'd go twitchy without something to do, wouldn't you?" She cocked her head to one side, as always when she had questions. "Steve, when are you going to rotate us again? I can't seem to get used to falling."

But she looked like she'd been born falling, he thought. Her small, slender form was meant for flying; gravity should never have touched her. "When I'm sure we won't need the drive. We might as well stay ready 'til then. Because I'm hoping you'll change back to a skirt."

She laughed, pleased. "Then you can turn it off. I'm not changing, and we won't be moving. Abel says the other ship did two hundred gee when it matched courses with us. How many can the *Angel's Pencil* do?"

Steve looked awed. "Just point zero five. And I was thinking of chasing them! Well, maybe we can be the ones to open communications. I just came from the radio room, by the way. Ann can't get anything."

"Too bad."

"We'll just have to wait."

"Steve, you're always so impatient. Do Belters always move at a run? Come here." She took a handhold and pulled him over to one of the thick windows which lined the forward side of the corridor. "There they are," she said, pointing out.

The star was both duller and larger than those around it. Among points which glowed arc-lamp blue-white with the Doppler shift, the alien ship showed as a dull red disk.

"I looked at it through the telescope," said Steve. "There are lumps and ridges all over it. And there's a circle of green dots and commas painted on one side. Looked like writing."

"How long have we been waiting to meet them? Five hundred thousand years? Well, there they are. Relax. They won't go away." Sue gazed out the window, her whole attention on the dull red circle, her gleaming jet hair floating out around her head. "The first aliens. I wonder what they'll be like."

"It's anyone's guess. They must be pretty strong to take punishment like that, unless they have some kind of acceleration shield, but free fall doesn't bother them either. That ship isn't designed to spin." He was staring intently, out at the stars, his big form characteristically motionless, his expression somber. Abruptly he said, "Sue, I'm worried."

"About what?"

"Suppose they're hostile?"

"Hostile?" She tasted the unfamiliar word, decided she didn't like it.

"After all, we know nothing about them. Suppose they want to fight? We'd—"

She gasped. Steve flinched before the horror in her face. "What—what put that idea in your head?"

"I'm sorry I shocked you, Sue."

"Oh, don't worry about that, but *why?* Did—shh."

Jim Davis had come into view. The *Angel's Pencil* had left Earth when he was twenty-seven; now he was a slightly paunchy thirty-eight, the oldest man on board, an amiable man with abnormally long, delicate fingers. His grandfather, with the same hands, had been a world-famous surgeon. Nowadays surgery was normally done by autodocs, and the arachnodactyls were to Davis merely an affliction. He bounced by, walking on magnetic sandals, looking like a comedian as he bobbed about the magnetic plates. "Hi, group," he called as he went by.

"Hello, Jim." Sue's voice was strained. She waited until he was out of sight before she spoke again.

Hoarsely she whispered, "Did you fight in the Belt?" She didn't really believe it; it was merely the worst thing she could think of.

Vehemently Steve snapped, "No!" Then, reluctantly, he added, "But it did happen occasionally." Quickly he tried to explain. "The trouble was that all the doctors, including the psychists, were at the big bases, like Ceres. It was the only way they could help the people who needed them—be where the miners could find them. But all the danger was out in the rocks.

"You noticed a habit of mine once. I never make gestures. All Belters have that trait. It's because on a small mining ship you could hit something waving your arms around. Something like the airlock button."

"Sometimes it's almost eerie. You don't move for minutes at a time."

"There's always tension out in the rocks. Sometimes a miner would see too much danger and boredom and frustration, too much cramping inside and too much room outside, and he wouldn't get to a psychist in time. He'd pick a fight in a bar. I saw it happen once. The guy was using his hands like mallets."

Steve had been looking far into the past. Now he turned back to Sue. She looked white and sick, like a novice nurse standing up to her first really bad case. His ears began to turn red. "Sorry," he said miserably.

She felt like running; she was as embarrassed as he was. Instead she said, and tried to mean it, "It doesn't matter. So you think the people in the other ship might want to, uh, make war?"

He nodded.

"Did you have history-of-Earth courses?"

He smiled ruefully. "No, I couldn't qualify. Sometimes I wonder how many people do."

"About one in twelve."

"That's not many."

"People in general have trouble assimilating the facts of life about their ancestors. You probably know that there used to be wars before—hmmm—three hundred years ago, but do you know what war is? Can you visualize one? Can you see a fusion electric point deliberately built to explode in the middle of the city? Do you know what a concentration camp is? A limited action? You probably think murder ended with war. Well, it didn't.

The last murder occurred in twenty-one something, just a hundred and sixty years ago.

"Anyone who says human nature can't be changed is out of his head. To make it stick, he's got to define human nature—and he can't. Three things gave us our present peaceful civilization, and each one was a technological change." Sue's voice had taken on a dry, remote lecture-hall tone, like the voice on a teacher tape. "One was the development of psychistry beyond the alchemist stage. Another was the full development of land for food production. The third was the Fertility Restriction Laws and the annual contraceptive shots. They gave us room to breathe. Maybe Belt mining and the stellar colonies had something to do with it, too; they gave us an inanimate enemy. Even the historians argue about that one.

"Here's the delicate point I'm trying to nail down." Sue rapped on the window. "Look at that spacecraft. It has enough power to move it around like a mail missile and enough fuel to move it up to our point eight light—right?"

"Right."

"—with plenty of power left for maneuvering. It's a better ship than ours. If they've had time to learn how to build a ship like that, they've had time to build up their own versions of psychistry, modern food production, contraception, economic theory, everything they need to abolish war. See?"

Steve had to smile at her earnestness. "Sure, Sue, it makes sense. But that guy in the bar came from our culture, and he was hostile enough. If we can't understand how he thinks, how can we guess about the mind of something whose very chemical makeup we can't guess at yet?"

"It's sentient. It builds tools."

"Right."

"And if Jim hears you talking like this, you'll be in psychistry treatment."

"That's the best argument you've given me," Steve grinned, and stroked her under the ear with two fingertips. He felt her go suddenly stiff, saw the pain in her face; and at the same time his own pain struck, a real tiger of a headache, as if his brain were trying to swell beyond his skull.

"I've got them, sir," the Telepath said blurrily. "Ask me anything."

The Captain hurried, knowing that the Telepath couldn't stand this for long. "How do they power their ship?"

"It's a light-pressure drive powered by incomplete hydrogen fusion. They use an electromagnetic ramscoop to get their own hydrogen from space."

"Clever . . . Can they get away from us?"

"No. Their drive is on idle, ready to go, but it won't help them. It's pitifully weak."

"What kind of weapons do they have?"

The Telepath remained silent for a long time. The others waited patiently for his answer. There was sound in the control dome, but it was the kind of sound one learns not to hear: the whine of heavy current, the muted purr of voices from below, the strange sound like continuously ripping cloth which came from the gravity motors.

"None at all, sir." The Kzin's voice became clearer; his hypnotic relaxation was broken by muscle twitches. He twisted as if in a nightmare. "Nothing aboard ship, not even a knife or a club. Wait, they've got cooking knives. But that's all they use them for. They don't fight."

"They don't fight?"

"No, sir. They don't expect us to fight, either. The idea has occurred to three of them, and each has dismissed it from his mind."

"But why?" the Captain asked, knowing the question was irrelevant, unable to hold it back.

"I don't know, sir. It's a science they use, or a religion. I don't understand," the Telepath whimpered. "I don't understand at all."

Which must be tough on him, the Captain thought. Completely alien thoughts . . . "What are they doing now?"

"Waiting for us to talk to them. They tried to talk to us, and they think we must be trying just as hard."

"But why?—never mind, it's not important. Can they be killed by heat?"

"Yes, sir."

"Break contact."

The Telepath shook his head violently. He looked like he'd been in a washing machine. The Captain touched a sensitized surface and bellowed, "Weapons Officer!"

"Here."

"Use the inductors on the enemy ship."

"But, sir! They're so slow! What if the alien attacks?"

"Don't argue with me, you—" Snarling, the Captain delivered an impassioned monologue on the virtues of unquestioning obedience. When he switched off, the Alien Technologies Officer was back at the viewer and the Telepath had gone to sleep.

The Captain purred happily, wishing that they were all this easy.

When the occupants had been killed by heat he would take the ship. He could tell everything he needed to know about their planet by examining their life-support system. He could locate it by tracing the ship's trajectory. Probably they hadn't even taken evasive action!

If they came from a Kzin-like world it would become a Kzin world. And he, as Conquest Leader, would command one percent of its wealth for the rest of his life! Truly, the future looked rich. No longer would he be called by his profession. He would bear a *name* . . .

"Incidental information," said the A-T Officer. "The ship was generating one and twelve sixty-fourth gee before it stopped rotating."

"Little heavy," the Captain mused. "Might be too much air, but it should be easy to Kzinform it. A-T, we find the strangest life forms. Remember the Chunquen?"

"Both sexes were sentient. They fought constantly."

"And that funny religion on Altair One. They thought they could travel in time."

"Yes, sir. When we landed the infantry they were all gone."

"They must have all committed suicide with disintegrators. But why? They knew we only wanted slaves. And I'm still trying to figure out how they got rid of the disintegrators afterward."

"Some beings," said the A-T Officer, "will do anything to keep their beliefs."

Eleven years beyond Pluto, eight years from her destination, the fourth colony ship to We Made It fell between the stars. Before her the stars were green-white and blue-white, blazing points against nascent black. Behind they were sparse, dying red embers. To the sides the constellations were strangely flattened. The universe was shorter than it had been.

For awhile Jim Davis was very busy. Everyone, including himself, had a throbbing blinding headache. To each patient, Dr. Davis handed a tiny pink pill from the dispenser slot of the huge autodoc which covered the back wall of the infirmary. They milled outside the door waiting for the pills to take effect, looking like a full-fledged mob in the narrow corridor; and then someone thought it would be a good idea to go to the lounge, and everyone followed him. It was an unusually silent mob. Nobody felt like talking while the pain was with them. Even the sound of magnetic sandals was lost in the plastic pile rug.

Steve saw Jim Davis behind him. "Hey, Doc," he called softly. "How long before the pain stops?"

"Mine's gone away. You got your pills a little after I did, right?"

"Right. Thanks, Doc."

They didn't take pain well, these people. They were unused to it.

In single file they walked or floated into the lounge. Low-pitched conversations started. People took couches, using the sticky plastic strips on their falling jumpers. Others stood or floated near walls. The lounge was big enough to hold them all in comfort.

Steve wriggled near the ceiling, trying to pull on his sandals.

"I hope they don't try that again," he heard Sue say. "It hurt."

"Try what?" Someone Steve didn't recognize, half-listening as he was.

"Whatever they tried. Telepathy, perhaps."

"No. I don't believe in telepathy. Could they have set up ultrasonic vibrations in the walls?"

Steve had his sandals on. He left the magnets turned off.

". . . a cold beer. Do you realize we'll never taste beer again?" Jim Davis' voice.

"I miss waterskiing." Ann Harrison sounded wistful. "The feel of a pusher unit shoving into the small of your back, the water beating against your feet, the sun . . ."

Steve pushed himself toward them. "Taboo subject," he called.

"We're on it anyway," Jim boomed cheerfully. "Unless you'd rather talk about the alien, which everyone else is doing. I'd rather drop it for the moment. What's your greatest regret at leaving Earth?"

"Only that I didn't stay long enough to really see it."

"Oh, of course." Jim suddenly remembered the drinking bulb in his hand. He drank from it, hospitably passed it to Steve.

"This waiting makes me restless," said Steve. "What are they likely to try next? Shake the ship in Morse code?"

Jim smiled. "Maybe they won't try anything next. They may give up and leave."

"Oh, I hope not!" said Ann.

"Would that be so bad?"

Steve had a start. What was Jim thinking?

"Of course!" Ann protested. "We've got to find out what they're like! And think of what they can teach us, Jim!"

When conversation got controversial it was good manners to change the subject. "Say," said Steve, "I happened to notice the wall was warm when I pushed off. Is that good or bad?"

"That's funny. It should be cold, if anything," said Jim. "There's nothing out there but starlight. Except—" A most peculiar expression flitted across his face. He drew his feet up and touched the magnetic soles with his fingertips.

"Eeeee! Jim! Jim!"

Steve tried to whirl around and got nowhere. That was Sue! He switched on his shoes, thumped to the floor, and went to help.

Sue was surrounded by bewildered people. They split to let Jim Davis through, and he tried to lead her out of the lounge. He looked frightened. Sue was moaning and thrashing, paying no attention to his efforts.

Steve pushed through to her. "All the metal is heating up," Davis shouted. "We've got to get her hearing aid out."

"Infirmary," Sue shouted.

Four of them took Sue down the hall to the infirmary. She was still crying and struggling feebly when they got her in, but Jim was there ahead of them with a spray hypo. He used it and she went to sleep.

The four watched anxiously as Jim went to work. The autodoc would have taken precious time for diagnosis. Jim operated by hand. He was able to do a fast job, for the tiny instrument was buried just below the skin behind her ear. Still, the scalpel must have burned his fingers before he was done. Steve could feel the growing warmth against the soles of his feet.

Did the aliens know what they were doing?

Did it matter? The ship was being attacked. His ship.

Steve slipped into the corridor and ran for the control room. Running on magnetic soles, he looked like a terrified penguin, but he moved fast. He knew he might be making a terrible mistake; the aliens might be trying desperately to reach the *Angel's Pencil*; he would never know. They had to be stopped before everyone was roasted.

The shoes burned his feet. He whimpered with the pain, but otherwise ignored it. The air burned in his mouth and throat. Even his teeth were hot.

He had to wrap his shirt around his hands to open the control-room door. The pain in his feet was unbearable; he tore off his sandals and swam to the control board. He kept his shirt over his hands to work the controls. A twist of a large white knob turned the drive on full, and he slipped into the pilot seat before the gentle light pressure could build up.

He turned to the rear-view telescope. It was aimed at the solar system, for the drive could be used for messages at this distance. He set it for short range and began to turn the ship.

❖   ❖   ❖

The enemy ship glowed in the high infrared.

"It will take longer to heat the crew-carrying section," reported the Alien Technologies Officer. "They'll have temperature control there."

"That's all right. When you think they should all be dead, wake up the Telepath and have him check." The Captain continued to brush his fur, killing time. "You know, if they hadn't been so completely helpless I wouldn't have tried this slow method. I'd have cut the ring free of the motor section first. Maybe I should have done that anyway. Safer."

The A-T Officer wanted all the credit he could get. "Sir, they couldn't have any big weapons. There isn't room. With a reaction drive, the motor and the fuel tanks take up most of the available space."

The other ship began to turn away from its tormentor. Its drive end glowed red.

"They're trying to get away," the Captain said, as the glowing end swung toward them. "Are you sure they can't?"

"Yes, sir. That light drive won't take them anywhere."

The Captain purred thoughtfully. "What would happen if the light hit our ship?"

"Just a bright light, I think. The lens is flat, so it must be emitting a very wide beam. They'd need a parabolic reflector to be dangerous. Unless—" His ears went straight up.

"Unless what?" The Captain spoke softly, demandingly.

"A laser. But that's all right, sir. They don't have any weapons."

The Captain sprang at the control board. "Stupid!" he spat. "They don't know weapons from sthondat blood. Weapons Officer! How could a telepath find out what they don't know? WEAPONS OFFICER!"

"Here, sir."

"Burn—"

An awful light shone in the control dome. The Captain burst into flame, then blew out as the air left through a glowing split in the dome.

Steve was lying on his back. The ship was spinning again, pressing him into what felt like his own bunk.

He opened his eyes.

Jim Davis crossed the room and stood over him. "You awake?"

Steve sat bolt upright, his eyes wide.

"Easy." Jim's gray eyes were concerned.

Steve blinked up at him. "What happened?" he asked, and discovered how hoarse he was.

Jim sat down in one of the chairs. "You tell me. We tried to get to the control room when the ship started moving. Why didn't you ring the strap-down? You turned off the drive just as Ann came through the door. Then you fainted."

"How about the other ship?" Steve tried to repress the urgency in his voice, and couldn't.

"Some of the others are over there now, examining the wreckage." Steve felt his heart stop. "I guess I was afraid from the start that alien ship was dangerous. I'm more psychist than emdee, and I qualified for history class, so maybe I know more than is good for me about human nature. Too much to think that beings with space travel will automatically be peaceful. I tried to think so, but they aren't. They've got things any self-respecting human being would be ashamed to have nightmares about. Bomb missiles, fusion bombs, lasers, that induction injector they used on us. And antimissiles. You know what that means? They've got enemies like themselves, Steve. Maybe nearby."

"So I killed them." The room seemed to swoop around him, but his voice came out miraculously steady.

"You saved the ship."

"It was an accident. I was trying to get us away."

"No, you weren't." Davis' accusation was as casual as if he were describing the chemical makeup of urea. "That ship was four hundred miles away. You would have had to sight on it with a telescope to hit it. You knew what you were doing, too, because you turned off the drive as soon as you'd burned through the ship."

Steve's back muscles would no longer support him. He flopped back to horizontal. "All right, you know," he told the ceiling. "Do the others?"

"I doubt it. Killing in self-defense is too far outside their experience. I think Sue's guessed."

"Oooo."

"If she has, she's taking it well," Davis said briskly. "Better than most of them will, when they find out the universe is full of warriors. This is the end of the world, Steve."

"What?"

"I'm being theatrical. But it is. Three hundred years of the peaceful life for everyone. They'll call it the Golden Age. No starvation, no war, no physical sickness other than senescence, no permanent mental sickness at all, even by our rigid standards. When someone over fourteen tries to use his fist on someone else we say he's sick, and we cure him. And now it's over. Peace isn't a stable condition, not for us. Maybe not for anything that lives."

"Can I see the ship from here?"

"Yes. It's just behind us."

Steve rolled out of bed, went to the window.

Someone had steered the ships much closer together. The kzinti ship was a huge red sphere with ugly projections scattered at seeming random over the hull. The beam had sliced it into two unequal halves, sliced it like an ax through an egg. Steve watched, unable to turn aside, as the big half rotated to show its honeycombed interior.

"In a little while," said Jim, "the men will be coming back. They'll be frightened. Someone will probably insist that we arm ourselves against the next attacks, using weapons from the other ship. I'll have to agree with him.

"Maybe they'll think I'm sick myself. Maybe I am. But it's the kind of sickness we'll need." Jim looked desperately unhappy. "We're going to become an armed society. And of course we'll have to warn the Earth . . ."

MADNESS HAS ITS PLACE

•

Larry Niven

• **CHAPTER ONE**

A lucky few of us know the good days before they're gone.

I remember my eighties. My job kept me in shape, and gave me enough variety to keep my mind occupied. My love life was imperfect but interesting. Modern medicine makes the old fairy tales look insipid; I almost never worried about my health.

Those were the good days, and I knew them. I could remember worse.

I can remember when my memory was better too. That's what this file is for. I keep it updated for that reason, and also to maintain my sense of purpose.

The Monobloc had been a singles bar since the 2320s.

In the '30s I'd been a regular. I'd found Charlotte there. We held our wedding reception at the Monobloc, then dropped out for twenty-eight years. My first marriage, hers too, both in our forties. After the children grew up and moved away, after Charlotte left me too, I came back.

The place was much changed.

I remembered a couple of hundred bottles in the

hologram bar display. Now the display was twice as large and seemed more realistic—better equipment, maybe—but only a score of bottles in the middle were liquors. The rest were flavored or carbonated water, high-energy drinks, electrolytes, a thousand kinds of tea; food to match, raw vegetables and fruits kept fresh by high-tech means, arrayed with low-cholesterol dips; bran in every conceivable form short of injections.

The Monobloc had swallowed its neighbors. It was bigger, with curtained alcoves, and a small gym upstairs for working out or for dating.

Herbert and Tina Schroeder still owned the place. Their marriage had been open in the '30s. They'd aged since. So had their clientele. Some of us had married or drifted away or died of alcoholism; but word of mouth and the Velvet Net had maintained a continuous tradition. Twenty-eight years later they looked better than ever . . . wrinkled, of course, but lean and muscular, both ready for the Gray Olympics. Tina let me know before I could ask: she and Herb were lockstepped now.

To me it was like coming home.

For the next twelve years the Monobloc was an intermittent part of my life.

I would find a lady, or she would find me, and we'd drop out. Or we'd visit the Monobloc and sometimes trade partners; and one evening we'd go together and leave separately. I was not evading marriage. Every woman I found worth knowing, ultimately seemed to want to know someone else.

I was nearly bald even then. Thick white hair covered my arms and legs and torso, as if my head hairs had migrated. Twelve years of running construction robots had turned me burly. From time to time some muscular lady would look me over and claim me. I had no trouble finding company.

But company never stayed. Had I become dull? The notion struck me as funny.

I had settled myself alone at a table for two, early on a Thursday evening in 2375. The Monobloc was half empty. The earlies were all keeping one eye on the door when Anton Brillov came in.

Anton was shorter than me, and much narrower, with a face like an axe. I hadn't see him in thirteen years. Still, I'd mentioned the Monobloc once or twice; he must have remembered.

I semaphored my arms. Anton squinted, then came over, exaggeratedly cautious until he saw who it was.

"Jack Strather!"

"Hi, Anton. So you decided to try the place?"

"Yah." He sat. "You look good." He looked a moment longer and said, "Relaxed. Placid. How's Charlotte?"

"Left me after I retired. Just under a year after. There was too much of me around and I . . . maybe I was too placid? Anyway. How are you?"

"Fine."

Twitchy. Anton looked twitchy. I was amused. "Still with the Holy Office?"

"Only citizens call it that, Jack."

"I'm a citizen. Still gives me a kick. How's your chemistry?"

Anton knew what I meant and didn't pretend otherwise. "I'm okay. I'm down."

"Kid, you're looking over both shoulders at once."

Anton managed a credible laugh. "I'm not the kid any more. I'm a weekly."

The ARM had made me a weekly at forty-eight. They couldn't turn me loose at the end of the day any more, because my body chemistry couldn't shift fast enough. So they kept me in the ARM building Monday through Thursday, and gave me all of Thursday afternoon to shed the schitz madness. Twenty years of that and I was even less flexible, so they retired me.

I said, "You do have to remember. When you're in the ARM building, you're a paranoid schizophrenic. You have to be able to file that when you're outside."

"*Hah*. How can anyone—"

"You get used to the schitz. After I quit, the difference was *amazing*. No fears, no tension, no ambition."

"No Charlotte?"

"Well . . . I turned boring. And what are you doing here?"

Anton looked around him. "Much the same thing you are, I guess. Jack, am I the youngest one here?"

"Maybe." I looked around, double-checking. A woman was distracting me, though I could see only her back and a flash of a laughing profile. Her back was slender and strong, and a thick white braid ran down her spine, centered, two and a half feet of clean, thick white hair. She was in animated conversation with a blond companion of Anton's age plus a few.

But they were at a table for two: they weren't inviting company. I forced my attention back. "We're gray singles, Anton. The young ones tend to get the message quick. We're slower than we used to be. We *date*. You want to order?"

Alcohol wasn't popular here. Anton must have noticed, but he ordered guava juice and vodka and drank as if he needed it. This looked worse than Thursday jitters. I let him half finish, then said, "Assuming you can tell me—"

"I don't know anything."

"I know the feeling. What *should* you know?"

A tension eased behind Anton's eyes. "There was a message from the *Angel's Pencil*."

"*Pencil* . . . oh." My mental reflexes had slowed down. The *Angel's Pencil* had departed twenty years ago for . . .

was it Epsilon Eridani? "Come on, kid, it'll be in the boob cubes before you have quite finished speaking. Anything from deep space is public property."

"*Hah!* No. It's restricted. I haven't seen it myself. Only a reference, and it must be more than ten years old."

That was peculiar. And if the Belt stations hadn't spread the news through the solar system, *that* was peculiar. No wonder Anton was antsy. ARMs react that way to puzzles.

Anton seemed to jerk himself back to here and now, back to the gray singles regime. "Am I cramping your style?"

"No problem. Nobody hurries in the Monobloc. If you see someone you like—" My fingers danced over lighted symbols on the rim of the table. "This gets you a map. Locate where she's sitting, put the cursor on it. That gets you a display . . . hmm."

I'd set the cursor on the white-haired lady. I liked the readout. "Phoebe Garrison, seventy-nine, eleven or twelve years older than you. Straight. Won a Second in the Gray Jumps last year . . . that's the America's Skiing Matches for seventy and over. She could kick your tail if you don't watch your manners. It says she's smarter than we are, too.

"Point is, she can check you out the same way. Or me. And she probably found this place through the Velvet Net, which is the computer network for unlocked lifestyles."

"So. Two males sitting together—"

"Anyone who thinks we're bent can check if she cares enough. Bends don't come to the Monobloc anyway. But if we want company, we should move to a bigger table."

We did that. I caught Phoebe Garrison's companion's eye. They played with their table controls, discussed, and presently wandered over.

Dinner turned into a carouse. Alcohol was involved, but we'd left the Monobloc by then. When we split up, Anton was with Michiko. I went home with Phoebe.

Phoebe had fine legs, as I'd anticipated, though both knees were teflon and plastic. Her face was lovely even in morning sunlight. Wrinkled, of course. She was two weeks short of eighty and wincing in anticipation. She ate with a cross-country skier's appetite. We told of our lives as we ate.

She'd come to Santa Maria to visit her oldest grandson. In her youth she'd done critical work in nanoengineering. The Board had allowed her four children. (I'd known I was outclassed.) All were married, scattered across the Earth, and so were the grandkids.

My two sons had emigrated to the Belt while still in their twenties. I'd visited them once during an investigation, trip paid for by the United Nations—

"You were an ARM? Really? How interesting! Tell me a story . . . if you can."

"That's the problem, all right."

The interesting tales were all classified. The ARM suppresses dangerous technology. What the ARM buries is supposed to stay buried. I remembered a kind of time compressor, and a field that would catalyze combustion, both centuries old. Both were first used for murder. If turned loose or rediscovered, either would generate more interesting tales yet.

I said, "I don't know anything current. They bounced me out when I got too old. Now I run construction robots at various spaceports."

"Interesting?"

"Mostly placid." She wanted a story? Okay. The ARM enforced more than the killer-tech laws, and some of those tales I could tell.

"We don't get many mother hunts these days. This

one was wished on us by the Belt—" And I told her of
a lunie who'd sired two clones. One he'd raised on the
Moon and one he'd left in the Saturn Conserve. He'd
moved to Earth, where one clone is any normal citizen's
entire birthright. When we found him he was arranging
to culture a third clone . . .

I dreamed a bloody dream.

It was one of those: I was able to take control, to defeat
what had attacked me. In the black of an early Sunday
morning the shreds of the dream dissolved before I could
touch them; but the sensations remained. I felt strong,
balanced, powerful, victorious.

It took me a few minutes to become suspicious of
this particular flavor of wonderful, but I'd had practice.
I eased out from under Phoebe's arm and leg and out
of bed. I lurched into the medical alcove, linked myself
up and fell asleep on the table.

Phoebe found me there in the morning. She asked,
"Couldn't that wait till after breakfast?"

"I've got four years on you and I'm going for infinity.
So I'm careful," I told her. It wasn't quite a lie . . . and
she didn't quite believe me either.

On Monday Phoebe went off to let her eldest grandson
show her the local museums. I went back to work.

In Death Valley a semicircle of twenty lasers points
at an axial array of mirrors. Tracks run across the desert
to a platform that looks like strands of spun caramel.
Every hour or so a spacecraft trundles along the tracks,
poses above the mirrors, and rises into the sky on a
blinding, searing pillar of light.

Here was where I and three companions and twenty-
eight robots worked between emergencies. Emergencies
were common enough. From time to time Glenn and
Skii and ten or twenty machines had to be shipped off

to Outback Field or Baikonur, while I held the fort at Death Valley Field.

All of the equipment was old. The original mirrors had all been slaved to one system, and those had been replaced again and again. Newer mirrors were independently mounted and had their own computers, but even these were up to fifty years old and losing their flexibility. The lasers had to be replaced somewhat more often. Nothing was ready to fall apart, quite.

But the mirrors have to adjust their shapes to match distorting air currents all the way up to vacuum, because the distortions themselves must focus the drive beam. A laser at 99.3% efficiency is keeping too much energy, getting too hot. At 99.1% something would melt, lost power would blow the laser into shrapnel, and a cargo would not reach orbit.

My team had been replacing mirrors and lasers long before I came on the scene. This circuit was nearly complete. We had already reconfigured some robots to begin replacing track.

The robots worked alone while we entertained ourselves in the monitor room. If the robots ran into anything unfamiliar, they stopped and beeped. Then a story or songfest or poker game would stop just as abruptly.

Usually the beep meant that the robot had found an acute angle, an uneven surface, a surface not strong enough to bear a loaded robot, a bend in a pipe, a pipe where it shouldn't be . . . a geometrical problem. The robots couldn't navigate just anywhere. Sometimes we'd have to unload it and move the load to a cart, by hand. Sometimes we had to pick it up with a crane and move it or turn it. Lots of it was muscle work.

Phoebe joined me for dinner Thursday evening.

She'd whipped her grandson at laser tag. They'd gone through the museum at Edward AFB. They'd skied . . .

he needed to get serious about that, and maybe get some surgery too . . .

I listened and smiled and presently tried to tell her about my work. She nodded; her eyes glazed. I tried to tell her how good it was, how restful, after all those years in the ARM.

The ARM: that got her interest back. *Stet*. I told her about the Henry Program.

I'd been saving that. It was an embezzling system good enough to ruin the economy. It made Zachariah Henry rich. He might have stayed rich if he'd quit in time . . . and if his system hadn't been so good, so dangerous, he might have ended in prison. Instead . . . well, let his tongue whisper secrets to the ears in the organ banks.

I could speak of it because they'd changed the system. I didn't say that it had happened twenty years before I joined the ARM. But I was still running out of declassified stories. I told her, "If a lot of people know something can be done, somebody'll do it. We can suppress it and suppress it again—"

She pounced. "Like what?"

"Like . . . well, the usual example is the first cold fusion system. They did it with palladium and platinum, but half a dozen other metals work. And organic superconductors: the patents listed a wrong ingredient. Various grad students tried it wrong and still got it. If there's a way to do it, there's probably a lot of ways."

"That was before there was an ARM. Would you have suppressed superconductors?"

"No. What for?"

"Or cold fusion?"

"No."

"Cold fusion releases neutrons," she said. "Sheath the generator with spent uranium, what do you get?"

"Plutonium, I think. So?"

"They used to make bombs out of plutonium."

"Bothers you?"

"Jack, the fission bomb was *it* in the mass murder department. Like the crossbow. Like the Ayatollah's Asteroid." Phoebe's eyes held mine. Her voice had dropped; we didn't want to broadcast this all over the restaurant. "Don't you ever wonder just how *much* of human knowledge is lost in that . . . black limbo inside the ARM building? Things that could solve problems. Warm the Earth again. Ease us through the lightspeed wall."

"We don't suppress inventions unless they're dangerous," I said.

I could have backed out of the argument; but that too would have disappointed Phoebe. Phoebe liked a good argument. My problem was that what I gave her wasn't good enough. Maybe I couldn't get angry enough . . . maybe my most forceful arguments were classified . . .

Monday morning, Phoebe left for Dallas and a granddaughter. There had been no war, no ultimatum, but it felt final.

Thursday evening I was back in the Monobloc.

So was Anton. "I've played it," he said. "Can't talk about it, of course."

He looked mildly bored. His hands looked like they were trying to break chunks off the edge of the table.

I nodded placidly.

Anton shouldn't have told me about the broadcast from *Angel's Pencil*. But he *had*; and if the ARM had noticed, he'd better mention it again.

Company joined us, sampled and departed. Anton and I spoke to a pair of ladies who turned out to have other tastes. (Some bends like to bug the straights.) A younger woman joined us for a time. She couldn't have been over thirty, and was lovely in the modern style . . . but hard, sharply defined muscle isn't my sole standard of beauty . . .

I remarked to Anton, "Sometimes the vibes just aren't right."

"Yeah. Look, Jack, I have carefully concealed a prehistoric Calvados in my apt at Maya. There isn't really enough for four—"

"Sounds nice. Eat first?"

"Stet. There're *sixteen* restaurants in Maya."

A score of blazing rectangles meandered across the night, washing out the stars. The eye could still find a handful of other space artifacts, particularly around the Moon.

Anton flashed the beeper that would summon a taxi. I said, "So you viewed the call. So why so tense?"

Security devices no bigger than a basketball rode the glowing sky, but the casual eye would not find those. One must assume they were there. Patterns in their monitor chips would match vision and sound patterns of a mugging, a rape, an injury, a cry for help. Those chips had gigabytes to spare for words and word patterns the ARM might find of interest.

So: no key words.

Anton said, "Jack, they tell a hell of a story. A . . . foreign vehicle pulled alongside *Angela* at four-fifths of legal max. It tried to cook them."

I stared. *A spacecraft matched course with the* Angel's Pencil *at eighty percent of lightspeed? Nothing man-built could do that. And warlike?* Maybe I'd misinterpreted everything. That can happen when you make up your code as you go along.

But how could the Pencil *have escaped?* "How did Angela manage to phone home?"

A taxi dropped. Anton said, "She sliced the bread with the, you know, motor. I said it's a hell of a story."

❖   ❖   ❖

Anton's apartment was most of the way up the slope of Maya, the pyramidal arcology north of Santa Maria. Old wealth.

Anton led me through great doors, into an elevator, down corridors. He played tour guide: "The Fertility Board was just getting some real power about the time this place went up. It was built to house a million people. It's never been fully occupied."

"So?"

"So we're en route to the east face. Four restaurants, a dozen little bars. And here we stop—"

"This your apt?"

"No. It's empty, it's always been empty. I sweep it for bugs, but the authorities . . . I *think* they've never noticed."

"Is that your mattress?"

"No. Kids. They've got a club that's two generations old. My son tipped me off to this."

"Could we be interrupted?"

"No. *I'm* monitoring *them*. I've got the security system set to let them in, but only when I'm not here. Now I'll set it to recognize you. Don't forget the number: Apt 23309."

"What is the ARM going to think we're doing?"

"Eating. We went to one of the restaurants, then came back and drank Calvados . . . which we will do, later. I can fix the records at Buffalo Bill. Just don't argue about the credit charge, stet?"

"But— Yah, stet." Hope you won't be noticed, that's the real defense. I was thinking of bailing out . . . but curiosity is part of what gets you into the ARM. "Tell your story. You said she *sliced the bread with the, you know, motor?*"

"Maybe you don't remember. *Angel's Pencil* isn't your ordinary Bussard ramjet. The field scoops up interstellar hydrogen to feed a fusion-pumped laser. The idea was to use it for communications too. Blast a message half across the galaxy with that. A Belter crewman used it to cut the alien ship in half."

"*There's* a communication you can live without. Anton . . . What they taught us in school. A sapient species doesn't reach space unless the members learn to cooperate. They'll wreck the environment, one way or another, war or straight libertarianism or overbreeding . . . remember?"

"Sure."

"So do you believe all this?"

"I think so." He smiled painfully. "Director Bernhardt didn't. He classified the message and attached a memo too. Six years of flight aboard a ship of limited size, terminal boredom coupled with high intelligence and too much time, elaborate practical jokes, yadda yadda. Director Harms *left* it classified . . . with the cooperation of the Belt. Interesting?"

"But he *had* to have *that*."

"But they had to agree. There's been more since. *Angel's Pencil* sent us hundreds of detailed photos of the alien ship. It's unlikely they could be faked. There are corpses. Big sort-of cats, orange, up to three meters tall, big feet and elaborate hands with thumbs. We're in mucking great trouble if we have to face up to such beasties."

"Anton, we've had three hundred and fifty years of peace. We must be doing something right. The odds say we can negotiate."

"You haven't seen them."

It was almost funny. Jack was trying to make me nervous. Twenty years ago the terror would have been fizzing in my blood. Better living through chemistry! This was all frightening enough; but my fear was a cerebral thing, and I was its master.

I wasn't nervous enough for Anton. "Jack, this isn't

just vaporware. A lot of those photos show what's maybe a graviton generator, maybe not. Director Harms set up a lab on the Moon to build one for us."

"Funded?"

"Heavy funding. *Somebody* believes in this. But they're getting results! It *works!*"

I mulled it. "Alien contact. As a species we don't seem to handle that too well."

"Maybe this one can't be handled at all."

"What else is being done?"

"Nothing, or damn close. Silly suggestions, career-oriented crap designed to make a bureau bigger . . . Nobody wants to use the magic word. *War*."

"War. Three hundred and fifty years out of practice, we are. Maybe C. Cretemaster will save us." I smiled at Anton's bewilderment. "Look it up in the ARM records. There's supposed to be an alien of sorts living in the cometary halo. He's the force that's been keeping us at peace this past three and a half centuries."

"Very funny."

"Mmm. Well, Anton, this is a lot more real for you than me. *I* haven't yet seen anything upsetting."

I hadn't called him a liar. I'd only made him aware that I knew nothing to the contrary. For Anton there might be elaborate proofs; but I'd seen nothing, and heard only a scary tale.

Anton reacted gracefully. "Of course. Well, there's still that bottle."

Anton's Calvados was as special as he'd claimed, decades old and quite unique. He produced cheese and bread. Good thing; I was ready to eat his arm off. We managed to stick to harmless topics, and parted friends.

The big catlike aliens had taken up residence in my soul.

Aliens aren't implausible. Once upon a time, maybe.

But an ancient ETI in a stasis field had been in the Smithsonian since the opening of the twenty-second century, and a quite different creature—C. Cretemaster's real-life analog—had crashed on Mars before the century ended.

Two spacecraft matching course at near lightspeed, *that* was just short of ridiculous. Kinetic energy considerations . . . why, two such ships colliding might as well be made of antimatter! Nothing short of a gravity generator could make it work. But Anton was *claiming* a gravity generator.

His story was plausible in another sense. Faced with warrior aliens, the ARM would do only what they could not avoid. They would build a gravity generator because the ARM must control such a thing. Any further move was a step toward the unthinkable. The ARM took sole credit (and other branches of the United Nations also took sole credit) for the fact that Man had left war behind. I shuddered to think what force it would take to turn the ARM toward war.

I would continue to demand proof of Anton's story. Looking for proof was one way to learn more, and I resist seeing myself as stupid. But I believed him already.

On Thursday we returned to Suite 23309.

"I had to dig deep to find out, but they're not just sitting on their thumbs," he said. "There's a game going in Aristarchus Crater, Belt against flatlander. They're playing peace games."

"Huh?"

"They're making formats for contact and negotiation with hypothetical aliens. The models all have the look of those alien corpses, cats with bald tails, but they all think differently—"

"Good." Here was my proof. I could check this claim.

"Good. Sure. Peace games." Anton was brooding. Twitchy. "What about war games?"

"How would you run one? Half your soldiers would be dead at the end . . . unless you're thinking of rifles with paint bullets. War gets more violent than that."

Anton laughed. "Picture every building in Chicago covered with scarlet paint on one side. A nuclear war game."

"Now what? I mean for us."

"Yah. Jack, the ARM isn't *doing* anything to put the human race back on a war footing."

"Maybe they've done something they haven't told you about."

"Jack, I don't think so."

"They haven't let you read all their files, Anton. Two weeks ago you didn't know about peace games in Aristarchus. But okay. What *should* they be doing?"

"I don't *know*."

"How's your chemistry?"

Anton grimaced. "How's yours? Forget I said that. Maybe I'm back to normal and maybe I'm not."

"Yah, but you haven't thought of anything. How about weapons? Can't have a war without weapons, and the ARM's been suppressing weapons. We should dip into their files and make up a list. It would save some time, when and if. I know of an experiment that might have been turned into an inertialess drive if it hadn't been suppressed."

"Date?"

"Early twenty-second. And there was a field projector that would make things burn, late twenty-third."

"I'll find 'em." Anton's eyes took on a faraway look. "There's the archives. I don't mean just the stuff that was built and then destroyed. The archives reach all the way back to the early twentieth. Stuff that was proposed, tanks, orbital beam weapons, kinetic energy weapons, biologicals—"

"We don't want biologicals."

I thought he hadn't heard. "Picture crowbars six feet long. A short burn takes them out of orbit, and they steer themselves down to anything with the silhouette you want . . . a tank or a submarine or a limousine, say. Primitive stuff now, but at least it would *do* something." He was really getting into this. The technical terms he was tossing off were masks for horror. He stopped suddenly, then, "Why not biologicals?"

"Nasty bacteria tailored for *us* might not work on warcats. We want *their* biological weapons, and we don't want them to have ours."

". . . Stet. Now here's one for you. How would you adjust a 'doc to make a normal person into a soldier?"

My head snapped up. I saw the guilt spread across his face. He said, "I had to look up your dossier. *Had* to, Jack."

"Sure. All right, I'll see what I can find." I stood up. "The easiest way is to pick schitzies and train *them* as soldiers. We'd start with the same citizens the ARM has been training since . . . date classified, three hundred years or so. People who need the 'doc to keep their metabolism straight, or else they'll ram a car into a crowd, or strangle—"

"We wouldn't find enough. When you need soldiers, you need thousands. Maybe millions."

"True. It's a rare condition. Well, good night, Anton."

I fell asleep on the 'doc table again.

Dawn poked under my eyelids and I got up and moved toward the holophone. Caught a glimpse of myself in a mirror. Rethought. If David saw me looking like this, he'd be booking tickets to attend the funeral. So I took a shower and a cup of coffee first.

My eldest son looked like I had—decidedly rumpled. "Dad, can't you read a clock?"

"I'm sorry. Really." These calls are so expensive that

there's no point in hanging up. "How are things in Aristarchus?"

"Clavius. We've been moved out. We've got half the space we used to, and we needed twice the space to hold everything we own. Ah, the time change isn't your fault, Dad, we're all in Clavius now, all but Jennifer. She—" David vanished. A mechanically soothing voice said, "You have impinged on ARM police business. The cost of your call will be refunded."

I looked at the empty space where David's face had been. I *was* ARM . . . but maybe I'd already heard enough.

My granddaughter Jennifer is a medic. The censor program had reacted to her name in connection with David. David said she wasn't with him. The whole family had been moved out but for Jennifer.

If she'd stayed on in Aristarchus . . . or been kept on . . .

Human medics like Jennifer are needed when something unusual has happened to a human body or brain. Then they study what's going on, with an eye to writing more programs for the 'docs. The bulk of these problems are psychological.

Anton's "peace games" must be stressful as Hell.

• CHAPTER TWO

Anton wasn't at the Monobloc Thursday. That gave me another week to rethink and recheck the programs I'd put on a dime disk; but I didn't need it.

I came back the next Thursday. Anton Brillov and Phoebe Garrison were holding a table for four.

I paused—backlit in the doorway, knowing my expression was hidden—then moved on in. "When did you get back?"

"Saturday before last," Phoebe said gravely.

It felt awkward. Anton felt it too; but then, he would. I began to wish I didn't ever have to see him on a Thursday night.

I tried tact. "Shall we see if we can conscript a fourth?"

"It's not like that," Phoebe said. "Anton and I, we're *together*. We had to tell you."

But I'd never thought . . . I'd never *claimed* Phoebe. Dreams are private. This was coming from some wild direction. "Together as in?"

Anton said, "Well, not married, not yet, but thinking about it. And we wanted to talk privately."

"Like over dinner?"

"A good suggestion."

43

"I like Buffalo Bill. Let's go there."

Twenty-odd habitués of the Monobloc must have heard the exchange and watched us leave. *Those three long-timers seem friendly enough, but too serious . . . and three's an odd number . . .*

We didn't talk until we'd reached Suite 23309.

Anton closed the door before he spoke. "She's in, Jack. Everything."

I said, "It's really love, then."

Phoebe smiled. "Jack, don't be offended. Choosing is what humans do."

Trite, I thought, and *skip it*. "That bit there in the Monobloc seemed overdone. I felt excessively foolish."

"That was for *them*. My idea," Phoebe said. "After tonight, one of us may have to go away. This way we've got an all-purpose excuse. You leave because your best friend and favored lady closed you out. Or Phoebe leaves because she can't bear to ruin a friendship. Or big, burly Jack drives Anton away. See?"

She wasn't just in, she was taking over. Ah, well. "Phoebe, love, do you believe in murderous cats eight feet tall?"

"Do you have doubts, Jack?"

"Not any more. I called my son. Something secretive is happening in Aristarchus, something that requires a medic."

She only nodded. "What have you got for us?"

I showed them my dime disk. "Took me less than a week. Run it in an autodoc. Ten personality choices. The chemical differences aren't big, but . . . infantry, which means killing on foot and doesn't have anything to do with children . . . where was I? Yah. Infantry isn't at all like logistics, and neither is it like espionage, and Navy is different yet. We may have lost some of the military vocations over the centuries. We'll have to re-invent them. This is just a first cut. I wish we had a way to try it out."

Anton set a dime disk next to mine, and a small projector. "Mine's nearly full. The ARM's stored an incredible range of dangerous devices. We need to think hard about where to store this. I even wondered if one of us should be emigrating, which is why—"

"To the Belt? Further?"

"Jack, if this all adds up, we won't have time to reach another star."

We watched stills and flat motion pictures of weapons and tools in action. Much of it was quite primitive, copied out of deep archives. We watched rock and landscape being torn, aircraft exploding, machines destroying other machines . . . and imagined flesh shredding.

"I could get more, but I thought I'd better show you this first," Anton said.

I said, "Don't bother."

"What? Jack?"

"It only took us a week! Why risk our necks to do work that can be duplicated that fast?"

Anton looked lost. "We need to do *something*!"

"Well, maybe we don't. Maybe the ARM is doing it all for us."

Phoebe gripped Anton's wrist hard, and he swallowed some bitter retort. She said, "Maybe we're missing something. Maybe we're not looking at it right."

"What's on your mind?"

"Let's *find* a way to look at it differently." She was looking straight at me.

I said, "Stoned? Drunk? Fizzed? Wired?"

Phoebe shook her head. "We need the schitz view."

"Dangerous, love. Also, the chemicals you're talking about are massively illegal. *I* can't get them, and Anton would be caught for sure—" I saw the way she was smiling at me. "Anton, I'll break your scrawny neck."

"Huh? Jack?"

"No, no, he didn't tell me," Phoebe said hastily, "though frankly I'd think either of you might have trusted me that much, Jack! I remembered you in the 'doc that morning, and Anton coming down from that twitchy state on a Thursday night, and it all clicked."

"Okay."

"You're a schitz, Jack. But it's been a long time, hasn't it?"

"Thirteen years of peace," I said. "They pick us for it, you know. Paranoid schizophrenics, born with our chemistry screwed up, hair trigger temper and a skewed view of the universe. Most schitzies never have to feel that. We use the 'docs more regularly than you do and that's that. But some of us go into the ARM . . . Phoebe, your suggestion is still silly. Anton's crazy four days out of the week, just like I used to be. Anton's all you need."

"Phoebe, he's right."

"No. The ARM used to be *all* schitzies, right? The genes have thinned out over three hundred years."

Anton nodded. "They tell us in training. The ones who could be Hitler or Napoleon or Castro, they're the ones the ARM wants. They're the ones you can send on a mother hunt, the ones with no social sense . . . but the Fertility Board doesn't let them breed either, unless they've got something special. Jack, you were special, high intelligence or something—"

"Perfect teeth, and I don't get sick in free fall, and Charlotte's people never develop back problems. That helped. Yah . . . but every century there are less of us. So they hire some Antons too, and *make* you crazy—"

"But carefully," Phoebe said. "Anton's not evolved from paranoia, Jack. You are. When they juice Anton up they don't make him too crazy, just enough to get the viewpoint they want. I bet they leave the top management boringly sane. But *you*, Jack—"

"I *see* it." Centuries of ARM tradition were squarely on her side.

"*You* can go as crazy as you like. It's all natural, and medics have known how to handle it since Only One Earth. We need the schitz viewpoint, and we don't have to steal the chemicals."

"Stet. When do we start?"

Anton looked at Phoebe. Phoebe said, "Now?"

We played Anton's tape all the way through, to a running theme of graveyard humor.

"I took only what I thought we could use," Anton said. "You should have seen some of the rest. Agent Orange. Napalm. Murder stuff."

Phoebe said, "Isn't this murder?"

That remark might have been unfair. We were watching this bizarre chunky rotary-blade flyer. Fire leaped from underneath it, once and again . . . weapons of some kind.

Anton said, "Aircraft design isn't the same when you use it for murder. It changes when you expect to be shot at. Here—" The picture had changed. "That's another weapons platform. It's not just fast, it's supposed to hide in the sky. Jack, are you all right?"

"I'm scared green. I haven't felt any effects yet."

Phoebe said, "You need to relax. Anton delivers a terrific massage. I never learned."

She wasn't kidding. Anton didn't have my muscle, but he had big strangler's hands. I relaxed into it, talking as he worked, liking the way my voice wavered as his hands pounded my back.

"It hasn't been that long since a guy like me let his 'doc run out of beta-dammasomething. An indicator light ran out and he didn't notice. He tried to kill his business partner by bombing his partner's house, and got some family members instead."

"We're on watch," Phoebe said. "If you go berserk we can handle it. Do you want to see more of this?"

"We've missed something. Children, I'm a *registered* schitz. If I don't use my 'doc for three days, they'll be trying to find me before I remember I'm the Marsport Strangler."

Anton said, "He's right, love. Jack, give me your door codes. If I can get into your apt, I can fix the records."

"Keep talking. Finish the massage, at least. We might have other problems. Do we want fruit juice? Munchies? Foodlike substances?"

When Anton came back with groceries, Phoebe and I barely noticed.

Were the warcats real? Could we fight them with present tech? How long did Sol system have? And the other systems, the more sparsely settled colony worlds? Was it enough to make tapes and blueprints of the old murder machines, or must we set to building clandestine factories? Phoebe and I were spilling ideas past each other as fast as they came, and I had quite forgotten that I was doing something dangerous.

I noticed myself noticing that I was thinking much faster than thoughts could spill from my lips. I remembered knowing that Phoebe was brighter than I was, and that didn't matter either. But Anton was losing his Thursday edge.

We slept. The old airbed was a big one. We woke to fruit and bread and dived back in.

We re-invented the Navy using only what Anton had recorded of seagoing navies. We had to. There had never been space navies; the long peace had fallen first.

I'm not sure when I slid into schitz mode. I'd spent four days out of seven without the 'doc, every week for forty-one years excluding vacations. You'd think I'd remember the feel of my brain chemistry changing. Sometimes I do; but it's the central *me* that changes, and there's no way to control that.

Anton's machines were long out of date, and none had been developed even for interplanetary war. Mankind had found peace too soon. Pity. But if the warcats' gravity generators could be copied before the warcats arrived, that alone could save us!

Then again, whatever the cats had for weapons, kinetic energy was likely to be the ultimate weapon, *however* the mass was moved. Energy considerations don't lie . . . I stopped trying to anticipate individual war machines; what I needed was an overview.

Anton was saying very little.

I realized that I had been wasting my time making medical programs. Chemical enhancement was the most trivial of what we'd need to remake an army. Extensive testing would be needed, and then we might not get soldiers at all unless they retained *some* civil rights, or unless officers killed enough of them to impress the rest. Our limited pool of schitzies had better be trained as our officers. For that matter, we'd better start by taking over the ARM. They had all the brightest schitzies.

As for Anton's work in the ARM archives, the most powerful weapons had been entirely ignored. They were too obvious.

I saw how Phoebe was staring at me, and Anton too, both gape-jawed.

I tried to explain that our task was nothing less than the reorganization of humanity. Large numbers might have to die before the rest saw the wisdom in following our lead. The warcats would teach that lesson . . . but if we waited for them, we'd be too late. Time was breathing hot on our necks.

Anton didn't understand. Phoebe was following me,

though not well, but Anton's body language was pulling him back and closing him up while his face stayed blank. He feared me worse than he feared warcats.

I began to understand that I might have to kill Anton. I hated him for that.

We did not sleep Friday at all. By Saturday noon we should have been exhausted. I'd caught catnaps from time to time, we all had, but I was still blazing with ideas. In my mind the pattern of an interstellar invasion was shaping itself like a vast three-dimensional map.

Earlier I might have killed Anton, because he knew too much or too little, because he would steal Phoebe from me. Now I saw that that was foolish. Phoebe wouldn't follow him. He simply didn't have the . . . the internal power. As for knowledge, he was our only access to the ARM!

Saturday evening we ran out of food . . . and Anton and Phoebe saw the final flaw in their plan.

I found it hugely amusing. My 'doc was halfway across Santa Maria. They had to get me there. Me, a schitz.

We talked it around. Anton and Phoebe wanted to check my conclusions. Fine: we'd give them the schitz treatment. But for that we needed my disk (in my pocket) and my 'doc (at the apt). So we had to go to my apt.

With that in mind, we shaped plans for a farewell bacchanal.

Anton ordered supplies. Phoebe got me into a taxi. When I thought of other destinations she was persuasive. And the party was waiting . . .

We were a long time reaching the 'doc. There was beer to be dealt with, and a pizza the size of Arthur's Round Table. We sang, though Phoebe couldn't hold a tune. We took ourselves to bed. It had been years since my urge to rut ran so high, so deep, backed by a sadness that ran deeper yet and wouldn't go away.

When I was too relaxed to lift a finger, we staggered singing to the 'doc with me hanging limp between them. I produced my dime disk, but Anton took it away. What was this? They moved me onto the table and set it working. I tried to explain: they had to lie down, put the disk here . . . But the circuitry found my blood loaded with fatigue poisons, and put me to sleep.

Sunday noon:
Anton and Phoebe seemed embarrassed in my presence. My own memories were bizarre, embarrassing. I'd been guilty of egotism, arrogance, self-centered lack of consideration. Three dark blue dots on Phoebe's shoulder told me that I'd brushed the edge of violence. But the worst memory was of thinking like some red-handed conqueror, and out loud.

They'd never love me again.

But they could have brought me into the apt and straight to the 'doc. Why didn't they?

While Anton was out of the room I caught Phoebe's smile in the corner of my eye, and saw it fade as I turned. An old suspicion surfaced and has never faded since.

Suppose that the women I love are all attracted to Mad Jack. Somehow they recognize my schitz potential though they find my sane state dull. There must have been a place for madness throughout most of human history. So men and women seek in each other the capacity for madness . . .

And so what? Schitzies kill. The real Jack Strather is too dangerous to be let loose.

And yet . . . it had been worth doing. From that strange fifty-hour session I remembered one real insight. We spent the rest of Sunday discussing it, making plans, while my central nervous system returned to its accustomed, unnatural state. Sane Jack.

❖   ❖   ❖

Anton Brillov and Phoebe Garrison held their wedding reception in the Monobloc. I stood as best man, bravely cheerful, running over with congratulations, staying carefully sober.

A week later I was among the asteroids. At the Monobloc they said that Jack Strather had fled Earth after his favored lady deserted him for his best friend.

• CHAPTER THREE

Things ran smoother for me because John Junior had made a place for himself in Ceres.

Even so, they had to train me. Twenty years ago I'd spent a week in the Belt. It wasn't enough. Training and a Belt citizen's equipment used up most of my savings and two months of my time.

Time brought me to Mercury, and the lasers, eight years ago.

Light-sails are rare in the inner solar system. Between Venus and Mercury there are still light-sail races, an expensive, uncomfortable, and dangerous sport. Cargo craft once sailed throughout the asteroid belt, until fusion motors became cheaper and more dependable.

The last refuge of the light-sail is a huge, empty region: the cometary halo, Pluto and beyond. The light-sails are all cargo craft. So far from Sol, their thrust must be augmented by lasers, the same Mercury lasers that sometimes hurl an unmanned probe into interstellar space.

These were different from the launch lasers I was familiar with. They were enormously larger. In Mercury's lower gravity, in Mercury's windless environment, they looked like crystals caught in spiderwebs. When the lasers fired the fragile support structures wavered like a spiderweb in a wind.

Each stood in a wide black pool of solar collector, as if tar paper had been scattered at random. A collector sheet that lost fifty percent of power was not removed. We would add another sheet, but continue to use all the available power.

Their power output was dangerous to the point of fantasy. For safety's sake the Mercury lasers must be continually linked to the rest of the solar system across a lightspeed delay of several hours. The newer solar collectors also picked up broadcasts from space, or from the control center in Challenger Crater. Mercury's lasers must never lose contact. A beam that strayed where it wasn't supposed to could do untold damage.

They were spaced all along the planet's equator. They were hundreds of years apart in design, size, technology. They fired while the sun was up and feeding their square miles of collectors, with a few fusion generators for backup. They flicked from target to target as the horizon moved. When the sun set, it set for thirty-odd Earth days, and that was plenty of time to make repairs—

"In general, that is." Kathry Perritt watched my eyes to be sure I was paying attention. I felt like a schoolboy again. "In general we can repair and update each laser station in turn and *still* keep ahead of the dawn. But come a quake, we work in broad daylight and like it."

"Scary," I said, too cheerfully.

She looked at me. "You feel nice and cool? That's a million tons of soil, old man, and a layer cake of mirror sheeting on top of that, and these old heat exchangers are still the most powerful ever built. Daylight doesn't scare you? You'll get over that."

Kathry was a sixth generation Belter from Mercury,

taller than me by seven inches, not very strong, but extremely dexterous. She was my boss. I'd be sharing a room with her . . . and yes, she rapidly let me know that she expected us to be bedmates.

I was all for that. Two months in Ceres had showed me that Belters respond to social signals I don't know. I had no idea how to seduce anyone.

Sylvia and Myron had been born on Mars in an enclave of archeologists digging out the cities beneath the deserts. Companions from birth, they'd married at puberty. They were addicted to news broadcasts. News could get them arguing. Otherwise they behaved as if they could read each other's minds; they hardly talked to each other or to anyone else.

We'd sit around the duty room and wait, and polish our skills as storytellers. Then one of the lasers would go quiet, and a tractor the size of some old Chicago skyscraper would roll.

Rarely was there much of a hurry. One laser would fill in for another until the Monster Bug arrived. Then the robots, riding the Monster Bug like one of Anton's aircraft carriers, would scatter ahead of us and set to work.

Two years after my arrival, my first quake shook down six lasers in four different locations, and ripped a few more loose from the sunlight collectors. Landscape had been shaken into new shapes. The robots had some trouble. Sometimes Kathry could reprogram. Otherwise her team had to muscle them through, with Kathry to shout orders and me to supply most of the muscle.

Of the six lasers, five survived. They seemed built to survive almost anything. The robots were equipped to spin new support structure and to lift the things into place, with a separate program for each design.

Maybe John Junior *hadn't* used influence in my behalf.

Flatlander muscle was useful, when the robots couldn't get over the dust pools or through the broken rock. For that matter, maybe it wasn't some Belt tradition that made Kathry claim me on sight. Sylvia and Myron weren't sharing; and I might have been female, or bent. Maybe she thought she was lucky.

After we'd remounted the lasers that survived, Kathry said, "They're all obsolete anyway. They're not being replaced."

"That's not good," I said.

"Well, good and bad. Light-sail cargos are slow. If the light wasn't almost free, why bother? The interstellar probes haven't sent much back yet, and we might as well wait. At least the Belt Speakers think so."

"Do I gather I've fallen into a kind of a blind alley?"

She glared at me. "You're an immigrant flatlander. What did you expect, First Speaker for the Belt? You thinking of moving on?"

"Not really. But if the job's about to fold—"

"Another twenty years, maybe. Jack, I'd miss you. Those two—"

"It's all right, Kathry. I'm not going." I waved both arms at the blazing dead landscape and said, "I like it here," and smiled into her bellow of laughter.

I beamed a tape to Anton when I got the chance.

> *"If I was ever angry, I got over it, as I hope you've forgotten anything I said or did while I was, let's say, running on automatic. I've found another life in deep space, not much different from what I was doing on Earth . . . though that may not last. These light-sail pusher lasers are a blast from the past. Time gets them, the quakes get them, and they're not being replaced. Kathry says twenty years.*
>
> *"You said Phoebe left Earth too. Working with*

an asteroid mining setup? If you're still trading
tapes, tell her I'm all right and I hope she is too.
Her career choice was better than mine, I expect . . ."

I couldn't think of anything else to do.

Three years after I expected it, Kathry asked. "Why
did you come out here? It's none of my business, of
course—"

Customs differ: it took her three years in my bed to
work up to this. I said, "Time for a change," and "I've
got children and grandchildren on the Moon and Ceres
and Floating Jupiter."

"Do you miss them?"

I had to say yes. The result was that I took half a year
off to bounce around the solar system. I found Phoebe,
too, and we did some catching up; but I still came back
early. My being away made us both antsy.

Kathry asked again a year later. I said, "What I did
on Earth was not like this. The difference is, on Earth
I'm dull. Here—am I dull?"

"You're fascinating. You won't talk about the ARM,
so you're fascinating and mysterious. I can't believe you'd
be dull just because of where you are. Why did you
leave, really?"

So I said, "There was a woman."

"What was she like?"

"She was smarter than me. I was a little dull for her.
So she left, and that would have been okay. But she
came back to my best friend." I shifted uncomfortably
and said, "Not that they drove me off Earth."

"No?"

"No. I've got everything I once had herding construction robots on Earth, plus one thing I wasn't bright
enough to miss. I lost my sense of purpose when I left
the ARM."

I noticed that Myron was listening. Sylvia was watching the holo walls, the three that showed the face of Mercury: rocks blazing like coals in fading twilight, with only the robots and the lasers to give the illusion of life. The fourth we kept changing. Just then it showed a view up the trunk into the waving branches of the tremendous redwood they've been growing for three hundred years, in Hovestraydt City on the Moon.

"These are the good times," I said. "You have to notice, or they'll go right past. We're holding the stars together. Notice how much dancing we do? On Earth I'd be too old and creaky for that—Sylvia, *what?*"

Sylvia was shaking my shoulder. I heard it as soon as I stopped talking: *"Tombaugh Station relayed this picture, the last broadcast from the* Fantasy Prince. *Once again, the* Fantasy Prince *has apparently been—"*

Starscape glowed within the fourth holo wall. Something came out of nowhere, moving hellishly fast, and stopped so quickly that it might have been a toy. It was egg-shaped, studded with what I remembered as weapons.

Phoebe won't have made her move yet. The warcats will have to be deep in the solar system before her asteroid mining setup can be any deterrent. Then one or another warcat ship will find streams of slag sprayed across its path, impacting at comet speeds.

By now Anton must know whether the ARM actually has plans to repel an interstellar invasion.

Me, I've already done my part. I worked on the computer shortly after I first arrived. Nobody's tampered with it since. The dime disk is in place.

We kept the program relatively simple. Until and unless the warcats destroy something that's being pushed by a laser from Mercury, nothing will happen. The warcats must condemn themselves. Then the affected laser will lock onto the warcat ship . . . and so will every Mercury laser that's getting sunlight. Twenty seconds, then the system goes back to normal until another target disappears.

If the warcats can be persuaded that Sol system is defended, maybe they'll give us time to build defenses.

Asteroid miners dig deep for fear of solar storms and meteors. Phoebe might survive. We might survive here too, with shielding built to block the hellish sun, and laser cannon to battle incoming ships. But that's not the way to bet.

We might get one ship.

It might be worth doing.

THE MAN WHO
WOULD BE KZIN

•

Greg Bear and
S.M. Stirling

"I am become overlord of a fleet of transports, supply ships, and wrecks!" Kfraksha-Admiral said. "No wonder the First Fleet did not return; our Intelligence reports claimed these *humans* were leaf-eaters without a weapon to their name, and they have destroyed a fourth of our combat strength!"

He turned his face down to the holographic display before him; it was set for exterior-visual, and showed only bright unwinking points of light and the schematics that indicated the hundreds of vessels of the Second Fleet. Here beyond the orbit of Neptune the humans' sun was just another star . . . *we will eat you yet*, he vowed silently. A spacer's eye could identify those suns whose worlds obeyed the Patriarch. More that did not, unvisited, or unconquered yet like the Pierin holdouts on Zeta Reticuli. *Yes, you and all like you!* So many suns, so many . . .

The kzin commander's tail was not lashing; he was beyond that, and the naked pink length of that organ now stood out rigid as he paced the command deck of the *Sons Contend With Bloody Fangs*. The orange fur around his blunt muzzle bristled, and the reddish washcloth of his tongue kept sweeping up to moisten his black nostrils. The other kzinti on the bridge stayed prudently silent, forcing their batwing ears not to fold into the fur of their heads at the spicy scent of high-status anger. The lower-ranked bent above the consoles and readouts of their duty stations, taking refuge in work; the immediate staff prostrated themselves around the central display tank, laying their facial fur flat. Aide-to-Commanders covered his nose with his hands in an excess of servility; irritated, Kfraksha kicked him in the ribs as he went by. There was no satisfaction to the gesture, since they were all in space-combat armor save for the unhinged helmets, but the subordinate went spinning a meter or so across the deck.

"Well? Advise me," the kzin admiral spat. "Surely *something* can be learned from the loss of a squadron of *Gut Tearer*-class cruisers?"

Reawii-Intelligence-Analyst raised tufted eyebrows and fluttered his lips against his fangs.

"Frrrr. The . . . rrrr, humans have devoted great resources to the defense of the gas-giant moons, whose resources are crucial."

As Kfraksha-Admiral bared teeth, the Intelligence officer hurried on. Reawii's Homeworld accent irritated Kfraksha-Admiral at the best of times. His birth was better than his status, and it would not do to anger the supreme commander, who had risen from the ranks and was proud of it. He hurried beyond the obvious.

"Their laser cannon opened fire with uncanny accuracy. We were unprepared for weapons of this type because such large fixed installations are seldom tactically worthwhile; also, our preliminary surveys did not indicate space defenses of any type. It is worth the risk to further fleet units to recover any possible Intelligence data from wreckage or survivors on appropriate trajectories."

Kfraksha-Admiral's facial pelt rippled in patterns equivalent to a human nod.

"Prepare summaries of projected operations for data and survivors," he said. Then he paused; now his tail did lash, sign of deep worry or concentration. "Hrrr. It is time we stopped being surprised by the Earth-monkeys and started springing unseen from the long grass ourselves. Bring me a transcript of all astronomical anomalies in this system."

The staff officers rose and left at his gesture, and Kfraksha-Admiral remained staring into the display tank; he keyed it to a close-in view of the animal planet. Blue and white, more ocean than Homeworld, slightly lighter gravity. A rich world. A soft world, or so the telepaths said, no weapons, a species that was so without shame that it deliberately shunned the honorable path of war. Thousands of thousands squared of the animals. Unconsciously, he licked his lips. *All the more for the feeding.*

The game was wary, though. He must throttle his leap, though it was like squeezing his own throat in his claws.

"I must *know* before I fight," he muttered.

He was the perfect spy.

He could also be the perfect saboteur.

Lawrence Halloran was a strong projecting telepath.

He could read the minds of most people with ease. The remaining select few he could invade, with steady concentration, within a week or two. Using what he found in those minds, Halloran could appear to be anybody or anything.

He could also make suggestions, convincing his subjects—or victims—that they were undergoing some physical experience. In this, he relied in large measure on auto-suggestion; sometimes it was enough to plant a subliminal hint and have the victims convince themselves that they actually experienced something. The problem was that the Earth of the twenty-fourth century had little use for spies or saboteurs. Earth had been at peace for three hundred years. Everyone was prosperous; many were rich. The planet was a little crowded, but those who strongly disliked that could leave. Psychists and autodocs saw that nobody was violent or angry or unhappy for long. Most people were only vaguely aware that things had ever been very different, and the ARM, the UN technological police, kept it that way, ensuring that no revolutionary changes upset the comfortable status quo.

Lawrence Halloran had an unusual ability that seemed to be completely useless. He had first used his talents in a most undignified way, appearing as the headmaster of his private Pacific Grove secondary school, *sans* apparel, in the middle of the quad during an exercise break. The headmaster had come within a hair's-breadth of being relieved of duty; an airtight alibi, that he had in fact been in conference with five teachers across the campus, had saved his job and reputation. Halloran's secret had not been revealed. But Halloran had learned an important object lesson: foolish use of his talents could have grave consequences. He had been raised to feel strong guilt at any hint of aggression. Children who scuffled in the schoolyard were sick and needed treatment.

Human society was not so very different from an ant's nest, at the end of the Long Peace; a stick, inserted from an unexpected direction, could raise hell. And woe to the wielder if he stayed around long enough to let the ants crawl up the stick.

That Halloran had not manifested his ability as an infant—not until his sixteenth year, in fact—was something of a miracle. The talent had undoubtedly existed in some form, but had kept itself hidden until five years after Halloran's first twinges of pubescence.

At first, such a wild talent had been exhilarating. After the headmaster fiasco, and several weirder if less immediately foolish manifestations (a dinosaur on a slidewalk at night, Christ in a sacristy), and string of romantic successes everyone else found bewildering, he had undergone what amounted to a religious conversion. Halloran came to realize that he could not use his talent without destroying himself, and those around him. The only thing it was good for was deception and domination.

He buried it. Studied music. Specialized in Haydn.

In his dreams, he became Haydn. It beat being himself.

When awake, he was merely Lawrence Halloran Jr., perpetual student: slightly raucous, highly intuitive (he could not keep his subconscious from exercising certain small forays) and generally regarded by his peers as someone to avoid. His only real friend was his cat. He knew that his cat loved him, because he fed her. Cats were neither altruists nor hypocrites, and nobody expected them to be noble. If he could not be Haydn, he would rather have been a cat.

Halloran resented his social standing. *If only they knew how noble I am.* He had a talent he could use to enslave people, and by sublimating it he became an irritating son of a bitch; that, he thought, was highly commendable self-sacrifice.

And they hate me for it, he realized. *I don't much love them either. Lucky for them I'm an altruist.*

Then the war had come; invaders from beyond human space. The kzinti: catlike aliens, carnivores, aggressive imperialists. Human society was turned upside down once again, although the process was swift only from a historical perspective. With the war eight years along, Halloran had grown sick of this masquerade. Against his better judgment, he had made himself available to the UN Space Navy; UNSN, for short. Almost immediately, he had been sequestered and prepared for just such an eventuality as the capture of a kzinti vessel. In the second kzin attack on the Sol system, a cruiser named *War Loot* was chopped into several pieces by converted launch lasers and fell into human hands.

In this, Earth's most desperate hour, neither Halloran nor any of his commanding officers considered his life to be worth much in and of itself. Nobility of purpose . . .

And if Halloran's subconscious thought differently—

Halloran knew himself to be in control. Had he not sublimated the worst of his talent? Had he not let girls pour drinks on his head?

Halloran's job was to study the kzin. Then to *become* one, well enough to fool another kzin. After all, if he could convince humans he was a dinosaur—which was obviously an impossibility—why not fool aliens into seeing what they expected?

The first test of Halloran-Kzin was brief and simple. Halloran entered the laboratory where doctors struggled to keep two mangled kzin from the *War Loot* alive. In the cool ice-blue maximum isolation ward, he approached the flotation bed with its forest of pipes and wires and tubing. Huddled beneath the apparatus, the kzin known to its fellows as Telepath dreamed away his final hours on drugs custom-designed for his physiology.

Telepaths were the most despised and yet valued of kzinti, something of an analogue to Halloran—a mind reader. To kzinti, any kind of addiction was an unbearably shameful thing—a weakness of discipline and concentration, a giving in to the body whose territorial impulses established so much of the rigid Kzinti social ritual. To be addicted was to be less self-controlled than a kzin already was, and that was pushing things very close to the edge. And yet addiction to a drug was what produced kzinti telepaths.

This kzin would not have looked very good in the best of times, despite his two hundred and twenty centimeters of height and bull-gorilla bulk; now he was shrunken and pitiful, his ribs showing through matted fur, his limbs reduced to lumpy bone, lips pulled back from yellow teeth and stinking gums. Telepath had been without his fix for weeks. How much this lack, and the presence of anesthetics, had dulled his talents nobody could say, but his kind offered the greatest risk to the success of Halloran's mission. The kzin had been wearing a supply of the telepath drug on a leather belt when captured. Administered to him now, it would allow him to reach into the mind of another, with considerable effort . . .

Halloran-Kzin had to pass this test.

He signaled the doctors with a nod, and from behind their one-way glass they began altering the concentration of drugs in Telepath's blood. They added some of the kzinti drug. A monitor wheeped softly, pitifully, indicating that their kzin would soon be awake and that he would be in pain.

The kzin opened his eyes, rolled his head, and stared in surprise at Halloran-Kzin. The dying Telepath concealed his pain well.

"I have been returned?" he said, in the hiss-spit-snarl of what his race called the Hero's Tongue.

"You have been returned," Halloran-Kzin replied.

"And am I too valuable to terminate?" the kzin asked sadly.

"You will die soon," Halloran-Kzin said, sensing that this would comfort him.

"Animals . . . eaters of plants. I have had nightmares, dreams of being pursued by herbivores. The shame. And no meat, or only cold rotten meat . . ."

"Are you still capable?" Halloran-Kzin asked. He had learned enough about kzinti social structure from the relatively undamaged prisoner designated Fixer-of-Weapons to understand that Telepath would have no position if he was not telepathic. Fixer was the persona Halloran would assume. "Show me you are still capable."

The kzin had shielded himself against stray sensations from human minds. But now he closed his eyes and knotted his black, leathery hands into fists. With an intense effort, he reached out and tapped Halloran's thoughts. Telepath's eyes widened until the rheumy circles around the wide pupils were clearly visible. His ears contracted into tight knots beneath the fur. Then he emitted a horrifying scream, like a jaguar in pain. Against all his restraints, he thrashed and twisted until he had torn loose the internal connections that kept him alive. Orange-red blood pooled around the flotation bed and the monitor began a steady, funereal tone.

Halloran left the ward. Colonel Buford Early waited for him outside; as usual, his case officer exuded an air of massive, unwilling patience.

"Just a minor problem," Halloran said, shaken more than he wished the other man to know.

"Minor?"

"Telepath is dead. He saw my thoughts."

"He thought you were a kzin?"

"Yes. He wouldn't have tried reading me if he thought I was human."

"What happened?"

"I drove him crazy," Halloran said. "He was close to the edge anyway . . . I pushed him over."

"How could you do that?" Colonel Early asked, brow lowered incredulously.

"I had a salad for lunch," Halloran replied.

Halloran knew better than to wake a kzin in the middle of a nightmare. Fixer-of-Weapons had not rested peacefully the last four sleeps, and no wonder, with Halloran testing so many hypotheses, hour by hour, on the captive.

The chamber in which the kzin slept was roomy enough, five meters on a side and three meters high, the walls colored a soothing mottled green. The air was warm and dry; Halloran had chapped lips from spending hours and days in the hapless kzin's company.

Thinking of a kzin as hapless was difficult. Fixer-of-Weapons had been Chief Weapons Engineer and Alien Technologies Officer aboard the invasion cruiser *War Loot*, a position demanding great strength and stamina even with the wartime dueling restrictions, for many other kzinti coveted such a billet.

War Loot had been on a mission to probe human defenses within the ecliptic; to that extent, the kzinti mission had succeeded. The cruiser had been disabled within the outer limits of the asteroid belt by converted propulsion beam lasers three weeks before, and against all odds, Fixer-of-Weapons and two other kzin had been captured. The others had been severely injured, one almost cut in half by a shorn and warped bulkhead. The same bulkhead had sealed Fixer-of-Weapons in a cabin corner, equipped with a functional vent giving access to seven hours of trapped air. At the end of six and a half hours, Fixer-of-Weapons had passed out. Human investigators had cut him free . . .

And brought him to Ceres, largest of the asteroids, to be put in a cage with Halloran.

To Fixer-of-Weapons, in his more lucid moments, Halloran looked like a particularly clumsy and socially inept kzin. But Halloran was a California boy, born and bred, a graduate of UCLA's revered school of music. Halloran did not look like a kzin unless he wanted to.

Four years past, to prove to himself that his life was not a complete waste, he had spent his time learning to differentiate one Haydn piano sonata or string quartet from another, not a terribly exciting task, but peaceful and rewarding. He had developed a great respect for Haydn, coming to love the richness and subtle invention of the eighteenth century composer's music.

To Earth-bound flatlanders, the war at the top of the

solar system's gravity well, with fleets maneuvering over periods of months and years, was a distant and dimly perceived threat. Halloran had hardly known how to feel about his own existence, much less the survival of the human race. Haydn suited him to a tee. Glory did not seem important. Nobody would appreciate him anyway.

Halloran's parents, and their fathers and mothers before them for two and a half centuries, had known an Earth of peace and relative prosperity. If any of them had desired glory and excitement, they could have volunteered for a decades-long journey by slow-boat to new colonies. None had.

It was a Halloran tradition; careful study, avoidance of risk, lifetimes of productive peace. The tradition had gained his grandfather a long and productive life—one hundred and fifty years of it, and at least a century more to come. His father, Lawrence Halloran Sr., had made his fortune streamlining commodities distribution; a brilliant move into a neglected field, less crowded than information shunting. Lawrence Halloran Jr., after the death of his mother in an earthquake in Alaska, had bounced from school to school, promising to be a perpetual student, gadding from one subject to another, trying to lose himself . . .

And then peace had ended. The kzinti—not the first visitors from beyond the Solar System, but certainly the most aggressive—had made their presence known. Presence, to a kzin, was tantamount to conquest. For hundreds of thousands of kzin warriors, serving their Patriarchy, Earth and the other human worlds represented advancement; many females, higher status, and lifetime sinecures, without competition.

Humans had been drawn into the war with no weapons as such. To defend themselves, all they had were the massive planet- and asteroid-mounted propulsion lasers and fusion drives that powered their starships. These technologies, some of them now converted to thoroughgoing weapons by Belters and UN engineers, provided what little hope humans had . . .

And there was the bare likelihood—unconfirmed as yet—that humans were innately more clever than kzinti, or at least more measured and restrained. Human fusion drives were certainly more efficient—but then, the kzinti had gravity polarizers, not unlike that found on the Pak ship piloted by Jack Brennan, and never understood. The Brennan polarizer still worked, but nobody knew how to control it—or build another like it. Gradually, scientists and UNSN commanders were realizing that capture of kzinti vessels, rather than complete destruction, could provide invaluable knowledge about such advanced technology.

Gravity polarizers gave kzin ships the ability to travel at eight-tenths the speed of light, with rapid acceleration and artificial gravitation . . . The kzinti did not *need* super-efficient fusion drives.

Halloran waited patiently for the Fixer-of-Weapons to awaken. An hour passed. He rehearsed the personality he was constructing, and toned the image he presented for the kzin. He also studied, for the hundredth time, the black markings of fur in the kzin's face and along his back, contrasting with the brownish-red undercoat. The kzin's ears were ornately tattooed in patterns Halloran had learned symbolized the intermeshed bones of kzinti enemies. This was how the kzinti recognized each other, beyond scent and gross physical features; failure to know and project such facial fur patterns and ear tattoos would mean discovery and death. The kzinti's own mind would supply the scent, given the visual clues; their noses were less sensitive than a dog's, much more so than a human's.

Another hour, and Halloran felt a touch of impatience. Kzinti were supposed to be light and short-term sleepers. Fixer-of-Weapons seemed to have joined his warrior ancestors; he barely breathed.

At last, the captive stirred and opened his eyes, glazed nictitating membranes pulling back to reveal the large, gorgeous purple-rimmed golden eyes with their surprisingly humanlike round irises. Fixer-of-Weapons's wedge-shaped, blunt-muzzled face froze into a blank mask, as it always did when he confronted Halloran-Kzin, who stood on the opposite side of the containment room, tapping his elbow with one finger. Distance from the captive was imperative, even when he was "restrained" by imaginary bonds suggested by Halloran. A kzin did not give warning when he was about to attack, and Fixer-of-Weapons was being driven to emotional extremes.

The kzin laid back his ears in furious misery. "I have done nothing to deserve such treatment," he growled. He believed he was being detained on a kzinti fleet flagship. Halloran, had he truly been a kzin, would have preferred human capture to kzinti detention. *I can't say I like the ratcat*, he thought, with a twinge of guilt, quickly suppressed. *But you've got to admit he's about as tough as he thinks he is*.

"That is for your superiors to decide," Halloran-Kzin said. "You behaved with suspected cowardice, you allowed an invasion cruiser to be disabled and captured—"

"I was not Kufcha-Captain! I cannot be responsible for the incompetence of my commander." Fixer-of-Weapons rose to his full two hundred and twenty centimeters, short for a kzin, and flexed against the imaginary bonds. The muscles beneath the smooth-furred limbs and barrel chest were awesome, despite weight loss under weeks of captivity. "This is a travesty! Why are you doing this to me?"

"You will tell us exactly what happened, step by step,

and how you allowed animals—plant-eaters—to capture *War Loot*."

Fixer-of-Weapons slumped in abject despair. "I have told, again and again."

Halloran-Kzin showed no signs of relenting. Fixer-of-Weapons lashed his long pink rat-tail, sitting in a tight ball on the floor, swallowed hard and began his tale again, and again Halloran used the familiar litany as a cover to probe the kzin's inner thoughts.

If Halloran was going to be a kzin, and think like one for days on end, then he had to have everything exactly right. His deception would be of the utmost delicacy. The smallest flaw could get him killed immediately.

Kzinti, unlike the UN Space Navy, did not take prisoners except for Intelligence and culinary purposes.

Fixer-of-Weapons finished his story. Halloran pulled back from the kzin's mind.

"If I have disgraced myself, then at least allow me to die," Fixer-of-Weapons said softly.

That's one wish you can be granted, Halloran thought. One way or another, the kzin would be dead soon; his species did not survive in captivity.

Halloran exited the cell and faced three men and two women in the antechamber. Two of the men wore the new uniform—barely ten years old—of the UN Space Navy. The third man was a Belter cultural scientist, the only one in the group actually native to Ceres, dressed in bright lab spotter orange. The two women Halloran had never seen before; they were also Belters, though their Belter tans had faded. All three wore the broad Belter Mohawk. The taller of the two offered Halloran her hand and introduced herself.

"I'm Kelly Ysyvry," she said. "Don't bother trying to spell it."

"Y-S-Y-V-R-Y," Halloran said, displaying the show-off mentality that had made his social life so difficult at times.

"Right," Ysyvry said, unflappable. "This," she nodded at her female companion, "is Henrietta Olsen."

Colonel Buford Early, the shortest and most muscular of the three men, nodded impatiently at the introductions; he was an Earther, coal-black and much older than he looked, something Ultra Secret in the ARM before the war. Early had recruited Halloran four years ago, trained him meticulously, and shown remarkable patience toward his peculiarities.

"When are you going to be ready?" he asked Halloran.

"Ready for what?" Halloran asked.

"Insertion."

Halloran, fully understanding the Colonel's meaning, inspected the women roguishly.

"I'm confused," he said, smiling.

"What he means," Ysyvry said, "is that we're all impatient, and you've been the stumbling block throughout this mission."

"What is she?" Halloran asked Early.

"We are the plunger of your syringe," Henrietta Olsen answered. "We're Belter pilots. We've been getting special training in the kzinti hulk."

"Pleased to meet you," Halloran said. He glanced back at the hatch to the cell airlock. "Fixer-of-Weapons will be dead within a week. I can't learn any more from him. So . . . I'm ready for a test."

Early stared at him. Halloran knew the Colonel was restraining an urge to ask him, *Are you sure?*, after having displayed such impatience.

"How do you know Fixer-of-Weapons will die?" the black man said.

Halloran's smile stiffened. He disliked being challenged. "Because if I were him, and part of me is, I would have reached my limit."

"It hasn't been an easy assignment," the cultural scientist commented.

"Easier for us than Fixer-of-Weapons," Halloran said, smirking inwardly as the scientist winced.

There would be many problems, of course. Halloran would never be as strong as a kzin, and if there were any sort of combat, he would quickly lose . . .

Halloran, among the kzinti, thinking himself a kzin, would have to carefully preprogram himself to avoid such dangerous situations, to keep a low profile concomitant with his status, whatever that might be. That would be difficult. A high-status kzin had retainers, sons, flunkies, to handle status-challenges; many of the retainers picked carefully for a combination of dim wits and excellent reflexes. An officer with recognized rank could not be challenged while on a warship; punishments for trying included blinding, castration, and execution of all descendants—all more terrible than mere death to a kzin. Nameless ratings could duel as they pleased, provided they had a senior's permission . . . and Halloran-Kzin would be outside the rank structure, with no protector.

Fixer-Halloran, when he returned to the kzinti feet, would likely find all suitable billets on other vessels filled. To regain his position and keep face among his fellows, he could not simply "fit in" and be docile. But there were more ways than open combat to gain social status.

The kzinti social structure was delicately tuned, though how delicately perhaps not even the kzinti understood. Halloran could wreak his own kind of havoc and none would suspect him of anything but overweening ambition.

All of this, he knew, would have to be accomplished in less than three hundred hours: just twelve days. His body would be worn out by that time. Bad diet—all meat, and raw at that, though digestible, with little chance for supplements of the vitamins a human needed and the life of a kzin did not produce; mental strain; luck running out.

He did not expect to return.

Halloran's hope was that his death would come in the capture or destruction of one or more kzinti ships.

The chance for such a victory, however negligible it might be in the overall strategy of the war, was easily worth one's life, certainly his own life.

The truth was, Halloran thought he was a thorough shit, not of much use to anyone in the long run, a petty dilettante with an unlikely ability, more a handicap than an asset.

Self-sacrifice would give him a peculiar satisfaction: *See, I'm not so bad*.

Nobility of purpose.

And something deeper: *to actually be a kzin*. A kzin could be all the things Halloran had trained himself not to be, and not feel guilty about it. Dominant. Vicious. Competitive.

Kzinti were allowed to have fun.

The short broadcast good-byes to his friends and relatives on Earth, as yet unassailed by kzinti:

His father, now one hundred and twenty, he was able to say farewell to; but his grandfather, a Struldbrug and still one of the foremost collectors of Norman Rockwell art and memorabilia, was unavailable.

He disliked his father, yet respected him, and loved his grandfather, but felt a kind of contempt for the man's sentimental passion.

His grandfather's answering service did not know where the oldest living Halloran was. That brought on a sharp tinge of disappointment, against which he quickly raised a shield of aloofness. For a moment, a very young Lawrence—Larry—had surfaced, wanting, desperately needing to see Grandpa. And there was no room for such active sub-personalities, not with Fixer-of-Weapons filling much of his cranium. Or so he told himself, drowning the disappointment as an old farmer might have discarded a sack of unwanted kittens.

Halloran met his father on the family estate at the cap of Arcosanti Two in Arizona. The man barely looked fifty and was with his fifth wife, who was older than Halloran but only by five or ten years. The sky was gorgeous robin's egg at the horizon and lapis overhead and the green desert spread for ten kilometers around in a network of canals and recreational sluices. Amosanti Two prided itself on its ecological balance, but in fact the city had taken a wide tract of Arizona desert and made it into something else entirely, something in which bobbing lizards and roadrunners would soon go crazy or die. Halloran felt just as much out of place on the broad open-air portico at two kilometers above sea level. Infrared heaters kept the high autumn chill away.

"I'm volunteering for a slowboat," Halloran told his father.

"I thought they'd been suspended," said Rose Petal, the new wife, a very attractive natural blonde with oriental features. "I mean, all that expense, and we're bound to lose them to the, mmm, outsiders . . ." She looked slightly embarrassed; even after nearly a decade, the words *war* and *enemy* still carried a strong flavor of obscenity to most Earthers.

"There's one going out in a few weeks, a private venture. No announcements. Tacit government support; if we survive, they send more."

"That does not sound like my son," Halloran Sr. ventured.

When I tried to assert myself, you told me it was wrong. When I didn't, you despised me. Thanks, Dad.

"I think it is wonderful," Rose Petal said. "Whether characteristic or not."

"It's a way out from under family," Halloran Jr. said with a little smile.

"*That* sounds like my son. Though I'd be much more impressed if you were doing something to help your own people . . ."

"Colonization," Halloran Jr. interjected, leaving the word to stand on its own.

"More directly," Halloran Sr. finished.

"Can't keep all our eggs in one basket," his son continued, amused by arguing a case denied by his own actions. *So tell him.*

But that wasn't possible. Halloran Jr. knew his father too well; a fine entrepreneur, but no keeper of secrets. In truth, his father, despite the aggressive attitude, was even more unsuited to a world of war and discipline than his son.

"That's not what you're doing," Halloran Sr. said. Rose Petal stood by, wisely keeping out from this point on.

"That's what I'm saying I'm doing."

His father gave him a peculiar look then, and Halloran Jr. felt a brief moment of camaraderie and shared secrets. *He has a little bit of the touch too, doesn't he? He knows. Not consciously, but . . .*

He's proud.

Against his own expectations for the meeting and farewell, Halloran left Arcosanti Two, his father, and Rose Petal, feeling he might have more to lose than he had guessed, and more to learn about things very close to him. He left feeling good.

He hadn't parted from his father with positive feelings in at least ten years.

There were no longer lovers or good friends to take leave of. He had stripped himself of these social accoutrements over the last five years. It was difficult to have friends who couldn't lie to you, and he always felt guilty with women. How could he know he hadn't influenced them subconsciously? Knowing this, as he returned to the port and took a shuttle to orbit, brought back the necessary feeling of isolation. He would not be human much longer. Things would be easier if he had very little to regret losing.

Insertion. The hulk of the kzin cruiser, its gravity polarizer destroyed by the kzin crew to keep it out of human hands, was propelled by a NEO mass-driver down the solar gravity well to graze the orbital path of Venus, piloted by the two Belter women to the diffuse outer reaches of the asteroids, there set adrift with the bodies of Telepath and the other unknown kzin restored to the places where they would have died. The Belters would take a small cargo craft back home. Halloran would ride an even smaller lifeboat from *War Loot* toward the kzin fleet. He might or might not be picked up, depending on how hungry the kzin strategists were for information about the loss.

The fleet might or might not be in a good position; it might be mounting another year-long attack against Saturn's moons, on the opposite side of the sun; it might be moving inward for a massive blow against Earth. With the gravity polarizers, the kzin vessels were faster and far more maneuverable than any human ships.

And there could be more than one fleet.

The confined interior of the cargo vessel gave none of its three occupants much privacy. To compensate, they seldom spoke to each other. At the end of a week, Halloran began to get depressed, and it took him another week to express himself to his companions.

While Henrietta Olsen buried herself in reading, when she wasn't tending the computers, Kelly Ysyvry spent much of her time apparently doing nothing. Eyes open, blinking every few seconds, she would stare at a bulkhead for hours at a stretch. This depressed Halloran further. Were all Belters so inner-directed? If they were, then what just God would place him in the company of Belters during his last few weeks as a human being?

He finally approached Olsen with something more than polite words to punctuate the silence. *A kzin wouldn't have to put up with this*, he thought. Kzinti females were subsapient, morons incapable of speech. *That would have its advantages*, Halloran thought half-jokingly.

Women frightened him. He knew too much about what they thought of him.

"I suppose lack of conversation is one way of staying sane," he said.

Olsen looked up from her page projector and blinked. "Flatlanders talk all the time?"

"No," Halloran admitted. "But they talk."

"We talk," Olsen said, returning to her reading. "When we want to, or need to."

"I need to talk," Halloran said.

Olsen put her book down. Perversely guilty, Halloran asked what she had been reading.

"Montagu, *The Man Who Never Was*," she replied.

"What's it about?"

"It's ancient history," she said. "Forbidden stuff. Twentieth century. During the Second World War— remember that?"

"I'm educated," he said. As much as such obscene subjects had been taught in school. Pacific Grove had been progressive.

"The Allies dressed up a corpse in one of their uniforms and gave him a courier's bag with false information. Then they dumped him where he could be picked up by the Axis.

Halloran gawped for a moment. "Sounds grim."

"I doubt the corpse minded."

"And I'm the corpse?"

Olsen grinned. "You don't fit the profile at all. You're not *The Man Who Never Was*. You're one of those soldiers trained to speak the enemy's language and dropped behind the lines in the enemy's uniforms to wreak havoc."

"Why are you so interested in World War Two?"

"Fits our times. This stuff used to be pornography— or whatever the equivalent is for literature about violence and destruction, and they'd send you to the psychist if they caught you with it. Now it's available anywhere. Psychological refitting. Still, the thought of . . ." She shook her head. "Killing. Even thinking like one of *them*—so ready to kill . . ."

Ysyvry broke her meditation by blinking three times in quick succession and turned pointedly to face Halloran.

"To the normal person of a few years ago, what you've become would be unspeakably disgusting."

"And what about now?"

"It's necessity," Ysyvry said. That word again. "We're no better than you. We're all soldiers now. Killers."

"So we're too ashamed to speak to each other?"

"We didn't know you wanted to talk," Olsen said.

Throughout his life, even as insensitive as he had tried to become, he had been amazed at how others, especially women, could be so ignorant of their fellows. "I'll probably be dead in a month," he said.

"So you want sympathy?" Olsen said, wide-eyed. "The Man Who Would be Kzin wants sympathy? Such bad technique . . ."

"Forget it," Halloran said, feeling his stomach twist.

"We learned a lot about you," Ysyvry continued. "What you might do in a moment of weakness, how you had once been a troublemaker, using your abilities to fool people . . . Belters value ingenuity and independence, but we also value respect. Simple politeness."

Halloran felt a deep void open up beneath him. "I was young when I did those things." His eyes filled with tears. "Tanjit, I'm sacrificing myself for my people, and you treat me as if I'm a bleeping dog turd!"

"Yeah," Olsen said, turning away. "We don't like flatlanders, anyway, and . . . I suppose we're not used to this whole war thing. We've had friends die. We'd just as soon it all went away. Even you."

"So," Ysyvry said, taking a deep breath. "Tell us about yourself. You studied music?"

The turnabout startled him. He wiped his eyes with his sleeve. "Yes. Concentrating on Josef Haydn."

"Play us something," Olsen suggested, reaching into a hidden corner slot to pull out a portable music keyboard he hadn't known the ship carried. "Haydn, Glenn Miller, Sting, anything classical."

For the merest instant, he had the impulse to become Halloran-Kzin. Instead, he took the keyboard and stared at the black and white arrangement. Then he played the first movement of Sonata Number 40 in E Flat, a familiar piece for him. Ysyvry and Olsen listened intently.

As he lightly completed the last few bars, Halloran closed his eyes and imagined the portraits of Haydn, powdered wig and all. He glanced at the Belter pilots from the corners of his eyes.

Ysyvry flinched and Olsen released a small squeak of surprise. He lifted his fingers from the keyboard and rotated to face them.

"Stop that," Olsen requested, obviously impressed.

Halloran dropped the illusion.

"That was beautiful," Ysyvry said.

"I'm human after all, even if I am a flatlander, no?"

"We'll give you that much," Olsen said. "You can look like anything you want to?"

"I'd rather talk about the music," Halloran said, adjusting tones on the musicomp to mimic harpsichord.

"We've never seen a kzin up close, for real," Ysyvry said. The expression on their faces was grimly anticipatory: Come on, scare us.

"I'm not a freak."

"So we've already established that much," Olsen said. "But you're a bit of a show-off, aren't you?"

"And a mind-reader," Ysyvry said.

He had deliberately avoided looking into their thoughts. Nobility of purpose.

"Perfect companion for a long voyage," Olsen added. "You can be whatever, whomever you want to be." Their expressions had become almost salacious. Now Halloran was sorry he had ever initiated conversation. How much of this was teasing, how much—actual cruelty?

Or were they simply testing his stability before insertion?

"You'd like to see a kzin?" he asked quietly.

"We'd like to see Fixer-of-Weapons," Ysyvry affirmed. "We were told you'd need to test the illusion before we release the hulk and your lifeship."

"It's a bit early—we still have two hundred hours."

"All the more time to turn back if you don't convince us," Olsen said.

"It's not just a hat I can put on and take off." He glanced between them, finding little apparent sympathy. Belters were polite, individualistic, but not the most socially adept of people. No wonder their mainstay on long voyages was silence. "I won't wear Fixer-of-Weapons unless I become him."

"You won't consciously know you're human?"

Halloran shook his head. "I'd rather not have the dichotomy to deal with. I'll be too busy with other activities."

"So the kzinti will think you're one of them, and . . . will *you*?"

"I will be Fixer-of-Weapons, or as close as I can become," Halloran said.

"Then you're worse than the fake soldiers in World War II," Olsen commented dryly.

"Show us," Ysyvry said, over her companion's words.

Halloran tapped his fingers on the edge of the keyboard for a few seconds. He could show them Halloran-Kzin—the generic kzin he had manufactured from Fixer-of-Weapons's memories. That would not be difficult.

"No," he said. "You've implied that there's something wrong, somehow, in what I'm going to do. And you're right. I only volunteered to do this sort of thing 'cause we're desperate. But it's not a game. I'm no freak, and I'm not going to provide a sideshow for a couple of bored and crass Belters."

He tapped out the serenade from Haydn's string quartet Opus 3 number 5.

Ysyvry smiled: "All right, Mr. Halloran. Looks like the UNSN made a good choice—not that they had much choice."

"I don't need your respect, either," Halloran said, a little surprised at how deeply he had been hurt. *I thought I was way beyond that.*

"What she's saying," Olsen elaborated, "is that we were asked to isolate you, and harass you a little. See if you're as much of a show-off as your records indicate you might be."

"Fine," Halloran said. "Now it's back to the silence?"

"No," Ysyvry said. "The music is beautiful. We'd appreciate your playing more for us."

Halloran swore under his breath and shook his head.

"Nobody said it would be easy, being a hero . . . did they?" Ysyvry asked.

"I'm no hero," Halloran said.

"I think you have the makings for one," Olsen told him, regarding him steadily with her clear green eyes. "Whatever kind of bastard you were on Earth. Really."

Will a flatlander ever understand Belters? They were

so mercurial, strong, and more than a little arrogant. Perhaps that was because space left so little room for niceties.

"If you accept it," Ysyvry said, "we've decided we'll make you an honorary Belter."

Halloran stopped playing.

"Please accept," Olsen said, not wheedling or even trying to placate; a simple, polite request.

"Okay," Halloran said.

"Good," Ysyvry said. "I think you'll like the ceremony."

He did, though it made him realize even more deeply how much he had to lose . . .

And why do I have to die before people start treating me decently?

The Belter pilots dropped the hulk a hundred and three hours after his induction into the ranks. They cut loose the kzin lifeship, with Halloran inside, five hours later, and then turned a shielded ion drive against their orbital path to drop inward and lose themselves in the Belt.

There were beacons on the lifeship, but no sensors. In the kzinti fleet, rescue of survivors was strictly at the discretion of the commanding officers. Halloran entered the digitized odor-signature and serial number of Fixer-of-Weapons into the beacon's transmitter and sat back to wait.

The lifeship had a month's supplies for an individual kzin. What few supplements he dared to carry, all consumable, would be gone in a week, and his time would start running out from that moment.

Still, Halloran half hoped he would not be found. He almost preferred the thought of failure to the prospect of carrying out his mission. It would be an ordeal. The worst thing that had ever happened to him. His greatest challenge in a relatively peaceful lifetime.

For a few days, he nursed dark thoughts about manifest destiny, the possibility that the kzinti really were the destined rulers of interstellar space, and that he was simply blowing against a hurricane.

Then came a signal from the kzinti fleet. Fixer-of-Weapons was still of some value. He was going to be rescued.

"Bullshit," Halloran said, grinning and hugging his arms tightly around himself. "Bullshit, bullshit, bullshit."

Now he was *really* afraid.

Wherever you are, whether in the crowded asteroid belt or beyond the furthest reaches of Pluto, space appears the same. Facing away from the sun—negligible anyway past the Belt—the same vista of indecipherable immensity presents itself. You say, yes, I know those are stars, and those are galaxies, and nebulae; I know there is life out there, and strangeness, and incident and death and change. But to the eye, and the animal mind, the universe is a flat tapestry sprinkled with meaningless points of fire. Nothing meaningful can emerge from such a tapestry.

The approach of a ship from the beautiful flat darkness and cold is itself a miracle of high order. The animal mind asks, *Where did it come from?*

Halloran, essentially two beings in one body, watched the kzinti dreadnought with two reactions. As Fixer-of-Weapons, now seating himself in the center of Halloran's mind, the ship—a rough-textured spire with an X cross at the "bow"—was both rescue and challenge. Fixer-of-Weapons had lost his status. He would have to struggle to regain his position, perhaps wheedle permission to challenge and supplant a Chief Weapons Officer and Alien Technologies Officer. He hoped—and Halloran prayed—that the positions on the rescue ship were held by one kzin, not two.

The battleship would pick up his lifeship within an

hour. In that time, Halloran adjusted the personality that would mask his own.

Halloran would exist in a preprogrammed slumber, to emerge only at certain key points of his plan. Fixer-of-Weapons would project continuously, aware and active, but with limitations; he would not challenge another kzin to physical combat, and he would flee at an opportune moment (if any came) if so challenged.

Halloran did not have a kzin's shining black claws or vicious fangs. He could project images of these to other kzinti, but they had only a limited effectiveness in action. For a moment, a kzin might think himself slashed by Fixer-of-Weapons's claws (although Halloran did not know how strong the stigmata effect was with kzinti), but that moment would pass. Halloran did not think he could convince a kzin to die . . .

He had never done such a thing with people. Exploring those aspects of his abilities had been too horrifying to contemplate. If he was pushed to such a test, and succeeded, he would destroy himself rather than return to Earth. Or so he thought, now . . .

Foolishness, Fixer-of-Weapons's persona grumbled. *A weapon is a weapon.*

Halloran shuddered.

The battleship communicated with the lifeship; first difficulty. The coughing growl and silky dissonance of the Hero's Tongue could not be readily mimicked, and Halloran could not project his illusion beyond a few miles; he did not respond by voice, but by coded signal. The signal was not challenged.

The kzinti could not conceive of an interloper invading their fold.

"Madness," he said as the ships closed. Humming the Haydn serenade, Lawrence Halloran Jr. slipped behind the scenes, and Fixer-of-Weapons came on center stage.

❖   ❖   ❖

The interior of the *Sons Contend With Bloody Fangs*—or any kzinti vessel, for that matter—smelled of death. It aroused in a human the deepest and most primordial fears. Imagine a neolithic hunter, trapped in a tiger's cave, surrounded by the stench of big cats and dead, decaying prey—and that was how the behind-the-scenes Halloran felt.

Fixer-of-Weapons salivated at the smells of food, but trembled at the same time.

"You are not well?" the escorting Aide-to-Commanders asked hopefully; Fixer's presence on the battleship could mean much disruption. The kzin's thoughts were quite clear to Fixer: *Why did Kfraksha-Admiral allow this one aboard? He smells of confinement . . . and . . .*

Fixer did not worry about these insights, which might be expected of a pitiful telepath; he would use whatever information was available to re-establish his rank and position. He lifted his lip at the subordinate, lowest of ranks aboard the battleship, a *servant* and licker-of-others'-fur. Aide-to-Commanders shrank back, spreading his ears and curling his thick, unscarred pink tail to signify non-aggression.

"Do not forget yourself," Fixer reminded him. "Kfraksha-Admiral is my ally. He chose to rescue me."

"So it is," Aide-to-Commanders acknowledged. He led Fixer down a steep corridor, with no corners for hiding would-be assailants, and straightened before the hatch to Kfraksha-Admiral's quarters. "I obey the instructions of the Dominant One."

That the commander did not allow Fixer to groom or eat before debriefing signified in how little regard he was held. Any survivor of a warship lost to animals carried much if not all the disgrace that would adhere to a surviving commander.

Kfraksha-Admiral bade him enter and growled to Aide-to-Commanders that they would be alone. This was how the kzin commander maintained his position without losing respect, by never exhibiting weakness or fear. Loss of respect could mean constant challenge, once they were out of a combat zone with its restrictions. As a kzin without rank, Fixer might be especially volatile; perhaps deranged by long confinement in a tiny lifeship, he might attack the commander in a foolish effort to regain and then better his status with one combat. But Kfraksha-Admiral apparently ignored all this, spider inviting spider into a very attractive parlor.

"Is your shame bearable?" Kfraksha-Admiral asked, a rhetorical question since Fixer was here, and not immediately contemplating suicide.

"I am not responsible for the actions of the commander of *War Loot*, Dominant One," Fixer replied.

"Yes, but you advised Kufcha-Captain of alien technologies, did you not?"

"I now advise you. Your advantage that I am here, and able to tell you what the animals can do."

Kfraksha-Admiral regarded Fixer with undisguised contempt and mild interest. "Animals destroyed your home. How did this happen?"

This is why I am aboard, Fixer thought. *Kfraksha-Admiral overcomes his disgust to learn things that will give him an edge.*

"They did not engage *War Loot* or any of our sortie. There is still no evidence that they have armed their worlds, no signs of an industry preparing for manufacture of offensive weapons—"

"They defeated you without weapons?"

"They have laser-propulsion systems of enormous strength. You recall, in our first meetings, the animals used their fusion drives against our vessels—"

"And allowed us to track their spoor back to their home worlds. The Patriarchy is grateful for such uneven exchanges. How might we balance this loss?"

Fixer puzzled over his reluctance to tell Kfraksha-Admiral everything. Then: *My knowledge is my life.*

"I am of no use to the fleet," Fixer said, with the slightest undertone of menace. He was gratified to feel—but not see—Kfraksha-Admiral tense his muscles. Fixer could measure the commander's resolve with ease.

"I do not believe that," Kfraksha-Admiral said. "But it is true that if you are no use to me, you are of no use to anybody . . . and not welcome."

Fixer pretended to think this over, and then showed signs of submission. "I am without position," he said sadly. "I might as well be dead."

"You have position as long as you are useful to me," Kfraksha-Admiral said. "I will allow you to groom and feed . . . if you can demonstrate how useful you might be."

Fixer cocked his fan-shaped ears forward in reluctant obeisance. These maneuvers were delicate—he could not concede too much, or Kfraksha-Admiral would come to believe he had no knowledge. "The humans must be skipping industrialization for offensive weapons. They are converting peaceful—"

Kfraksha-Admiral showed irritation at that word, not commonly used by kzinti.

"—propulsion systems into defensive weapons."

"This contradicts reports of their weakness," Kfraksha-Admiral said. "Our telepaths have reported the animals are reluctant to fight."

"They are adaptable," Fixer said.

"So much can be deduced. Is this all that you know?"

"I learned the positions from which two of the propulsion beams were fired. It should be easy to calculate their present locations . . ."

Kfraksha-Admiral spread his fingers before him, unsheathing long, black and highly polished claws. Now it was Fixer's turn to tense.

"You are my subordinate," the commander said. "You will pass these facts on to me alone."

"What is my position?" Fixer asked.

"Fleet records of your accomplishments have been relayed to me. Your fitness for position is acceptable." The days when mere prowess in personal combat decided rank were long gone, of course; qualifications had to be met before challenges could be made. "You will replace the Alien Technologies Officer on this ship."

"By combat?" A commander could grant permission . . . which was tantamount to an order to fight. Another means of intimidating subordinates.

"By my command. There will be no combat. Your presence here will not be disruptive, so do not become too ambitious, or you will face me . . . on unequal terms."

"And the present officer?"

"I have a new position he will not be unhappy with. That is not your concern. Now stand and receive my mark."

Halloran-Fixer could not anticipate what the commander intended quickly enough to respond with anything more than compliance. Kfraksha-Admiral lifted his powerful leg and swiftly, humiliatingly, peed on Halloran-Fixer, distinctly marking him as the commander's charge. Then Kfraksha-Admiral sat on a broad curving bench and regarded him coldly.

Deeply ashamed but docile—what else could he be?— Fixer studied the commander intently. It would not be so difficult to . . . what?

That thought was swept away even before it took shape.

Fixer-of-Weapons had no physical post as such aboard the flagship. He carried a reader the size of a kzin hand slung over his shoulder—with some difficulty, which did not immediately concern him—and went from point to point on the ship to complete his tasks, which were many, and unusually tiring.

The interior spaces of the *Sons Contend With Bloody Fangs* were strangely unfamiliar to him. Halloran had not had time (nor the capacity) to absorb all of his kzin subject's memories. He did not consciously realize he was giving himself a primary education in kzinti technology and naval architecture. His disorientation would have been an infuriating and goading sign of weakness to any inferior seeking his status, but he was marked by Kfraksha-Admiral—physically marked with the commander's odor, like female or a litter—and that warned aggressive subordinates away. They would have to combat Kfraksha-Admiral, not just Fixer.

And Fixer was proving himself useful to Kfraksha-Admiral. This aspect of Halloran's mission had been carefully thought out by Colonel Early and the Intelligence Staff—what could humans afford to have kzinti know about their technology? What would Fixer logically have deduced from his experience aboard the *War Loot*?

Kfraksha-Admiral, luckily, expected Fixer to draw out his revelations for maximum advantage. The small lumps of information deemed reasonable and safe—past locations of two Belter laser projectors that had since burned out their mirrors and lasing field coils, now abandoned and useless except as scrap—could be meted out parsimoniously.

Fixer could limp and cavil, and nobody would find it strange. He had, after all, been defeated by animals and lost all status. His current status was bound to be temporary. Kfraksha-Admiral would coax the important facts from him, and then—

So Fixer was not harassed. He studied his library, with some difficulty deciphering the enigmatic commas-and-dots script and mathematical symbologies. Unconsciously, he tapped the understanding of his fellows to buttress his knowledge.

And that was how he attracted the attention of somebody far more valuable than he, and of even lower status—Kfraksha-Admiral's personal telepath.

Kzinti preferred to eat alone, unless they had killed a large animal by common endeavor. The sight of another eating was likely to arouse deep-seated jealousies not conducive to good digestion; the quality of one's food aboard the flagship was often raised with rank, and rank was a smoothly ascending scale. Thus, the officers could not eat together safely, because there were no officers at the same level, and if there was no difference in the food, differences could be imagined. No. It was simply better to eat alone.

This suited Fixer. He had little satisfaction from his meals. He received his chunks of reconstituted meat-substitute heated to blood temperature—common low-status battle rations from the commissary officer, and retired to his quarters with the sealed container to open it and feed. His head hurt after eating the apparent raw slabs of gristle, bone and meager muscle; he preferred the simulated vegetable intestinal contents and soft organs, which were the kzinti equivalent of dessert. A kzin could bolt chunks the size of paired fists . . . But none of it actually pleased him. What he did not eat, he disposed of rapidly: pitiful, barely chewed-fragments it would have shamed a kzin to leave behind. Fixer did not notice the few pills he took afterwards, from a pouch seemingly beneath his chest muscles.

After receiving a foil-wrapped meal, he traversed the broad central hall of the dining area and encountered the worst-looking kzin he had ever seen. Fur matted, tail actually *kinked* in two places, expression sickly-sycophantic, ears recoiled as if permanently afraid of being attacked. Telepath scrambled from Fixer's path, as might be expected, and then—

Addressed him from behind.

"We are alike, in some respects—are we not?"

Fixer spun around and snarled furiously. One did not address a superior, or even an equal, from behind.

"No anger necessary," Telepath said, curling obeisantly, hands extended to show all claws sheathed. "There is an odd sound about you . . . it makes me curious. I have not permission to read you, but you are strong. You send. You *leak*."

Halloran-Fixer felt his fury redouble, for reasons besides the obvious impertinence. "You will stand clear of me and not address me, *Addict*," he spat.

"Not offending, but the sound is interesting, whatever it is. Does it come from time spent in solitude?"

Fixer quelled his rage and bounded down the Hall— or so it appeared to Telepath. The mind reader dropped his chin to his neck and resumed his halfhearted attempts to exercise and groom, his thoughts obviously lingering on his next session with the drug that gave him his abilities.

Fixer could easily tell what the commander and crew were up to, if not what they actually thought at any given moment. But Telepath was a blank slate. Nothing "leaked."

He returned to his private space, near the commander's quarters, and settled in for more sessions in the library. There was something that puzzled him greatly, and might be very important—something called a ghost star. The few mentions in the library files were unrevealing; whatever it was, it appeared to be somewhere about ten system radii outside the planetary orbits. It seemed that a ghost star was nothing surprising, and therefore not clearly explicated; this worried Fixer, for he did not know what a ghost star was.

❖   ❖   ❖

Kzinti aboard spaceships underwent constant training, self-imposed and otherwise. There were no recreation areas as such aboard the flagship; there were four exercise and mock-combat rooms, however, for the four rough gradations of rank from executive officers to servants. When kzinti entered a mock-combat room, they doffed all markings of rank, wearing masks to disguise their facial characteristics and strong mesh gloves over their claws to prevent unsheathing and lethal damage. Few kzinti were actually killed in mock-combat exercise, but severe injury was not uncommon. The ship's autodocs could take care of most of it, and kzinti considered scars ornamental. Anonymity also prevented ordinary sparring from affecting rank; even if the combatants *knew* the other's identity, it could be ignored through social fiction.

Fixer, in his unusual position of commander's charge, did not receive the challenges to mock-combat common among officers. But there was nothing in the rules, written or otherwise, that prevented subordinates from challenging each other, unless their officers interfered. Such combats were rare because most crewkzin knew their relative strengths, and who would be clearly outmatched.

Telepath, the lowest-ranked and most despised kzin aboard the flagship, challenged Fixer to mock-combat four day-cycles after his arrival. Fixer could not refuse; not even the commander's protection would have prevented his complete ostracization had he done so. His existence would have been an insult to the whole kzinti species. A simple command not to fight would have spared him—but the commander did not imagine that even the despised Fixer would face much of a fight from Telepath. And Fixer could not afford to be shunned; ostensibly, he had his position to regain.

So it was that Halloran faced a kzin in mock-combat. Fixer—the kzin persona—did not fall by the wayside, because Fixer could more easily handle the notion of combat. But Halloran did not remain completely in the background. For while Fixer was "fighting" Telepath, Halloran had to convince any observers—including Telepath—that he was winning.

Fixer's advantages were several. First, both combatants could emerge unharmed from the fray without raising undue suspicions. Second, there would be no remote observers—no broadcasts of the fight.

The major disadvantage was that of all the kzinti, a telepath should be most aware of having psychic tricks played on him.

The exercise chambers were cylindrical, gravitation oriented along one flat surface at Kzin normal, or higher for more strenuous regimens. The walls were sand-colored and a constant hot dry wind blew through hidden vents, conditions deemed comfortable in the culture that had dominated Kzin when the species achieved spaceflight. The floor was sprinkled with a flaked fluid-absorbing material. Kzinti rules for combat were few, and did not include prohibitions against surprise targeting of eye-stinging urine. The flakes were more generally soaked with blood, however. The rooms were foul with the odors of fear and exertion and injury.

Telepath was puny for a kzin. He weighed only a hundred and fifty kilograms and stood only two hundred and five centimeters from crown to toes, reduced somewhat by a compliant stoop. He was not in good shape, but he had little difficulty bending the smallest of the ten steel bars adjacent to his assigned half of the combat area—a little gesture legally mandated to give a referee some idea how the combatants were matched in sheer strength. This smallest bar was two centimeters in diameter.

Halloran-Fixer made as if to bend the next bar up, and then ostentatiously re-bent it straight, hoping nobody would examine it closely and find the metal completely unmarked. Probably nobody would; kzinti were less given to idle curiosity than humans.

Telepath screamed and leaped, arms spread wide. The image of Fixer was a bare ten centimeters to one side of his true position, and that allowed one of the kzin's feet to pass a hair's-breadth to one side of Halloran's head. Halloran convinced Telepath he had received a glancing blow across one arm. Telepath recovered somewhat sloppily, for a kzin, and sized up the situation.

There were only the mandated two observers in the antechamber. This fight was regarded as little more than comedy, and comedy, to kzinti, was shameful and demeaning. The observers' attentions were not sharply focused. Halloran-Fixer took advantage of that to dull their perceptions further. This allowed him to concentrate on Telepath.

Fixer did not crouch or make any overt signs of impending attack. He hardly breathed. Telepath circled at the outside of the combat area, nonchalant, apparently faintly amused.

Halloran had little experience with fighting. Fortunately, Fixer-of-Weapons had been an old hand at all kinds of combat, including the mortal kind that had quickly moved him up in rank while the fleet was in base, and much of that information had become lodged in the Fixer persona. Halloran waited for Telepath to make another energy-wasting move.

Kzinti combat was a matter of slight advantages. Possibly Telepath knew this, and sensed something not right about Fixer. Something weak . . .

But Telepath could not read Fixer's thoughts in any concentrated fashion; that required a great effort for the kzin, and debilitating physical weakness afterward. Halloran's powers were much more efficient and much less draining.

Fixer snarled and feigned a jump. Telepath leaped to one side, but Fixer had not completed his attack. He stood with tail twitching furiously several meters from the kzin, needle teeth bared in a hideous grin.

Telepath had good reason to be puzzled. It was rare for a threatened attack to be aborted, from a kzin so much larger and stronger than his opponent. Now the miserable kzin was truly angry, and afraid. Several times he rushed Fixer, but Fixer was never quite where he appeared to be. Several times, Halloran came near to having his head crushed by a passing swipe of the weak kzin's gloved hand, but managed to avoid the blow by centimeters. Something was goading Telepath beyond the usual emotions aroused by mock combat.

"Fight, you sexless female!" Telepath shrieked. A deeply obscene curse, and the observers did some of their own growling now. Telepath had done nothing to increase their esteem.

Fixer used the kzin's anger to his own advantage. The fight would have to end quickly—he was tiring rapidly, far faster than his puny opponent. Fixer seemed to run to a curved wall, leaping and rebounding, crossing the chamber in a flash—and bypassing Telepath without a blow. Telepath screamed with rage and tried to remove his gloves, but they were locked, and only the observers had the keys.

While Telepath was yowling fury and frustration, Fixer-Halloran delivered a bolt of suggestion that staggered the kzin, sending him to all fours with an apparent cuff to the jaw. The position was not as dangerous for a kzin—they could run more quickly on fours than erect—but Halloran-Kzin's image loomed over the stunned Telepath and kicked downward. The observers did not see the maneuver precisely, and Telepath was on the floor writhing in pain, his ear and the side of his head swelling with auto-suggestion injury.

Fixer offered his gloves to the observers and they were unlocked. He had not harmed Telepath, and had not received so much as a scratch himself. Fixer had acquitted himself; he still wore Kfraksha-Admiral's stink, but he was not the lowest of the kzinti on *Sons Contend With Bloody Fangs*.

"The humans obviously have a way of tracking our ships, yet they do not have the gravity polarizer . . ." Kfraksha-Admiral sat on his curved bench, legs raised, black-leather fingers clasped behind his thick neck, seeming quite casual and relaxed. "What is our weakness, that they spy on us and can aim their miserable adapted weapons upon us?"

Fixer's turmoil was not apparent. He knew the answer but of course he could not give it. He had to maneuver this conversation to determine if the commander was asking a rhetorical question, or testing him in some way.

"By our drives," he suggested.

"Yes, of course, but not by spectral signatures or flare temperatures, for in fact we do not use our fusion drives when we enter the system. And without polarizer technology, gravitational gradient warps cannot be detected . . . short of system wide detectors, which these animals do not have, correct?"

Fixer rippled his fur in agreement.

"No. They detect not the effects of our drives, but the power sources themselves. It is obvious they have discovered magnetic monopoles. I have suspected as much for years, but now plans are taking shape . . ."

Fixer-Halloran was relieved, and horrified, at once. This was indeed how kzinti ships were tracked; in fact, it was a little slow of the enemy not to have thought of it before. The cultural scientists back on Ceres had been puzzled as well; the kzinti had a science and technology more advanced than the human, but they seemed curiously inept at pure research. Almost as if the knowledge had been pasted onto a prescientific culture . . .

Every Belter prospector had monopole detection equipment; mining the super-massive particles was a major source of income for individual Belters, and for huge Belt corporations. Known monopole storage centers and power stations were automatically compensated for in even the cheapest detector. In an emergency, a detector could be used to determine position in the Belt—or anywhere else in the solar system—by triangulation from those known sources. An unknown—or kzinti—monopole source set detectors off throughout the solar system. And the newly-converted propulsion lasers could then be locked onto their targets . . .

"This much is now obvious. It explains our losses. Do you concur?"

"This is a fact," Fixer said.

"And how do you know it is a fact?" Kfraksha-Admiral challenged.

"The lifeship from *War Loot* is not powered by monopoles. I survived. Animals would not distinguish monopole sources by the size of the vessel—they would attack all sources."

Kfraksha-Admiral pressed his lips tight together and twitched whiskers with satisfaction. "Precisely so. We must have patience in our strategies, then. We cannot enter the system using our monopole-powered gravity polarizers. But there is the ghost star . . . if we enter the system without monopoles, and without approaching the gas-giant planets, where we might be expected . . . We can enter from an apparently empty region of space, unexpectedly, and destroy the animal populations of many worlds and asteroids. This plan's success is my sinecure. Many females, much territory—glory. We are moving outward now to pass around the ghost star and gain momentum."

Fixer-Halloran again felt a chill. Truly, without the monopoles, the kzinti ships would be difficult to detect.

Fixer pressed his hands together before his chest, a sign of deep respect. Kfraksha-Admiral nodded in condescending fashion.

"You have proven valuable, in your own reluctant, rankless way," he acknowledged, staring at him with irises reduced to pinpoints in the wide golden eyes. "You have endured humiliation with surprising fortitude. Some, our more enlightened and patient warriors, might call it courage." The commander drew a rag soaked in some pale liquid from a bucket behind his bench. He threw it at Fixer, who caught it.

The rag had been soaked in diluted acetic acid vinegar. "You may remove my mark," Kfraksha-Admiral said. "Henceforth, you have the status of full officer, on my formal staff, and you will be in charge of interpreting the alien technologies we capture. Your combat with Telepath . . . has been reported to me. It was not strictly honorable, but your forbearance was remarkable. In part, this earns you a position."

Fixer now had status. He could not relax his vigilance, for he would no longer be under the commander's protection, but he could assume the armor of a true billet; separate quarters, specific duties, a place in the ritual of the kzinti flagship. Presumably the commander would not grant permission for many challenges, and as a direct subordinate he would count as one of the commander's faction, who would retaliate for any unprovoked attack.

The *Sons Contend With Bloody Fangs* had pulled its way out of the sun's gravity well at a prodigious four-tenths of the speed of light, faster than was safe within a planetary system, and was racing for the ghost star a hundred billion kilometers from the sun. Sol was now an anonymous point of light in the vastness of the Sagittarius arm of the galaxy; the outer limits of the solar system were almost as far behind.

The commander's plans for the whiplash trip around the ghost star were secret to all but a few. Fixer was still not even certain what the ghost star was—it was not listed under that name in the libraries, and there was obviously a concept he was not connecting with. But it was fairly easy to calculate that to accomplish the orbital maneuvers the commander proposed, the ghost star would have to be of at least one-half solar mass. Nothing that size had ever been detected from Earth; it was therefore dark and absolutely cold. There would be no perturbed orbits to give it away; its distance was too great.

So for the time being, Fixer assumed they were approaching a rendezvous with either a dark, dead hulk of a star, or perhaps a black hole.

A hundred billion kilometers was still close to the solar neighborhood, as far as interstellar distances were concerned. That kzinti knew more about these regions than humans worried the sublimated Halloran. What other advantages would they gain? The time had come for Halloran to examine what he had found. With his personality split in half, and locked into a kzin mentality, he might easily overlook something crucial to his mission.

In his quarters, with the door securely bolted, Halloran came to the surface. Seven days in the kzinti flagship had taken a terrible toll on him; in a small mirror, he saw himself almost cadaverous, his face deeply lined. Kzinti did not use water to groom themselves, and there were no taps in his private quarters—the aliens were descended from a pack-hunting desert carnivore, and had efficient metabolisms—so his skin and clothing would remain dirty. He took a medicinal towelette, used to treat minor scratches received during combats, and wiped as much of his face and hands clean as he could. The astringent solution in the towelette served to sharpen his wits. After so long in Fixer's charge, there seemed little brilliance and fire left in Halloran himself.

And Fixer is just not very bright, he thought sourly. *Think, monkey, think!*

He looked old.

"Bleep that," he murmured, and picked up the library pack. As Fixer, he had subliminally marked interesting passages in the kzinti records. Now he set out to learn what the ghost star was, and what he might expect in the next few hours, as they approached and parabolically orbited. A half-hour of inquiry, his eyes reddening under the strain of reading the kzinti script without Fixer's intercession, brought no substantial progress.

"Ghost," he muttered. "Specter. Spirit. Ancestors. A star known to ancestors? Not likely—they would have come on into the solar system and destroyed or enslaved us centuries ago . . . what the tanj *is* a ghost star?"

He queried the library on all concepts incorporating the words ghost, specter, ancestor, and other synonyms in the Hero's Tongue. Another half-hour of concentrated and fruitless study, and he was ready to give up, when the projector displayed an entry. *Specter Mass*.

He cued the entry. A flagged warning came up; the symbol for shame-and-disgrace, a Patriarchal equivalent of Most Secret.

Fixer recoiled; Halloran had to intervene instantly to stop his hand before it halted the search. Curiosity was not a powerful drive for a kzin, and shame was a *very* effective deterrent.

A basic definition flashed up. *"That mass created during the first instants of the universe, separated from kzinti space-time and detectable only by weak gravitational interaction. No light or other communication possible between the domain of specter mass and kzinti space-time."*

Halloran grinned for the first time in seven days.

Now he had it—he could *feel* the solution coming. He cued more detail.

"Stellar masses of specter matter have been detected, but are rare. None has been found in living memory. These masses, in the specter domain, must be enormous, on the order of hundreds of masses of the sun"—the star of Kzin, more massive and a little cooler than Sol— *"for their gravitational influence is on the order of .6 [base 8] Kzin suns. The physics of the specter domain must differ widely from our own. Legends warn against searching for ghost stars, though details are lost or forbidden by the Patriarchy."*

Not a black hole or a dark star, but a star in a counter-universe. Human physicists had discovered the possible existence of *shadow mass* in the late twentieth century— Halloran remembered that much from his physics classes. The enormously powerful superstring theory of particles implied *shadow mass* pretty much as the kzinti entry described it. None had been detected . . .

Who would have thought the Earth was so near to a ghost star?

And now, Kfraksha-Admiral was recommending what the kzinti had heretofore forbidden—lose approach to a ghost star to gain a gravitational advantage. The kzinti ships would appear, to human monopole detectors, to be leaving the system—retreating, although slowly. Then the fleet would decelerate and discard its monopoles, sending them on the same outward course, and swing around the ghost star, gaining speed from the star's angular momentum. No fusion drives would be used, so as not to alarm human sentries. Slowly, the fleet would swing back into the solar system, and within a kzinti year, attack the worlds of men. Undetected, unsuspected, the kzinti fleet could end the war then and there. The monopoles would be within retrieval distance.

And all it would require was a little kzinti patience, a rare virtue indeed.

Someone scratched softly at the ID plate on his hatch. Halloran did not assume the Fixer persona, but projected the Fixer image, before answering. The hatch opened a safe crack, and Halloran saw the baleful, rheumy eye of Telepath peering in.

"I have bested you already," the Fixer image growled. "You wish to challenge for a shameful rematch?" Not something Fixer need grant in any case, now that his status was established.

"I have a problem which I must soon bring to the attention of Kfraksha-Admiral," Telepath said, with the edge of a despicable whimper.

"Why come to me?"

"You are the problem. I hear sounds from you. I *remember* things from you. And I have dreams in which you appear, but not as you are now . . . sometimes I am you. I am the lowest, but I am important to this fleet, especially with the death of *War Loot*'s Telepath. I am the last Telepath in the fleet. My health is important—"

"Yes, yes! What do you want?"

"Have you been taking the telepath drug?"

"No."

"I can tell . . . you speak truth, yet you hide something."

The kzin could not now deeply read Halloran without making an effort, but Halloran was "leaking." Just as he had never been able to quell his "intuition," he could not stop this basic hemorrhage of mental contents. The kzin's drug-weakened mind was there to receive, perhaps more vulnerable because the subconscious trickle of sensation and memory was alien to it.

"I hide nothing. Go away," the Fixer-image demanded harshly.

"Questions first. What is an 'Esterhazy'? What are these sounds I hear, and what is a 'Haydn'? Why do I feel emotions which have no names?"

The kzin's pronunciation was not precise, but it was close enough. "I do not know. Go away."

Halloran began to close the door, but Telepath wailed and stuck his leathery digits into the crack. Halloran instinctively stopped the hatch to prevent damage. A kzin would not have . . .

"I cannot see Kfraksha-Admiral. I am the lowest . . . but I feel danger! We are approaching very great danger. My shields are weakening and my sensitivity increases even with lower doses of the drug . . . Do you know where we are going? I can feel this danger deep, in a place my addiction has only lightly touched . . . Others feel it too. There is restlessness. I must report what I feel! Tell the commander—"

Cringing, Halloran pressed the lever and the door continued to close. Telepath screamed and pulled out his digits in time to avoid losing more than a tip and one sheathed claw.

That did it. Halloran began to shake uncontrollably. Sobbing, he buried his face in his hands. Death seemed very immediate, and pain, and brutality. He had stepped into the lion's den. The lions were closing in, and he was weakening. He had never faced anything so horrible before. The kzinti were insane. They had no softer feelings, nothing but war and destruction and conquest . . .

And yet, within him there were fragments of Fixer-of-Weapons to tell him differently. There was courage, incredible strength, great vitality.

"Not enough," he whispered, removing his face from his hands. Not enough to redeem them, certainly, and not enough to make him feel any less revulsion. If he could, he would wipe all kzinti out of existence. If he could just expand his mind enough, reach out across time and space to the distant home-world of kzin, touch them with a deadliness . . .

The main problem with a talent like Halloran's was hubris. Aspiring to god-like ascendancy over others, even kzinti. That way lay more certain madness.

A kzin wouldn't think that way, Halloran knew. *A kzin would scream and leap upon a tool of power like that.* "Kzin have it easier," he muttered.

Time to marshal his resources. How long could he stay alive on the kzinti flagship?

If he assumed the Fixer persona, no more than three days. They would still be rounding the ghost star . . .

If he somehow managed to take control of the ship, and could be Halloran all the time, he might last much longer. And to what end?

To bring the *Sons Contend With Bloody Fangs* back to human space? That would be useful, but not terribly important—the kzinti would have discarded their gravity polarizers. Human engineers had already studied the hulk of *War Loot*, not substantially different from *Sons Contend*.

But he wanted to *survive*. On that Halloran and Fixer-Halloran were agreed. He could feel survival as a clean, metallic necessity, cutting him off from all other considerations. The Belter pilots and their initiation . . . Coming to an understanding of sorts with his father. Early's wish-list. What he knew about kzinti . . .

That could be transmitted back. He did not need to survive to deliver that. But such a transmission would take time, a debriefing of weeks would be invaluable.

Survival.

Simple life.

To *win*.

Thorough shit or not, Halloran valued his miserable life.

Perhaps I'm weak, like Telepath. Sympathetic. Particularly towards myself.

But the summing up was clear and unavoidable. The best thing he could do would be to find some way to inactivate at least this ship, and perhaps the whole kzinti fleet. Grandiose scheme. At the very top of Early's wishlist. All else by the wayside.

And he could not do it by going on a rampage. He had to be smarter than the kzinti; he had to show how humans, with all their love of life and self-sympathy, could beat the self-confident, savage invaders.

No more being Fixer. Time to use Fixer as a front, and be a complete, fully aware Halloran.

Telepath whimpered in his sleep. There was no one near to hear him in this corridor; disgust could be as effective as status and fear in securing privacy.

Hands were lifting him. *Huge* hands, tearing him away from Mother's side. His own hands were tiny, so tiny as he clung with all four limbs to Mother's fur.

She was growling, screaming at the males with the Y-shaped poles who pinned her to the wicker mats, lashing out at them as they laughed and dodged. Hate and fury stank through the dark air of the hut. "Maaaa!" he screamed. "Maaaa!"

The hands bore him up, crushed him against a muscular side that smelled of leather and metal and kzin-tosh, male kzin.

They will eat me, they will eat me! cried instinct. He lashed out with needle-sharp baby claws, and the booming voice above him laughed and swore, holding the wriggling bundle out at arm's length.

"This one has spirit," the Voice said.

"Puny," another replied dismissively. *"I will not rear it. Send it to the crèche."*

They carried him out into the bright sunlight, and

he blinked against the pain of it. Fangs loomed above him, and he hissed and spat; a hand pushed meat into his mouth. It was good, warm and bloody; he tore loose chunks and bolted them, ears still folded down. From the other enclosures came the growls and screams of females frightened by the scent of loss, and behind him his mother gave one howl of grief after another.

Telepath half-woke, grunting and starting, pink bat-ears flaring wide as he took in the familiar subliminal noises of pumps and ventilators.

He was laughing, walking across the quadrangle. Faces turned toward him

—*naked faces?*—

Mouths turning to round O shapes of shock.

—*Flat mouths? Flat teeth?*—

Students and teachers were turning toward him, and he knew they saw the headmaster, buck-naked and priapically erect. He laughed and waved again, thinking how Old Man Velasquez would explain *this*—

Telepath struggled. Something struck him on the nose and he started upright, pink tongue reflexively washing at the source of the welcome, welcome pain. The horror of the nightmare slipped away, too alien to comprehend with the waking mind.

"Silence, *sthondat*-sucker!" Third Gunner snarled, aiming a kick that thudded drumlike on Telepath's ribs. Another harness-buckle was in one hand, ready to throw. "Stop screaming in your sleep!"

Telepath widened his ears and flattened his fur in propitiation as he crouched; Third Gunner was not a great intellect, but he was enormous and touchy even for a young kzin. After a moment the hulking shape turned and padded off down the corridor to his own doss, grumbling and twitching his whiskers. The smaller kzin sank down again to his thin pallet, curling into a fetal ball and covering his nose with his hands, wrapping his tail around the whole bundle of misery. He quivered, his matted fur wrinkling in odd patterns, and forced his eyes to close.

I must sleep, he thought. His fingers twitched toward the pouch with his drag, but that only made things worse. *I must sleep; my health is important to the fleet.* Unless he was rested he could not read minds on command. Without that, he was useless and therefore dead, and Telepath did not want to die.

But if he slept, he dreamed. For the last four sleeps the dreams of his kittenhood had been almost welcome. Eerie combinations of sound plucked at the corners of his mind as he dozed, as precise as mathematics but carrying overtones of feelings that were not *his*—

He jerked awake again. *Mother*, he thought, through a haze of fatigue. *I want my mother.*

The alienness of the dreams no longer frightened him so much.

What was really terrifying was the feeling he was beginning to *understand* them . . .

Halloran flexed and raised his hands, crouching and growling. Technician's-Assistant stepped aside at the junction of the two corridors, but Fire-Control-Technician retracted his ears and snarled, dropping his lower jaw toward his chest. Aide-to-Commanders had gone down on his belly, crawling aside. Beside the disguised human Chief-Operations-Officer bulked out his fur and responded in kind.

Sure looks different without Fixer, Halloran thought as he sidled around the confrontation.

The kzinti were almost muzzle-to-muzzle, roaring at each other in tones that set the metal around them to vibrating in sympathy; thin black lips curled back from wet half-inch fangs, and the ruffled fur turned their bodies into bristling sausage shapes. The black-leather shapes of their four-fingered hands were almost skeletal, the long claws shining like curves of liquid jet. Dim orange-red light made Halloran squint and peer. The walls here in this section of officer country were covered with holographic murals; a necessity, since kzinti were very vulnerable to sensory deprivation. Twisted thorny orange vegetation crawled across shattered rock under a lowering sky the color of powdered brickdust, and in the foreground two Kzinti had overturned something that looked like a giant spiked turtle with a bone club for a tail. They were burying their muzzles in its belly, ripping out long stretches of intestine.

Abruptly, the two high-ranking kzin stepped back and let their fur fall into normal position, walking past each other as if nothing had happened.

Nothing did, a ghost of Fixer said at the back of Halloran's head; the thin psychic voice was mildly puzzled. *Normal courtesy*. Passing by without playing at challenge would be an insult, showing contempt for one not worthy of interest. Real challenge would be against regulations, now.

Chief-Operations-Officer scratched at the ID plate on the commander's door, releasing Kfraksha-Admiral's coded scent. A muffled growl answered.

Kfraksha-Admiral was seated at his desk, worrying the flesh off a heavy bone held down with his hands. A long shred of tendon came off as he snapped his head back and forth, and his jaws made a wet *clop* sound as he bolted it.

"Is all proceeding according to plan?" he asked.

"Yes, Dominant One," Chief-Operations-Officer said humbly.

"Then why are you taking up my valuable time?" Kfraksha-Admiral screamed, extending his claws.

"Abasement," Chief-Operations-Officer said. He flattened to the floor in formal mode; the others joined him. "The jettisoning of the monopoles and gravity polarizer components has proceeded according to your plans. There are problems."

"Describe them."

"A much higher than normal rate of replacement for all solid-state electronic components, Kfraksha-Admiral," the engineer said. "Computers and control systems particularly. Increasing as a function of our approach to the ghost star. Also personnel problems."

Kfraksha-Admiral's whiskers and fur moved in patterns that meant lively curiosity; discipline was the problem any Kzin commander would anticipate, although perhaps not so soon.

"Mutiny?" he said almost eagerly.

"No. Increased rates of impromptu dueling, sometimes against regulations. Allegations of murderous intent unsupported by evidence. Superstitions. Several cases of catatonia and insanity leading to liquidation by superiors. Suicides. Also rumors."

"*Hrrrr!*" Kfraksha-Admiral said. Suicide was an admission of cowardice, and very rare.

Time to fish or be *bait*, Halloran decided.

Gently, he probed at the consciousness of the kzin, feeling the three-things-at-once sensation of indecision. Kfraksha-Admiral knew something of why the Patriarchy forbade mention of phenomenon; because the Conservors of the Ancestral Past couldn't figure out what was involved. Inexplicable and repeated bad luck, usually; the kzin was feeling his fur try to bristle. Kzinti *believed* in luck, as firmly as they believed in games theory. Eternal shame for Kfraksha-Admiral if he turned back now. His cunning suggested aborting the mission; an unwary male would never have become a fleet commander. Gut feeling warred with it; even for a kzin, Kfraksha-Admiral was aggressive; otherwise he could never have achieved or held his position.

Shame, Halloran whispered, ever so gently. It was not difficult. Easier than it had ever been before, and now he felt *justified*.

Eternal disgrace for retreating, his mind intruded softly. *Two years of futility already. Defeat by plant-eaters.* Sickening images of unpointed grinding teeth chewing roots. *Endless challenges.* A commander turned cautious had a line of potential rivals light-years long, waiting for stand-down from Active Status. Kzin were extremely territorial; modern kzin had transferred the instinct from physical position to rank.

Glory if we win. More glory for great dangers overcome. Conquest Hero Kfraksha-Admiral—no, Kfraksha-Tchee, a full name, unimaginable wealth, planetary systems of slaves with a fully industrialized society. Many sons. Generations to worship my memory. The commander's ears unfolded as he relaxed, decisions made. "This is a perilous course. Notify *Flashing Claws*"—a Swift Hunter-class courier, lightly armed but lavishly equipped with drive and fuel—"to stand by on constant datalink." The Patriarchy would know what happened. "The fleet will proceed as planned. Slingshot formation, with *Sons Contend With Bloody Fangs* occupying the innermost trajectory."

That would put the flagship at the point of the roughly conical formation the fleet was to assume; the troopships with their loads of infantry would be at the rear. "Redouble training schedules. Increase rations." Well-fed kzin were more amenable to discipline. And—"Rumors of what?"

"That we approach the Darkstar of Ill-Omen, Dominant One."

Kfraksha-Admiral leaned forward, his claws prickling at the files of printout on his desk. *"That was confidential information!"* He glared steadily at Chief-Operations-Officer, extreme discourtesy among carnivores. The subordinate extended hands and ears, with an aura of sullenness.

"I have told no one of the nature of the object we approach," he said. Few kzinti would trouble to prod and poke for information not immediately useful, either. "The ship and squadron commanders have been informed; so have the senior staff."

"Hrrr. Chirrru. You—" a jerk of the tail towards Aide-to-Commanders. "Fetch me Telepath."

Halloran slumped down on the mat in his quarters, head cradled in his hands, fighting to control his nausea. *Murphy, don't tell me I'm developing an allergy to kzin*, he thought, holding his shaking hands out before him. The mottled spots were probably some deficiency disease, or his immune system might be giving up under the strain of ingesting all these not-quite-earthlike proteins. He belched acid, swallowed past a painfully dry throat, remembering his last meeting with his father. A kzin ship was like the *real* Arizona desert, and it was sucking the moisture out of his tissues, no matter how much he drank. A dry cold, though. It held down the soupy smell of dried rancid sweat that surrounded him; that had nearly given him away half a dozen times.

A sharp pain thrilled up one finger. Halloran looked down and found he had been absently stropping non-existent claws on the panel of corklike material set next to the pallet. A broken fingernail was bent back halfway. He prodded it back into place, shuddering, tied one of the antiseptic pads around it and secured it with a strip of cloth before he lowered himself with painful slowness to his back. Slow salt-heavy tears filled the corners of his eyes and ran painfully down the chapped skin of his face.

It was easier to be Fixer. Fixer did not hurt. Fixer was not lonely. Fixer did not feel guilt; shame, perhaps, but never guilt.

Fixer doesn't exist. I am Lawrence Halloran, Jr. He closed his eyes and tried to let his breathing sink into a regular rhythm. It was difficult for more reasons than the pain; every time he began to drop off, he would jerk awake again with unreasoning dread. Not of the nightmares, just dread of *something.*

Intuition. Halloran had always believed in intuition. Or maybe just the trickle of fear from the crew, but he should not be *that* sensitive, even with fatigue and weakness wearing down his shields. His talent should be weaker, not stronger.

Enough. "My status is that of a complete shit, but my health is important to the mission," he mumbled sardonically to himself. Sleep was like falling—

—and the others were chasing him again, through the corridors of the crèche. Pain shot in under his ribs as he bounded along four-footed, and his tongue lolled dry and grainy. They were all bigger than him, and there were a double handful of them! Bright light stabbed at his eyes as he ran out into the exercise yard, up the tumbled rocks of the pile in the center, gritty ocher sandstone under his hands and feet. Nowhere to run but the highest . . .

Fear cut through his fatigue as he came erect on the central spire. He was above them! The high-status kits would think he was challenging them!

Squalls of rage confirmed it as the orange-and-spotted tide boiled out of the doorway and into the vast quadrangle of scrub and sand. Tails went rigid, claws raked toward him; he stood and screamed back, but he could hear the quaver in it, and the impulse to grovel and spread his ears was almost irresistible. Hate flowed over him with the scent of burning ginger, varied only by the individual smells of the other children. Rocks flew around him as they poured up the miniature crags; something struck him over one eye. Vision blurred as the nictitating membranes swept down, and blood poured over one. The smell of it was like death, but the others screeched louder as they caught the waft.

Hands and feet gripped him as he slumped down on the hard rock, clawing and yanking hair and lifting, and then he was flying. Instinct rotated his head down, but he was already too stunned to get his hands and feet well under him; he landed sprawling across an edge of sandstone and felt ribs crack. Then the others were on him, mauling, and he curled into a protective ball but two of them had his tail, they were stretching it out and raising rocks in their free hands and *crack* and *crack*—

Halloran woke, shuddering and wincing at pain in an organ he did not possess. Several corridors away, Telepath screamed until the ratings dossed near him lost all patience and broke open an arms locker to get a stunner.

"Dreams? Explain yourself, *kshat*," Kfraksha-Admiral growled.

Telepath ventured a nervous lick of his nose, eyes darting around, too genuinely terrified to resent being called the kzin equivalent of a rabbit.

"Nothing. I said nothing of dreams," he said, then shrieked as the commander's claws raked along the side of his muzzle.

"*You dare to contradict me?*"

"I abase mysel—"

"Silence! You distinctly said 'dreams' when I asked you to determine the leakage of secret information."

"Leaks. First Fixer-of-Weapons was leaking. He is strong. He *leaks*. I run from him but I cannot hide in sleep. Such shame. Now *more* are leaking. The officers dream of the Ghost Star. Ancestors who died without honor haunt it . . . their hands reach up to drag us down to nameless rot. One feels it. All feel it—"

"Silence! Silence!" Kfraksha-Admiral roared, striking open-handed. Even then he retained enough control not to use his claws; this thing *was* the last Telepath in the fleet, after all, even if insanity was reducing its usefulness.

And even such a sorry excuse for a kzin shouldn't be much harmed by being beaten unconscious.

"You find time to groom?" Kfraksha-Admiral asked sullenly.

Finagle, Halloran swore inwardly, drawing the Fixer persona more tightly around him. The last sleep-cycle had seen a drastic deterioration in *everyone's* grooming, except his memorized projection. The commander's pelt was not quite matted; it would be a long time before he looked as miserable as Telepath—Finagle alone knew what Telepath looked like now, he seemed to have vanished—but he was definitely scruffy. The entire bridge crew looked peaked, and several were absent, their places taken by younger, less-scarred understudies. Some of those understudies had new bandages, evidence that their superiors' usefulness had deteriorated to the point where the commander would allow self-promotion. The human's talent told him the dark cavern of the command deck smelled of fear and throttled rage and bewilderment; the skin crawled down his spine as he sensed it.

Kzinti did not respond well to frustration. They also did not expect answers to rhetorical questions.

Kfraksha-Admiral turned to Chrung-Fleet-Communications Officer. "Summarize."

"*Hero's Lair* still does not report," that kzin said dully.

That was the first of the troop-transports, going in on a trajectory that would leave them "behind" the cruisers, dreadnoughts, and stingship carriers when the fleet finally made its out-of-elliptic slingshot approach to Earth. Kfraksha-Admiral had calculated that Earth was probably the softest major human target, and less likely to be alert. Go in undetected, take out major defenses and space-industrial centers, land the surface-troops; the witless hordes of humankind's fifteen billions would be hostages against counterattack.

If things go well, Halloran thought, easing a delicate tendril into the commander's consciousness. *Murphy rules the kzin, as well as humans.* Wearily: *When do things ever go well?*

—and the long silky grass blew in the dry cool wind, that was infinitely clean and empty. His Sire and the other grown males were grouped around the carcass, replete, lapping at drinks in shallow, beautifully fashioned silver cups. He and the other kits were round-stomached and content, play-sparring lazily, and he lay on his back batting at the bright-winged insect that hovered over his nose, until Sire put a hand on his chest and leaned over to rasp a roughly loving tongue across his ears—

"It is well, it is well," Kfraksha-Admiral crooned softly, almost inaudibly. Then he came to himself with a start, looking around as heads turned toward him.

Finagle, I set him off on a memory-fugue! Halloran thought, feeling the kzin's panic and rising anger, the tinge of suspicion beneath that.

"All must admire Kfraksha-Admiral's strategic sense," Halloran-Fixer said hastily. "Light losses, for a strategic gain of the size this operation promises."

Kfraksha-Admiral signed curt assent, turning his attention from the worthless sycophant. Behind Fixer's mask, Halloran's human face contorted in a savage grin. Manipulating Kfraksha-Admiral's subconscious was more fun than haunting the other kzin. *Even for a ratcat, he's a son-of-a . . . pussy, I suppose. Singleminded, too.* Relatively easy to keep from wondering what was causing all this—*I wish I knew*—and tightly, tightly focus on getting through the next few hours. Closest approach soon.

And it was all so *easy*. He was *unstoppable* . . .

Scabs broke and he tasted the salt of blood. *I'm not going to make it.* He ground his jaws and felt the loosening teeth wobble in their sockets. Death was a bitterness, no glory in it, only this foul decay. *Maybe I shouldn't make it. I'm too dangerous.* His face had been pockmarked with open sores, the last time he looked. Maybe that was how he looked inside.

So easy, sucking the kzinti crews down into a cycle of waking nightmare. As if they were doing it to themselves. Fixer howled laughter from within his soul.

"I have the information by the throat, but I still do not understand," Physicist said, staring around wildly. He was making the *chiruu-chiruu* sounds of kzinti distress. *Dealer-With-Very-Small-and-Large* was a better translation of his name/title. "I do not understand!"

Most of the bridge equipment was closed down. Ventilation still functioned, internal fields, all based on simple feedback systems. Computers, weapons, communications, all had grown too erratic to trust. A few lasers still linked the functioning units of the fleet.

Outside, the stars shone with jeering brightness. Of the Ghost Star there was no trace; no visible light, no occlusion of the background . . . and instruments more sophisticated had given out hours ago. Many of the bridge crew still stayed at their posts, but their scent had soured; the steel *wtsai* knives at their belts attracted fingers like unconscious lures.

"Explain," Kfraksha-Admiral rasped.

"The values, the records just say that physical law in the shadow-matter realm is unlike kzinti timespace . . . and there is crossover this close! The effect increases exponentially as we approach the center of mass; we must be within the radius the object occupies in the other continuum. The cosmological constants are varying. Quantum effects. The U/R threshold of quantum probability functions itself is increasing, that is why all electronic equipment becomes unreliable—probability cascades are approaching the macrocosmic level."

Kfraksha-Admiral's tail was quivering-rigid, and he panted until thin threads of spittle drooled down from the comers of his mouth.

"Then we shall win! We are nearly at point of closest approach. Our course is purely ballistic. Systems will regain their integrity as we recede from the area of singularity."

Murphy wins again, Halloran thought wearily, slumping back against the metal wall. His body was shaking, and he felt a warm trickle down one leg. *He's right*. The irony of it was enough to make him laugh, except that that would have hurt too much. Halloran had done the *noble* thing. He had put everything into controlling Kfraksha-Admiral, blinding him to the voices of prudence . . .

And the bleeping ratcat was right *after all*.

His shields frayed as the human despaired. Frayed more strongly than he had ever felt, even drunk or coming, until he felt/was Kfraksha-Admiral's ferocious triumph, Physicist's jumble of shifting equations, Telepath's hand pressing the ampule of his last drug capsule against his throat in massive overdose, *why have the kzinti disintegrated like this—*

Halloran would never have understood it. He lacked the knowledge of physics—the ARM had spent centuries discouraging that—but Physicist was next to him, and the datalink was strong. No kzinti could have understood it; they were simply not introspective enough. Halloran-Fixer *knew*, with the whole-argument suddenness of revelation; knew as a composite creature that had experienced the inwardness of Kzin and Man together.

The conscious brain is a computer, but one of a very special kind. Not anything like a digital system; that was one reason why true Artificial Intelligence had taken so long to achieve, and had proven so worthless once found. Consciousness does not operate on mathematical algorithms, with their prefixed structures. It is a quantum process, indeterminate in the most literal sense. Thoughts became conscious—decision was taken, will exercised— when the nervous system amplified them past the one-graviton threshold level. So was insight, a direct contact with the paramathematical frame of reality.

They couldn't know, Halloran realized. Kzinti physics was excellent but their biological sciences primitive by human standards.

And I know what's driving them crazy, he realized. Telepathy was another threshold effect. Any conscious creature possessed *some* ability. The Ghost Star was amplifying it to a terrifying level, even as it disabled the computers by turning their off/on synapses to off *and* on. Humans might be able to endure it; Man is a gregarious species.

Not the kzinti. Not those hard, stoic, isolated killer souls. Forever guarded, forever wary, disgusted by the very thought of such an involuntary sharing . . . whose only glimpse of telepathy was creatures like Telepath. Utter horror, to feel the boundaries of their personalities fraying, merging, becoming *not-self*.

Halloran knew what he had to do. *It's the right thing.* Fixer-of-Weapons stirred exultantly in his tomb of flesh. *Die like a Hero!* he battle-screeched.

Letting go was like thinning out, like dying, like being free for the first time in all his life. Halloran's awareness flared out, free of the constraints of distance, touching lightly at the raw newly-forged connections between thousands of minds in the Ghost Sun's grip. *I get to be omnipotent just before the end*, he thought in some distant corner. To his involuntary audience: *MEET EACH OTHER*.

The shock of the steel was almost irrelevant, the reflex that wrenched him around to face Telepath automatic. Undeceived at last, the kzin's drug-dilated eyes met the human's. Halloran slumped forward, opening his mouth, but there was no sound or breath as

—he—

"Get out of my dreams!"

—the human—

—fell—

—released—

"Shit," Halloran murmured. His heels drummed on the deck. *Mom.*

The roar from Colonel Buford Early's office was enough to bring his aide-de-camp's head through the door. One glance at his Earther superior was enough to send it back through the hatch.

Early swore again, more quietly but with a scatological breadth that showed both his inventiveness and his age; it had been *many* generations since some of those Anglo-Saxon monosyllables had been in common use.

Then he played the audio again; without correction, but listening carefully for the rhythm of the phrasing under the accent imposed by a vocal system and palate very unlike that of *Homo sapiens sapiens*:

"—so you see"—it sounded more like *zo uru t'zee*—"it's not really relevant whether I'm Halloran or whether he's dead and I'm a kzinti with delusions. Halloran's . . . memories were more used to having an alien in his head than Telepath's were, poor bleeping bastard. The Fleet won't be giving you any trouble, the few that are still alive will be pretty thoroughly insane.

"On the other hand," the harsh nonhuman voice

continued, "remembering what happened to Fixer I really don't think it would be all that advisable to come back. And you know what? I've decided that I really don't owe any of you that much. Died for the cause already, haven't I?"

A rasping sound, something between a growl and a purr: kzinti laughter. "I'm seeing a lot of things more clearly now. Amazing what a different set of nerves and hormones can do. My talent's almost as strong now as it was . . . before, and I've got a *lot* less in the way of inhibitions. It's the Patriarchy that ought to be worried, but of course they'll never know."

Then a hesitation: "Tell my Sire . . . tell Dad I died a Hero, would you, Colonel?"

• EPILOGUE

The kzin finished grooming his pelt to a lustrous shine before he followed Medical-Technician to the deepsleep chamber of the Swift Hunter courier *Flashing Claws*. His face was expressionless as the cover lowered above him, and then his ears wrinkled with glee; there would be nobody to see until they arrived in the Alpha Centauri system a decade from now.

The Patriarchy had never had a Telepath who earned a full name before.

Too risky! Telepath wailed.

Kshat, Fixer thought with contempt.

Shut up both of you, Halloran replied. *Or I'll start thinking about salads again.* All of them understood the grin that showed his/their fangs.

The Patriarchy had never had one like Halloran before, either.

IN THE HALL OF THE
MOUNTAIN KING

·

Jerry Pournelle and
S.M. Stirling

• **PROLOGUE**

Durvash the tnuctipun knew he was dying. The thought did not bother him overmuch—he was a warrior of a peculiar and desperate kind and had never expected to survive the War—but the consciousness of failure was far worse than the wound along his side.

Breath rasped harsh between his fangs. Thin fringed lips drew back from them, flecked with purple blood from his injured airsac. Unbending will kept all fourteen digits splayed on the rough rock; the light gravity of this world helped, as well. Cold wind hooted down from the heights, plucking at him until he came to a crack that was deep enough for a leg and an arm; the long flexible fingers on both wound into irregularities, anchoring him. He turned his head back down into the valley and closed both visible-light eyes, opening the third in the center of his forehead and straining against the dark into the depths of the valley. Yes. Multiple heat-sources in the thrintun-size range, and there were no large endothermic animals on this world. Nothing but thrintun and their slaves and foodyeast in the oceans and huge bandersnatch worms to convert it into protein.

Light-headed, Durvash giggled at that. There *had* been

bandersnatch on this world, until the supposedly
nonsentient worms had all turned on their thrint masters
one day. Just as the sunflowers that guarded Slaver estates
had all focused their beams inward. A thousand other
surprises had happened that day; two centuries before
Durvash was born, at the beginning of the War. The
Slavers had never suspected, never suspected that the
tnuctipun engineers had devised a barrier against their
telepathic hypnosis, never suspected that the tnuctipun
fleet that vanished into space when the Slavers found
their homeworld would return one day. Thrint were
fewer now.

So are tnuctipun, he thought, sobering; it did not do
to depend on Slaver stupidity anymore. Most of the very
stupid ones had died early in the conflict, along with a
dozen thrintun slave species. The survivors were
desperate. The information he had weaseled out of the
base on this world was proof of that.

Durvash continued scanning, straining his eye up into
the lower electromagnetic spectra. Over a dozen
thrintun were toiling up the slopes below him. They
had slave trackers—a species of borderline sapience
but very sensitive noses—and hand weapons, and a
powered sled with limited flight capabilities. He drew
his sidearm, a round ball of energy with a handle, and
whispered to it. The tool writhed and settled into a
pistol-shape; he spoke instructions and an aiming-grid
opened out above it. The map of the valley showed
geological fault lines, but he would have to be very
careful.

A word marked a spot on the map. "Twenty
nanoseconds," he said, and turned to jam his head
against the rock and squeeze all three eyes shut. Holding
the weapon behind him he pulled the trigger. It would
fire only for the specified time, on the specified spot . . .
whuump. *CRACK*. Hot air blasted at him, slamming

him back and forth, until broken shards of bone in his thorax gnawed at the edges of his breathing-sac. Automatic reflex clamped his nostril shut and made him want to curl into a ball, but tnuctipun had evolved as arboreal carnivores on a world of very active geology. They had a well-founded instinct about hanging on tight when the ground shook. Then rock groaned all around him, loud enough almost to drown out the sound of a falling mountainside across the valley, megatons of mass avalanching down on the slaver and the thrint hunters.

Total matter-energy conversion is a very active thing, even if only for twenty nanoseconds in a limited space.

Instinct kept his digits clamped tight on rock and weapon. When he woke again, he thought it was night for a moment. Then he realized it was only blackness before his eyes, and the pain began. It came and went in waves, in time to the thundering in his resonator membranes; his neck hurt from the loudness of it. Durvash spat blood and phlegm and growled deep in his throat. He crawled up the rock, crawled and crawled until he left a broad dark smear on the stone, fresh trail for the thrint hunters that would follow. He almost missed the cover of his hidehole.

Opening it was more pain, the pain of full consciousness to tap out the code sequence. By the time he reached the end of the tunnel bored through the mountain and sank into the control chamber of the tiny spaceship, he was whimpering for his mother. He made it, though, and slapped a palm down on the controls. Medical sensors sedated him and began the process of healing as best they could; other machines activated remote eyes and prepared to lift off as soon as practical.

I made it, he knew, as pain lifted and darkness drifted down. Compensators whined as the ship lifted. *We can stop Suicide Night.*

❖   ❖   ❖

Halfway around the planet a single unwinking eye looked down on a display. A hand like a three-fingered mechanical grab touched controls.

"Launch a God fist at these coordinates," the thrint officer rasped, his tendrils clenched tight to his mouth in determination.

"Master—" the three-armed slave technician said in agitation. A Godfist was a heavy bombardment weapon, a small spaceship in itself with a high-level computer, and well-armed for self-defense. The warhead held nearly a kilogram of antimatter. After it landed there would be very little left of the continent.

OBEY, the thrint commanded. The Power clamped down brutally; the Slaver could feel the technicians acute desire to be elsewhere.

I wish I were elsewhere too, the thrint thought bitterly, watching the God fist lift on the remote screens. *I wish I were at the racetrack or with a female. I wish I were small and back home with Mother.*

"What does it matter?" he said to the air. "We're all going to die anyway." In about twenty years; the garrison here was to withdraw and leave only the foodyeast-supervisor quite soon. Dubious if they would make it to the next thrint-held system, anyway. The Power was of little use in a space battle against shielded tnuctipun vessels. "At least this powerloss-sucking tnuctipun spy will die before us."

As it turned out, he was wrong.

• CHAPTER ONE

Mixed crowd tonight, Harold thought, as he watched Suuomalisen's broad and dissatisfied back push through the crowd and the beaded curtain over the entrance. Sweat stained the fat man's white linen suit, and a haze of smoke hung below the ceiling as the fresher system fought overstrain. The screened booths along the walls and the tables around the sunken dance-floor were crowded, figures writhing there to the musicomp's Meddlehoffer beat, a three-deep mob along the long brass-railed bar. Blue uniforms of the United Nations Space Navy, gray-green of the Free Wunderland forces, gaudy-glitzy dress of civilian hangers-on and the new civilian elite of ex-guerrillas and war profiteers grown rich on contracts and confiscated collabo properties. Drinking, eating, talking, doing business ranging from the romantic to the economic, or combinations; and most were smoking as well. Some of the xenosophont customers would be uncomfortable in the extreme; *Homo sapiens sapiens* is almost unique in its ability to tolerate tobacco.

Tough, he decided. Outside the holosign would be floating before the brick: *HAROLD'S TERRAN BAR:*

A WORLD ON ITS OWN. Below that in lower-case print: *humans only.* The fat man had chosen to ignore that in his brief spell as quasi-owner, and Harold agreed with the decision. The sign had been a small raised finger to the kzinti during the occupation years; now that humans ruled the Alpha Centauri system again, anyone who could pay was welcome. There were even a depressed-looking pair of kzin in a booth off at the far corner, the hiss-spit-snarl of the Hero's Tongue coming faintly through their privacy screen. That was the only table not crowded, but quarter-ton felinoid carnivores did not make for brash intrusion.

But it's a human *hangout, and if the aliens don't like it, they can go elsewhere,* he decided.

"Glad to see the last of *him,* boss," the waitress said, laying a platter and a stein in front of him. "I'd rather work for a kzin."

"Good thing you didn't have to, then," Harold said, a grin creasing his basset-hound features between the jug ears. Suuomalisen had bought under the impression—correct—that Harold was on the run from the collaborationist government, right towards the end of the kzinti occupation. He had also been under the impression—false—that he was buying a controlling interest; in fact, the fine print had left real control with a consortium of employees. He had been glad to resell back to the original owner, and at a tasty profit for Harold.

Akvavit, beer chaser, and plate of grilled grumblies with dipping sauce called; he added a cigarette and decided the evening was nearly complete.

"*Completely* complete," he murmured, as his wife joined him; he stood and bowed over a hand.

"What's complete?" she said. Ingrid Schotter-Yarthkin was tall, Belter-slim; the strip-cut of her hair looked exotic above the evening gown she wore to oversee the backroom gambling operation.

"Life, sweetheart."

"At seventy-three?" she said; Wunderland years, slightly shorter than Terran. She had been only two years younger than he when they were growing up in the old Wunderland before the ratcat invasion. Now, time-dilation and interstellar cold sleep had left her less than half his biological age. "Middle-aged spread already?"

"I'm spreading myself thin, personally," Claude Montferrat-Palme said, sliding in to join them.

Harold grunted. The ex-policeman *was* thin, with the elongated build and mobile ears of a purebred Wunderland *Herrenmann*. He also wore the asymmetric beard favored by the old aristocracy.

"Seems sort of strange to be back to private life," Harold said musingly.

Claude shuddered. "Count it lucky we weren't put before a court," he said.

"Speak for yourself."

Claude winced slightly; he had been police chief of Munchen under the kzinti occupation. Resister before Wunderland surrendered to the invaders, then a genuine collaborator; someone had to hold society together, to get whatever was possible from the kzin. Earth was losing the war. But then—

Then Ingrid came back, with the Belter captain, and Claude's world came apart. His help to the resistance had been effective, and timely enough to save him from a firing squad. Not timely enough to save his job as police commissioner, of course. Harold was tarred with the edge of the same brush; anyone who made money under the occupation was suspect in these new puritanical days, as were the aristocrats who had perforce cooperated with the alien invaders. *There* was irony for you . . . especially considering how the commons had groveled to the kzin, and worked to keep their war factories going during the invasions of Sol System. Double irony for

Harold, since he was a Herrenmann's bastard and so never really accepted by his father's kindred. That might have changed if folk knew exactly what Harold and Ingrid and that Sol-Belter Jonah Matthieson *done* out in the Serpent Swarm.

It would be too an exaggeration to say that the three of them—well, they three plus Jonah Matthieson—had won the war; but it wouldn't be too large an expansion of the truth to say that without them the war would have been lost.

"Heroes are not without honor," Claude said. "Save in their own countries. Perhaps we should write a book to tell our true story."

"Sure," Harold said. "That would really make that ARM bastard happy. Right now he's happy, but—"

Claude's knowing grin stopped him. "Yes, of course. No books." He shrugged. "So we know, but no one else does."

And at that General Early had been tempted to make all four of them vanish, no matter their service to the UN. There would have been no trials. Freedom or a quiet disappearance, and for some reason—perhaps Early really had some human emotions—they'd been turned loose with their memories more or less intact.

They all frowned; Harold thoughtfully, looking down at the wineglass he rolled between his palms.

"I don't like it," Ingrid said. "Oh, I don't miss the fame—more trouble than it's worth, we'd have to beat off publicity-seekers and vibrobrains with clubs. I don't like General Buford Early—remember, I worked for him back in Sol System"—Ingrid had escaped the original kzin attack on Alpha Centauri and made the twenty-year trip back to Sol in suspended animation—"and I don't like the ARM getting a foothold here. What did our ancestors come here *for*, if not to get away from them?"

Both men nodded agreement. In theory, the ARM were the technological police of the United Nations, charged with keeping track of new developments and controlling those that menaced social peace. That turned out to be *all* new technology, and the ARM had grown until it more-or-less set UN policy. For three centuries they had kept Sol System locked in pacifistic stasis, to the point where even the memory of conflict was fading and a minor scuffle got people sent to the psychists for "repair." That placid changelessness and the growing sameness of life in the overcrowded, over-regulated solar system had been a strong force behind the interstellar exodus.

The ARM had kept Solar humanity from making ready after the first kzinti warship attacked a human vessel, right up to the arrival of the First Fleet from conquered Alpha Centauri. The operators of the big launch-lasers on Mercury had had to virtually *mutiny* to fight back, even when the kzin battlecruisers started beaming asteroid habitats.

"*I* don't like the way Early's so cozy with the new government," Harold growled.

"In the long run, luck goes only to the efficient," Claude said, and the others nodded again, because it wasn't hard to guess his train of thought.

The war was ended by pure luck: the weird aliens who sold the faster-than-light spacedrive to the human colonists on We Made It had really won the war for Sol. The kzin Fifth Fleet would have crushed all resistance, if there had been time for it to launch from Alpha Centauri and cover the 4.3 light-years at .8 *c*. Chuut-Riit, the last kzin Governor; had been a strategic genius; even more rare in his species, he never attacked until he was *ready*. Fortunately for humanity, that Chuut-Riit hadn't lived to send that fleet.

It had been Buford Early's idea to send in an assassin

team with the scoopship *Yamamoto*'s raid as a cover. Jonah, and Ingrid, and an intelligent ship that had gone insane. A mad scheme, one that shouldn't have worked, but it was all Earth could try—and it had worked. Was General Early a military genius, or incredibly lucky?

Now the hyperdrive would open the universe to Man. The problem was that it eliminated the moat of distance; the hyperwave, the communications version of the device, gave contact with Earth in mere hours. Cultures grown alien in centuries of isolation were thrown together . . . and serious interstellar politics became possible once more, and ARM General Buford Early was right in the middle of it all.

"I thoroughly agree," Claude said. "He's got Markham under his thumb, and a number of others. It's already unwise to cross him."

"As Jonah found out," Ingrid sighed.

Harold felt a prickle of irritation. True, Ingrid had chosen him—when both Claude and the Sol-Belter were very much available—but he didn't like to be reminded of it. Even less he didn't want to be reminded that she and Jonah had been lovers as well as teammates. It hadn't helped that the younger man refused all help from them, later.

She shook her head. "Poor Jonah. He should not have been so . . . so brusque with General Early. Buford is older than the Long Peace, and he can be . . . uncivilized."

• CHAPTER TWO

Jonah Matthieson belched and settled his back against the granite of the plinth. The long sunset of Wunderland was well under way. Tall clouds hung hot-gold nearly to the zenith of the pale blue sky, where the dome of night was darkening. Along the western horizon bands of purple shaded down to crimson and salmon pink. War had done that, the *Yamamoto*'s raid two years ago pounding the northern pole with kinetic-energy missiles at near light speed, then the fighting with the Crashlander armada later, which had included a fair number of high-yield weapons on kzinti holdouts. There was a *lot* of dust in the atmosphere. Wunderland is a small planet, half Earth's diameter and much less dense, a super-Mars; the gravitational gradient was small, and the air extended proportionately farther out. Hence there was a lot of atmosphere for it to fill.

And a wonderful sunset for one mustered-out stingship pilot to sit and savor, particularly if he was drunk enough. Unfortunately the bottle was empty.

A sudden spasm of rage sent it flying, out to crash among the other debris along the front of the Ritterhaus. The ancient government house had been a last strongpoint for the kzinti garrison in Munchen. Scaffolding covered the front of the mellow stone, but the work went slowly while more essential repairs were attended to. Much Centauran industry had been converted to war production during the occupation, and what survived was now producing for the United Nations Space Navy and Wunderland's own growing forces.

Jonah lurched erect, mouth working against the foul taste, blinking gritty eyes. For a moment the sensation reminded him—

"Oh, Finagle, I hurt."

They had come from Earth, Jonah and Ingrid and the artificial intelligence ship *Catskinner*, and the ship's computer had found something that shouldn't have been there. A ship that had floated in the Belt for so long that it had accreted enough dust to become an asteroid. A ship held unchanging in stasis, unchanging for billions of years, until it was awakened. Not just the ship. The Master.

Jonah shuddered.

That had been one of the times the thrint's mind-control had slipped. It had been busy, keeping control of all the minds of the Free Wunderland flotilla, trying to find out what had gone on during the several billion years it had lain in timeless stasis.

Eyes blurring, burning, skin hanging loose and gray and old around the wrists of bleeding hands, speckled with ground-in dirt.

Thrint tended to forget to tell their slaves to remember personal maintenance; they were not a very bright species. What humans would call an IQ of 80 was about average for Thrintun, and Dnivtopun hadn't been a genius by Slaver standards. That had been almost the worst of the subconscious humiliation. The Master had been so *stupid*—and under the Power you couldn't help but try to change that, to rack your brains for helpful solutions. Help the Master!

Jonah had been the one to crack the problem of making a new amplifier helmet to increase the psionic powers of the revenant Slaver. *That* would have made Dnivtopun master of the Alpha Centauri system and every human and kzin living there. Made him ruler of a new Slaver empire, because there had been fertile thrint females and young in the ship, the ship encased in its stasis field and the asteroid that had accreted about it over the thousands of millennia.

He moaned and pressed the heels of his hands to his temples. Yes, he'd broken free for an instant at the end, enough to struggle with Markham. Ulf Reichstein-Markham, who had *liked* the telepathic hypnosis the Slaver imposed. The psychists had erased Markham's memories of that; now he was a hero, space-guerrilla kzin-killing Resistance fighter and stalwart of the Provisional Government. The psychists hadn't been nearly as thorough with Jonah Matthieson, one-time Terran Belter, ex-combat pilot in the UNSN, assassin of Chuut-Riit. They'd just given him a strong block about the secret aspects of the affair, and turned him loose. He was supposed to recover fully in time, too. Not soon enough to have his job back, of course. No one wanted an unstable combat pilot. They'd give him his rank, but he'd be a paper shuffler, a useless man in a useless job. So he'd asked to go home. Belter prospectors were slightly mad anyway. And he learned that a hyperdrive transport back to Sol was out of the question, and there wasn't even a place for him in cold sleep aboard a slowship. Shuffle paper or get lost. Of course they'd hinted there was one other possibility, one he'd hated even more than shuffling paper.

He'd been bitter about that. That had led to more trouble . . .

A man was walking by, with the brisk step of someone with a purpose and somewhere to go.

"Gut Herr, spare some money to feed a veteran?" Jonah asked. He despised himself each time he did this, but it was the price of the oblivion he craved.

"*Lieber Herr Gott,*" the man's voice rasped. Wunderland was like that, conservative: they even swore by God instead of Finagle. It had been settled by North European plutocrats uneasy with the way Earth was heading under the UN and the ARM. "You again! This is the third time today!"

Startled, Jonah looked up. The face was unfamiliar, clenched and hostile under a wide-brimmed straw hat. The man's suit was offensively white and clean, a linen bush-jacket. Some well-to-do outbacker in town on business.

"Sorry, sir," Jonah said, backing up slightly. "Honest— I didn't look at your face, just your hands and the money. Please, I won't hit on you again, I promise."

"Here." A solid gold-alloy coin, another Wunderlander anachronism. "And here, another. To keep your memory fresh. Do not bother me again, or the polezi I will call." Frowning: "How did a combat veteran come to this?"

Jonah ground the coins together in his fist, almost tempted to throw them after the retreating back of the spindly low-gravity. *Because the bloody ARM is punishing me!* he screamed mentally. *Because I spoke out!* Not anything treasonable, no secrets, no attempt to evade the blocks in his mind. Just the truth, that they were still holding back technological secrets—had even while Earth faced defeat at kzinti hands—that they were conspiring to put the whole human race back into stasis, the way they had in the three centuries of the Long Peace, before the kzinti came. That the ARM had secret links, secret organizations on all the human-settled worlds. *Buford Early, Prehistoric Man, has frozen me out.* The ARM general probably thought he was giving a gentle warning, tugging on his clandestine contacts until every regular employment was closed to Matthieson. So that Matthieson would come crawling back, eventually.

Early was at least two centuries old, probably more. Old enough to remember when military history was taught in the schools, not forbidden as pornography. Possibly old enough to have *fought* against other humans in a war. He was very patient . . . and he had hinted that Jonah would make a good recruit for the ARM, if he altered his attitudes. Perhaps even for something *more* secret than the ARM, the thing hinted at by the collaboration with the *oyabun* crimelords here in the Alpha Centauri system. Jonah had threatened to reveal that.

Go right ahead, Lieutenant, Buford had said, laughing. It creased his carved-ebony face, gave you some idea of how ancient he really was, how little was left of humanity in him. Laughter in the gravel voice: *It's been done before. Whole books published about it. Nobody believes the books, and then they somehow don't get reprinted or copied.*

"Finagle eat my eyes if I'll crawl to you, you bleeping tyrant," Jonah whispered softly to himself.

He looked down at the coins in his hand; a five-krona and a ten. Enough to eat on for a couple of weeks, if you didn't mind sleeping outside in the mild subtropical nights. Of course, that made it more likely someone would kick your head in and rob you, in the areas where they let vagrants settle. Another figure was crossing the square, a woman this time, in rough but serviceable overalls and a heavy strakkaker in a holster on one hip.

"Ma'am?" Jonah asked. "Spare some eating money for a veteran down on his luck?"

She stopped, looking him up and down shrewdly. Stocky and middle-aged, pushing seventy, with rims of black under her fingernails. Not one of the tall slim mobile-eared aristocrats of the Nineteen Families, the ones who had first settled Wunderland. A commoner, with a hint of a nasal accent to her Wunderlander that suggested the German-Balt-Dutch-Danish hybrid was not her native tongue.

"Pilot?" she said skeptically.

"I was, yes," Jonah said, bracing erect. He felt a slight prickle of surprise when she read off the unit and section tabs still woven into the grimy synthetic of his undersuit.

"Then you'll know systems . . . atmosphere training?"

"Of course."

"We'll see." The questions stabbed out, quick and knowledgeable. "All right," she said at last. "I won't give you a fennig for a handout, but I could have a job for you."

Hope was more painful than hunger or hangover. "Who do I have to kill?" he said.

She raised her brows, then showed teeth. "Ach, you joke. Good, spirit you have."

She held out a belt unit, and he laid a palm on it as hope flickered out. There would be a trace on it from the net, General Early would have seen to that. There had been other prospects.

"Hmm," she grunted. "Well, a good record would not have you squatting in the ruins, smelling . . ." She wrinkled her nose and seemed to consider. "Here." She pulled out a printer and keyed it, then handed him the sheet it extruded, together with a credit chip. "I am Heldja Eladsson, project manager for Skognara Minerals, a Suuomalisen company.

"If you show up at the listed address in two days, there will be work. I am short several hands; skilled labor is scarce, and my contract will not wait. The work is hard but the pay is good. There's enough money in the chip to keep you blind drunk for a week, if that's your problem. And enough for a backcountry kit, working clothes and such, if you want the job. Be there or not, as you please."

She turned on her heel and left. Alpha Centauri had set, but the eye-straining point source that was Beta was still aloft, and the moon.

"I won't spend the chip on booze," he said to himself. "But by Murphy's ghost, I'm going to celebrate with the coins that smug-faced farmer gave me."

The question of where to do it remained. Then his eyes narrowed defiantly. Somewhere to clean up first, then—yes, then he'd hit Harold's Terran Bar. It would be good to sit down and order. *Damned* if he would have taken Harold Yarthkin's charity, though. Not if he were starving.

The chances were he'd be the only Terran there, anyway.

• CHAPTER THREE

Minister the Honorable Ulf Reichstein-Markham regarded the Terran with suspicion. The office of the Minister for War of the Provisional Government was as austere as the man himself, a stark stone rectangle on the top floor of the Ritterhaus. Its only luxuries were size and the sweeping view of the Founder's Memorial and Hans-Jorge Square; for the rest it held a severely practical desk and retrieval system, a cot for occasional sleep, and a few knickknacks. The dried ear of a kzin warrior, a picture of Markham's mother—who had the same bleakly handsome, hatchet-faced Herrenmann looks with a steel-trap jaw—and a model of the *Nietzsche*, Markham's ship during most of his years as a leader of Resistance guerrillas in the Serpent Swarm, the asteroid belt around Alpha Centauri. Markham himself was a young man, only a little over thirty-five; blond asymmetric beard and wiry close-cropped hair, tall lean body held ramrod-tight in his plain gray uniform.

"Why, exactly, do you wish to block further renovation of the Munchen Scholarium?" he said, in his pedantic Wunderlander-flavored English. It held less of that guttural undertone than it had a year ago.

146

General Buford Early, UN Space Navy, lounged back in the chair and drew on his cheroot. He looked to be in late middle age, perhaps eighty or ninety, a thick-bodied black man with massive shoulders and arms and a rumpled blue undress uniform. The look was a finely crafted artifact.

"Duplication of effort," he said. "Earth and We Made It are producing technological innovations as quickly as interstellar industry can assimilate them—faster than the industries of Wunderland and the Serpent Swarm can assimilate them. Much cheaper to send data and high-end equipment directly here, now that we have the hyperdrive, and hyperwave communications. You're our forward base for the push into kzinti space; the war's going to last another couple of years at least, possibly a decade, depending on how many systems we have to take before the kzin cry uncle."

Markham's brow furrowed for a moment, then caught the meaning behind the unfamiliar idiom.

"The assault on Hssin went well," he pointed out.

That was the nearest kzin-held system, a dim red dwarf with a nonterrestrial planet; the assault that took the Alpha Centauri system had been mounted from there. UN superluminal warships and transports had ferried Wunderlander troops in for the attack. Early could read Markham's momentary, slightly dreamy expression well. *Schadenfreude*, sadistic delight in another's misfortune. Hammerblows from space, utterly unexpected, wrecking the ground defenses and what small warships were deployed at Hssin. Then the landing craft floating down on gravity polarizer drive, hunting through the shattered habitats and cracking them one by one. Hssin had unbreathable air, and it had been constructed as a maintenance base more than a fortress.

"True," Early nodded. "And that's just what Wunderlanders should concentrate their efforts on—

direct military efforts. Times have changed; it doesn't take decades to travel between Sol and Alpha Centauri any more. With the Outsider's Gift"—the hyperdrive had been sold to the human colonists of We Made It by aliens so alien they made kzinti look familiar—"star systems don't have to be so self-sufficient anymore."

Markham's frown deepened. "Wunderland is an independent state and not signatory to the United Nations treaties," he pointed out acerbically.

Early made a soothing gesture, spreading his hands. The fingers moved in a rhythmic pattern. Markham's eyes followed them, the pupils growing wider until they almost swallowed the last gray rim of the iris.

"You really don't care much about the Scholarium, do you?" the Terran said soothingly.

Markham nodded, his head moving slowly up and down as if pulled on a string.

"True. It vas of no use to us during the occupation, und now makes endless trouble about necessary measures." His accent had grown a little thicker.

"There are so many other calls on resources. And it really is politically troublesome."

Another nod. "Pressing for early elections. *Schweinerie!* What does nose-counting matter? Ve soldiers haf the understanding of Vunderland's problems. The riots against the Landholders must be put down! Too many of my colleagues prejudices against their social superiors haff."

"The alliance with the UN is important. We have to stand by our allies while the war is on, after all."

This time Markham seemed to frown slightly, his head jerking as if it tried to escape some confinement. Early moved his fingers again and again in the rhythmic dance, until the Wunderlander's face grew calm once more. "True. For ze present."

"So you'll deny their application for additional funds."

"'*Ja.*" Early snapped his fingers, and Markham started.

"And if you have no further matters to discuss, Herr General?" he said, impatiently keying the system on his desk.

"Thank you for your time, sir," Early replied, standing and saluting.

"You got what you wanted?" the man who called himself Shigehero Hirose said, as they walked out the guarded front entrance of the Ritterhaus.

The mosaic murals were under repair, their marble and iridescent glass tesserae still ripped and stained by the close-quarter fighting that had retaken the building. It would have been safer to use heavy weapons from a distance, but the Wunderlanders had been willing to pay in blood to keep the structure intact. Here the Founders had landed; here the Nineteen Families had taken the Oath. Early shook his head slightly at that; too much love of tradition and custom, even now; too much sense of connection to the past. The ARM would have to deal with that. That sort of thinking made people uncomfortably independent. Isolated anomic individuals were much easier to deal with, and also more likely to accept suitably slanted versions of past, present, and future.

There was still a slight scent of scorch in the lobby's air, and an even fainter one of old blood. The volunteer repair crews were cleaning each section by hand with vibrosweeps and soft brushes before they began adding new material.

"Most of what *we* wanted," Early said, with deliberate emphasis.

Hirose was the *oyabun* of his clan, and a man of some weight on this planet. The organization had grown during the lawless occupation years, and they were putting their accumulated wealth and power into shrewd investments now. Nevertheless, he bowed his head slightly as he answered:

"We, of course. Still, did not your psychists plant sufficient key commands last year?"

"We had to be careful. Markham was unstable, of course"—no wonder, after the resurrected thrint had used him as an organic waldo mechanism for weeks on end—"and besides, he'd be no use if we altered his psyche too much. We were counting on his subconscious craving for an authority figure, but evidently that's not as vulnerable as we thought. And he's getting more and more steamed about the political situation here, the anti-aristocratic reaction. Ironic."

"Which in turn is favorable to us," Hirose said.

"Oh, in the long run, yes. Nothing more susceptible to secret manipulation than democracy."

He sighed; in many ways, the Long Peace back on Earth had been more restful. A successful end to the long clandestine struggle, with an official agency, the ARM, openly allowed to close down disrupting technology. There had been fierce struggles within the Brotherhood over releasing the hoarded knowledge, any of it, even in the face of the kzin invasion. Necessary, of course; but the hyperdrive was *another* complicating factor. Now the other colonized systems were no longer merely dumping-grounds for malcontents, safely insulated by unimaginable distance. They were only a hyperwave call away, and each one was a potentially destabilizing factor.

He sighed. Perhaps the struggle was futile . . . *Never*.

"There is another factor I'd like you to check into," he went on. "Montferrat and his friends, and Matthieson. They know entirely too much."

"An isolated group," Hirose said dismissively. "Matthieson is disintegrating, and alienated from the others."

"Perhaps; but knowledge is always dangerous. Why

else do we spend most of our time suppressing it? And"—
he paused—"there's a . . . *synchronicity* to that crew.
They're the sort of people things happen around;
threatening things."

"As you wish, Elder Brother," Hirose said.

"Indeed."

• CHAPTER FOUR

"My nose is dry," Large-Son of Chotrz-Shaa said, leaning forward to lap at the heated single-malt: *I'm worried.* "We are impoverished beyond hope."

His brother Spots-Son made a *meeow-ur* of sardonic amusement, and poured some cream from the pitcher into his saucer of Glen Rorksbergen. Thick Jersey mixed sluggishly with the hot amber fluid as he stirred it with an extended claw. Both the young kzin males were somewhat drunk, and neither was feeling cheerful in his cups.

"Which is why you order fifty-year whiskey and grouper," he said, gesturing at the table. The two-meter fish was a mess of clean-picked bones on the platter; he picked up the head and crunched it for the brains, salty and delicious.

Large-Son flattened his batwing ears and wrinkled his upper lip to expose long wet dagger-teeth. "You eat your share, hairball-maker-who-never-matured." Spots growled around the mouthful; he had never entirely lost the juvenile mottles in his orange pelt. Dueling scars and batwing ears at his belt showed how he usually dealt with those who reminded him of it.

"And the price of a meal is nothing compared to what we owe."

Spots-Son flared his facial pelt in the equivalent of a shrug. Kzinti rarely lie; it is beneath a warrior's honor, and in any case few of them can control the characteristic scent of falsehood.

"Truth," Spots said. "My liver is chill with worry; we are poor beyond redemption. But if we must die, at least let us do it full and soothed."

A shape brushed past the shimmer of the privacy screen. "Owe? Poor?"

They both wheeled, grinning and folding their ears into combat-position. Long claws slid out of four-digit hands like knives at the tips of black leather gloves. A human had spoken, mangling the Hero's Tongue with his monkey palate. During the kzinti occupation, a human would have had his tongue removed for so insulting the language of the Heroic Race.

"You intrude," Spots-Son said coldly in Wunderlander.

"This is a public booth," the man pointed out. "And the only one not full. Besides, we all seem to have something in common."

That *was* an insult. The fur lay flat on their muzzles, and they grinned wider, threads of saliva falling from thin carnivore lips.

"Cease to intrude, monkey," Large-Son said; this time he used the Hero's Tongue, in the Menacing Tense.

"We're all warriors, for one thing," the human continued, smelling of reckless self-confidence.

Both kzin relaxed, blinking and studying the monkey. He was a tall male, with a strip of dark head-fur; the clothes he wore were uniform and also thermally adjustable padding for wear under ground-combat armor. They blinked again, noting the ribbons and unit-markings, looked at each other.

He speaks truth, Spots-Son signaled with a twitch of

eyebrows. Both of them had been junior engineering officers in an underground installation before the human counterattack on the Alpha Centauri system; both had been knocked out with stungas toward the end. The human was actually more of a warrior than either of them; their defense battery might or might not have made a kill during the tag-end of atmospheric combat, but this monkey had beaten kzinti fighters at close quarters. The pips on his sleeve were so many dried kzin ears dangling from a coup belt. It was permissible to talk to him, although not agreeable.

The human smiled in his turn, although he kept his teeth covered. "Besides, we're all broke, too. My name is Jonah Matthieson, ex-Pilot, ex-Captain, United Nations Space Navy. Let me order the next round of drinks."

". . . and so we inherit the care of our dams, our Sire's other wives, now ours, and our siblings and half-siblings," Spots-Son said morosely some hours later, upending the whiskey decanter over his dish. "Honor demands it."

Harold's was half-empty now; a waiter came quickly enough when the long orange-furred arm waved the crystal in the air, setting out fresh liquor and cream. Spots-Son slopped the amber fluid into his bowl and into Jonah's glass. Large-Son was lying with his muzzle in his dish, tongue protruding slightly as he snored. Thin black lips flopped against his fangs, and his eyes were nearly shut.

"Kzinti females take much care," Spots continued, lowering his muzzle. Despite his care it went too far into the heated drink as he nearly toppled, making him sneeze and slap at his nose. "And much feeding. The properties have been confiscated by the military government—all the fine ranchlands and hunting-grounds our Sire possessed, all except the house. Where once we feasted on blood-dripping fresh beef and screaming zianyas, now our families must trade heirlooms for synthetic protein. Soon we will have no alternative but honorable suicide."

"Thas—that's a shame," Jonah said. "Yeah, after th' war the fighters get nothin' and the politicians get rich, like always." He hiccuped and drank. "Goddam UN Space Navy doesn't need no loudmouths who think for themselves, either. Say, what did you say you did before the war?"

"I," Spots said with slow care and some pride, "was a Senior Weapons System Repairworker. And my sibling, too."

Jonah blinked owlishly. "Reminds me." He fumbled a sheet of printout from a pocket. "Lookit this. Decided it was a good deal so I'd come in here an' spend my last *krona*. Here."

He spread the crumpled paper on the damp surface of the table. The kzin craned to look; it was in the spiky fourteen-point gothic script most commonly used for public announcements on Wunderland. Printed notices were common; during the occupation the kzin overlords had restricted human use of the information net, and since then wartime damage had kept facilities scarce.

Technical personnel wanted, he read, *for heavy salvage operation*. Categories of skills were listed. *Heavy work, some danger, high pay. Suuomalisen Contracting, vid. 97-777-4321A Munchen*.

"Urrrowra," Spots said mournfully. "Such would be suitable—if we were not kzinti. Surely none will hire us. No, suicide is our fate—we must cut our throats with our own *wtsai* and immolate our households. Woe! Woe for a dishonored death in poverty, among furless omnivores! No shrine will enclose our bones and ashes; only eating-grass will cover our graves. Perhaps Kdapt-Preacher is right, and the God has a hairless face!"

Large-Son whimpered in half-conscious agreement

and slapped his hands over his eyes to blank out the horrible vision of the heretic's new creed, that God had created Man in His own image.

"Naw," Jonah said. "I talked to the boss, she don't care anything but you can do the job. Or wouldn't have hired me, with a black mark next to my discharge. C'mon—bring the bottle. Talk to her tomorrow."

"You are right!" Spots bellowed, standing to his full two meters and a half of massive, orange-furred height. His naked pink tail lashed. "We will fight against debt and empty-accountness. We leap and rip the throat of circumstance. We will conquer!"

From the other side of the long room beads rustled as a tall black-skinned human stuck his head through the curtain. He was dressed in archaic white tie and tuxedo, but there was a fully functional military-grade stunner in his fist. Behind the bar several other employees reached down and came up with shockrods as guests' heads turned toward the booth.

"Shhhhh!" Jonah said, tugging recklessly at the felinoid alien's fur. "The bouncers."

"Rrrrr. True." There was no dignity in being stunned and thrown out in the gutter. "Where shall we go? Our quarters are far outside Munchen, and transport for kzin costs much." Sleeping outside would not be very wise, given the number of exterminationist fanatics ready to attack a helpless kzin.

"C'mon. I know a doss where they don't care 'bout anything but your coin, and it's cheap."

They weaved their way to the door, Spots half-carrying his brother and Jonah lifting the unconscious kzin's tail with exaggerated care.

• CHAPTER FIVE

". . . still worth lookin', oh, yes," the old man said.

Jonah yawned and looked over at him. The two kzin were unrolling their pallets up a level in the framework; the human had a stack of blankets and a pillow instead, all natural fiber in the rather primitive way of Wunderland, and all smelling dubious and looking worse. It must be even more difficult for the felinoids, with their sensitive noses.

"Look at 'er this way," the man was saying. "You take hafnium—"

It was hard to estimate his age; he could be as young as seventy or as old as one-fifty, depending on how much medical care he had been able to afford during the occupation.

"—good useful industrial metal; or gold, likewise, and we use it as monetary backing. Usually don't pay to mine it anywhere but in the Swarm, in normal times. But there *ain't* been any normal times, not since the pussies came, no sirree. So people've been out in the Jotuns for a dog's age now, finding deposits. Don't pay to bring in heavy equipment; deposits are rich but small. You can make yourself rich that way, and that's not counting salvage on all the equipment the pussies abandoned out there, all very salable these days. I'd go myself, don't you doubt it, go again like a shot."

"Hey," Jonah called. "You sound like you've done that before; what're you doing *here*?"

The great room was noisy with the sounds of humans settling down to sleep, snores, snatches of drunken song. There were still tens of thousands of displaced from the war years.

"Made me a fortune, oh, yes, more than one," the old man said. His wrinkled-apple face looked over at Jonah, eyes twinkling. "Lost 'em all. Some the government took, and I spent the others going back and looking for a bigger strike. Most people get into that game don't know where to stop. Get thirty thousand crowns worth, they want sixty. Get sixty, spend it trying to find half a million. Stands to reason, of course; that's why the heavy metals are so valuable. Value of 'em includes all the time and labor and money spent by those who *don't* find anything, you see."

"Wouldn't be like that with me," Jonah said, unrolling the blankets. *Finagle, but I'm tired of being poor*, he thought. Odd; poverty had never come up before he got to Alpha Centauri. Before then he'd been a Navy pilot, or a rockjack asteroid prospector. The Navy fed you, and rockjacks generally made enough to get by certainly during the war, with industry sucking in all the materials it could find. "Just enough to set me up. Software business." He had a first-rate Solarian education in it, and the locals were behind. "That's all I'd want."

"Likely so, stranger, likely so," the old man said. "Well, don't signify, does it?"

"Finagle!" Jonah swore, as the beam jerked backward towards him. He heaved at the bight of control line. "Get it, Spots!"

"Hrrrrr," Spots growled, and caught the end of it. His pelt laid itself flat under the harness, and the long steel balk slowed and then touched gently on the junction-point. A little less power in the stubby plump-cat limbs and they would both have been crushed against the uprights of the frame.

"Slack off!" Jonah called down.

Large-Son flapped his ears in amusement thirty meters below and turned the control rheostat of the winch. The woven-wire cable slacked, and together man and kzin guided the end of the beam into its slot Jonah clamped the sonic melder's leads to the corners and stepped back onto the scaffolding.

"Sound on the line," he called, and keyed his belt unit.

That flashed the alarm and began the process of sintering the beam into a single homogenous unit with the rest of the frame; it worked by vibrational generation of a heat-interface, and Spots winced and crouched beside him, hands clamped firmly over furled ears. The human took the opportunity to flip up his sight goggles and take a mouthful of water from his canteen; when he noticed the kzin's dangling tongue he poured some into a saucer the felinoid had clipped to his harness. Around them the complex geometries of the retrieval rig were growing into a latticework around the hill. Humans and the odd alien—there was a kdatlyno, and a couple of unbelievably agile five-armed Jotoki, and the brothers Kzinamaratsov, as he had named them in a private joke. Beyond was a flat terrain of swamp, livid-green Terrestrial reeds and mangrove, olive-green palmlike things native to Wunderland.

He slapped at his neck; it was *hot* here, right on the equator. The bugs were native, but they would cheerfully bite humans, or kzinti if they could get through the fur and thick hide. The brothers were suffering more than he. Their species shed excess heat through tongue and nose and the palms of hands and feet, more than enough on savagely dry Kzin. Difficult in this steambath, although the kzinti's high natural body-temperature and the fight gravity of Wunderland helped a little. Jonah shook his head. He had been fighting kzin for most of his adult life: in space back in Sol System, by sabotage, and even hand-to-hand in a hunting preserve when he'd been sent in as a clandestine operative. Now he was working with a couple of them, and they turned out to be a pretty good team. Stronger than humans by far, which was valuable on this archaeological relic of a project—the contractor was too cheap to rent much of what little modern equipment could be spared for civilian projects—and quicker. Their abilities were well balanced by his superior hands and better head for heights; kzinti had evolved on a world of 1.5 gravities, climbing low hills rather than trees. They were not quite as good with their fingers as humans, and a long vertical drop made them nervous.

"More water?" he offered the other.

No, Spots signaled with a twitch of his ruff, scratching vigorously a moment later. Then, aloud: "Is that not the Contractor Human?"

"It *is*, by Finagle's ghost," Jonah muttered. "*Hey, Biggie! We're coming down!*"

Jonah did so with a graceless rush down the cat-walks; he had always been athletic for a Belter, and the last two months had left him in the best condition he had ever been, but he was still a child of zero-G. The kzin followed with oil-smooth grace, and they dropped in front of the project supervisor. Fairly soon the contract would be over . . .

"Looks like it'll be finished soon," Jonah said amiably. "Should be, with the extra time we've been putting in."

"And the bonuses you'll be getting, don't forget that," she replied, wiping at her face with a stained neckerchief.

"Yeah, they sound real good on the screen—the problem is, we haven't seen anything deposited to our accounts."

Heldja made an impatient gesture, then smiled—carefully, because the two kzin were looming behind Jonah like oil-streaked walls of orange fur. Their teeth were very white, and all were showing.

"What vould you with money be doing *here*?" she said reasonably, waving a hand. There were pressmet huts standing on the dredged island; beyond the six-meter reeds of the swamp began, stretching beyond sight. Tens of thousands of square kilometers of them, and the closest thing to humanity in there was wild pigs gone feral, fighting it out with the tigripards. "Except to gamble and lose it? I ride the float of your money—all the hands' money—this is true, because it furnishes working capital; but the bonuses more than make up for it. Transfer will be made as soon as the hovercraft gets back to Munchen."

• CHAPTER SIX

"No, Ib," Tyra Nordbo said, lowering her rifle.

"Fire!" the young man said.

"No!"

One of the prisoners looked up from his slump; tears rolled slowly down through the dirt on his cheeks and the thin wispy adolescent beard. His lips moved soundlessly.

"Squad—fire!"

The magrifles gave their whispering grunt, and the five prisoners toppled into the graves they had spent the last half-hour digging. Behind, the villagers gave a murmur, halfway between shock and approval; they were Amish, men in dark suits and women in long black skirts. The half-ruined houses of the farmtown beyond were slipping into shadow as Alpha Centauri set; the moon was up, and Beta, leaving it just too dark to tell a black thread from a white. The air smelled of death and of moist turned earth from the graves, and from the plowed fields beyond, purple-black rolling hills amid the yellow of reaped grain and the dusty green of pasture. Orchards and vineyards spotted the land, and small lakes behind dams. Woodlots were the deep green of Terran oak and the orange-green of Kzin, tall frondlike growths in Wunderland's reddish ocher. Westward the last sunlight touched the glaciers and crags of the Jotuns, floating like a mirage seen through glass. The mountains were close, the dense forest of the foothills less than a day's walk away.

It was hard to imagine war had passed this way, until you saw the graves. Many fresh ones in the churchyard, and these five outside it, along the graveled main street. The other soldiers in the squad lowered their weapons and turned to watch the exchange between brother and sister.

Tyra Nordbo was 180 centimeters, as tall as her brother, but she lacked the ordinary low-gravity lankiness of Wunderlanders; she was robust and full-bosomed, and strikingly athletic for a girl of eighteen. Her brother was only four years older and much alike in his high-cheeked, snub-nosed looks. There was a hardness to his face that she lacked, although she matched the anger when he swung to confront her.

"Karl, Yungblut," he snapped over his shoulder, "bury them. Kekkonen, get the dogs back to the van." He raised his voice to the villagers. "You people, return to your homes. Justice has been done."

The black-clad farmers stirred and settled their hats and turned back to their houses.

"Justice, Ib?" Tyra said, her voice full of quiet fury. She slung her rifle and reached to tear off the Provisional Gendarmerie badge sewn to the arm of her bush jacket. It landed at Ib's feet with a quiet *plop* of dust. Her holoprinted ID card followed it.

"Those were bandits!" Ib said, jerking his head at the graves where earth fell shovelful by shovelful.

"Thieves, murderers, and rapists," Tyra said, nodding jerkily. The sight was not too bad; the prefrag penetrators were highly lethal but did not mangle flesh much. She had seen much worse, working in an aid station for the underground army, during the street fighting in Munchen at Liberation. "They deserved to die—after a fair trial."

The Amish here were strict in their pacifist faith, and had made little resistance when the gang moved in; the investigation had been ugly hearing. This part of the Jotun foothills had been guerrilla country during the last days of the occupation, full of folk on the run from the collaborationist police, from the forced-labor gangs, or simply from spreading poverty and chaos. Not all of them had gone back to the lowlands when peace came, to the sort of badly-paid hard work that was available. Many had turned to raiding, and were difficult to catch. The Wunderlander armed forces were stretched thin, and most of their efforts had to go to the fighting farther into the kzinti sphere, as the human fleets pressed the aliens back.

"They were guilty," she went on. "They still deserved a trial, and it wouldn't have taken any effort at all to carry them back to Arhus," she went on bitterly. Her eyes stung, and she blinked back anger and grief. *I will not cry.*

"General Markham—"

"You and your precious Ulf Reichstein-Markham. He's as bad as a kzin!" she snapped. Some of the other troopers scowled at that. Ulf Markham had been among the fiercest of the space-based Resistance fighters in the Serpent Swarm, and he had a considerable following in the military. "Compared to a *real* hero, like Jonah Matthieson, or— Enough. I quit. My pay's in arrears"—everyone's was—"so I'll take the horse and rifle in lieu. Goodbye."

"Stop—" Ib called to her back. "You're running away, running away like Father did!"

"Don't you ever mention Father like that again," she said coldly, forcing her hand away from the weapon slung

at her back. Her hands were mechanical as she unhitched the horse and vaulted into the saddle, an easy feat on Wunderland.

His voice followed her as she cantered out into the falling night.

And so the Commission leaves us only the home farm, the Teufelberg forest, and the Kraki, of the properties, Tyra Nordbo read, tilting the paper towards the firelight. The letter took on the tones of her mother's voice, deliberately cheerful and utterly sad, as it had been ever since Dada left. Was taken away on that crazy astrophysical expedition by the kzin, Yiao-Captain. *But this is more than enough to keep all of us here busy. It is a relief not to have the management of so much else, and we must remember how many others are wanting even for bread.*

She started to crumple the printout in one hand, then carefully smoothed it out and folded it, tucking it back into the saddlebags and leaning back against the saddle. In the clearing on the other side of the fire her horse reached down and took another mouthful of grass, the rich *kerush* sound followed by wet munching and the slight jingle of the hobble chain. Her new dog Garm looked up and thumped his tail on the grass, the firelight ruddy on the Irish Setter—mostly Setter—hairs of his coat. Elsewhere the flicker caught at grass, trees, bushes, the overhanging rock of the cliff behind her and the gnarled trunk and branches of an oak that grew out of the sandstone ten meters above her head. Overhead the stars were many and very bright; in the far distance a tigripard squalled, and the horse threw up its head for a moment in alarm. Nowhere in the wilderness about her was there a hint of Man—save that the tree and the grass, woman and horse and dog were all of the soft and blood and bone of Sol.

"So," she whispered to herself. "It is not enough that we are stripped of our honor, they must make us paupers as well."

Not quite *paupers*, she admitted.

That had been among the first things her father taught her; not to lie, first and foremost not to lie to herself. They would be quite comfortably off; the home farm was several thousand hectares, the timber concession would be profitable enough now that the economy was recovering, and the pelagic-harvester *Hrolf Kraki* was a sturdy old craft. The household staff were all old retainers, loyal to *Mutti*, and very competent. *It's not the money*, she knew; it was a matter of pride. The Nordbos had been the first humans to settle Skognara District, back when the Nineteen Families arrived. They had been pioneers, ecological engineers adapting Terran life to a biosphere not meant for it and a planet not much like Earth; then guides, helpers, kindly landfathers to the ones who came after and settled in as tenants-in-chief, subtenants, workers.

It was not the loss of the lands and factories and mines; in practice the family had merely levied a small percentage in return for governing, a thankless privilege these past two generations. But Gerning and Skognara *belonged* to the Nordbos, they had *made* them with blood and sweat and the bones of their dead. For the Commission to take the rights away was to spit on the memories. Of Friedreich Nordbo, who had sponsored a tenth-share of the First Fleet, of Ulrike Nordbo, who discovered how to put Terran nitrogen-fixing soft bacteria in fruitful symbiosis with the native equivalents, of Sigurd Nordbo, who lost his life fighting to save a stranded schoolbus during the Great Flood. Of her aunt Siglide Nordbo, who had piloted her singleship right up to the moment it rammed a kzinti assault transport during the invasion.

And of Peter Nordbo, who had stood like a rock between the folk of Skognara and the conquerors' demands, every day that he was able. Who was ten years gone, shanghaied into space because he told a kzin who was half a friend of an astronomical curiosity, leaving a wife who had no choice but to yield more than he had, as conditions grew worse. Condemned for a traitor *in absentia*, by a court that thought it was merciful . . . and *Mutti* was all alone now in the big silent house on the headland at Kor-hess, looking out over the waves. Few friends had been willing to visit, much less speak in her defense.

"*Dada-mann*," Tyra whispered, laying her head on her knees and weeping aloud, because there was nobody to hear. That was what she had cried out when he left. There had been no words he could say to a child of eight . . . Presently Garm came, creeping on his stomach and whining at her distress, sticking his anxious cold nose against her face; she clutched him and sobbed until there was no more.

When she was functional again she took the coffee pot off the heater coil—the fire was for comfort, and predators—and poured herself a cup. The other letter was still sealed; she had nearly discarded it, until the return address caught her eye. Claude Montferrat-Palme, a Herrenmann of ambiguous reputation. Frowning, she pressed her thumb to the seal to deactivate the privacy lock and then opened it.

"Dear Fra Nordbo," she read. "A possible juncture of interests—"

"Yes, there are workings in the mountains," the old villager said.

At least, that was what Tyra *thought* he had said. These backwoodsmen had been up in the high country for the better part of two centuries, pioneers before the kzinti came and isolated by choice and necessity since. Their dialect was so archaic it was almost *Pletterdeutz*, without the simplified grammar and many of the loan-words from the Baltic and Scandinavian languages that characterized modern Wunderlander. Back further in the Jotuns were tiny enclaves even more cut off, remnants of the ethnic separatists who had come with the third through seventh slowship fleets from Sol System.

"What sort of workings?" she said, slowly. Her own accent was Skognaran, more influenced by Swedish and Norse than the central dialect of Munchen; modified by a Herrenmann-class education, of course. The Nordbos were formerly of the Freunchen clan, one of the Nineteen Families. *Formerly*. Luckily, these primitives were out of touch with the news; they barely comprehended that the alien conquerors were gone.

"Ja, many sorts, *Fra* Nordbo," the old man said deferentially.

The von Gelitz family had owned these lands—still did, pending the Reform Commission's findings—but that ownership had always been purely theoretical, except for a hunting lodge or two. Nobody but the Ecological Service ever paid much official attention to this area, and they had gotten careless during the occupation. There was an old manor house outside Neu Friborg's common fields, but it had been ruins for the better part of a century. He had called them the "old herr's place."

Old, she thought with a shiver, looking at the man. They were getting by on home remedies here, and what knowledge their healer could drag out of an ancient first-aid program. The wrinkles, wispy white hair, liver spots . . . this man might be no more than seventy or eighty, barely middle-aged with decent medicine. *Markham should spend less on his precious fleet—the UN Navy is fighting the war now—and more on people and places like this!*

Apart from premature aging and the odd cripple, it was not too bad as backcountry towns in the Jotuns went. Built of white-plastered fieldstone and homemade tile, around a central square with the mayor's office, the nationalpolezi station—long disused—and the Reformed Catholic church. There was a central fountain, and plenty of shade from eucalyptus and pepper and featherfrond trees. They were sitting under an awning outside the little *gasthaus*, watching the sleepy traffic of midafternoon: bullock-carts and burros bringing in firewood or vegetables, a girl switching along a milch cow, tow-haired children in shorts tumbling through the dust in some running, shouting game. A rattletrap hovertruck went by in a cloud of grit, and a waitress went about watering the flowers that hung from the arches behind them in earthenware pots.

That was all there *was* to see: the town and its four-hundred-odd inhabitants, the cluster of orchards and fields around it in the little pocket of arable land, and wilderness beyond—mostly scrubby, in the immediate vicinity, but you could find anything from native jungle to forest to desert in a few days' journey. All about the peaks of the Jotuns reared in scree and talus and glacier; half a continent of mountains, taller than Earth's Himalayas and much wider. Wunderland had intermittent plate tectonics, but when they were active they were *active*, and the light gravity reduced the power of erosive forces. These were the oldest mountains on the planet, and not the highest by any means.

The old man finished fanning himself with his straw hat and continued:

"Jade, of course. No mines, but from the high mountain rivers; that is how we paid our tribute to the kzin. We are not ignorant *knuzen* here, Fra Nordbo!"

There was a pathetic pride to that; a hovertruck had come once a month from the lowlands, until the final disruption at liberation. Tyra felt a slight stinging in her eyes. Once even the most isolated settlement had been linked to Munchen, with virtual-schools and instant emergency services . . .

"Then, sometimes hunters come through; hunting for tigripard hides, quetzbird feathers. Or prospectors. There is gold, hafnium . . . when I was a small boy, scholars also from the Scholarium in Munchen."

"Scholars?" she said, pricking up her ears.

"Yes; they said little—this was just after the War, you understand, people were suspicious then—but there were rumors of formations that could not be accounted for. But they found nothing, and had to return to Munchen when so much of the Scholarium was closed by the government." The collaborationist authorities had other priorities than education; their own profits, primarily. "And—but your supplies, they have arrived!" He rose and left, bowing and murmuring good wishes.

Another hovertruck pulled into the square; big and gleaming by contrast with the single ancient relic the village of Neu Friborg owned, although shabby enough by Munchen standards, much less Earth's. The man who stepped down from it was tall, 190 centimeters at least; his black hair was worn in a shag cut, although she knew he had kept it in a military-style crop while he was Police Chief of Munchen. Chief for the collaborationists, and notoriously corrupt even by the gang's standards. Claude Montferrat-Palme, of the Sydow clan. He wore expensive outbacker clothes, leather boots and grey usthcloth jacket and breeches, with a holstered strakkaker, and a beret. A small, nearly clipped black mustache lay on his upper lip, and his mouth quirked in a slight smile.

"Fra Nordbo," he said, bowing formally over her hand with a click of heels.

"Fro Palme," she replied, inclining her head with equal

formality. A server bustled up with steins of the local beer.

"Prosit," he said.

"Skaal," she replied. "Now that the amenities are over, could you tell me exactly what you had in mind?"

Her voice held a chilly correctness; he seemed to recognize the tone, and smiled wryly.

"Fra Nordbo, I'm very strongly reminded of your father."

"You knew him?" she said, with a raised eyebrow. "Perhaps you will claim to have been his friend, next?"

He surprised her by letting the smile grow into a deep laugh. "Quite the contrary," he said, shaking his head. "He treated me with the most frigid *politesse*, as be fitted an honorable Landholder forced to deal with noxious collaborationist scum."

She relaxed slightly. "He couldn't have known you were involved with the Resistance," she said.

"Ach, at the time I wasn't," he replied frankly. "I *was* a collaborationist at that point. My conversion came later; people do change. As some claim your father did, later."

"That is a lie!" she said. More calmly: "My father was an astrophysicist, it was his . . . hobby, since he had to govern Skognara from a sense of duty. How was he to know the enemy would think a mere energy-anomaly a thing of potential military importance? The kzin—Yiao-Captain—forced him to accompany them on the expedition."

"From which he has never returned, and hence cannot defend himself. And the Commission has been in no charitable mood."

Tyra's blond head drooped slightly. "I know," she said quietly. "Ib . . . my brother and I, we have discussed resigning the Nordbos from the Freunchen clan."

"Advisable, but it may make little difference. Unless I've lost my political feelers—and I haven't—the

Reformers are going to strip the Nineteen Families of everything but ceremonial power. And from all but their strictly private property, as well."

Tyra nodded jerkily, feeling the hair stir on her neck as her ears laid back. That mutation was a mark of her heritage, of the old breed that had won this planet for humankind.

"It is unjust! Men like my father did everything they could to shield—" She shrugged and fell silent again, taking a mouthful of the beer.

"Granted, but most of the kzin are gone, and a great deal of repressed hatred has to have a target." He turned one hand up in a spare gesture. "Even our dear Grand Admiral Ulf Reichstein-Markham has been able to do little to halt the growth of anti-Families feeling. Which means we of the Families—as individuals—had better look to our own interests."

Tyra looked down into her mug. Montferrat laughed again.

"How tactful you are for one so young, Fra Nordbo. I have a reputation for looking after my own interests, do I not? *Old Sock* is the nickname now; because I fit on either foot, having changed sides at just the right moment. Unfortunately, most of my accumulated wealth went on securing my vindication."

He nodded dryly at her startled glance. "Yes, our great and good government of liberation is very nearly as corrupt as the collaborationists they hunt down so vigorously. Not Markham; his vice is power, not wealth. A little too nakedly apparent, however, and I doubt he will retain much of it past the elections, when the junta steps down. Which it will, given that the UN Space Navy is overseeing the process . . . but I digress."

"Ja, Herr," Tyra said. "You spoke of a matter of mutual interest?"

"Indeed." He took out a slim gold cigarette case,

opening it at her nod and selecting a brown cigarillo. His gaze sought the mountains as he took a meditative puff. "After *you* mentioned rumors of something . . . strange in these mountains."

"I was a student at the Scholarium before the liberation, and afterwards a little. Before my brother . . . Well, he greatly admires Admiral Markham."

"Of whom you no longer think highly, and who is notoriously unfond of myself, thus showing his bad taste," Montferrat said suavely. "Yes. Thank you for the information on that little atrocity, by the way; it may come in useful as a stick for the Admiral's spokes." He frowned slightly, looking at the glowing tip of the cigarillo.

"I don't believe in fate, but there's a . . . synchronicity to events, sometimes. Your father vanished, seeking an artifact of inexplicable characteristics, near this system. You come across evidence of another here in these mountains. And I—"

Tyra made an inquiring sound.

"Well, let us say that this is the third instance," Montferrat went on. "More would be unsafe for you to know; it has to do with General Markham, and his Sol-System patrons the ARM. It would *certainly* be unsafe for me to be openly involved in any such search."

"You implied that you would be commissioning a search?" Tyra said.

"No. *Searchers*. Who will be looking, but not specifically for that. It *is* necessary that someone guard these unaware guardians; and since this presents me with an opportunity to do a lovely lady a service—"

He smiled gallantly; Tyra retained her look of stony politeness. Montferrat sighed.

"As you will." A puff made the cigarillo a crimson ember for a moment. "First I must tell you a story, about a man named Jonah, and some friends he has made recently. Unusual friends—"

• CHAPTER SEVEN

The hovercraft that carried the outgoing shift back to the Munchen docks was an antique. Not only would the design be completely obsolete once gravity polarizers were available for ordinary civilian work; it had been built before the kzinti frontier world of Hssin had decided to send a probing fleet to investigate the promising electromagnetic traffic from Alpha Centauri. That was nearly sixty Terran years ago, fifty Wunderlander, and it had soldiered on ever since, carrying cargo and passengers up and down the Donau river and out into the sheltered waters of Spitzer Bay. It was simplicity itself, a flat rectangle of light-metal alloy with a control cabin at the right front corner and ducted fans on pivots at the rear. Other fans pumped air into the plenum chamber beneath, held in by skirts of tough synthmesh; power came from molecular-distortion batteries.

Jonah and the kzinti squatted on their bedrolls in the center of the cargo bay, with the hunched backs of the other workers and the waist-high bulwarks at the edge between them and the spray cast up by the river. Spots hated to get his pelt wet, spitting and snarling under his breath, while Bigs endured stolidly. The human rolled a cigarette of *teufelshag*, ignoring the felinoids' *urrows* of protest. They were well up into the settled areas now. Thinly settled, but the banks of the middle Donau had been where humans first came to Wunderland. The floodplain and benchland were mostly cleared, or in planted woodlots; farther back from the floodplain the old Herrenmann estates stood, bowered in gardens, whitewashed stone and tile roofs. Many were broken and abandoned, during the occupation, by kzin nobles who had seized a good deal of this country for their own, or by anticollaborationist mobs after the liberation. They passed robot combines gathering rice, blocks of orange grove fragrant with cream-white flowers, herds of beefalo and kzinti *zitragor* under the watch of mounted herdsmen. Villages were planted among small farms, many of them worked by hand; machinery had gotten very scarce while the kzinti were masters.

The hovercraft slowed as traffic thickened on the river, strings of barges, hydrofoils, pleasure craft: with their colored sails taut in the stiff southerly breeze. The steel spire of St. Joachim's Cathedral blazed in the light of Alpha, with Beta high in the sky as well. Farther north there were parks along the waterside, with palm groves and frangipani, but the section the hovercraft edged toward was workaday and bustling, sparkling with welding torches as the old wrecked autocranes were replaced with temporary steel frames; in the meantime stevedores sweated to haul rope pulleys. Jonah flicked the butt of his cigarette into the water like a minor meteor undergoing reentry.

"Nice to be affluent," he said cheerfully.

Bigs made an indescribable sound and turned away from the irritating human, lying flat on the decking with his chin extended. Spots waggled his ears in the kzin equivalent of an ironic chuckle.

"Three thousand krona each," he said dryly. "The

prospect heats my liver—I truly feel one of Heaven's Admirals. This for thirty diurnal periods of laboring like a slave in a swamp and improvising machinery out of muck and junk. There is fungus growing on my fur. I may never be able to eat fish again."

"Let's collect, then," Jonah answered.

They heaved themselves erect under the burden of their kitbags and shouldered their way to the bows as the big vehicle ran up on a concrete landing ramp and sank to the surface. It was easy enough, although the cargo well was crowded; nobody on Wunderland was going to jostle a kzin, liberation or no. Legal prosecution would be cold comfort after you fell to the ground in several pieces. The surf-noise of voices sounded tinny after the long hours of engine roar.

"Fra Eldasson," Jonah called. The contractor was slipping out of the control cabin and walking up the ramp. "Finagle dammit, wait for us!"

She turned, frowning, then smiled without showing her teeth as she saw the three of them wading through the crowd toward her.

"Problem you haf?" she said brusquely.

"I thought you were going to pay us as soon as we got back to Munchen," Jonah said.

"Certainly," she replied, glancing out of the corner of her eyes at the two towering orange figures behind him. They grinned at her. "I've told everyone"—a hand waved at the others disembarking—"credit chips or account transfers will be made at the opening of bank hours tomorrow. It *is* Sunday, you know."

Jonah blinked in bewilderment for a moment, then realized what she meant. Wunderland was a *very* conservative place; about what you would expect from a settlement founded by North European plutocrats in the late twenty-first century. Even now they still observed religious holidays.

"May we eat it if it attempts to snatch away our gain/ prey?" Bigs snarled in the Hero's Tongue: in the Menacing Tense, at that.

"Shut up," Jonah whispered; Bigs was uncivilized, even for a kzin. "A lot of people around here understand that language—do you want to start a riot, talking about eating a human?" Far too many *had* been eaten; compulsory holocasts of kzinti hunting parties chasing down political prisoners had been a staple of the occupation.

Tanjit, I was the quarry *for a kzinti hunting party,* he reminded himself. *Me and Ingrid.* He pushed the memory out of his mind; thinking about Ingrid was too painful. Besides, the kzin hunting him had died.

From Eldasson's narrowed eyes and slight smile, he suspected that she had understood. *Tanjit. If there's a disturbance, she might* really *try to stiff us.* Kzinti were not popular with the courts, understandably enough—although Jonah's war record would help. It was not everyone who had assassinated a Planetary Governor like Chuut-Riit.

"Look, Fra Eldasson, we're broke until we get paid—we don't even have enough to buy a drink," he said reasonably.

"*Ja.* Hmmm. Here"—She took him by the arm and lead him to one side, behind a wrecked crane. The thick synthetic bars had frayed out into tangled fiber fragments; heavy beam-rifle hit, from the look of it. Composites did not weather, so it might have been from last year, or from the street-fighting fifty years ago when the kzin landed.

"Here's four hundred in cash," she said. "Don't let any of the others know, or everyone will be about me like grisflies. Meet me at Suuomalisen's Sauna later tonight, and I'll transfer the rest for you and your two ratcats."

"All right."

"*Hrraer.*"

✧   ✧   ✧

"I thank Eldasson for the drink and the meat," Spots said, "but the delay is irksome. We will have much to set at rights in our households; our younger siblings are still immature, of shrunken liver and rattlepate."

Bigs wrinkled his upper lip in agreement and stropped his claws on the table. Shavings of tekdar curled back, creamy yellow beneath the darker patina of the surface.

Jonah nodded. They were in one of the quieter rooms of the Sauna, which despite its name was an entertainment center of varied attractions, some shocking even to him; the tamer floor shows were interesting, but of course wasted on non-humans. The kzinti had eaten on their own—no human felt comfortable with a feeding kzin, and the felinoids detested the smell of what men ate—but had returned to wait with him.

"Yeah; I'm anxious to get the credit deposited myself," he said. *And you're not bad company for ratcats, but you're not half as pretty as what I have in mind*, he thought: it had been a long month in the swamps. "Eldasson had better show up soon."

"Eldasson?" a voice said.

Jonah looked up, slightly surprised. A man who associated with kzinti got used to being ignored, or left to his own thoughts, whichever way you preferred to look at it. The speaker was a thickset man for a Wunderlander, with a blue-jowled stubble of beard and a grubby turban; from one of the little ethnic enclaves that hung on even here in Munchen. The light from the stained-glass overhead lamps flickered across his olive skin.

"She owes you money?" the man went on.

"A fair bit," Jonah replied.

The other man giggled and lifted his drink; the steel bracelets on his wrist tinkled.

"Then you had better have a written contract," he said. "Notarized."

"Notarized?" Jonah said in alarm. "We've got the contracts, right here." He tapped his belt-unit. "With mods for bonuses and overtime."

"A personal recording?" the turbaned man said scornfully. "How long *have* you been on Wunderland, flatlander?"

Jonah bristled and ran a reflexive hand down his Sol-Belter strip of hair; his great-great-grandmother had been the last of his family to be born on Earth.

"Sorry—I knew by your accent you were Sol-system," the other said, raising a placating hand. "I just wanted to warn you; Eldasson and Suuomalisen are like *that*"—he held up two fingers, twined about each other—"and they're both crooked as a kzin's hind leg. You'd better be ready to sue for that money."

A gingery scent filled the air; the stranger backed off in alarm, as the two kzin stood and grinned, lines of slaver falling from their thin black lips. The same thought had occurred to Jonah; a kzin was not likely to receive much justice from the Wunderland junta's courts, these days.

"Let's go hunting," he said.

"*Hraareow.*"

Munchen was the biggest city Jonah had ever traveled: over a quarter of a million people. There were many times that in the Belt, but not even Gibraltar Base had as much in one habitat. Of course, much of Earth was one huge city—over eighteen billion, an impossible number—but he had been born to the Belt and the war against the Kzin. The other problem was that it wasn't a habitat at all; it was uncontained, sprawling with the disregard for distances of a thinly settled planet and a people who had been wealthy enough to give most families their own aircar. The open space above still made him a little nervous; he pretended it was the blue dome of a bubbleworld, one of the larger farming ones with a high spin. Luckily, it was unlikely that Eldasson was in the residential neighborhoods, or the slums that had grown up during the occupation. Nor was she at the address Public Info listed as her home, which had turned out to be a townhouse with several loud, extremely xenophobic—or at least anti-kzinti—dogs.

"Hrunge k'tze hvrafo *tui*," Bigs said; he stopped, opened his mouth and wet his nose with his tongue. *"Tui, tza!"*

I think I scent the prey, Jonah translated mentally. He let the length of skeelwood he was carrying up the sleeve of his overall drop until the tip rested on his fingers. *The prey is* here.

The nightspot they were staking out was a few hundred meters behind them, around a slight curve in the tree-lined road. It was a converted house, and the buildings here stood well apart; hedges lined the outer lawns, making the turf roadway a glimmer of green-black under the glowglobes. The summer night was quiet and dark, the moon and Beta both down and the stars little dimmed by city lights; the smell of dew was stronger than that of men's engines. Feet came walking, several pair. Then he saw them. Eldasson right enough, but dressed in a fancy outfit of black embroidered tunic and ballooning indigo trousers. A dark woman in a tight shipsuit to one side of her, arm in arm, talking and laughing. Another behind them, tall even for a Wunderlander but thick-built, almost a giant, shaggy ash-blond hair . . .

"Fra Eldasson," Jonah said, stepping into the pool of light under one of the globes that hung from the treebranches; they were biologicals, hitched into the tree's sap system. "How pleasant to meet you."

He could sense the kzinti spreading out behind him. Not hear them—their padded feet were soundless on the grass—but a whisper of movement, a hint of sour-ginger scent. Kzin anger: it sent the hair on his own backbone to bristling as conditioned reflex said *danger*. His smile was grim. Danger in truth, but not to him.

Eldasson stopped, blinking at him. "What are you doing here?" she snapped. Her companions looked at Jonah, then recoiled slightly at the sudden looming appearance of Spots and Bigs. The tall blond rumbled a challenge; the two women crouched slightly, spreading to either side.

Finagle, Jonah thought. *These aren't flatlanders. I miscalculated.* Even after decades of war between Man and Kzin, most Earthers were still culturally conditioned against violence. That had never gone as far on Wunderland, and there had been little law here for humans while the kzinti ruled. Nobody who prospered in those years was likely to be a pacifist. Jonah tapped his belt unit, for emphasis and for a record of what followed.

"We got a little tired of waiting for you to show up with our money, Fra Eldasson," he said calmly. "We'd like it now, if you please."

"You'll get it as soon as the transfer to me clears," she said. The voice was flat and wary; her right hand was behind her back.

Calm settled on Jonah, a comforting familiarity. The feeling of being completely immersed in reality and completely detached at the same time, what the adepts who trained him for war had said was the closest he would ever approach *satori*. For the first time in a year, the wounds within his mind ceased to itch.

"Not good enough. We want it *now*."

"No! Now get out of this neighborhood; you're not welcome here."

Bigs spoke; his Wunderlander was more thickly accented than his sibling's and distorted by anger as well:

"Why do you think you can cheat a Hero and live, monkey?"

"Ah, a racial slur," Eldasson said, smiling tightly. "Jilla, von Sydow, remember that." To the kzin: *"Go ch'rowl your Patriarch, ratcat."*

Bigs screamed and leaped. Everything seemed to move very slowly after that. Jonah dove forward and down, the yawara-stick snapping out into his hand, then sweeping toward Eldasson's wrist as it came out with the chunky shape of a military-grade stunner. She was throwing herself backward; the wood met the synthetic of the weapon instead of flesh, and there was a high karking buzz before the stunner flew off into darkness. Bigs's leap turned from fluid perfection into a ballistic arch, and his body met the earth with a thud that shook through Jonah's body. The human came up coiling off his hands, one long leg pistoning out into Eldasson's stomach.

That *hurt*. She was wearing impact armor, memory-plastic that stiffened under rapid stress. The heelstrike still sent her back winded and wheezing against the hedge. Spots came on in a hunching four-footed rush, like a giant orange weasel; the blond giant roared and swept out a chopping cut with a Gurkha knife. They circled, eight claws against a knife. The kzin was limping as he turned, dark-red blood running down one columnar thigh, naked pink tail held out rigidly to sweep around as a weapon in itself. The man had been wearing armor too; it showed through the rents in his tunic, glittering where the claws had scraped. Bigs was stirring and muttering, no longer a mute limp pile of orange fur. Only the edge of the beam could have clipped him.

Enough. The woman in the skinsuit came for Jonah, hands stripping two black-plastic rods out of sheaths along her thighs, each baton a meter long. Shockrods; the touch would bring utter pain, possible brain damage or even death in the wrong place. She had delicate Oriental features, lynx-calm, and the movements were unmistakable. Well, Nipponjin were common in the Alpha Centauri system too, out in the Serpent Swarm. He lunged, using the length of arm and leg, the point of his yawara punching out for her throat.

This is uncivilized. Maybe the ARM were right.

The hard wood clacked on plastic as both rods came around, one smashing at the stick, the second driving for his elbow with bone-breaking force. He let the force of the blow help him pivot the stick to block the second rod. *Clack.* Faint brushing contact against his left arm. *Pain!* A datum, nothing more. Pain did not hurt; paying attention to it hurt. Snap-kick to the inside of her knee, damage done but she rolled forward with the fall and backflipped, coming up crouching with the rods before her in an X, guard position.

Eldasson was straightening up, whooping for breath. Her hand snapped out a flat black lozenge and clenched; a shimmering appeared in the air before it, and a tooth-gritting whine. Jonah knew what that was; ratchet knife, a wire blade stiffened and set trembling thousands of times a second by a magnetic field. It would slash through tissue and bone as if they were jelly.

Things just became more serious, he thought, feeling his testicles trying to draw themselves up into his abdomen.

He rushed toward the woman with the shockrods, bringing his yawara down in a straight overarm blow. It smacked into the X, and she slid the shockrods down toward his hand. Jonah accepted it, accepted the sudden agony that froze his lungs and sent shimmers of random light across his pupils. His other hand flashed up to her wrists and he bore forward with his full weight and strength. They went over backward; he landed with a knee in her stomach, and the rods came down across her throat. The face beneath him convulsed, the galvanic reaction tossing him aside before she slumped into unconsciousness. Wheezing with pain he shoulder-rolled erect, both arms trembling as he brought them back to guard position.

Eldasson was on her feet and shuffling toward him, the ratchet knife extended. Behind her the big human and Spots were still circling. It could only have been thirty seconds or so. She lunged at him, the blade invisible in the dimness, but he could hear it keening malevolently. Jonah twisted aside desperately, felt something like a hot thread stroke along his side. He tried for a kick and snatched the foot back when the knife moved down, backing and feeling at the cut along his side. *Not too deep*, he realized with a hot surge of relief; only enough to break the skin. Blood flowed down his flank and soaked into his coverall around the waistband. He retreated a little faster, looking around for something to use.

Then Bigs rose in the shadows by the sidewalk.

"Look behind you," Jonah suggested helpfully, flexing his arms to try and work the feeling back into them. Eldasson snorted contempt and bored in, holding the ratchet knife before her like a ribbon saber and lunging as he skipped away. She was breathing more normally now, and the twin red spots on her cheekbones might have been anger as much as the aftereffects of being gut-kicked. A grunt of triumph as he dodged to the side and went down on the pavement; the ratchet knife went up for a slash, night air peeling back from its buzzing wire edge. There was a yawp of sound; the woman's eyes rolled up in their sockets, and the knife went silent as fingers released it. She crumpled bonelessly to the ground, her head going *thock* on the asphalt.

Bigs clipped the stunner to his belt. Spots unlocked his jaws from the knife-man's right shoulder and threw him a dozen paces to crumple bonelessly on the soft turf of a lawn. Jonah swept up the ratchet knife and flipped the hilt in his hand, the molecur-distortion battery making it heavy even in the .61-G field of Wunderland. The contractor's eyes were open; Bigs had taken time to reset the stunner's field to *light*. That meant that Eldasson could feel and see, although not move the main voluntary muscles. The Sol-Belter drove his heel into her ribs with judiciously calculated force.

"Paytime, Fra Eldasson," he said. "Payback time."

Her lips worked, trying to spit at him. Bigs picked her up by the back of her tunic and shook her at arm's length, as effortlessly as he might have a rag doll. When he was finished he brought her close and smiled in her face, tongue dangling and carnivore breath hot.

"How . . . how much?" she croaked.

"Just what you owe us," Jonah said. "Not one fennig more . . . in money."

General Buford Early looked a little less out of place in Munchen than he did in his native Sol System, these days; men as black as he were rare on Wunderland, and mostly from the Krio enclaves. They were even rarer in the polyglot genetic stew of Earth. That was not true at the time of his birth. He had been born while there were still distinct human sub-races, a fact he took some care to disguise. Not least by keeping a careful ear for the changes in language, and by muting the inhuman gracefulness learned through the centuries. Other things he hid more deeply; but the power he held from his rank in the UN Space Navy, from his role in the ARM, and from his own force of personality, he did not bother to conceal. Heldja Eldasson looked a little intimidated, sitting across the wide oak desk in the upper offices of the Ritterhaus, once more headquarters of Wunderland's government.

"What else could I do?" she said sullenly. The autodoc had healed the worst of her injuries, but she had not been allowed enough time to clear up the bruises that marked her face with red and blue splotches. "The ratcat-lover had his tame kzin *grin* at me until I transferred the funds and authenticated the contract."

"You could have gone to the police," he pointed out, lighting a cigar. That was also more common here on Wunderland than on Earth, among the many archaisms he found rather pleasant.

"Teufelheim! They had the contracts—and would the police believe me, with my record? I wouldn't have chanced stiffing them, if you hadn't suggested it."

He stared at her for a moment, and she dropped her eyes before the steady yellowish glare of his.

"Excellency," she finished sullenly.

"It should have occurred to you that—" Early stopped. *That I have influence with the courts, and the police.* Both quite true, although not to the extent he would on Earth. There, opponents of the ARM—or the Brotherhood, if they were unlucky enough to learn of its existence—could be ignored so completely that they found nobody even acknowledged their existence any longer. Harsher measures were rarely necessary; overt fear was a crude tool. The Secret Reign had survived the centuries by manipulating men, not by trying to rule them directly. It was already far older than any mere state in the year Buford Early was born . . .

"Never mind," he continued. "You'll be compensated for your loss." *Loss of stolen money*, he thought ironically. "And keep me informed of *anything* to do with Matthieson. Understood?"

"Jawul," she replied.

• **CHAPTER EIGHT**

Jonah pulled his head out of the fountain and shook it; the two kzin looked up from tending their wounds and complained with yeowls as drops hit their fur. The human restrained an impulse to grin at them; from the way they were wagging their ears back at him, they felt the same way.

"Well, we're rich," he said. "Comparatively speaking. Rich in spirit, too—I never did like being cheated." *And this time I got to do something about it*, he added silently. *Finagle, but I feel good!* Better than he had in a year. Better than he had since the psychists released him and Early began his campaign of persecution.

Bigs grunt-snarled. Spots answered aloud: "We have fought side by side," he said. His whiskers drooped. "Although there will be little enough left of this money when our debts are paid and supplies laid in for our households."

"Considering that you were contemplating suicide the night I met you, that's not bad," Jonah observed dryly, turning and sitting on the cornice of the fountain. "How much *will* you have left?"

"If we pay no more than the most pressing of our

debts . . ." Spots turned and consulted with his sibling in the Hero's Tongue; kzin felt uneasy with a language as verbal as English. "A thousand each."

"Hmmm. The idea is to let money make money," Jonah replied. "You ought to invest it."

Bigs folded his ears in anger, and the pelt laid itself flat on his face, sculpting against the massive bones. Spots lifted his upper lip and let his tail twitch in derision.

"If we had the skill, we would not have the opportunity. Business—who would do business of that sort with a kzin?"

"Well, I—" Jonah snapped his fingers. "Wait a minute! Remember that dosshouse we stayed at, the night I told you about the job?"

"I would rather forget," Spots said.

"Vermin," Bigs rasped. "Human-specific vermin at that. If the Fanged God is humorous, they will die from ingesting kzin blood."

"No, the old man I talked to—he'd been on prospecting expeditions into the Jotuns."

Spots had bent his head to lap at the water in the fountain; now he raised it, hands still braced on the rim, long pink washcloth-sized tongue lapping at his jowls and whiskers.

"You are altruistic, for a monk—for a human," he said suspiciously.

"Tanj," Jonah replied. "There Ain't No Justice. You two are out of luck because your side lost the war; I'm in bad odor with . . . hmmm, an influential patriarch, let's say. And we've just pounded on some people who, if not respectable, are certainly established citizens of Munchen. Reason and health both say we should get out of town. If nothing else, living's cheaper in the countryside. The Jotuns are pretty wild; we could hunt most of our food."

That brought the kzinti heads up, both of them. The

aliens stared at him with their huge round lion-colored eyes for a moment, then looked at each other.

"I've got three thousand, you've got thirty-five hundred, our two friends here have a thousand apiece. No, that's not enough. Mm-hm. Need about twice that."

The old man's name was Hans Shwartz, and he had been perfectly willing to discuss an expedition. His honesty was reassuring, if depressing.

"Why so much?" Jonah asked. "I've done rockjack work, back in the Sol-Belt, but this is planetside—the air's free."

"*Ja*, but nothing else is," Hans said. "Look. You've got animals—no sense in trying to take ground vehicles, it's too rough in there—and you've got personal supplies, you've got weapons—"

"Weapons?"

"Bandits. Worse now than during the war. Weapons, then there's detector equipment. Southern Jotuns have funny geography, difficult—that's why it's worthwhile going in there. Scattered pockets of high-yield stuff; doesn't pay for large-scale mining, even these days."

Jonah nodded, and the two kzin flared their nostrils in agreement. The Serpent Swarm had been stripped of experienced rockjacks; they made the best stingship fighter-pilots, and the Alpha Centauran space-navy had inherited plenty of shipbuilding capacity from the occupation. Thousands of small strike craft built in Tiamat and the other space fabrication plants were riding in UN carriers deeper and deeper into kzinti space. Even so, the natural superiority of asteroid mining was only somewhat diminished. There would have been little or no mining and industry on the surface of Wunderland but for the kzinti. Kzin had been in its late Iron Age when the Jotok arrived and brought with them the full panoply of fusion power and gravity polarizers. The polarizer made surface-to-orbit travel fantastically cheap, and with fusion power pollution had never been a problem either.

"Ja, lot of stuff we'd need to make it worthwhile going. I'm willing to invest my savings, but not lose them— why do you think I'm sleeping in flophouses with three thousand krona in the bank? The return would be worth it, but only if we're properly equipped."

Jonah rubbed at his jaw; the stubble was bristly, and he reminded himself to pick up some depilatory, now that he could afford it.

"What prey is in prospect?" Bigs said.

Shwartz understood the idiom; he seemed to have had some experience with kzin. Enough to know basic etiquette like not staring, at least.

"Depends, *t'kzintar.*" *Warrior,* in the Hero's Tongue; a derivative of *kzintosh,* male. "Possibly, nothing at all! That's the risk. Have to go way outback; anything near a road or shipline's been surveyed to hell and back. Take in filter membranes, then build a hydraulic system if we discover anything. Pack it out. Only the heavy metals and rare earths worth enough. With luck, oh, maybe ten, twenty thousand krona each—profit, that is, after expenses. Depends on when you want to stop, of course."

"Twenty thousand sounds fine to me," Jonah said. About the price of a rockjack's singleship, in normal times. More than enough for independence, if he managed carefully; passage back to Sol System, if he wanted it. "Excuse us for a minute?"

"*Ja,*" the old man said mildly, stuffing his pipe and turning away to sit quietly on his cot, blowing smoke rings at the grimy ceiling of the dosshouse.

Jonah and the kzin brothers huddled in a corner; the half-ton of sentient flesh made a barrier as good as any privacy screen.

"Sounds like the best prospect going," he murmured.

"Yes," Spots said. He took a comp from his belt and tapped at the screen; a kzin military model, rather chunky, marked in the dots-and-commas of the aliens' script. "That would repurchase enough land to sustain our households. With an independent base, we could contract work to meet our cash-flow problems."

"I am tempted," Bigs cut in; they both looked at him in surprise. "My liver steams with the juices of anticipation. With enough wealth, we need no longer associate so much with humans." His ears folded away and he ducked his muzzle. "No offense, Jonah-Matthieson. You hardly seem like a monkey."

"None taken," Jonah said dryly. *Actually, he's quite reasonable . . . for a pussy*, he thought, using the old UN Space Navy slang for the felinoids. *That was flattery.* Accepting defeat violated kzin instincts as fundamental to them as sex was to a human. Walking among aliens who did not recognize kzinti dominance without lashing out at them took enormous strength of will.

"Hrrrr." Spots closed his eyes to a slit; the pink tip of his tongue protruded slightly. "How are we to raise the additional capital?" He brightened, unfurling ears. "A raid! We will—"

Jonah groaned; Bigs was grinning with enthusiasm . . . aggressive enthusiasm. How had these two survived since the liberation? *Badly*, he knew.

"No, no—do you want to end up in *prison*?"

That made them both wince. Kzinti were more vulnerable to sensory deprivation than humans; they were a cruel race, but rarely imprisoned their victims except as a temporary holding measure. Kzin imprisoned for long periods usually suicided by beating their own brains out against a wall, or died in raving insanity if restrained.

"No, we'll have to go with what the old coot had in mind," Jonah concluded.

Huge round amber-colored eyes blinked at him. "But he said he did not have access to sufficient funds," Spots pointed out reasonably, licking his nose and sniffling. Puzzlement: *I sniff for your reasoning.*

It was amazing how much you learned about kzinti, working with them for a month or two. Back in Sol System, nobody had known squat about the aliens, except that they kept attacking—even when they shouldn't. Now he knew kzin body language; he also knew their economic system was primitive to the point of absurdity. Not surprising, when a bunch of feudal-pastoral savages were hired as mercenaries by a star-faring race, given specialized educations, and then revolted and overthrew their employers. That had happened a long, long, *long* time ago, long enough to be quasi-legend among the kzin. They had never developed much sophistication, though; nor a real civilization.

What they had done was to freeze their own development. The kzin became a space-faring power long before they understood what that meant; and with space travel came access to genetic alteration techniques. The kzin used those, both on their captives and on themselves. The plan was to make them better; but better to the Race of Heroes meant to be even more primitive, even more dedicated to the Fanged God, even more loyal to the Patriarch. Civilization breeds for rationality; but the kzin used gene mechanics to build in proof against that.

While they were at it, they altered their social customs, then changed their genes so the new customs would be stable. The result was a race of barbarians, culturally well below the level of the Holy Roman Empire, roaming through space in wars of conquest and slavery.

Fortunately they had also changed their genes to make themselves more Heroic; and to a kzin, Heroes were rarely subtle and never deceptive.

Heroes don't lie, and they don't steal. *It should be enough*, Jonah thought. So—

"He'll have a backer in mind," Jonah said. "A beneath-the-grass patriarch. A silent partner." Explaining the concept took a few minutes. "Otherwise he wouldn't have talked to us at all."

The huge kzinti heads turned toward each other.

"*We need him*," Spots said. "*Badly*."

"*Truth*," Bigs replied morosely.

Each of them solemnly bared the skin on the inside of a wrist and scratched a red line with one claw, then stared at him expectantly.

Oh, Finagle, the human thought. "Can I use a knife?" he said aloud.

"I won't take money from Harold Yarthkin," Jonah said bluntly.

He stared narrow-eyed at the lean Herrenmann face across the table, with its arrogant asymmetric double spike of beard. The room was large, elegant, and airy in the manner of Old Munchen, on the third story of a townhouse overlooking the Donau and the gardens along its banks. Almost as elegant as Claude Montferrat-Palme in his tweeds and suede, looking for all the world like a squire just in from riding over the home farm. He lounged back in the tall carved-oak chair, framed against the bright sunlight and the wisteria and wrought iron of the balcony behind him. His smile was lazy and relaxed.

"Oh, I assure you, there's no money of his in this. We're . . . close, but not bosom companions, if you know what I mean."

Ingrid, Jonah's mind supplied. An old and tangled rivalry; resolved now, but the scratches must linger. His were about healed, but he hadn't spent forty years brooding on them.

"Although he probably *would* back you up. You did save both their lives, there at the end."

Jonah felt a cold shudder ripple his skin, but the sensation was fading. *There are no more thrint*, he told himself. None at all, except for the Sea Statue in the UN museum, and that was safely bottled in a stasis field until the primal monobloc recondensed. After an instant the sensation went away. A year ago the memory attacks had been overwhelming; now they were just very, very unpleasant. Progress, of a sort.

"Not interested," he said flatly. *For one thing, our dear friend Harold might have left me here for the pussies, if it wouldn't have made him look bad in front of Ingrid.* Harold Yarthkin was a hero of sorts; Jonah knew the breed, from the inside. As ruthless as a kzin, when he was crossed or almighty Principle was at stake.

"But as I said, it's my money."

"Why are you spending your time on this penny-ante stuff, then?" Jonah asked. His nod took in the room, the old paintings and wood shining with generations of labor and wax.

"I'm not as rich as all that," Montferrat said to Jonah's skeptical eyebrow. "Contrary to rumor, most of the money I, hmmm, disassociated from official channels during the occupation didn't stick. Much of the remainder went after the liberation—my vindication wasn't an automatic matter, you see. Too many ambiguous actions. And I'm not exactly in good odor with the new government. The ARM doesn't like any of us who were involved in . . . that business, you know. Therefore the most lucrative investments, like buying up confiscated estates, are barred to me. But yes, backing an expedition like yours isn't all that good a bet. I've funded a number, and no more than broken even."

"Why bother?"

"For some reason, the Provisional Government—our

acquaintance Markham, and General Early—doesn't really want exploration in that quarter. Among the many other things they dislike. Just to put a spoke in their wheels is satisfaction enough for me, so long as it doesn't *cost* money. And besides, perhaps the horse will learn to sing."

Jonah shrugged off the reference and sat in thought for a moment.

"Accepted," he said, and leaned forward to press his palm to the recorder.

". . . and that, my dear, was how Jonah Matthieson came to be prospecting in these hills," Montferrat finished.

Night had fallen during the tale, and the outdoor patio was lit by the dim light of the town's glowstrips. Insectoids fluttered around them, things the size of a palm with wings in swirling patterns of indigo and crimson; they smelled of burnt cinnamon and made a sound as of glass chimes. Tyra took a cigarette and leaned forward to accept the man's offer of a light; she leaned back and blew a meditative puff at the stars before answering him.

"You certainly don't believe in letting the left hand know what the right does, do you, Herr Montferrat-Palme. Claude."

His grin was raffish and his expression boyishly frank. "No," he said. "But I'll tell you everything . . ."

She raised a brow.

". . . that I think you need to know. I'm still uncertain of Jonah—uncertain of what the psychists did to him. I need someone to watch him; to report back to me, if there's any sign he's not what he pretends to be. And unobtrusively check up on any attempt to sabotage his expedition. You're the perfect choice, young and obscure . . . and Jonah is likely to trust you, if that's necessary."

"Well and good, and I can use the employment," Tyra said, giving him a level stare. "But what are your *purposes* here, myn Herr?"

"Money." After a moment he continued: "For a reason. I've got political plans. Not so much ambitions—with my history I'll never hold office—but I have candidates in mind. Harry, for one . . . I intend, in the long run, to put a glitch in Herrenmann Reichstein-Markham's program; he'd make a very bad *caudillo*, and I think he's got ambitions in that direction." Tyra nodded grimly. "Beyond that, I want to get the ARM out of Wunderlander politics—a long-term project—and ease the transition to democracy.

"Not," he went on with a slight grimace, "the form of government I'd have chosen, but we have little choice in the matter, do we? In any case, I need money, and I need information, which is power. This business is just one gambit in a very complicated game."

"I've never been called a pawn so graciously before," Tyra said, rising and extending her hand. The older aristocrat clicked heels and bent over it. "Consider it a deal, Claude."

• CHAPTER NINE

The convoy was crowded and slow as it ground up the switchbacks of the mountain road. Hovercraft had a greasy instability in rocky terrain like this, setting Jonah's teeth on edge. The *speed* was disconcerting, too. Insect-slow, in one sense, compared to the singleships and fighter stingcraft he had piloted in the War, but you could not see velocity in space. Uncomfortably fast in relation to the ground; he kept expecting a collision-alarm to sound. He ignored the sensation, as he ignored the now-familiar scent of kzin, and scrolled through the maps instead. The flatbed around them was crowded, with farmers and travelers and mothers nursing their squalling young, and a cage full of shoats that turned hysterical every time the wind shifted and they scented Bigs and Spots. The kzin were sleeping; they could do that eighteen hours a day when there was nothing else to occupy their time.

Hans tapped the screen. "No sense in looking anywhere near here, like I said," he went on. "Surveyors found it all, and then when it got worth taking the contractors took it all out, twenty, thirty years ago. We'll buy some animals in Gelitzberg and—"

An alarm *did* go off, up in the lead truck. Almost at once an explosion followed, and a slow tide of dirt and rock came down the hillslope to their right, with jerking trees riding atop it like surfboarders on a wave. The autogun on the truck pivoted with smooth robotic quickness and its multiple barrels fired with a noise like yapping dogs, streaks of light stabbing out at other lines of fire reaching down from the scrubby hillside. Magenta globes burst where the seeker missiles died, but more lived to smash their liquid-metal bolts into engines; then the guard truck took the avalanche broadside and went spinning down the slope to vanish in a searing actinic glare as its power core ruptured. Molecular distortion batteries could not explode, strictly speaking, but they contained a *lot* of energy.

By that time Jonah had already rolled off the flatbed and dived for the roadside bush; he had seen boarding actions during the war, and had trained hard in gravity. He landed belly-down and eeled his way into the thick reddish-brown native scrub, ignoring the thorns that ripped at his exposed hands and face. To his surprise, Hans was not far away and moving rather more quietly. The response of the two kzin was not surprising at all; they went over the heads of their human companions and up the hillside in a series of bounding leaps, then vanished into cover with an appalling suddenness.

Jonah licked at the sweat on his upper lip and took up the trigger slack on his magrifle. It was a cheap used model, and the holo sight that sprang into existence over the breech quivered slightly and never reached the promised x40 magnification. It was still much better than nothing, and he used it to scan the upper slope carefully, starting close and working back. The bandits were visible in short snatches, working their way cautiously toward the wrecked convoy. Fire still crackled overhead from passengers and guards; the bandits returned it with careful selectivity, not wanting to damage their loot more than was needful. One face showed through a gap between rocks for an instant, a heavy pug countenance with brown stubble and a gold tooth.

If they had seeker missiles, they've probably got a good jammer, Jonah thought. No help to be expected anytime soon.

"Here goes," he whispered softly, laid the sighting-bead on a blurred shape screened by bush, and stroked at the trigger.

His rifle was set for high-subsonic; the slug gave a sharp *pfut* and the weapon bumped gently at his shoulder. The bandit folded and dropped backward, screaming loud enough to be heard over a thousand meters. One of the weaknesses of impact armor; when there was *enough* kinetic energy behind the projectile, the suddenly-rigid surface could pulp square meters of your body surface. Very painful, if not fatal.

Hans was firing too, accurate and slow. Jonah snap-shot, raking the slope and clenching his teeth against the knowledge that they would be scanning for him, with better sensors than an overage rifle sight. They had heavy weapons, too.

Another scream, this time one of kzin triumph, inhumanly loud and fierce; instincts that remembered tiger and sabertooth raised hairs under the sweat-wet fabric of his jacket. A human body soared out and tumbled down the hillside, limp in death. Seconds later, a globe of flame rose from nearby, the discharge of a tripod-mounted beamer's power cell. Another heavy beamer cut loose, but this time directed back upslope at the bandits. Jonah's sights showed Bigs holding it like a hand weapon, screaming with gape-jawed joy as he hosed down the hillside. Bush flamed, and men ran through it burning. Jonah shot, shifted aimpoint, shot again, as much in mercy as anything else. When he shifted to wide-angle view for a scan, he saw a swarthy-faced bandit in the remnants of military kit rallying the gang, then leading them in a swift retreat over the hill.

And the two kzin pursuing. *"Come back!"* he screamed incredulously. Hans looked at him; the humans shrugged, and began to follow.

Horses did not like kzin. That, it seemed, was an immutable fact of life. Hans watched the last of them go bucking off across the dusty square of Neu Friborg with a philosophical air.

"Waste of time, horses, anyway," he said. "Die on you, like as not. Draw tigripards. Mules are what we need; mules for the gear, and we can walk. Kitties'd have to walk anyhow, too heavy for horses."

"I *eat* herbivores, I do not perch upon them," Bigs said, and stalked off to curl up on a rock and sulk.

"Will these . . . mules be more sensible?" Spots asked dubiously.

The stock pens had been set up for the day, collapsible metal frames old enough to be rickety; most of the work animals being offered for sale had been stunned into docility by the heat. High summer in the southern Jotuns was no joke, with both suns up and this lowish altitude. Jonah fanned himself with his straw hat, wiped sweat from his face and looked dubiously at the collection of bony animals who turned their long ears towards him. It was probably imagination, the look of malicious anticipation . . . *and planets have lousy climate control systems*, he added to himself. His underwear was chafing, and he was raw under his gunbelt. The pens stank with a hot, dry smell and buzzed with flies, Terran and the six-winged Wunderlander equivalents.

"I haven't had much to do with animals," he said dubiously. Except to eat them sometimes, and he preferred his meat prepared so its origin wasn't too obvious. In space you ate rodent, mostly, anyway, or decently synthesized protein. It made him slightly queasy, the thought of eating something with eyes that size and a large head.

"You'll learn," Hans said, running his hands expertly down the legs of one animal. "Won't do," he added to the owner, in outbacker dialect. "Galls. Let's see t'other one.

"Yep, you'll learn," he continued to Jonah. "Unless you want to carry three hundred kilos of gear yourself."

"I see your point," Jonah replied.

The mule stretched out its neck at Spots and gave a deafening bray with aggressive overtones. The kzin's fur bottled, and he hissed back at the mule, which blinked and fell silent. From the way its eyes rolled, it was keeping a wary watch on the big carnivore . . .

"Thiss'un 'll do," Hans told the owner. "And the other five."

The grizzled farmer nodded and whistled for the town registrar, who came over with a readout pistol and scanned the barcodes laser-marked into the mules' necks.

"Set down," she said, tucking the instrument into a holster in her skirts. "New system, just back on line— haven't had a computer link like this since way back in the occupation." She gave Spots a hard glare; that was extremely bad manners by kzinti standards, but the felinoid stared over her head.

Poor bleeping pussy must have had a lot of practice at that, Jonah thought with some compassion. Stares and jostling and tobacco smoke; life was not easy for kzin under human rule. *On the other hand, we don't enslave or eat them, so matters are rather more than even.*

"Might as well get started," Hans concluded, after slapping palms with the farmer. "You fellas need to learn how to do up a pack saddle. Got to be balanced, or you'll get saddle galls and then we'll be stuck without enough transport to carry our gear. Couldn't have that. All right, first lesson."

He handed one of the wood-and-leather frames to Spots, together with a blanket. "Fold the blanket, then put the saddle firmly across."

Spots picked up the gear in his stubby-fingered four-digit hands, conscious of the village loafers and small children watching him. So conscious that he did not realize what the mule's laid-back ears meant, and the way it turned its head to fix him with one distance-estimating eye. The kick was swift even by kzinti standards, and precisely aimed. Spots made a whistling sound as he flew back, folding around his middle. The onlookers laughed; he fought back to all fours. His back arched, fur bottled out, ears folded away in combat mode, and his tail stood out like a pink column behind him. He was beyond lashing it, in his rage, and his lower jaw sank down on his breast in the killing gape as he whooped for breath. Adrenaline surge and lack of oxygen sent gray across his eyes and narrowed his vision down to a tunnel. When a human moved at the corner of it, he whirled and began the upward gutting stroke with barred claws.

The motion froze. It was the human Jonah, and he stood calmly in the position of respectful-nonaggression, with no smell of fear. His teeth were decently concealed. Slowly, slowly, willpower beat down the aching need to kill and the rage-shame of mockery. The loafers had tumbled backward at the blurring-swift kzin leap that left Spots back on his feet, though some of the children had cried out in delight as at a wonder. Spots's pelt sank back toward normal, and he forced his ears to unfold, his tail to relax. Jonah bent and picked up the saddle and its blanket pad.

"Shall we do this together?" he said in an even voice. "I wouldn't care to be kicked by that thing, myself—I don't have cartilage armor across my middle the way you Heroes do."

Stiffly, Spots's ears waggled; the equivalent of a forced smile. "Mine is not in very good condition, at the moment. How shall we approach?"

"One on either side," Jonah said. "We shouldn't give him a target."

"Hrraaaeeeeeeee!" Bigs shrieked and leapt.

The gagrumpher froze for a fatal instant, its six legs tensed and head whipping backward, then spurted forward in a desperate bound. Spots rose out of the underbrush almost at its feet and lunged for the exposed throat, fastening himself with clawed hands and feet to the big animal and sinking his fangs into its throat. Blood bubbled between his teeth, hot and salty and spicy across his tongue, but he concentrated on squeezing his jaws shut. Air wheezed through the punctured windpipe and he gave a grunt of triumph as it closed beneath the bone-cracking pressure of his grip. Suffocation killed the prey, when you got a good throat-hold. The animal collapsed by the forelegs, then went over on its side with a thump as Bigs arrived and threw his massive form against its hindquarters. A few seconds more and it kicked and died.

They crouched for a moment, panting, forepaw-hands on the warm body. The soft night echoed to the throbbing killscream of triumph, and then they settled down to the enjoyable task of butchering and eating. Spots cuffed affectionately at his sibling as they ripped open the body cavity and squabbled over hearts—gagrumphers had two, one major and one secondary, like most Wunderland higher life-forms—and liver. It was a big beast, twice the weight of an adult male kzin, half a human ton, but they made an appreciable dint in it, before feeling replete enough to pile the remainder in torn-off segments of hide; it would be fresh enough to eat for a couple of days. With the chore done they could lie at leisure, cracking bones for marrow with rocks and the hilts of their wtsai-knives, nibbling at treats of organ and tripe, grooming the blood and bits out of each other's fur.

"It is well, it is well," Bigs crooned, working over the hard-to-reach places at the back of his sibling's neck. It was amazing where the blood got to, when you stuck your head into the prey's abdominal cavity.

"It is well," Spots confirmed, yawning cavernously. "If I never eat synthetic protein again, it will be far too soon. Nothing is lacking but ice cream, or some bourbon with milk."

"Your pride-mate provides," Bigs announced, unslinging a canteen and two flat dishes that collapsed against it. "The bourbon, at least."

A throaty purr resounded from both throats. *This is how the Fanged God meant kzinti to live*, Spots thought. The night was bright to their sight, full of interesting scents; a gratifying hush of terror was only gradually wearing off, as the native life reacted to the roar of hunting kzin.

It was how kzin *had* lived, for scores of scores of millennia, on the savannahs and in the jungles of Kzin itself. The scent of his brother was rich and comforting with their common blood. So had young warriors lived in the wandering years, cast out by their fathers and the home pride. They grouped together in the wastelands, brothers and half-brothers and cousins, growing strong in comradeship and skill, until they could raid the settled bands for females of their own—or even displace their fathers and become lords in their own right. From those bonds sprang the pride and the clan, foundations of kzinti culture. So had the Heroic Race lived through the long slow rise to sentience, through all the endless hunting time. Before iron and fire, before the first ranches. Long, long before the Jotoki came from space, with their two-edged gifts of technology and education to hire orange-furred mercenaries.

"I scent a path that might have been," Spots mused, over a second drink. "If the Jotok had never come to Kzin-home, would we ever have been more than wandering hunters, with castle-dwelling ranchers as the height of our civilization? My liver trembles with ambiguity—perhaps that would have been best?"

"And miss the Endless Hunt?" his more conventional sibling retorted. "The flesh of these excellent gagrumphers?"

"The Endless Hunt is endless time spent in spaceships and habitats, living on synthetic meat, never feeling wind in your fur," Spots replied. They had both done tours of duty offplanet during the war, and served longer in fortresses on the surface that might as well have been battlecraft. "And living among aliens."

"The Fanged God created them to serve us," Bigs said reasonably, rolling onto his back in the gesture of relaxed trust and looking at Spots upside-down. "Thus freeing the Heroes for the honorable path of war."

"So said the Conservors of the Patriarchal Past," Spots said, with a sardonic wave of his bat-wing ears. "You will note that there are few of them around. We *lost* this war."

Bigs's posture grew slightly rigid. "My nose is dry with worry," he said, in an attempt at lightness. "Our impoverished but noble line is about to be disgraced with a Kdaptist."

"Lick your nose, kshat-hunter; I do not yet imagine that God created Man in His image. Kdapt-Preacher I have seen; he is of great liver, but rattlebrain as a kit. As a kzinrett. His experiences in the war . . ."

Bigs nodded wisely. "Yet I will not challenge him claw-to-claw," he said.

Spots snorted, lips flapping against his teeth; the self-proclaimed prophet had made many converts among the remaining kzinti in the Alpha Centauri system. It was soothing to the self-esteem to blame defeat on God, Who was the ultimate Victor in every life. He had made even more with an uninterrupted series of personal victories in death-duels; his belt was like a dried-flesh kilt with the ear trophies he had garnered since proclaiming his mission. Luckily, he had also proclaimed his intention of voyaging to Kzin itself and trying to convert the Patriarch. The Riit would deal with him in due course, one assumed.

"Yet still, we lost."

"We have suffered a setback," Bigs replied stubbornly, scratching his belly. "It was unfair—the Outsiders intervened."

Spots twitched tail. The mysterious Outsiders *had* sold the hyperdrive to the human colonists of We Made It; it was still a matter of furious controversy among the Wunderland survivors whether the Fifth Fleet so painfully accumulated by the late, great Chuut-Riit would have overwhelmed the human homeworld. Neither species would have stumbled on the hyperdrive themselves, he thought, despite knowing some such thing had been made by the ancient thrint and tnuctipun. It was so . . . *unlikely*.

"Unfair," Bigs repeated.

"As the great Kztarr-Shuru said, fairness is the concept of those whose leap rams their nose into a stone wall. They open their eyes and complain. Four fleets were destroyed by the monkeys," Spots said meditatively, likewise scratching. The salt of blood made for a pleasantly itching skin; his belly was drum-tight with fresh meat he had killed with his own teeth and claws, an intensely satisfying feeling. "Even when they had no tradition of war. I have studied them."

"Too much, my brother," Bigs said, rolling over onto his stomach to talk seriously. "Even as you speak too much with the Jonah-monkey."

"The Jonah-monkey is a warrior," Spots said sharply. "He has saved our honor . . . not to mention our lives."

"For its own monkey purposes," Bigs grumbled, holding down a legbone with both hands and gnawing. The tough bone grated and chipped beneath his fangs. "Remember, in the end, there can be only Dominance toward such as it."

Spots rose and stretched, one limb at a time, his tongue curling pinkly. "When we are not paupers living on enemy territory . . ." he said, and rippled his fur in a shrug at the sharp scent of annoyance from his sibling. It faded; it was difficult for any young kzintosh to maintain anger on a full belly after a kill. "We should return to their camp. As Jonah said, the old one will have difficulty setting a decent pace—he needs his rest."

"Hrrraweo. Journeying with humans! Their cremated meats . . ."

Spots joined in the shudder "Yet we may hunt—we have not eaten so well since the war ended."

"Truth." Bigs looked around at the minor scavengers, already congregating for the scraps. "Yet in my inmost liver, I feel we are now such as these."

With a sigh, they slid off into the friendly night, back toward the human campfire.

• CHAPTER TEN

"ID cards? We don' need no ID cards! We don' need no stinkin' ID cards!"

The bandit chief struck his fist on the table and snarled; the jugs of drink jumped, and one flask of sake fell. The porcelain was ancient and priceless, an heirloom from Earth; one of the black-clad attendants had crossed the room to catch it before it had time to travel half the distance to the floor. Scalding-hot rice wine cascaded across his wrists and forearms, but there was no tremor in them as he set it reverently back in place, bowed, and stepped smoothly to his guard position along the wall. Shigehero Hirose spared him the indignity of sending him to the autodoc; repairs could be made at any time, but an opportunity to demonstrate true loyalty—and to accumulate *giri*—was more rare.

The bandit, Gruederman, lost some of his bluster. Hirose thought that was merely from the guard's speed, not from the true depths of disciplined obedience it showed; but any lesson learned by a barbarian was an improvement. "Herr Gruederman," the Nipponjin said. "I have gone to some trouble to secure false identities for you and your group as members of the Provisional

Gendarmerie. I am sure you will find them very useful."

Gruederman threw himself back in the chair, taking up his bottled beer and gulping at it. Hirose hid a cold distaste behind his bland smile. The other man was short and thickset, bouncy-muscular, which was something; many Wunderlanders who did no manual labor were obscenely flabby. Humanity had had only a few centuries to adapt to the .61 gravity, and millions to develop a physiology suited to 1.0. But for the rest he was a slobbering pig, not even bothering to depilate—Hirose suppressed a shudder at the sheer *hairiness* of *gaijin*—with great bands of sweat darkening his khaki tunic under the armpits and at the neck. Granted, the hotel room was hot, even with the ceiling fan. But . . .

He wrinkled his nose. Gruederman didn't wash very often, either, and he had the rank body odor of a red-meat eater.

"More guns is what we need, more equipment," he was saying. "Not stinkin' ID. Why can't you get us guns? You slants fence what we take, you've got to have good contacts."

"Our contacts are our concern," Hirose said quietly. "We have provided a valuable service; you may purchase weapons elsewhere with the valuata we supply." *And we are not going to make you so much of a menace that the Provisional Government looks too closely, which would happen if we provided you with the equipment you desire.* "In return, we ask only that you do an occasional favor . . ."

Gruederman frowned. "*Ja*, no problem, we boot some head. Who you want done?"

Hirose pushed the holos across the table and sipped delicately at his sake.

"Lieber Herr Gott!" Gruederman swore, taking another swig of beer. "Ratcats!"

"The humans are the crucial targets," the oyabun said quietly.

"I know these fuckers! They were on the convoy to Neu Friborg last week. Shot us up! You say they're goin' into the Jotuns?" Hirose inclined his head. "No problem, we boot their heads *good*."

"Excellent," Hirose said, nodding.

Gruederman belched hugely, pushed back his chair and swaggered to the door. "We boot them good." The bandit hitched at his belt and went out without bowing. The *oyabun* walked quickly to the window and flung it open; without needing orders, the others began to clean the room and lit incense.

The things I do for the Secret Rule, he thought ironically. *Or for* fear *of the Secret Rule*. Once your family was in the Brotherhood, there was no such thing as resignation. That was how the world had been knit together, back on Earth; slowly, but oh so surely. *"Until Holy Blood fills Holy Grail . . ."* he quoted to himself. And now, it seemed, the extra-solar colonies would go the same way. He sighed; it had been pleasant, the degree of autonomy four and a half light-years interposed between Earth and Alpha Centauri. Virtual independence, the way it must have been on Earth before Nippon was opened to the West, when the Eastern Way families had received their orders from the Elders only once or twice in a generation. All things came to an end, though; the kzinti had come, the hyperdrive had followed, and now the universe had shrunk drastically once more.

It was useless to think of resistance. Even more so to think of rebellion, or exposing the Brotherhood; it had been exposed a dozen times, and *it did not matter*. In more than one century investigators had managed to publish books with most of the details of the Brotherhood, its origin, many of the membership, even some of the signs of the Craft. They hadn't mattered. The books were not believed. They were buried under a mountain of disinformation, the tale-tellers ignored if outsiders, silenced if initiates. Outright rebels like Frederick Barbarossa and Lenin were crushed. Invincible, secret beyond secret, the conspiracy at the heart of all conspiracies and secret orders, the Brotherhood went on. Just at the moment it took the form of the ARM and Buford Early, and demanded that certain individuals vanish in the dangerous, bandit-haunted wastes of the Jotuns. That, at least, was easily arranged, with willing tools who knew nothing of what purpose they served.

"Go." He turned, nodding to the attendant who had caught the spilled wine. "See to your hurts."

He kept his voice curt, but the man sensed the approval. *When the time comes to silence Gruederman, I will send that one*, Hirose decided. None of Gruederman's band could be allowed to live, of course. They would be no loss to anyone.

"It's a very tempting proposition, Herr Early—or should I say Herr General Early?—but I'm afraid it's not what I had in mind at the present time," Claude Montferrat-Palme said.

His current mistress set a tray between the two men and withdrew; she was a spectacular blonde in red tights and slashed tunic, and Early's eyes followed her out of the lounge with appreciation. Low gravity could do some interesting things for the human figure, things only prosthetics or special effects could accomplish on Earth. Belters were usually too spindly to take advantage.

They were meeting on Montferrat's home ground, the manor-house of his grudgingly restored estate. Grudgingly, since his allegiance to the Resistance had been so late and politic, but the conversion had been spectacular when it came. Also he turned out to have used much of the graft that came the way of a *collabo* chief of police for Munchen to help refugees, most of whom had showed their gratitude in electorally solid ways . . . *Rather surprising me*, Montferrat chuckled inwardly. *Sometimes I wish the world would not keep chipping away at my cynicism so.* You needed the vigor of disillusioned youth to maintain a really black, bitter cynicism. In his seventh decade and settling into middle age, Claude felt a disconcerting mellowing effect.

Early leaned back, coffee cup in one hand and brandy snifter in the other. "Excellent," he said after sipping at one and then the other. Continuing: "I'm surprised you're not interested, *Herrenmann*. You struck me as an ambitious man."

"Pleasant to meet someone who appreciates the finer things," Montferrat said, swirling the amber liquid in his snifter and inhaling the scent. Most of the plutocrats who founded Wunderland had been German or Netherlander or Scandinavian; his Montferrat ancestors were a French exception, and they had worked long and hard to establish the true vines of Cognac on this property. Along with the coffee plantations, things were possible in Wunderland's climate that were not on earth.

"And I *am* ambitious, Herr General," he went on, setting it down and taking out his cigarette case.

Early accepted one of the cigarillos, and they both lit from the candle on the table. The big room was dimly lit, letting in moonlight and warm garden scents through the tall louvered windows on three sides. Blue smoke drifted up toward the molded plaster of the ceiling.

"Strange you should be willing to risk all this, then," he said, waving an arm at the outer wall; taking in the mansion and estate beyond, in spirit.

"If you mean the inheritance of the Nineteen Families," Montferrat said, blowing a smoke ring, "it's already more-or-less lost. And in any case, what business is it of yours?"

"I'm merely advising General Markham, as liaison with the UN Space Navy," Early said mildly.

"Advising him that his dreams of returning Wunderland

to the pre-War status quo can be accomplished," Montferrat said dryly. "Absurd. For a variety of reasons, good and bad, the Families were too closely involved in running the planet during the Occupation. Their rule is doomed, even if the Provisional Government's Gendarmerie has stopped the rioting and looting against them."

"You haven't thrown in with the Democrats, either," Early pointed out.

"No, because I recognize a certain fine Terrestrial hand behind them—you've been puppeting the new Radical Democrat party too—financing it, in fact."

"You'll never prove a word of *that*," Early replied.

"Of course not; I'm not entirely sure what you and your masters are after, but you're certainly no fool. There isn't even enough evidence to convince Markham, and he's a clinical paranoid, I wonder his autodoc doesn't fix him. My best guess is that you want to use Markham to restore order, infiltrating our military in the process— then use him to discredit the aristocrats completely with his ham-handed repression. Thus leaving the field to the Radical Democrats, who want a constitution that's a carbon copy of Earth's—complete with a technological police. Which the experience of the UN shows is equivalent to handing the government *over* to the technological police, since to control technology in a modern society you have to control everything."

For a moment the mask of affability slipped on Early's face, and Montferrat felt a slight prickling along his spine. *How much of that is genuine?* he thought. *The man is ancient, for Gott's sake.* At least three times older than himself . . . and he ought to be sitting wheezing in a computerized wheelchair in the Strudlebug's Club back on Earth. *Secrets of the ARM.*

"You *are* ambitious," Early said softly. "I'd hoped to talk you out of this party you're promoting."

"Many people are involved with the Centrists," Montferrat corrected; Early waved his hand.

"Please, I know the signs of secret influence when I see them." For some reason he grinned at that. "Separatism is not a viable alternative."

"Independence is," Montferrat said. "And Wunderland—the Alpha Centauri system—is going to be independent. Of the kzin, and of Earth and the UN."

"You'd better be sure you've got ample bargaining power before you sit down to bargain with me," Early warned.

"Oh, exactly, my dear General. Which is why, as you will have noticed, I'm not bargaining with you now."

Unexpectedly, Early laughed; it was a deep rich sound, thick as chocolate. "You aren't, are you?" He took another sip of the brandy. "Well, in that case—perhaps you could expand on the remark you made at dinner, about local performance techniques and classical Meddelhoffer?"

• **CHAPTER ELEVEN**

"He's not *human*," Jonah gasped, flopping down on a rock and watching Hans swing along up the mountainside.

Bigs rolled a baleful eye at him as he lay prone in the track, twitching expressive eyebrows; Spots carefully poured water from a plastic container over his body, from head to the base of his tail. Then he trudged down to the small stream and poured several more over his own head before returning to repeat the process with his brother. Both kzin were panting, their tongues lolling, the palms of their hands and feet and their tails oozing sweat. Those were the only ways kzinti *had* to shed excess heat; Kzin was a cooler planet than Earth or Wunderland. Besides . . .

"If—" Spots stopped, thrust his muzzle into the plastic container and lapped down a torrent "—if I remember my instructors, you monk-hrrreaow, you Men evolved into omnivores by taking to running down your prey in long chases."

"Think so," Jonah replied.

His feet hurt, and he felt dizzy from the amount he'd sweated. A swallow from his canteen to wash down salt tablets, and he poured more on a neckerchief and wiped

215

his face and neck. The hollow where they had halted was shady at least, big gum trees and whipsticks, but the steep rock to either side concentrated the sunlight, and it was humid as well. The air hummed and buzzed with insects, drawn to sweat, landing and biting and stinging. The human ignored them; there was no relief until they made camp and set up the sonics—and those had to be turned low or the sensitive ears of the kzin found them unbearable in frequencies humans could not hear.

"Well, we Heroes evolved from stalk-and-leap hunters!" Spot snapped. Literally: his jaws closed on the word with a wet *clomp*. "Of *course* we don't shed heat as well. We don't chase prey that escapes our ambush! We never needed to! We developed brains cunning enough to catch meat without following it for days!"

There was a teeth-gritting whine in the kzin's voice. Bigs was in worse shape, heavier and thicker-pelted; he simply lay with his tongue hanging out on the ground. Jonah nodded wordlessly, stumbling down to the stream and refilling his canteen. *He* had never had the slightest interest in chasing prey of any sort, except kzinti Vengeful Slasher-class fighters during the War—and that could be done in the decent comfort of a crashcouch, right next to a good food synthesizer and autodoc. Fighting in space was war for gentlemen: either you won or you died, usually quickly, and you did it in climate-conditioned comfort. There had been a couple of boarding actions when the Fourth Fleet was smashed, but even those had been done in space armor.

He shuddered slightly, swallowing hard. There had been *tubing* in the meat last night.

The water looked cool and inviting as he dipped his head once more. The pebbles in the bottom were unusual—he noticed the dull glitter of them through the rippling water, and idly lifted a handful. *Heavy*, he thought, and threw them skipping across the surface. One struck a shovel lashed to the pack-saddle of a mule, startling the animal out of its torpor and into a brief bucking frenzy. The sound of pebble on steel was a dull, metallic *clunk* . . .

"Wait a minute," Jonah whispered. He scrabbled at his belt for the sample spectroscope and scooped again for more pebbles; his hands were trembling as he shoved one into the trap of the instrument and flicked the activator. "*Platinum!*" he yelled. The kzinti unfurled their ears to maximum, like pink radar dishes. "54% platinum, by Finagle's ghost!"

Jonah Matthieson had been a rockjack, an asteroid prospector, in the brief intervals of peace in Sol System; the methods in that were a great deal more mechanized, but he knew what was valuable. He scrabbled in the streambed, then tore back to his mules for the pan. Pebbles and heavy sand washed out as he swirled the water and flicked off the lighter material. Readings glowed as he jammed more samples into the scanner: 57%, 72%, an incredible 88%. His stomach ached with the tension as he worked his way upstream; Bigs and Spot were following, howl-spitting at each other in the Hero's Tongue. At last he thought to call Hans. The Sol-Belter was still fumbling with the belt radio when the old man came up, leading his mules and looking nearly as phlegmatic.

"Ja," he said calmly. "Platinum all right. Nice heavy concentration." He took the pipe out of his mouth to spit aside. "Worthless."

Spot gave an ululating howl, jaws open at the sky. Bigs collapsed again, this time into the stream with only his eyebrows and black nostrils showing; his tail waved pink in the water, and little fish-analogues came to nibble at it. Jonah felt an overwhelming urge to break the spectroscope over the Wunderlander's head, and then a sick almost-headache at the back of his neck.

"It's a perfectly good industrial metal!" he protested, slogging to the bank of the stream and sitting down on a wet rock. A kermitoid croaked and thrashed away through the spiny underbrush. "It's used for everything from chemical synthesis to doping crystal fusion cores. Back in the Sol Belt, it was the first thing we looked for."

"Ja, so useful the kzinti hauled seven or eight asteroids from the Swarm to near-Wunderland orbit as reserves, back during the Fifth Fleet buildup," Hans nodded. "Still a lot of it left. We need something valuable but not so valuable they thought to get a supply set up," he went on. "Gold, hafnium, something like that. Well," he went on, "rest-period's over. Got to get a move on if we want to get anything done."

Spots and Bigs whined. So did Jonah.

"Give me two," Spots said, throwing two cards into the pile.

Jonah dealt, watching the kzin across the campfire narrowly. His scent was calm—he had long since learned to recognize the gingery smell of kzinti excitement—but that could simply be control enough to keep it down below the stun-your-nostrils level humans could recognize. Bigs seemed to be watching him intently, ears out and fur fluffed up around his face. Spots's tail was held rigidly and quivering just slightly at the tip . . .

"Fold," he decided. Nobody else wanted more cards.

Spots flapped his ears, and his eyebrows twitched. "See you and raise you three."

Three *krona*, to the humans; the brothers were playing each other for kzinretti, of which they both had more than they wanted, due to the surplus after most of the kzintosh—male kzin—in the system died. Evidently numbers in the harem were a status matter for kzinti.

"See you," Bigs said in Wunderlander: "*And smell you,*

you vatch-in-the-grass," he muttered under his breath in the Hero's Tongue, in the Mocking Tense.

"And two," Hans added. He puffed ostentatiously on his pipe, and the two kzin closed their nostrils in an exaggerated gesture. Their huge golden eyes caught the firelight occasionally, silver disks in the darkness.

Well, it is pretty foul, Jonah conceded. On the other hand, Hans was sitting downwind.

"Call." Bigs's tail was quivering visibly.

Spots sighed and let his ears droop. "Three queens," he said, flipping his hand upright.

Bigs lunged and snapped close to his nose. "I thought you were bluffing!" he said, throwing down his pair of tens.

"You should have listened to the Conservors and learned to control the juices of your liver," Spots said sanctimoniously, purring slightly and letting the tip of his tongue show through his teeth. The pelt rose around his neck, and his whiskers worked back and forth; he licked a wrist and smoothed them back. "That is fifteen kzinretti you owe me—my selection, remember."

"Sorry, fellers," Hans laughed. "That's fifteen krona you three owe *me*." He turned up his hand; three aces.

Spots shrieked, sending the mules snorting and pulling on their curb chains out at the edge of sight. Bigs waved his ears and thumped his tail back and forth, flapping his lips against his fangs in derision.

"Now whose liver is overheated?" he said, then stretched and yawned. "You have first watch."

Spots stalked off into the night, ears folded away and tail a rigid pink length behind him.

"I think even Hans is getting tired," Jonah said over his shoulder.

Then he raised the cutting bar and slashed again at the thick, matted vegetation ahead of him. It was almost all native, with the cinnamon scent of Wunderlander growth; the local varieties seemed to run mostly to thorns and silica-rich stems, though. The cutting bar was a thin-film of diamond sandwiched between vacuum-deposited layers of single-crystal iron, and it should have gone through vegetation with scarcely more effort than air. Two of the teeth had broken off on rocks, and the matted stems pulled irritatingly at his wrist.

Spots scarcely bothered to flap his ears; Bigs was morosely silent again. Last night he had even turned down the evening poker game, a very bad sign.

"Your turn," the human wheezed.

Bigs squeezed past him and began chopping methodically. From the way his lips moved and the slight murrling sounds from his chest, he was fantasizing each bush as an enemy to be killed. Hans was to their right and a thousand meters upslope, up in the open. Hotter up there, no shade, but at least there was some wind, a little air. The olive gloom around Jonah seemed as airless as the bottom of the sea; sweat clung and curdled, drying in the creases of his body, chafing at the small sores the thorns had left on his arms and face. Even the tough synthetic of his clothing was starting to give way, and the zitrigor leather of his boots had begun to wear thin in a place or two. He was leaner by about ten kilos than he had been at the beginning of the trip, and tough as the strip of dried meat he chewed at mechanically as he marched. The kzinti had lost weight too, and their pelts were so matted with tangles and burrs that even their obsessive nightly grooming could scarcely keep pace.

So much for the mighty hunters, he thought snidely. That was a little unfair; whatever their instincts, Wunderland kzin were the descendants of space travellers. Their immediate ancestors came from Hssin, a sealed-habitat colony on a world with poisonous atmosphere. Spots and Bigs had hunted in their father's preserves, but their home environment was as artificial as any human's.

"I begin to dream of talcum powder and blowdriers," Spots said unexpectedly. Bigs grunted. "And of kzinretti. My palazzo will be in chaos."

Jonah grunted in his turn. Thinking about women was a *bad* idea out here; easier for a kzin, since their responses were so conditioned on smell. They turned upslope to avoid an outcrop of granite and emerged blinking onto the steep brushy slopes of the hill; they were in an interior depression of the Jotuns, with eroded volcanic peaks on all sides, and it focused the summer heat like a lens. Wearily they all sank to the ground, letting the mules browse for a moment. The kzin had taken to wearing conical straw hats the humans wove for them, and now they fanned their dangling tongues. Jonah shook his canteen and decided half-full was still enough to warrant a drink; he sipped at the water, letting each drop soak into his tissues. Far above a contrail streaked across the sky, some vacationer in an aircar off to the beaches of Heleigoland Island. Sitting under an umbrella, sipping at drinks with fruit in them. Watching girls diving into the surf . . .

"There's not much point in going on," he said wearily. It was only the thought of retracing his steps that had kept him from saying it until now. Going forward with some hope was bad enough; going back with none was unbearable. "We've got those tigripard hides, that'll cover most of our expenses. We could sell the gear."

Bigs was lost in his brooding. "I begin to think you are correct, Jonah-human," his sibling said sadly. "My nose is dry with worry at what will befall our households—but still, we—"

Hans jumped down from a boulder near them. "Ready to give up, are we? The valiant Heroes, the UN Navy hotshot?" He cackled laughter, his ancient leathery face crinkling. "You're so stupid you don't know a fortune when you're standing on one. You're so stupid you'd shit on a plate and call it steak!" The Wunderlander was practically dancing around his bewildered companions. "Jonah, you're sitting down, you've got your thinking apparatus jammed on money—can't you tell when you're rubbing your cheeks on wealth?"

"Something hit so hard the planet *splashed*," Hans said, leaning on his pick.

They had been working up the side of the hill, following the gullies and taking samples. The gold was patchy, but the deposits caught in folds and ripples in the ground were increasingly rich. Off to their left a waterfall stretched down the surface of a cliff, a thread-thin line of silver against the pink granite rock; where it struck down in the valley bottom an explosion of mist blossomed, amid a great circle of whipstick and jacaranda trees, with tall silver-gums towering over all. Ahead the slope was jagged and eroded, soft crumbly rock and clay streaked with bright mineral colors. The scent of the scrub under their feet was dry and intense, like a perpetual almost-sneeze, cut occasionally by a drift of cooler air and mist from the falls. Kermitoids peeped and croaked, and a red-tailed hawk dove down the slope after a rabbit and then rose with the struggling beast in its claws, *skree-skree* as it flapped off heavily toward the cliffs.

"Ja, big astrobleme—way, way back. Punched right through the crust. Wunderland's got slow continental drift, you know, ja? Starts and stops. This made a hot-spot, kept burning through every time the crust moved across it. The whole line of the Jotuns, east-to-west across the Aeserheimer Continent is here because of it—this is the active part. Erosion . . . that's why you get pockets of metallics here. None very big, but by Herr Gott, they're rich."

"Where do we dig?" Spots asked. He was drooling slightly, always a sign of impatience in a kzin.

"Not down here," Hans said; the beatific smile still quirked at the edges of his mouth. "No, no use digging down here. Oh, there's gold, but we need water to set up the ripple membranes and get it out." He used the haft of his pick as a pointer. "Up there. We can cut a furrow 'cross the hillside from the creek."

"Tanj," Jonah said, measuring distances. Trivial by spatial terms, but he'd acquired a whole new perspective on "kilometer" since he started spending so much time dirtside. "That's quite a job, without any equipment."

"We've got cutter bars and thirty kilometers of monofilament," Hans said cheerfully. "My brains, and you three for strong backs and simple minds, plus four mules. That's plenty of equipment for what we'll need."

"There ain't no justice," Jonah muttered, dragging a forearm across his face. Still, it wasn't much harder than the contracting job, and promised to pay a good deal better.

"You said it, son. You said it," Hans chuckled.

"Hrreeeaaawww!" Bigs groaned, rising from all fours with a gut-straining effort; their flexible spines made a straight lift harder for a kzin than for a man. The timber across his shoulders was ten meters long, and even on Wunderland it weighed three times his body mass. The other three hauled on the cable rigged over a wood-frame block and tackle, and the long gum-tree timber rose slowly in swaying jerks until it settled into the predug hole with a rush and stood nearly upright, vibrating. The two kzin took turns bracing it upright and hammering rocks into the hole to hold it so. Three more of equal size stretched in a line across the gully; up on the lip the humans returned to slicing other trunks into square-cut troughs with the cutter bars. When the line of supports was complete, they would swing the troughs out and lash them to the poles with monofilament.

"We're doing the slave's part of this," Bigs complained to his brother, as they climbed down the boulders to where the next upright waited to be dragged up to its hole.

"Suck sthondat excrement," Spots said.

They set themselves on either side of the massive timber and braced themselves, securing a good hold on the oozing slab-cut timber with their claws. The sharp medicinal scent of eucalyptus sap was overwhelming.

"*Strike!*"

The kzin heaved in unison, lifting the end of the beam and running it half a dozen steps upslope before letting it fall.

"It's the heavy lifting," Bigs went on, as they rested for a second, panting. His tongue worked on nose and whiskers, reaching almost to his tufted eyebrows. "*They* slice planks off trees, we carry the trunks."

"We are larger and stronger," Spots pointed out reasonably. He had tied a wad of cloth over his head and soaked it in water; now he patted at it, and runnels fanned down his neck and muzzle, plastering the fur to his skin. Mud streaked his legs and the paler-colored pelt of his belly. "If the monkeys were hauling these trunks, they would go very slowly—or we would have to take more time to rig a dragway with a winch and tackle."

"Hrrrr. Then we should get more of the gold," Bigs went on. "Now—*strike*."

They moved the log another dozen meters. This time they dropped it next to a rock-pool full of water and crouched to lap up a drink; instinctively, their muzzles rose every second or two to scan the surroundings.

"We contributed less than a quarter of the capital, yet we are to have equal shares," Spots replied. "You would complain if a monkey brought you a zianya with its muzzle already taped."

Bigs yawned enormously and licked his lips. "Zianya— ah, the first mouthful, full of fear-juices! With dipping sauce and grashti on the side." He paused. "Yet I *would* complain if a monkey brought one. It is disgraceful to be dependent upon them."

"Silence, fool. You did not complain when they were our slaves—and we were even *more* dependent on them then! Ready—*strike*."

This rush carried them to the line of supports, where the next hole waited.

"You are a whisker-splitter," Bigs said, unlimbering his cutting bar. They had dropped the thigh-thick end of the log across a boulder, leaving it at comfortable chest height. With four swift strokes he trimmed the hard wood to a point.

"Besides," Spots continued, raising his voice slightly from the other end of the log, where he belayed a loop of cable to a hole punched through the wood. "There are probably no zianyas closer than Hssin."

They whined; zianyas were a homeworld beast, and they had never flourished in the ecology of Wunderland, unlike many other kzinti animals. Before the human hyperdrive armada arrived some kzin estates had specialized in rearing them, coaxing them to reproduce and investing in expensive gravity-polarizer sheds to rear them under homeworld gravity, 1.55 of Earth's. Most of those had been smashed in the fighting, or confiscated in the aftermath of liberation, and the markets were vanished now that kzinti were few and poor in a human-ruled Wunderland.

"Reason enough to shake the dust of this world from our paws," Bigs went on. "Push—slowly, slowly."

Spots heaved with a steady pressure on the smaller end of the log, as his brother guided the point to the lip of the hole. As he did, his ears waggled ostentatiously.

"Yes—I can see us prostrating ourselves before the Patriarch's Cushion. '*Admittedly we did surrender to the omnivores and obey them; nevertheless we long to have Full Names and be permitted to maintain the noble-sized households we, the penniless refugees, have brought.*' Aha! The Patriarch's liver overflows with kin-feeling for us! His pelt stands on end with joy at our scent! With his own hands, he serves us tuna ice cream. He awards us Names; he allows us possession of every one of our kzinretti; he grants us vast estates on the *extremely expensive* savannahs of Homeworld . . ."

His lips flapped derisively against his teeth in imitation of a kzinti snore; *you dreamer*, it implied. "We could not even afford passage to kzinti space without human help."

"That may change," Bigs said, grimly sliding out his claws. Long silvery needles against the black leather of his hands. "That may change . . ."

"Not without gold," Spots replied. He took the end of the cable in his mouth and climbed the wall of the canyon with a bounding four-footed rush; kzinti had evolved hands to help them climb rocks.

"Next one ready!" he called, dropping back into Wunderlander. Jonah and Hans straightened; the older man groaned, kneading his hands into the small of his back. "Reave this to the block line."

• **CHAPTER TWELVE**

Gracious lord God, but these are primitive! Tyra Nordbo thought.

Friendly enough, but so *backward*. The village was hidden, with dwellings of straw and bamboo tucked deep under an overhang of rock. There was a waterfall at one end of the little valley, and channels irrigated gardens of banana, citrus and vegetables. There were goats and sheep, a few horses . . . and that was all. There was plenty to eat here, but not a book, not a powered tool, not a single comp or receiver. The only metal or synthetic was what their ancestors had brought in, fleeing as refugees from the first wave of kzinti conquest. There were things here that had been only names to her before: opthamalia, cataracts, club-foot, harelip. She shuddered at the thought, even as she made herself smile and accept an opened coconut from a smiling woman. At least the settlement was fairly clean. And the people walked with pride.

I thought we were badly off in Skognara during the occupation, she mused. Machinery wearing out, more and more hand labor, the kzin tribute abating not one whit. *It was paradise compared to this*. The thought of the labor and loneliness these people had endured was chilling. Only by cutting themselves off completely from the money economy had they been able to stay out of the kzinti sight, but that meant no machinery, no medicine, no help in the disasters of everyday life . . . They were touchingly awed at having one of the Nineteen Families here, as well. There was no mistaking what she was, of course; everything from her accent to the mobile ears that twitched forward at a sound betrayed it. *It is humbling.*

"Why did you stay here?" she asked the leathery old headman of the . . . village seemed inappropriate. Compared to this, Neu Friborg was like downtown Munchen. And the headman was probably only fifty or so, not even middle-aged by civilized standards.

His grandfather had been a orbital shuttle pilot.

"We are *free*, Fra Nordbo," the man said proudly. "Here, we pay no tribute to the enemy. None of them has ever come here—except one on a hunting trip."

He nodded proudly to a ledge above the plaited-cane doorway. The skull that grinned with yellowed fangs looked much like a cat's, or a tigripard's, until you saw the long braincase that swept back from the heavy brows. A creature that thought, and made tools, and hunted Man. Until some Men hunted it . . .

"We had the pelt," the villager went on regretfully, "but it rotted in my father's time."

"The kzinti are gone," Tyra said gently. "Gone from all this world. None remain except those who accept human rule. You have no need to hide any more."

The man's face fell slightly. "I know," he said. "A fur hunter told us the news ten months ago." More slowly: "You are of the Herrenfolk, Fra Nordbo," he said. "Since the war is over, folk have come from the Great City. They speak of taxes, of land titles—of taking our children for schools."

"You understand," he went on, leaning closer earnestly.

"We do not want to be isolated any more . . . not really. We know we have forgotten much. But we are *free*. Some say the folk of Munchen wish to grind us down, that they think of us as ignorant savages."

You are, poor creatures. No fault of yours, Tyra thought sadly.

"What shall we do?" he said. "We know nothing of these matters—only what the officials of the new government tell us. Some say we should move again, as our ancestors did—move back even further into the mountains, and live free. There are others like us in the Jotuns, they might help."

"Even the Jotuns are not large enough to shield you from Time and Fate," Tyra said gently. "You need a friend who can intervene for you in Munchen. I know a good man, a Herrenmann, who would be your protector. But even so, change will come. It must; your children deserve to have the world opened up to them once more. Wunderland is once more a planet of Man, and there is no reason to deny them the stars."

"Thank you," the headman said, wiping at his eyes one palm; the calluses scraped against the blond-gray stubble on his cheeks. "We will try it."

The headman's daughter came in, with a tray: slices of roast wild boar and gagrumpher, steamed plantain, sauces, the rough homemade wine. Tyra's mouth filled at the smell; her own camp-cooking had grown tiresome.

"It is good of one of the Freunchen clan to take time for our troubles," the headman went on.

"Duty," Tyra mumbled. *Embarrassing*. Perhaps only in a place as out-of-the-way as this, as completely isolated from the past century, could you find that sort of faith in the Nineteen Families and their tradition of stewardship.

"We must do what we can for you, who helped those who were strangers," he said.

"Murphmmhg?" she replied, then swallowed. "You've already helped me," she said. Quite sincerely; a month in the wilderness with nobody but her horse and Garm to talk to had been a chastening experience.

"There are . . . bad people in the mountains," he said. "Some of them have been here for a long time—they fought the ratcats a little, stole from us more. The real fighters, to them we gave without asking, but they went back to the towns when the liberation came. The others have become worse, and more have joined them since. They do not come this far back into the mountains often—we have little to steal, and we will fight to keep what we have. When the police chase them, then they run deep into the Jotuns. Some of the ones who were here during the war, they know their way around, a little."

"Do you help the police?"

"Yes." Flat and decisive. "The outlaws, they are *advokats*." That was a small, scruffy, unpleasant-smelling carrion eater common to this part of the continent; it travelled in packs, attacked sick or wounded animals, and would eat anything including dung. Eat until it puked up, then eat the vomit. The beast was almost all mouth and legs, with very little in the way of a brain, an evolutionary holdover. "If we had more guns, we would shoot them ourselves."

"Thank you," she said. "I'll be cautious."

"And . . ." He looked down at his feet in their crude leather sandals. "You said, you were looking also for unusual things?"

Tyra felt a sudden prickle of interest. *Unusual* could mean anything, back in here; jadeite, a meerschaum deposit, abandoned kzinti equipment from a clandestine base . . . or news of the party she had been told to look out for. Business for herself, or for Herrenmann Montferrat-Palme. It was about time *something* turned up, it was cheap to live in the outback but not free, and she would be damned if she was going to be a burden on Mutti. Doubly damned if she would go asking Ib for help.

"Yes, if you please," she answered.

"Here."

He pulled out something small but heavy, wrapped in cloth, and placed it on the table between them. The work-gnarled fingers unfolded the homespun cotton with slow care and the young aristocrat leaned over, holding her breath. A dull-shining piece of . . . not metal, she thought. About the size of her palm, with a curved surface and a ragged edge, as if it had been torn lose from a larger sheet. Not any material she recognized, but there was a cure for that.

"Excuse me," she said, and rummaged in the pack-saddle braced against one bamboo wall. The sample scanner Montferrat had gotten for her was late-model, a featureless rectangle with a pistol grip and readout screen. She pressed it against the whatever-it-was and pulled the trigger.

No data, it told her.

"What do you mean, no data?" she muttered. Perhaps the contact wasn't close enough: she turned the piece over and made sure there was no airspace.

No data.

"Swine of a gadget!" she said, and tried it on the surroundings. No problem with the table, a rock on the floor, the bamboo wall, or her own hand. Tyra pressed it firmly against the artifact.

No data.

"Hmmpfh." The girl tapped at the back, running the diagnostic. Everything fine.

Her hand stopped in mid-motion. The scanner worked by firing a tiny but very intense burst of laser energy into the sample, then analyzing the result. The material involved was minuscule, too little to even feel if you used it on yourself, unless you pressed it to your eye, of course. But the laser was very energetic.

She tapped out *temperature*. At ambient, which was no surprise. Then she squeezed the trigger for the sample function—*no data*—and asked for hotspots. Nothing: still at ambient temperature. Whatever this was, it was absorbing the energy and not ablating; not even warming up.

Odd, she thought: *very odd*. Back home in Gerning, the manor-house had had a functioning computer system with good educational programs. Tyra Nordbo had received a sound university-entrance level scientific education, and offhand she could not think of *anything* with those characteristics. A moment's conference with her belt-comp's reference functions confirmed her ignorance. It could be a kzin product, or something military that was not in the general databases . . .

"Do you mind if I test this?" she said to the headman.

He grinned. "We tried shooting at it. Then we dropped large rocks on it. Nothing we could do would so much as scratch it. The smith's forge didn't even heat it up."

She nodded. That did not mean much, since the only thing these outbackers had in the way of weapons was old-fashioned chemical energy rifles. There were plenty of modern materials that would be untouchable to anything they could do, and which would reflect away a lot more thermal energy than charcoal could produce.

A crowd of children gathered as she came out into the sun, blinking for a moment in the brightness; all dressed alike in shorts, bare feet and varying degrees of grime. They clustered bright-eyed as she drew the magrifle from its sheath beside her saddle, on the porch of the hut, and held up the piece.

"Would one of you like to help me?" she said. A sea of hands waved at her amid eager clamor. She picked a girl of nine or so, with strawberry-blond braids and a gap in her teeth. "What's your name?"

The girl blushed and dug at the packed dirt with a toe. "Helge," she whispered.

"Well, Helge, why don't you take this all the way down there—down by that big boulder—and put it in at ground level? Jam it in tight, facing me. The rest of you," she went on, "get back—back behind me. Yes, that means you, too. One of you take the little one."

A few adults had come to look as well; some of them with envy at her equipment, more in curiosity. *Gracious lord Gott but it must be boring here*, she thought. The cassette of regular ammunition came out with a *clack* sound, and she slid in the red-flagged one from the bottom of her war-bag. The normal rounds were single-crystal iron, prefragmented for antipersonnel or hunting use. These were narrow penetrators of osmium, in a ferroplastic sabot that would peel off at the muzzle. Antiarmor darts, and at a hundred meters they would punch through two hundred millimeters of machinable steel plate. Much less of real armor, and it drained the batteries like the *teufel*, but she had a solar-charging tarpaulin spread out over a sunny patch of ground. She tapped the velocity control to maximum and set the weapon for semi-auto.

Helge ran like the wind, heels flashing, and used one to pound the piece of material into the angle between ground and rock. Tyra gave her a smile of thanks and waved her back into the crowd as she sat, pushed her hat back and brought the rifle up with her elbows on her knees. A final check to be sure that everyone was behind her—Dada-mann had taught her about firearms as soon as she could walk; even under the occupation Herrenmann families had been allowed hunting weapons—and she took up the slack on the trigger. The sighting holo sprang up before her eye on x5, and she laid the target blip on the center of the gray material. Squeeze gently—

Whack. The recoil was punishing, several times worse than normal; there was not all that much mass in the darts, but they were travelling *fast*. She let the tremor die out of her arms and shoulders and the sight settle back on the target as the muzzle came down with its own weight. *Whack. Whack. Whack. Whack*. Five rounds, as much as her shoulder could stand and more than should be necessary.

"Don't touch it!" she called sharply, as some of the children ran ahead of her.

The older ones pulled their younger siblings back, making a circle around her as she knelt. The impacts had driven the fragment back against the stone; into the stone, in fact, cutting a trough. The surface was shiny, plated with a film of osmium, and splashes had colored the earth and rock. She reached out with a stick, and it sizzled as the end came in contact with the shiny film. The osmium layer peeled away at the touch, falling to the battered earth below.

"Scheisse," she whispered. *Nothing. Gottdamned nothing*. The dull gray surface of the material was utterly unmarked, to the naked eye at least. She shifted the rifle to her left hand and pulled out the scanner. Another no data, and the temperature was still at ambient . . . no, about .002 of a degree higher. That after being struck with penetrator darts that splashed across its surface in a molten film!

Well, Herr Montferrat-Palme wanted the unusual, she thought. *And this is* certainly *unusual enough*.

Another thought struck her as she lifted the material and turned it. The edges were torn, twisted as if something had struck a sheet of whatever-it-was and belled this piece out beyond the breaking strain of the material. Considering what the tensile strength must be, that would have to be a fairly drastic event.

"Careful about that," she said to a curious child who was poking at the film of osmium; the edges would be razor sharp even though it was thinner than tinfoil. She crumpled it with the heel of her boot and stamped it into a harmless lump. Turning to the headman:

"Where did you find this stuff?"

"The Mutfiberg, Fra Nordbo. We pan a little gold in the rivers below it, to trade for things we must have. In the wash beneath—"

• **CHAPTER THIRTEEN**

"Let her rip!" Hans called into his beltphone. "Don't
get your underwear in a knot," he went on to Jonah.
"And that's enough dirt."

"My back agrees with you but my greed dissents,"
Jonah said, straightening up.

The water-furrow that fed their wash was nearly half
a kilometer long, dug along the hillside or carried in
troughs of log slab. Nothing in it had come with them,
except the monofilament line that held it together. The
wash itself was a series of stepped wooden boxes,
ingeniously rigged with baffles so that the flow of water
would shake them.

Their bottoms were different; memory-film, made in
Tiamat, the central manufacturing asteroid of the Serpent
Swarm asteroid. Leads hooked them to a wooden stand
where their computer and main distortion-battery lay.
A single keystroke would activate the memory-film; each
box's floor was set to form an intricate pattern of moving
ripples. Rushing water would dissolve the mixture of
water-deposited volcanic soil and gold granules Jonah
shoveled in to the first box; a thin layer of water would
then run over the rippling film. Gravity would leave the

heavier metal particles in the troughs of the ripples, and they would move slowly down each box to deposit the gold in a deep fold, ready to be scooped out. The surface had a differential stickiness, too, nearly frictionless to the useless garague, catching at any molecule the computer directed.

From higher up the water-furrow a rumbling sounded. Spots had lifted the sluicegate, and the flood was rumbling along. Raw timber vibrated and thuttered, and the beams reinforcing corners groaned as the first weight threw itself against them. A meter across and deep, the wave bore dirt and twigs before it, and a hapless kermitoid that peeped and thrashed. It curled and rose as it struck the pile of gold-rich dirt, then washed it away and into the settling tanks like a child's sand-castle. The tanks themselves began vibrating back and forth, their squealing groans almost deafening.

"Shovel, boy, shovel!" Hans called. "That's a pocketful of krona with every shovelful of dirt."

Jonah cursed and wiped at his face, covered in an oil of sweat and dirt; more moisture ran from the sodden rag around his forehead, trickling down to cut runnels over his face and drip onto his bare chest. He had always been muscular for a Belter, but the weeks of labor had thickened his arms and shoulders, besides burning his face and body nearly the color of teak. The loads of dirt still felt heavy as he swung the long handle. Hans was spindly and wrinkled beside him, but his movements were as regular as a metronome.

"You're putting too much heave into it," the old man said after a moment. "Remember what I told you. Don't jerk at it. Just enough to get the shovel moving, then turn your wrists and let the dirt slide off into the water. No need to waste sweat *sticking* it in."

Jonah grunted resentfully, but he followed Hans' advice. He was right; it *was* easier that way. Zazen helped too. His training was coming back to him, more and more these days. Use the movements to end thought; become the eye that does not seek to see itself, the sword that does not seek to cut itself, the unself-contemplating mind. Feel sensation without stopping its flow with introspection, pull of muscle, deep smooth breath, aware without being aware of being aware. The two humans fell into lockstep, working at the high pile of precious dirt. Presently the pile grew smaller, and Spots came up with more. He was dragging it on a sled made from more of the film, set to be nearly frictionless on the packed earth of the trail. There was a rope yoke around his neck and shoulders, and he pulled leaning far forward, hands helping him along. When he was level with the men he collapsed to earth, panting.

Jonah stuck his shovel in the pile and helped him out of the rope harness, then handed him a bucket made from a section of log. The kzin lapped down a gallon or so and then poured the rest over his head, scooping out another from the trough and repeating the process. Then he licked his whiskers back into shape and shook himself, showering Jonah and Hans with welcome drops from his fur. The air was full of the smell of a quarter ton of hot wet carnivore.

"Bigs needs someone to help with the shoring," he rasped, drinking again. "He digs more quickly than we thought."

"Guess I'd better," Hans said, rubbing a fist into the small of his back. "See you later, youngster." He walked off up the trail to the shaft they had sunk into the hillside, whistling.

Spots paused as he gathered up the drag harness and the film. "Ah—adventure!" he said. "Travelling to far-off lands; ripping out the gizzards of hardship and danger; winning fortune and Name. Is it not glorious? Does your liver not steam with—"

"Go scratch fleas," Jonah muttered, spitting on his hands and reaching for the shovel.

"Better that than hauling freight like a zitragor," the kzin replied, flapping his ears ironically as he turned to go for the next load. "Far better."

"I cannot believe it! I do not believe the testimony of my own nose!" Bigs said, pawing through a pile of datachips.

"Believe what?" Spots replied.

Across the campfire Jonah looked up at the sound; the hiss-and-spit of the Hero's Tongue *always* sounded like a quarrel, but this was probably the real thing.

"That I was stupid enough to let you pack the virtual-reality kit!" Bigs said.

That was a late-model type, with nose implants for scents as well as ear and eye coverings for visual and aural data.

"It's in perfect working order."

"The chips, fool, the chips—you forgot the *Siege of Zeeroau*, the *Hero Chruung Upon the Ramparts*, no *Warlord Chmee at the Pillars*—all our good stuff. None of the classics at all!"

Spots flapped his ears and fluttered his lips against his teeth. "You run too many of that graypelt sthondat excrement," he said. "You will curdle your liver and stultify your brain living in the past that way; you should pay more attention to the modern world, sibling. Renovate your tastes! Entertainment should be instructive!"

"Modern—heeraaeeow—*The Kzinrette's Rump*?" Bigs said sarcastically, throwing one chip aside and digging for more. His voice rose an octave as he listed titles, and his tail quivered and then began to lash.

"*Blood and Ch'rowl*? *The Lost Patriarch of the Hareem Planet*? *Energy Swords at the Black Sun*?" He screamed, a raw sound of rage. "Is there *nothing* here but smut and cheap, trashy science fiction adventures?"

He abandoned the carton of chips. The two kzinti faced each other, crouching low and claws extended: their ears were folded away and their tails held rigid. The air smelled of ginger as they growled through their grins, and their fur bottled out. Jonah started to rise in genuine alarm; most of the siblings' spats were half in fun, but this looked like the real thing—and when kzinti got angry enough to stop exchanging insults in the Mocking Tense, they were milliseconds away from screaming and leaping. It must be the sheer frustration of the hard labor . . .

Hans broke in first: "You two tabbies interested in our results, or are you too set on killing each other and leaving it all for us monkeys?" he said dryly.

The kzin relaxed, breaking the lock of their unwinking eye-to-eye stare. The huge golden orbs turned on the old man instead, and they both licked their lips with washcloth-sized pink tongues. After a moment their fur sank back and their tails relaxed, but they both drooled slightly with tongues lolling. Hans brought out the portable scale and a set of bags of tough thermoplastic, setting a heatrod at one hand.

"That's the last of it," Hans said.

He took the container off the scales and dropped the dust into a bag; then wrote the weight on the outside and sealed it shut with the rod. Jonah watched the digital readout blink back to zero. They were sitting in front of the humans' tent—the shelters of the felinoids were longer but much lower—and the sunken firelight was flickering on their faces, shining in the eyes of the kzin. Tonight it was scarcely brighter than the moon, full and larger than Luna from earth, leaving a circle of blackness in the sky where the stars were outshone. The dust had not looked like gold, save for a few granules larger than pinheads. Mostly it was blackish.

"Not much to look at," he said, hefting one of the bags. It was a little larger than his fist, but heavy enough to bring a grunt of surprise.

"No nuggets," Hans nodded. "It's rich, but not that rich. We've cleared about three thousand krona. Not bad for the first day's work."

"First month's work," Bigs grunted, lying flat on his belly with his hands on either side of his chin. "Not counting walking *in* to this verminous spot."

"There is that, yes," Hans went on cheerfully, and spat into the fire before lighting his pipe with a twig. "Thing is, we'll get as much tomorrow. For a while, too. Sort of time for it all to pay off. Remember what I said back in Munchen; getting the benefit of all the labor that everyone *else* who went looking put into it. Now we reap the results. Should be tasty, very tasty."

Spot's tongue moistened his nose. "How much?" he said. At their looks: "How much shall we take out before we stop?"

Hans pursed his mouth. "Twenty thousand over our expenses would do me fine. Twenty thousand's enough to get the shop I've had my eye on."

"Not enough for me," Bigs said; the humans looked at him in slight surprise. Usually the larger kzin spoke as little to them as he could. "For what I want . . . I need more."

"More is good," Jonah nodded, remembering to turn away his eyes. *Never stare at a kzin.* Seven times, *never stare at a* hostile *kzin*. "I'd like forty thousand myself. Starting a business is risky. Plenty of people have gone bust just because they didn't have enough cash to tide them over until the returns started."

"Forty thousand would satisfy me," Spots mused, using a branch he had whittled to scratch himself on one cheek, then under his chin. He slitted his eyes and purred, tongue showing slightly. "Plenty of land coming on the market; we might even be able to buy back some of our Sire's lost estate. Enough over to start a consulting firm; there are kzinti in the Serpent Swarm, on Tiamat, who would be glad to have Wunderland agents."

"Forty thousand it is, then," Hans said. He hooked the coffeepot off the fire and poured himself a cup. "Nothing like a cup of hot coffee to settle you for sleep."

Bigs spoke up. "When shall we divide it?"

The old man's hands stopped and he looked up, face carefully calm. "Well, that's a question. We could split it up when we leave, or when we get back to civilization, or each day. Something to be said for all three."

"Each day, where I can see it," Bigs snarled. Literally; talking with kzinti made you realize that humans never really snarled. "I labor in the earth like a slave. The prey I toil for shall rest in no monkey's larder."

Spots hissed at him; he turned and hissed back through open jaws, and the smaller kzin shrugged with an elaborate ripple of spotted orange fur.

"I will be content either way," he said. "By all means, divide it. It makes no difference."

Jonah locked eyes with Bigs for a moment, then shrugged himself. It *didn't* make any difference. Except . . . why was the kzin so insistent? A surly brute, to be sure—if Jonah had been in the habit of naming kzinti, he would have christened him Coon—but it was also a little strange he had never so much as mentioned what he intended to do with the money. In modern kzin society few ever satisfied the longing for physical territory with game on it, and their harem and retainers about them; that was reserved for the patriarchs. It must have been doubly cruel for a noble's sons to have the prospect snatched away; Spots daydreamed about it constantly, and Jonah could see him imagining the wilderness about them to be his own. Whereas Bigs seemed more and more withdrawn, as if Wunderland were not really real to him any more.

Again, he shrugged. Kzinti psychology was still a mystery to those humans expert in it. Jonah Matthieson had killed quite a few kzin, and worked a few months with two. That was no basis for easy judgment—in fact, just enough to lull your sense of difference and put you most at risk of anthromorphizing them. That could be dangerous; besides the weird culture the orange-furred aliens had produced, dragged straight from the Iron Age into an interstellar civilization, their basic mental reflexes were not like a human being's. And never had been, even before they used the new technology to alter their own genes.

They wanted to be more like their folk heroes. So they did genetic engineering to make it so. That was what the ARM intelligence people decided was the only plausible explanation for Kzinti behavior and customs. Usually civilization changes things. Defects don't result in death. Evolution stops, then works backwards. Bad genes are preserved. *Not with the kzin. They really are like the Heroes they admire.*

Hans wordlessly set out the scales, checking that each bag was identical. Then he divided them into four piles, and silently invited his partners to take their pick. Bigs scooped his up and disappeared into the dark; they heard him stop and make a long leap onto bare rock further up the slope, hiding his trail. Spots sighed and trotted out into the night in the opposite direction.

"Of course, now we've each got to wonder about our goods," Hans added; the smaller kzin hesitated for a second, then continued. "Wonder if any of the others has found them, you see. Couldn't tell *who*, not if some of it just disappeared."

Jonah halted with an armful of small, heavy bags. "Finagle's hairy arse, *now* you mention that?"

"Well, son, if it was all in one place it'd also be a teufel of a temptation, now, wouldn't it?" There was a twinkle in the little blue eyes beside the button nose, but they were as hard as any Jonah had ever seen. "Been at this business quite a few years now. Not the first time I've had partners, no indeed. Something to be said for all the methods."

Jonah yawned cavernously over his morning coffee, then hauled the crisp air deep into his lungs as he stretched work-stiffened muscles. It was a cool morning, a relief before the long blazing heat of the day. Alpha Centauri was rising red over the mountains to the east, and the eye-hurting bright speck of Beta hung on a peak like a jewel on a wizard's staff. No mountain on Earth could have been so slender and so steep, but Wunderland pulled its heights less fiercely. Birds and orthinoids were waking down in the ribbon of forest that filled the valley, purling and cheeping. None of the kzin were present, which was not surprising in itself. The aliens had fallen into a gorge-and-fast cycle which seemed to be natural to them, and the bacon and eggs frying in the pan would be repulsive to them.

They used to be that way to me, he admitted: far too natural. After this much pick-and-shovel work, he just felt hungry all the time.

"Want some hash-browns?" Hans asked.

"You're bleeping right I do," Jonah said, yawning again.

"See you didn't get any more sleep than the rest of us," Hans said.

"The rest of us?" Jonah paused with his fork raised over his loaded plate.

"Oh, I may be getting on, but that don't make me sleep any sounder. Just the opposite. First the big ratcat goes out to check nobody's found his goods—then the little one. Then you. Then the big one again . . ."

Jonah flushed. "I just had to piss," he said.

"Funny you went in that direction, then," Hans said, and cackled with laughter. "This'll get worse the longer we're out here. That's why I wanted to stop at twenty thousand, mostly. Now we'll all have to check nightly. And each of us worry about the others ganging up on him."

Jonah forced himself to eat. His body remembered his hunger, even if his mind was telling him his stomach was full of lead.

"You don't seem too worried," he said.

"Well, it's a matter of possibilities," Hans said. "The two ratcats could take us out—but they don't get on too well, you may have noticed. Still, blood counts for something. Or you and Spots could take the rest of us— Spots will be seeing Bigs as a real challenge down in his balls, while we're just monkeys. Or—"

"Or you could know where it all is and just take it and clear out," Jonah said harshly, feeling the hair on his back creep. As a programmer, he knew what an infinite regression setup could do to your logic; also how the Prisoner's Dilemma generally worked out in real life.

Hans lit his first pipe of the day with a stick from the fire. "No, don't think so. You three are a lot tougher than you were when we started. You'd catch me and kill me. Still, it's something to think about, isn't it?" He blew a cloud of smoke. "Enough lollygagging—nobody told us to stop working."

"Sure," Jonah muttered to himself. "Send *me* back to Neu Friborg for supplies. Why *me*?"

Another charge of water went down the sluice, to his left past the beaten trail up to the shaft. The wood groaned less now after a week of operation; water had swollen it until the pegged joints were tight, and there was less leakage too. He ignored it, concentrating on strapping the pack-saddle tight; the mule just seemed quietly relieved to be free from hauling loads out of the mine. The pack was mostly empty, except for some hides and dried meat to lend credence to their cover-story of hunting for pelts. The *last* thing they needed was contact with the authorities. The Provisional Government was hard-up and had even more than the usual official determination to see that the citizenry and their money were soon parted. All four of them agreed on that, if nothing else, although it had been a bleeping struggle to get the kzinti to skin their kills before they ate them.

Is Hans out of his mind? Or is he in it with them? Jonah thought. It would be a four-day trip. Four days he'd be unable to check on his goods, and that was nearly fifteen thousand krona by now. Without that gold he'd be back cadging handouts in Munchen soon enough. *I put up more money than the others*, he thought bitterly. *As it is, I'm getting less than my share. Tanjit, but it's hot.* He reached for the canteen and poured more water on the cloth draped over his head. He could hear Spots coming down the trail, dragging another load of dirt for the boxes. With a scowl, he led the mule behind a boulder; it was downwind from the trail this time of day, so he wouldn't have to talk to the kzin.

Spots stopped for a moment, moaning softly and pulling the rope yoke over his head. His effort at grooming the matted, worn spots on his sloping shoulders seemed half-hearted, and after a few swipes he simply lay down in the roadway, groaning more loudly. Something he would never do if he were aware of being watched, of course . . . Jonah felt a moment's guilt. *I should cough or something*, he thought. Then: *No*. If he did, he would have to explain why he was hiding behind the rock—and that would make Spots more suspicious than he was already. At least they were still talking when business made it necessary, while Bigs was barely speaking even to his sibling and not at all to the humans.

The kzin lay still, panting in the sparse shade a pile of rocks threw over the path. Then his head came up, the big pink bat-ears swiveling downslope. Jonah held his breath, eyes narrowing in suspicion. Spots drew his wtsai and headed down the steeper slope, leaping over the water furrow and dodging along agile and swift as the hillside grew steeper. When the kzin stopped to cut a pole from a broombush and began prying up a large flat rock suspicion grew to rage. Jonah drew his magrifle out of its slings along the pack saddle and stepped out from behind the rock.

I should let him have it right now, he thought, taking up the slack. *No*, he decided, as the back of the kzin's head sprang into the holosight. *No, I want him to see it coming.*

"Freeze, ratcat!" he shouted, and sent a round *whack* through the air over him.

Spots whirled and leaped backward instead, the stone thumping back down on the others that supported it. His ears flared wide with surprise, as did the wet black nostrils, then folded away in anger. He crouched, opening his mouth wide and extending his hands to either side; one gripped the wtsai, and the claws slid out on the other, needles against the black leather of the hand.

"What—put that rifle down, monkey!"

"Right," Jonah sneered; the ratcat had gotten good enough at Wunderlander to put indignation into its tones. "So you can cut me up—and then take my goods."

Spots's pupils flared wider still, in surprise. "Oh, so *that* was where you put them," he said. "Clever, clever, the spray from the furrow would obscure your scent."

The human had been moving downslope; he climbed across the furrow carefully, not that there was any danger with sixty-nine rounds still in the cassette, and halted beyond leaping distance.

"Drop the knife," he said, his voice flat and ugly.

"I saw a fuzzball crawling under there," Spots went on, staring at him in deliberate rudeness. "I was going to pry up the rock and kill it."

"Murphy, can't you invent something more plausible than that?" Jonah jeered. There was a bounty on fuzzballs . . . although they were commoner here in the Jotuns than in more settled regions.

Another footfall sounded on the trail. Jonah risked a quick glance upslope; it was Hans, trotting up with his rifle at high port. He stopped at the sight of the tableau below and then climbed down, standing midway between Spots and Jonah but out of the line of fire, with the muzzle of his weapon carefully down.

"You fellers mind telling me what's going on?" he said mildly.

They both began to speak at once. Jonah gestured Spots into silence with the rifle.

"The bleeping ratcat found my goods, and I caught him trying to lift the rock"—he nodded at the lever still jutting into the air, and then at the boulder upslope where the mule still stood—"and clean me out."

He tensed slightly; Hans *might* be in it with the alien. Not likely, since Hans had voted to send Jonah off for the supplies. If it was Hans, they would have waited until he was gone and they could do it safely. Or wait—Spots could be double-crossing *Hans* by promising to wait until Jonah was gone, and then looting the cache first himself!

"Of course," Jonah went on sardonically, "he *claims* it was all because he saw a fuzzball crawl under there."

Spots had risen from his crouch. Ostentatiously, he sheathed the wtsai and stood up to his full two-meters plus of height, staring down his muzzle at Jonah with ears half-unfurled. That was an insult as well; it was the Posture of Assured Dominance, rather than the fighting crouch used to confront an adversary.

"There is an easy way to find out, monkey," he said. "Put your arm in through the gap you used to hide the bags of gold. If there is no fuzzball, it is perfectly safe."

He backed up along the slope, still in clear sight but more than leaping distance away from the tumbled rocks. Jonah licked his lips, tasting the salt of sweat, and moved closer to his once-secret cache.

"Of course, you know that fuzzballs never let go once they bite, don't you?" Spots said, as Jonah bent toward the hole. "The jaws have to be broken and pried loose. Not that that matters a great deal. The neurotoxin venom is quite deadly. Convulsions, bleeding from all the orifices, hallucinations and agonizing death."

Jonah snorted and bent further. Then he stopped, looking at Spots. *Kzin don't lie well*, he thought. The slick film of sweat that covered his body suddenly seemed to cool. *They don't get enough practice—they can smell each other lying*. Spots could be relying on human inability to smell, nearly total by kzinti standards . . . but Jonah knew enough of their body language to know that he really was relaxed. Even amused. And if there was a Beam's Beast hiding down there— With a convulsive movement he turned and hauled one-handed on the lever. The big volcanic slab toppled backwards slowly in Wunderland's .61 G, and the fuzzball cowered for a second as the light stabbed its dark-adapted eyes.

"Pappy-*eek!*" it shrilled, the characteristic warning cry.

Jonah gave a shout of loathing and pumped two rounds into the vermin. The little biped flew backward, half its torso torn away, but still snapping at the air. Beam's Beast—the origin of the name was lost in the early settlement of the planet—was about half a meter long, covered in titan-blond fur. They had huge eyes, filling nearly half their faces, and clever monkey-like hands to match their demonic cunning. They could even be considered cute, if you didn't notice the over-lapping fangs. In a frenzy of disgust the human leaped forward and stamped the heavy heel of his boot into the big-eyed face. Then he had to spend a minute using the muzzle of his magrifle to pry the jaws out of the tough synthetic.

That was a welcome distraction. When he looked up Hans had slung his rifle and was looking at him with a speculative stare; Spots was grinning in contempt-threat. Jonah clicked his rifle onto safety.

"Guess I'd better get back to the mules—" he began. Then the earth shook, and a cloud of dust rose from over the ridge where the mineshaft lay.

None of them wasted words as they ran.

Spots was the first to reach the entrance, but he hesitated. The exterior shoring on the hillside was still intact, but choking dust and grit billowed out. Most kzin are natural claustrophobes unless they are lactating females, and it had raised his opinion of his brother's courage, if not his intelligence, when he volunteered for the job at the pit-face. It also kept Bigs more out of contact with the humans . . .

Without a word, Jonah plunged past him into the interior.

The outer stretch was intact, but the air broiled with metallic-tasting debris; hacking and coughing, he stopped for an instant to tie the wet headcloth over his mouth and nose and snatch a glowrod from the wall. Murk surrounded him, glowing with reflected light, thickening as he advanced wiping his streaming eyes. Ten meters in the roof had collapsed, and a tangle of dirt, rock, broken timbers and planking lay across his way. He dropped to the floor and raised the glowrod. A triangle of empty space in the lower right-hand corner of the pile gaped at him like a toothless mouth. He crawled close and shouted:

"Bigs! Can you hear me?"

Nothing; nothing but the trickling sound of dirt falling, and the groan of raw timber stressed to its limits. The rest might come down at any moment. He repeated the call in the Hero's Tongue, shouting as loud as he could, grit raw in his throat and lungs.

A sound; faint, and it could be wood collapsing as readily as a kzin moaning in pain. Spots and Hans came up behind him, and he turned urgently.

"This looks like it might go through. Get me a cutter-bar and a rope."

Spots stared at him oddly as Hans handed him the tools. Jonah tied the rope around his waist and went down on his belly.

"I'm—" he hesitated for a moment and took a deep breath. "I'm going to go in head-first. I'll tie a loop under Bigs's forelimbs, if I can, and you pull him out."

That might work with a kzin; they were so flexibly jointed that they could get through any space big enough to pass their head with a centimeter to spare on either side of the skull. That was a conscious kzin, of course.

"You are going in that hole?" Spots asked, in a low voice. His pelt was bristling in a ripple pattern, as if he tried to order it flat and his nerves rebelled. He looked over his shoulder; the entrance was a spot of light. More dirt trickled down from above. "Bigs might be dead."

"I *said* I'm going, didn't I?" Jonah asked, his voice rough with more than the bad air. A wave of gooseflesh ran over his own skin; he looked at the hole, and remembered the piping cry of the fuzzball. *Don't try to talk me out of it. You might succeed.*

"Pain does not hurt," he muttered to himself. "Death does not cause fear; fear of death causes fear."

The mantra was little protection as he squirmed into the hole. He could feel it shifting above him, and the jagged edges of broken wood clawed at his back and flanks. He could feel the blood trickling down, feel the salt sweat stinging in the wounds. One meter, then ten, infinitely cautious. Controlling his breathing helped control the overwhelming impulse to squirm backward. The glowrod was little help, in air so thick with floating dust, and his passage stirred up more.

At least it's fairly straight. After a time that could have been a minute or twenty, his outstretched hand touched something softer. Kzinti fur, that twitched under his hand. Timber creaked.

"Brother?" Bigs whispered, in the Hero's Tongue.

"Jonah," the man said, and felt the kzin start again. "Careful, it's still unstable! Can you understand me?"

"Yes," the alien rasped. The heavy scent of its fear was detectable even through the dirt; he could smell urine, too.

"Are you badly injured?"

A moment's silence, full of heavy panting. "No. I think not. There is a timber resting on my thighs, but they are only bruised, not broken. My shoulder is dislocated." That hurt a kzin less than a human, but it meant the arm was useless until the joint was set back. "I am bleeding a little, but I cannot move."

Jonah had been feeling around, raising the glowrod. Bigs was in a bubble of space, spindle-shaped with the narrow end at his feet. There was a main vertical support across his legs just down from the crotch; one jagged end of a fastening peg had driven into the flesh for a centimeter or so.

"I'm—" Jonah paused to cough. "I'm going to have to get in there with you," he said. *Tanjit. There Ain't No Justice. I don't even like the bleeping pussy—never did.* It was mutual, too. "I'll tie this rope under your forelimbs and then sever the timber with my cutter-bar. Then we'll slide you out on your back. I'll follow and get you past the obstacles. Understand?"

"Brother," the kzin whispered again, and something in his own language too fast and faint for Jonah to follow.

The human shook him, and barely dodged the instinctive snap that followed.

"Finagle shave you bald, *do you understand me?*"

"Yesss . . ." followed by a mumble.

Oh, joy. Concussed. Jonah shone the light into the big golden eyes. One pupil was slightly larger than the other, and that was a cross-species indicator. No blood from the nose or ears, though.

"Here I come," Jonah said, keeping up a flow of words to maintain Bigs's attention. *And to boost* my *morale too.* "I'm going to have to do a forwards somersault." That took an eternity, but when it was completed he was lying along the kzin's side. "Here comes the rope. Can you lift your forequarters?"

Another eternity before the dazed kzin understood, and the slipknot loop went under his armpits. He made a short convulsive sound between clenched fangs as the rope touched his dislocated shoulder, and the claws of his other hand stabbed into the dirt close to Jonah's stomach.

"Be a Hero," Jonah said sharply, in that language. Bigs twitched his whiskers affirmatively. It was not that the kzin was unable to control his fear, but the blow to the head was leaving him wavering in and out of full consciousness. A quarter-ton of kzin acting from instinct and reflex was not something you wanted to have with you in a confined space.

"Here we go," the human muttered, and reached down with the cutter bar.

This was the one with no broken teeth, and it sliced smoothly through the tough gumtree wood. Pale curls of shavings came free as he drew and pushed, with a faint *shirrr-shirrr* sound. His own pelvis was under the timber. If it was bearing weight, it would shift when he cut through and smash his hipbones to splinters. Not that that would be of much interest to either of them when the dirt closed 'round . . . Halfway through, and the log had not pinched shut on the cutter bar, that was a good sign. Three quarters of the way, and something went *crack* over his head. Man and kzin froze, peering upwards. Another *crack* and the sound of rock grinding on wood. Jonah's arm resumed movement, more quickly this time. He closed his eyes for the last cut. There was a deep *tung* sound as the wood was cut and the severed end rode *up*, not down towards him.

He let out a shaky breath, suddenly conscious of how thirsty he was. No time for that. He dropped the cutter-bar, carefully, and wedged his knee under the end of the timber that now lay across Bigs's thighs.

"This is going to hurt," Jonah said, and repeated it until he was sure Bigs was fully conscious. "Here goes."

"Eeeeraaeeewwooww!"

The kzin scream was deafening in the strait space, like being in a closet with a berserk speaker system. After the jagged wood was free of his flesh Bigs was silent save for rapid shallow panting.

"All right," Jonah shouted, mouth to the hole. "Get ready to pull!" The slack on the rope came taut. "Carefully. If the rope gets caught on a timber, it could bring the whole thing down on us."

The ten meters of passage might as well have been a kilometer. Jonah had to follow behind Bigs's nearly inert form, pushing on his feet and easing the cable-thick tail over obstacles; when the rope caught, he had to crawl millimeter by millimeter along the hairy body until his hands could reach and free the obstruction. More skin scraped off his back and shoulders as he did so, a lubrication of sweat and human and kzinti blood that made the wiggling, gasping effort a little easier. After the first few minutes he lost track of progress; there was only effort in the dark, an endless labor. Until light that was dazzling to his dark-adapted eyes made him blink, and a draft of air cool and pure by comparison brought on another coughing fit. Hands human and inhuman pulled him and the comatose kzin out of the last bodylength of the wormhole.

Jonah had only an instant to lie and wheeze. The groaning and creaking from above became a series of gunshot cracks, and streams of loose dirt poured down. A board followed, ripped free as the scantlings twisted under the force of the earth above and weakened with the forward sections brought down in the first fall. He told his body to rise and run, but nothing happened but a boneless flopping sensation; there was nothing left, no reserve against extremity. Death was coming, smothering in the dark, coming at the instant of victory.

Spots had been squatting while Hans maneuvered the larger, heavier body of his sibling across his shoulders. One hand was up, steadying that; the other reached out and gathered Jonah to his orange-furred chest.

"*Run*," he grunted.

Hans ran beside him—a staggering trot was a better description—steadying the load on his back and taking some of the dragging weight. Jonah was clutched beneath him, turning his progress into a three-limbed hobble that turned into a scrambling rush as the innermost section of the shoring gave way behind them. Wood screamed as each successive section took the full weight for a moment and yielded; the collapse nipped at their heels, its billow of choking dust enclosing them like the hot breath of a carnivore in pursuit. They shot out of the mouth of the diggings like a melon-seed squeezed between fingers and collapsed half a dozen meters from it; Spots was barely conscious enough to turn sideways and avoid crushing Jonah beneath the half-ton weight of two grown kzintosh.

Jonah was still sitting with his head in his hands when Hans returned with the medical kit and water.

"Better look at Bigs first," he coughed, drinking a full dipper in one long ecstatic draught and blinking up at the sun. It had hardly moved; less than two hours since the cave in, difficult to believe.

"Hmmm-*hmm*," Hans agreed.

He and Spots went to work. "No broken bones," Spots pronounced. "There is a lump on the skull but the bone is sound beneath it. Reflexes are within parameters. Concussion, but I doubt any major damage."

"Speak for yourself," Bigs whispered. "More water." He drank rather than lapping, to wash down the handful of antibios and hormonal healing stimulants his brother handed him.

Hans had been examining the thigh wound. "Splinters in here," he said, slipping his hand into the debrilidator glove. "Want a pain-killer?"

"I am a Hero—" Bigs began. Then the miniature hooks in the computer-controlled glove began extracting foreign matter from the wound. "—*so of course I do*," he went on, in a thready whisper.

The work was quickly done, and Hans stepped over to Jonah; then he whistled, watching as the younger man doused himself with water. Fresh blood slicked great patches of skin and raw flesh.

"You done a good job on yourself, youngster," he said, rummaging for the synthskin sprayer. "Hold on."

Jonah did his best to ignore the itching sting of the tiny hooks cleaning dirt and dead skin out of the scrapes. The synthskin was cooling relief in comparison, sprayed on as each area was cleansed.

"What the tanjit were you doing digging that deep?"

he asked Bigs. "You were way beyond the shored-up section. You know the routine; timber and shore *every* meter you go in."

Bigs's eyes were glazed. "Hull," he mumbled. "I found the hull."

"You found the *what?*" Jonah asked, looking up sharply; then he gasped. Hans had done likewise, and braced himself against a flayed area. Spots halted with his muzzle halfway into a bucket.

"Hull," Bigs said more distinctly. "Like nothing I've seen before. Spaceship hull. Small."

• CHAPTER FOURTEEN

The little trading post had a dusty, abandoned feel. There was the adobe store, two houses and a paddock, all planted where three faint mule-tracks crossed a creek. Tile houses had roofs of tile with tiles missing, carrying solar-power panels with some of the panels missing; the pump that filled the watering troughs before the veranda of the store was still functioning, and the metered charger available to anyone who wanted to top up their batteries. The satellite dish on the rooftree looked to be out of order for some time, though. A straggly pepper tree shaded the notional street, and a big kitchen garden lay behind a dun-colored earth wall.

Tyra Nordbo tethered her horses where they could drink; Garm stood on his hind paws to lap beside them. Two meters further down two pack-mules looked up at her animals, then returned to their indifferent doze. She blinked at them thoughtfully as she loosened girths and patted her horse's neck, put a hand to the stock of her rifle where it rested before the fight stirrup in its saddle scabbard, then shook her head.

"Hello the house," she called, from outside the front door; outback courtesy.

The inside was just as shabby as the exterior, if a little cooler from the thick walls, and the fan-and-wet-canvas arrangement over the interior door. A counter split the room in half, with a sleepy-looking outbacker standing behind it; boxes and bales were heaped up against the walls. And another man was at the customer's side, reading from a list:

". . . two four-kilo boxes of the talcum powder. Two kilos of vac-packed vanilla ice cream. One kilo radiated pseudotuna. A thousand meters of number-six Munchenwerk Monofilament, with a cutter and tacker. Ten hundred-nail cassettes for a standard nailgun . . ."

Both men looked up, then looked again, squinting against the sunlight behind her. A third look, when she stepped fully inside and became more than an outline; the storekeeper straightened and unconsciously slicked back his thinning brown hair. Tyra sighed inwardly. There were times when being twenty and a pattern of Herrenmann good looks was something of an inconvenience. Here in the back of beyond it made you stand out, even in smelly leathers with a centimeter of caked dust on your face and a bowie tucked into the right boot-top. Then her eyes narrowed slightly; after the first involuntary reaction, the customer was looking at her with suspicion, not appreciation.

He's changed, she realized. Harder and stronger-looking than the holo Montferrat had shown her. Burned dark-brown from outdoor work, dressed in shabby leather pants and boots with a holstered strakkaker at his waist and a sleeveless jerkin. The Belter crest still stood alone on his head, legacy of a long-term depilation job, but it had grown longer and tangled.

"Guetag, herr," she said politely, nodding.

What the tanj is she doing out here? Jonah thought suspiciously. His gaze travelled from head to toe. Young, very pretty, with the indefinable something—perhaps her accent—that indicated Herrenmann birth. Definitely not an outbacker. Not the sort to be bashing the bundu. Although there were plenty of Herrenmann families down on their luck these days, of course. He started to estimate what she would look like without the bush jacket and leather pants . . .

Get back to business, mind, he admonished himself, with a mental slap on the wrist. *Think of ice and sulphur.* Besides that, his experience with Wunderlander women had not exactly been overly positive.

"Been out here long?" she asked.

"Not long," he said shortly.

"Prospecting? Odd to find a Sol-Belter prospecting dirtside."

Jonah stopped, a finger of cold fear trailing across his neck. His crest marked him, and his accent. For that matter the standard Sol System caucasoid-asian mix of his own genetic background was uncommon here, where unmixed European stock was in the majority.

"Hunting," he grunted, jerking his head at the pile of pelts on the counter.

Suddenly they looked completely unconvincing. The beautiful wavy lines of tigripard, the fawn and red of gagrumphers, all might as well have been cheap extrudate. She met his eyes and smiled, face unlined but crinkles forming in the reddish-grey dust on her skin. It was a charming smile.

"Hunting good?" she asked. "Enough to keep all of you in business?"

"Good enough," Jonah replied, lifting a sack of beans to his shoulder. Then he turned back. "All of us?" he said.

"Not really smart to be out in the bundu alone," she pointed out. "Let me give you a hand."

Before he could prevent her she scooped up a double armful of sacks—a very respectable armful, for a Wunderlander born and raised in this gravity—and carried them out the door. Jonah followed, torn between fear and embarrassment. Outside, she was tying them down to a mule's packsaddle with brisk efficiency.

"What's wrong with hunting alone?" he asked, when the silence began to be suspicious in itself. She turned and looked at him with open-eyed surprise; blue eyes, he noticed, with a faint darker rim.

"Break a leg and die," she said. "Or a dozen other things. Not to mention the bandits."

Jonah moved to the other side of the mule and began strapping the sack of beans to the frame of the saddle, moving it a little to be sure the load was balanced. She had neat hands, slender for a tall woman but strong-looking; her nails were clipped short and clean enough to make him feel self-conscious about the rim of black grime under his. It was difficult to object to the lecture; coming out here alone *would* be insanely risky. Too risky even for a flatlander.

"Heard the Provisional Police have the bandits under control," he said.

"Oh, they're getting there. Not much on trials and procedures, but they track well enough. Big job, though. It'll be a while before these hills are safe for a man alone—or a woman, of course. Tempting fate to go out there with a mule-train of supplies, too."

Jonah worked on in silence, turning on his heel for another load and ignoring the presence at his heel.

"Tyra Nordbo, clan Freunchen," she said after a moment. "Besides which, a man alone usually doesn't require that much tuna and ice cream. You don't look like you drink that much bourbon by yourself, either."

"Manse Chung," he replied shortly. "I've got unusual tastes."

"Not Jonah Matthieson?" she enquired sweetly. "The man with the unusual, large, hairy *friends*?"

Jonah stepped back half a pace, snarling and reaching for his strakkaker; he paused with the vicious machine-pistol half out of the holster, half from prudence and half from the genuine shock on her face.

"Please, be calm, Mr. Matthieson," she said soothingly, hands held palm-down before her. "We have a mutual friend in Munchen who asked me to look you up. And," she added with a gamine grin, "you're a girlhood hero of mine, anyway—some people did hear a *little* of what went on out in the Serpent Swarm, you know."

"I don't have any friends in Munchen, and I don't have any here either," Jonah barked. *Montferrat. He's checking up on us, the scheming bastard.* "I've got a *backer* in Munchen, and he'll get the return on his capital he was promised, *if* he leaves me alone to do my work. Now if you'll pardon me, Fra Nordbo or whatever your name is, I'm a busy man."

"What took you so long?" Hans said.

"Making sure I wasn't followed," Jonah said. "Got it out?"

"Out to the mouth of the diggings," the old man said. "Didn't think it would be all that smart to leave it out in plain view."

"Show me."

Film sheeting had been rigged over the mouth of the shaft and covered with dirt and vegetation. Jonah ducked through into the interior chamber, lit by glowrods stapled to the timbers of the shoring, and whistled silently.

The . . . craft, he supposed . . . was a wasp-waisted spindle four meters long and three wide. One end flared with enigmatic pods; a hole had been torn in it there, the only sign of damage. Through the hole showed the unmistakable sheen of a stasis field. A Slaver stasis field, except that no thrint could be held in a ship this size; the thrintun were Man-tall and much more thickly built. Jonah shuddered at the memory of icy tendrils of certainty ramming into his mind . . . but he knew thrint naval architecture as few men living did, and *they* had been programmed to forget it. Thrintun ships were always large; the thrint were plains-dwelling carnivores by inheritance, and not intelligent enough to suppress their instincts.

"Tnuctipun," he breathed.

The Slavers' engineers, the ones whose revolt had brought down the Slaver Empire three billion years before. The revolt had wiped out both races and every other sentient in the galaxy save for the bandersnatch; humans and kzinti alike had evolved from Slaver-era tailored foodyeasts, along with the entire ecosystems of their respective planets. As a master race, the thrint had not been too impressive, apart from their power of telepathic hypnosis—with the Power, they did not *need* intelligence. An IQ equivalent to human 80 was normal for thrintun. Little was known of the tnuctipun, but it was clear that they had been very clever indeed.

"Or something else from then," Hans said. "That hull's like nothing in Known Space, that's for sure. Tensile strength and radiation resistance is right off the scale; none of the gear we brought can even test it." He scratched in the perpetual white three day's beard that covered his chin. "Wish we hadn't found it. Gold I understand. This I don't. Don't like it."

"This could make us one bleeping lot richer than all the gold on Wunderland," Jonah said.

"We do not know if there is *anything* valuable in the artifact," Spots said. "Not yet."

"There is a stasis field!" Bigs replied. "Neither the Patriarchy nor the monkeys have that as yet. There is the hull material. Think of the naval implications of such ships! We know the ancients had superluminal drives—undoubtedly the secret of that is inside as well. Matter conversion . . ."

He licked his chops and forced his voice to quietness; they were near the disused gold-washing boxes, but the humans could be anywhere and both of them had some command of the Hero's Tongue.

"You said we could not return to the Patriarchy—we, defeated cowards with nothing to offer. Now we can return. Now we can return as *Heroes*, assured of Full Names—assured of harems stocked from the Patriarch's daughters, and a position second only to his!"

Spots nodded thoughtfully. "There is some truth in that," he said judiciously; his voice was calm, but his eyes gleamed and the wet fangs beneath showed white and strong in the morning light. "*If* we could get the secrets, and *if* we can get them offplanet—you do not hope to ride aloft in the alien craft, I hope," he added dryly.

Bigs snorted; neither of the humans could fit in any likely passenger compartment, much less a kzin.

"We must get the pilot, or download the data from the craft's computers," he said decisively.

"Easy to say," Spots said, flapping his ears. Bigs grinned at the reminder that his sibling had always been better with information systems. "The hardware and programs both will be totally incompatible—fewer similarities in design architecture than kzinti-human system interfaces have. At least we and the monkeys have comparable capacities, and integrating *those* systems was a reborn-as-kzinrett nightmare. I did some of that during the war. What kind of computer would the monkey slaves of the thrintun build?"

"And yet. To be a true Hero, to have a name, it never was easy. Until now it was not possible. Now it is."

Spots paused thoughtfully, scratching himself under the jaw. "And the monkey authorities—if they sniff one trace scent of this, they will bury us so deep that we will stay submerged as long as that spacecraft did."

Bigs's fur rippled, and he gave an involuntary dry retch. Ever since the cave-in he had been unable to force himself closer than the outer entrance of the shaft. The darkness, the stifling *closeness* . . . he retched again. As nearly as they could estimate the tnuctipun spaceship had spent the last three thousand million years in the planetary magma, bobbing around beneath the Aeserheimer Continent's crustal plate. The hot spot must be connected with it, somehow—the how of it was beyond them; none of them was a specialist in planetary mechanics—and only chance had ever brought it to the surface again. Vanishingly unlikely that it should be then, although erosion would have revealed it in another few centuries. On the other paw, it had to be discovered *sometime*. It looked to be eternal.

To be buried *that long*, though. His mind knew that it had been less than an instant; inside a stasis field, the entropy gradient was disconnected from that of the universe as a whole. Less than a single second would pass inside during the entire duration of the universe, from the explosion of the primal monobloc to the final inward collapse into singularity. His mind knew that, but his gut knew otherwise.

Spots chirred. "For that matter, what of the humans here? They seem no more anxious than we to attract the *government's*"—he fell into Wunderlander for that; the Hero's Tongue had no precise equivalent—"attention. Yet they may be reluctant to allow us to depart with the data—they are monkeys, after all."

"We can bury their bones. They are outcasts, not dear to the livers of the monkeys in authority. Who will miss their scent?"

The smell of anger warned him; he looked up just in time to jerk his head backward, and Spots's claws fanned the air over his nose rather than raking through the sensitive flesh.

"Honorless sthondat!" the smaller kzin hissed. "Did you forget the oath we swore with Jonah-human? You are alive because of the Jonah-human! Oath-breaker! Are you without regard for the bones of your ancestors? The Fanged God will regurgitate your soul."

Bigs bristled, swelling up to a third again his size; his ears folded back.

"They are *monkeys*," he growled back; the sound was a steady *urrreeuueeerree* beneath the modulations of his words. The Menacing Tense in Imperative Mode.

"That *monkey* crawled into the darkness to rescue you as you lay helpless," Spots said; he stood higher, unwilling to let Bigs' height give him dominance. All eight claws on his hands were out. "Blood for blood."

They began to circle, tails rigid. "What of our duty to the Patriarch?" Bigs spat.

"Our first duty to the Patriarch is to be Heroes," Spots replied. "Heroes do not break their solemn oath!"

They both sank on their haunches for the final leap. Then Bigs let his fur fall and looked aside.

"There is a true trail among the prints of your words," he admitted with sullen reluctance. *Earth rumbling and the walls closing around*—"If the monke . . . if Jonah-human refuses to let us leave with the data, I will challenge him to honorable single combat."

Spots straightened suspiciously; he sniffed with his jaw open and licked his nose for a second try.

"I smell reservations. They smell stronger than a dead kshat," he warned. "Be sure, I will not permit less. No under-the-grass killing. And if you duel Jonah-human, you must preserve his head for the Ancestral Museum of our line."

"Agreed. We shall all act as Heroes. Even the Jonah-human."

Spots's pelt rippled in a shrug. "We quarrel over the intestines of a prey that grazes yet," he said. "So far, all we have is an impenetrable mystery."

• CHAPTER FIFTEEN

"What did you *do*?" Spots demanded, springing back and bruising his tail against a timber upright. He rubbed at it absently, eyes locked on the tnuctipun spacecraft with the same intent longing that they might have fixed on a zianya bound in the blood trough of a feasting table.

"I did *nothing*," Bigs said.

Jonah grunted, and Hans whistled softly. For the better part of a week, nothing. And now the stasis field had vanished, seemingly of its own accord.

The hull had turned . . . translucent, as well. Much of the interior seemed to be packed solid with equipment of various sorts; none of it familiar, although he thought he recognized something like the wave-guides of a gravity polarizer. *If it's that small, and can lift this ship, it's better than anything we or the kzin can make*, he thought. Nothing this size could make space on its own—the power-plant alone would be too large—and nothing this size could possibly mount a superluminal drive, from what little was publicly known about them. On the other hand, nothing humans or kzinti knew would stand three billion years of immersion in liquid metal, either.

"Tnuctipun," he whispered, awed. In the center of

the forward bulge was a capsule, and inside that he could dimly see the outline of a body inside a cocoon of tubes and wires.

Small, was his first thought. He knew from his time on the thrintun ship *Ruling Mind* that tnuctipun were small; they had built that thrintun vessel, and many of the crawlspaces were too cramped for a human to enter. Long limbs in proportion to the body, and twelve digits, longer and more jointed than human fingers. Another indication; there was a rough correlation between manual dexterity and the length of time a species had been sentient. Dolphins and bandersnatch were exceptions, of course. Overall he thought it would come to about his waist standing erect, but the arms were as long as his. A single nostril in the long snout, ahead of an even longer swelling of braincase; a pattern of holes on either side of the head that might correspond to ears, or might not; two large eyes and a smaller one set where the forehead would be if there was one. The eyelids closed side-to-side rather than up and down.

I'm the first human ever to see a tnuctipun, Jonah thought, slightly dazed. He stepped forward, acutely conscious of the smell of his own sweat, of the ginger scent of the kzin. They were staying well back; not that they were more fearful than he, just less driven by curiosity.

"It's hurt," he said, peering closely with his hands on the absolute smoothness of the hull; it was an odd sensation, the palms always trying to slip away.

Whatever the tnuctipun was floating in was liquid, and reddish blood was hazing the egg-shaped chamber; it thinned and flowed away as he watched. An *autodoc*, he realized. Doubling as a pilot's crash couch. Some small scoutcraft and atmosphere flyers used that arrangement, with a high-oxygen liquid for breathing. A body with open air spaces inside it was much more vulnerable to acceleration than one whose lungs were solidly filled with incompressible liquid. *Why bother, if they had gravity polarizers?* he wondered. Then: *ah.* Gravity waves were detectable, and the ones from a polarizer much more so than the natural variety. A clandestine operations craft, no doubt. The tnuctipun had probably been a spy, and the ship designed to slip onto thrintun-held planets during the war of the Revolt. Jonah was willing to bet a great deal that the hull material was superlatively stealthed, as well as near-as-no-matter invulnerable.

"You realize what this means?" he said, looking at the others. "It means we four are potentially the richest beings in known space."

"Means we could all lose our heads, hearts and testicles when the gov'mint gets its claws on us," Hans said dourly. The kzin both snapped their jaws shut: *We are meat.*

"We certainly are if Markham or the ARM get hold of us," Jonah mused.

And the bleeping ARM wouldn't even use this stuff, particularly now we're beating the pussies. At that thought his head came up, raking his eyes across the kzin. Both returned his glance blandly, looking aside in carnivore courtesy. *The Patriarchy would use it,* he knew. Kzinti had never been able to afford antitech prejudice; they had less natural inventiveness than humans to begin with. *Tanj. And we were ready to kill each other over gold, much less this.*

A voice spoke in his ear, in the Hero's Tongue: *"What did you do?"*

Jonah jumped backwards; then he noticed everyone else around the spacecraft had done likewise; the kzinamaratsov brothers were whirling in place, trying to find whatever was speaking beside their ears.

"It's hurt," the voice said, in Wunderlander with a trace of Sol Belt accent. The wet sound of kzin jaws closing on air followed.

The kzin were bristling. "Haunted weapons," Spots said, snapping twice.

"Translator program," Jonah said. "The systems are active, if not the pilot. It's trying to talk to us." It was vibrating the air beside their ears somehow, not too startling compared to the rest of the technology.

"That is beyond my parameters," the computer said. "I must consult my operator before I can make further judgments."

Jonah opened his mouth to reply, and found himself croaking. A startled glance outside showed darkness.

"We'd better knock it off for a while," he said. *Nerve-wracking work.*

Especially when the translator program had spent an hour trying to find out which side they were on in the tnuctipun-thrintun war; it seemed to have a bee in its bonnet about that, understandably enough. He strongly suspected that it also had a self-destruct subroutine, and would engage it if it 'thought' that they were part of a thrint slave-species. The type of suicide bomb available to a culture whose basic energy source was matter conversion did not bear thinking of. You could tell a good deal about the people who designed an infosystem by talking to one of their programs, and there was a pristine ruthlessness to this one that even the kzin found chilling.

No wonder the Revolt wiped out intelligent life, he thought. They had had to take a datalink out and show the ship's system the stars before it really seemed to believe them about the length of time that had passed. At that, it was probably fortunate that the pilot was still comatose. The computer had limited autonomy; it was very powerful, right up with the great machines that ran the UN Space Navy from Gibraltar Base in the Sol Belt, but not a true personality, as far as he could tell.

Neither human nor kzinti designers had ever been able to make a really sentient system that did not go catatonic within months. Evidently the ancient world of the Slaver Empire had been no more successful. At least the AI was completely logical; Finagle alone knew what a conscious but traumatized tnuctipun would do on realizing it was the only member of its species left in a universe changed beyond recognition.

Jonah shivered again. That did not bear thinking about either. When the *Yamamoto* dropped him and Ingrid Raines off into the kzin-occupied Alpha Centauri system two years ago they had decelerated by using a stasis field—one of the few the UN had been able to make— and skidding through the photosphere of the star. A little, little mistake and they would have spent the next several billion years in stasis themselves—until Alpha Centauri went nova, perhaps. Then the invulnerable bubble of not-time might have been flung out, eventually to land on a planet. To wait while intelligent life arose or arrived, then be opened. He swallowed, mind exploring the concept the way a tongue might probe at a sore tooth. *At that, there would have been two of us*, he thought. *And I'd still have gone off the deep end.*

Jonah was preoccupied enough not to notice the extra figure at the campfire, as he walked downslope to the tents. Spots and Bigs had better senses; he looked up sharply at their angry hisses of territorial violation.

"You all seemed to be busy," Tyra Nordbo said, crouched by the fire. "So I thought I'd help myself to some of this coffee."

With her free hand, she pitched something small and heavy out into the firelight. All of them recognized the material. After a moment, they recognized the shape; the hole in the rear section of the tnuctipun ship's hull matched it exactly.

❖   ❖   ❖

"No, of *course* I haven't reported back to Herrenmann Montferrat," Tyra said. "How could I? The government—which means the ARM, remember—is monitoring all frequencies and all the cable and satellite links. There is still a state of military emergency on, you know."

Jonah relaxed slightly; out of the corner of his eye, he could see Spots and Bigs doing likewise, the ruffs of fur around their throats and shoulders sinking back to the level of the rest of their pelts. Their eyes stayed locked on the young woman, ominously steady, glints of silver and red in the gathering dark against the ruddy orange of their fur. Hans was imperturbable as he sucked his pipe to a glowing ember.

"You really don't have much choice but to go through with your agreement, as far as I can see," she went on.

"Oh?" Jonah said, softly. "We didn't bargain to hand over the Secret of the Ages for a pat on the head and a few thousand krona."

Bigs snorted agreement, followed by a low growl. Spots was silent, but the tip of his tongue showed as he panted slightly.

"It's *too* big," Tyra said. "The ARM would give anything to suppress this—they'll take the tnuctipun back to Earth, put it in the museum next to the Sea Statue, that thrint they bottled up again, and that'll be that. You know them. They have a *lot* of influence here on Wunderland these days. To make any use of the secret, you'd have to have a powerful patron of your own—or," she added with a gamine chuckle that made her look twelve for a second, "you could take it and sell it to the Outsiders or the Patriarch of Kzin. No offense," she added in the brothers' direction.

Bigs snarled, a sound like ripping canvass. Spots snorted, a *flupp* sound. "None taken," he said.

"Besides which," she went on, "*I* know about it, and it's my duty to see that the most responsible authority takes charge of it for the benefit of Wunderland—of everyone, eventually. That means Montferrat. Of course, you could kill me and bury my body." She leaned back against her saddle. "Up to you, mein herren."

Blast, she had to go and say it, Jonah thought. His palms were damp. *I'm a—moderately—law-abiding type,* he mused. *And normally, I'd be against offing anyone that good-looking on general principle. But* Finagle *there's a lot at stake here!*

Odd, how ambition struck. He had never been conscious of wealth as something he lacked, before. Enough to be comfortable, yes; the loss of that had been shocking when Early had him railroaded out of the UN Space Navy and then blacklisted. A little more of the gold, yes; independence had looked awfully desirable. The tnuctipun's secrets were more than wealth, they were *power.* The problem was, they were proportionately risky.

"Ja, Fra Nordbo," Hans said mildly. "Those look to be the alternatives, don't they?" Tyra stiffened; she had not meant to be taken literally. "If you'd let us talk it over in private, for a minute?" He waggled his pipe towards the kzinti; it would be futile to try and run in the dark, with them ready to scent-track as accurately as hounds and with intelligence to boot.

As soon as she had withdrawn, Bigs spoke: "Kill him. I mean her." Kzinti females were mute and subsentient, probably another consequence of genetic engineering, and kzintosh—male kzin—had trouble remembering that sexual dimorphism was not so extreme among the race of Man. The matter was academic to them, of course. "We owe the monke—hrreaheerr, Montferrat-human only money. We can pay him off with gold. The secrets in that craft will make us Patriarchs!"

"Or make us dead," Hans said. "Killing the girl—the Provisional Gendarmerie, they don't worry about trifles like proof. They just shoot you. Can't spend if you're dead. I wish we hadn't found it, I truly do."

"I also," Spots said surprisingly. "But it is done." His breed wasted little time on regrets. "My sibling is right—in potential. Hans-human is also right—as to the risk. I scratch dirt upon the dung of risk . . . but there is no glory in defeat. It is a difficult matter."

"We can't kill Tyra—the girl," Jonah said reasonably.

The two kzin looked at each other. Bigs rolled his eyes toward Jonah and made a complex gesture, involving fingers wiggling at the muzzle, flapping ears, a ripple of the fur and an arch of the back. It meant *mating frenzy*; also *stupidity* and *madness*.

"Hrrrr." Spots lay his chin on his hands and turned his eyes on Jonah. "We must agree, whatever we do. Or else fight each other." He added kindly: "If all agree to kill the female, we will do it; you need not watch. We will even forgo eating it."

"Bleeping hell you—" Jonah forced calm. *Breath in. Breath out. Ommmm*— "Look, I know it's tempting for you, but I've decided; we really can't do anything but sell to Montferrat. Wunderland's our only market. They won't let us get off planet! Montferrat is the only market on Wunderland that won't slap us in a psychist's chair. And kill you two, by the way."

"I think Fra Nordbo should go," Hans said. He gestured with his pipe as Jonah stared round. "Nothing against her personal. No, seems a nice enough sort. Still, I'm a Wunderlander—commoner, like my parents before me. Don't like the thought that we hand this to the new government; too cozy by half with the Earthers. Don't like the idea of the Herrenmenn getting it, either—tired of them running things, and throwing us scraps." He smiled across at the kzin without showing his teeth. "Since you fellers' friends back home *can't* get it, that don't come into the picture."

Tanjit! Jonah thought. Aloud: "Look, we've had a long day. What say we turn in? She isn't going anywhere. We can consider it in the morning."

"Logic will be the same in the morning," Spots said reasonably. "Also, you will not find the decision easier once you have mated."

"I don't *intend* to mate!" Jonah snapped. *Although Finagle knows I'd like to.* Aliens had trouble with the details of human social interaction. "And I say let's think it over in the morning."

• **CHAPTER SIXTEEN**

Spots-Son of Chotrz-Shaa whimpered softly in his sleep. He was hiding from his father. Chotrz-Shaa had seen the vids from the Fourth Fleet sent against Man-Home. Three elder sons and a brother had sailed with the Fourth Fleet; Ssis-Captain, Second Gunner and Squadron Analyst. Chotrz-Shaa raged through the home complex; the scent of his anger was terrible. In the palazzos of the harem, mothers tucked their kittens into cupboards or piles of pillows and yowled their fear and defiance, prepared to fight to the death to keep the enraged male from eating the young. That was an instinct older than the Patriarchy, older than speech and tools.

Spots-Son followed in his father's wake; the smell of killing rage repelled and led. Occasionally a faint *euuuw-euuuw* trickled past the young kzin's lips; his brother the Big One gave him a contemptuous look, that was the infant's distress call. They followed down corridors of black basalt with trophies of ceremonial weapons, into the communications room. Sometimes their father brought them there for lessons with the teaching machines, but now it was in turmoil; smashed crockery, modules thrown here and there. A human servant huddled bleeding in one corner, then scuffled out as the youngsters entered.

Pictures were up on the wall holo. For a long time the two youngsters stared at them without comprehension, until Spots recognized the face in one.

"Uncle Ssis-Captain!" he cried. "Sire's Brother!"

Bigs reared back beside him with a *reeearrwowow* of protest, hair bottling out and tail stiff. Uncle Ssis-Captain was *dead*. He was floating in zero-G, with the bottom half of him *gone*. The brothers were old enough for preliminary education; they both knew about spacecraft, and kzinti anatomy.

"But . . . but Uncle Ssis-Captain went to conquer the monkeys!" Spots wailed.

Uncle Ssis-Captain had picked him up and swung him around, and promised him an elephant-hunt when he came to visit on the estate on Earth . . .

"The monkeys killed Uncle Ssis-Captain," Bigs said shakily. "That . . . that is Brother and Brother." The other two forms in the holo were calcinated to ash and bone, but one had a chased-tungsten arm ring. Their father had given that when the Fleet left on its mission of conquest.

Two shrill cries of grief and rage rose, higher and higher until an adult roar cut them off.

"What are you doing here?" it bellowed.

Spots threw himself down flat, paws over eyes and fur laid flat. Bigs was more reckless; he stood upright, met his father's eyes.

"I shall kill all the monkeys—they killed Uncle and—"

"Silence, cub!" Chotrz-Shaa bellowed, backhanding the youngling into the wall and whimpering silence. The huge face bent low, filling Spots's vision, all glaring eyes and teeth and rage-smell.

"No, Father!" he cried, and woke.

❖   ❖   ❖

I detest that dream, he thought, shaking his head and rolling up to all fours.

It was the hour before dawn, with the moon down and the air chilly; it felt good to be comfortable in his fur, and scents were marvelously clear. Eyesight was flatter and less color-sensitive than in daylight, but otherwise not much less as the pupils of his eyes expanded until the iris was only a yellow thread around the black pits of sight. Something moved, a human—he sniffed deeply—yes, the blander, earthier odor of the female.

Good, he thought. That dream usually came when something serious disturbed him in his sleep. If the human-female was trying to escape, he could kill it without angering Jonah-human; that would be best. *Jonah is a fine monkey*, he thought. If the thought were not slightly blasphemous, one could wish that he had been born a Hero. *I will make him my Chief Slave when we reconquer Wunderland.* As they would, if Bigs was right. If only. *My liver says yes, but my brain disagrees. Enough. The longest leap begins with setting your hindclaws. First the Tyra-human.*

He crept forward, belly to the earth, tail straight back to balance his weight and hands touching down occasionally to guide it. Ready for the sudden overwhelming rush, the final leap; he needed no weapon for this. Excitement folded his ears back into knots and drew lips back from teeth, brought the claws sliding out on all eight digits. Almost, he was reluctant to end it; Tyra-human moved very quietly, for a monkey, and he might have had trouble following her if the breeze had not been with him. Eagerness brought him forward faster, but with only a little more noise; a pebble displaced, a thorn snagging his fur and snapping. Then he went rigid with shock.

"*Quiet,*" she said, turning and calling softly. "They're moving up the valley."

She looked directly at him, with the bulbous shape of nightsight glasses hiding her eyes. She spoke in the Hero's Tongue, as closely as a monkey could come to pronouncing it; in the Warning Tense. He nearly screamed and leapt then; only caution at the sight of her magrifle gave him pause. Then the sense of the words sank home.

They? he thought. Quickly he came level with her and followed her pointing hand. Motion, over a kilometer away; he took the glasses from his belt and looked. Humans on horseback, leading other horses. Octal to the second of them, all heavily armed, and he recognized the shapes of knock-down beamers on the lead horses.

"Who?" he breathed. *I lay my fur flat in shame. Claw your own nose and roll in sthondat excrement, Spotted Fool! We should have kept lookouts.*

"Don't know," she replied. Even now a thought flickered, how easy it would be to reach out—only arm's reach—and slash her throat open.

No. Not with an unknown factor . . . unless she led them to us? His lips went further back in rage, but it was unlikely.

"Could be the Provisional Gendarmerie," she said softly. "Or it could be bandits. Either way, bad news for us. They'll be here by dawn at that rate. Can't miss the trail and the water-furrow."

Us, Spots thought mournfully. *Us expands to too many monkeys.* The Fanged God would have his jokes on those so lost to honor that they surrendered.

I will rip your throat yet, he thought, staring resentfully up into the sky for a second. The God appreciated a good fight.

"I will wake the others," he went on aloud.

"Well, they've got Provisional Gendarmerie *armbands*," Jonah said, lowering the magnifier.

"Cloth's cheap," Hans replied.

Jonah nodded, mind busy. "All right. Spots, you take your beamer and dig in behind those rocks over there. Hans, get the mules back into the diggings and then set up on the hill over the entrance."

Hans was the best shot of all of them; it was difficult to be a *bad* shot with a military magrifle, but he was superb.

"I'll take the center, here."

"What about me?" Tyra Nordbo said.

I wish to Finagle you were far, far away, Jonah thought. Aloud: "Ever used that rifle?"

"Yes."

The reply was bitten off, and from the expression she hadn't enjoyed it. All to the good; he'd known people in the UN Navy who enjoyed combat, and none of them were types he'd like to have backing him up. They tended to fly off the handle like . . . like kzinti, come to think of it.

"You get about ten meters to the east of me and take that little knoll." He turned to eye the two kzin. "And *nobody* fires unless they open up, or I give the order. Understood?"

Bigs looked skeptical. "What if they flank us?" Spots asked. "There are enough of them."

"Then we'll retreat," Jonah said. "And someone else will have the headache of what to do with *that*." He jerked a thumb towards the entrance to the diggings.

The mounted column wove over the ridge opposite and down into the morning shadow of the valley, disappearing into the dense vegetation along the streambed. Jonah burrowed deeper into cover, showing nothing but the lenses of his field glasses, their systems keyed to passive receptors only. IR would show their locations, of course; a good deal depended on how much the whatever-they-were had in the way of detection systems. Quite a bit if they really were Provisionals, anything from the Eyeball Mark I to military issue if they were bandits. The dawn was coming up in the east, to his right; the snowpeaks and clouds around the summits of the Jotuns turned red as blood, while Beta was a point of white fire overhead. The waterfall toned and thundered to his right, mist rising out of darkness into light.

He pulled the audio jack on his field glasses out and put it in his ear. The instrument clicked, sorting out sound not in the human-voice frequencies. Then:

". . . *boot some head* . . ."

"Shut up, scheisskopf! Turn it on!"

A crackling hiss filled his ear. *Wonders of modern technology*, he reflected sourly; it was always easier to make things not happen than to make them happen, so countermeasures generally ran ahead of detection. The rustle of boots and the clink of equipment came more clearly, and the *tock . . . tock . . .* of synthetic horseshoes on firm ground or rock. The strangers were in no hurry. They stopped to water their horses and picket them, to set up a firing line along the edge of the brush, before two walked out from under the trees and began climbing the hill.

"Everybody stay calm," Jonah warned again, as the pair halted and looked upslope.

They looked tough, shabby and a little hungry; or at least the rat-faced thin one did. The leader had a beer belly that hung over his gunbelt, and even in the cool morning sweat stains marked his armpits. He carried a strakkaker at his belt and a magrifle in his hands; his companion had the chunky shape of a jazzer slung from an assault sling. That fired miniature molecular-distortion batteries set to discharge into any living tissue they met. An unpleasant weapon.

The big-bellied leader smiled, a false grin creasing

his stubbled face. His Wunderlander had a thick accent, maybe regional, or he might have come from one of the many ethnic enclaves that dotted the planet:

"Hey, you up there? Why you hiding?"

"Why are you here?" Jonah replied. "Ride on. We'll mind our business, you mind yours."

"Hey, we can't do that, man!" the other man said. "We're the Provisional Gendarmerie—you know, the mounted police? We're inspecting the area for illegal weapons. New order, to confiscate all illegal weapons, peace and order, you know?"

"What's illegal?" Jonah asked.

"Just military stuff, man. You know, magrifles, jazzers, beamers—hunting rifles, they are fine."

"Let's see some ID, then."

"ID? We got *plenty* of ID. Here, I show you."

The fat man pulled something out of a leg-pocket on his stained pants and handed it to the smaller figure beside him. He murmured an order, which the other seemed to resent; then he took off his hat and began thrashing the little man over the head and shoulders.

"Ja, boss, Ja, I'll *take* it," the small man with the big nose said.

"Here!" he called out, climbing towards Jonah's position.

"Toss it over that rock and get back down," Jonah shouted.

Ratface scuttled to obey, and Jonah signed to Tyra. She leopard-crawled with her rifle across her elbows, over to the plastic card and examined it with a frown of puzzlement; then she ran it past the scanner of her beltcomp. That brought another frown, and she kept crawling to within arm's length of him to pass the ID. He glanced down at it; a holo of the fat man's face, looking indecent without its stubble. Serial number, and *Leutnant Edward Gruedermann, Provizional Staatspolezi.*

"My comp recognizes the codes, and I updated about a month ago, but . . ."

"But?" Jonah bit out. If he had stood off a real Gendarmerie Lieutenant, they were all in serious trouble. Wunderland was under martial law, and out here a mounted police officer could be judge, jury and executioner all in one. Staging a shoot-out with the police would be absolute suicide, even if he won. Jonah Matthieson's ambiguous status would harden into "desperate criminal" quite quickly, then.

"But if that lot are Provisionals, I'm a kzinrette." She bit her lip; even then it was interesting . . . "Look, herr Matthieson—up until two months ago, I was *in* the Provisional Gendarmerie. My brother Ib's a captain. I spent six months riding with them. That lot down there smell wrong, completely."

Jonah met her eyes, a changeable sea-blue; tinted with gray this morning, desperately sincere. *Tanj, why couldn't she be a middle-aged battleaxe of eighty?*

"All right," he said. "I'll play it safe." *Because if we do give up our guns, there's our options gone right there.* "You get over there east of the Brothers Kzinamaratsov; they might come up the gully."

To his surprise, he heard her chuckle—he had only taken up ancient literature in the last year himself; data was free, if nothing else—and she touched a finger to her brow before heading off east with an expert's use of cover.

"If this ID is genuine," Jonah called down to the man halfway up the slope, "then you won't mind me calling in to Munchen for confirmation. Leutnant Gruederman."

Gruederman began a snarl, and forced it back into a smile. *Docking contact*, Jonah told himself. *Tyra was right.*

"Hey, man, we don't want to *steal* your guns—it's the law, you know. Here—" he shoved the other man "—we'll give you compensation."

"See," the little man said, rummaging in his knapsack. "This is worth three, maybe four hundred krona!" He held up a briefcase-sized box, an obsolete model of musicomp and library. "Good stuff, pre-war!"

Stolen from some farmer you bushwacked, Jonah thought grimly. He took up the slack on his trigger and put the aiming point on the musicomp. *Whack*. The casing exploded and the little bandit went howling and whirling away, face slashed by the fragments. The sharp sound of the high-velocity round went echoing off down the valley in a *whack*-whackkkkk of fading repetitions.

"Get moving," Jonah called flatly.

The bandit chief's face convulsed, going from a broad grin to an expression that was worthy of a kzin. Spittle flecked out as he screamed:

"You can't do this to Ed Gruederman! I will boot your head!"

The smaller bandit had recovered enough to unlimber his jazzer. A round cracked over Jonah's head; by reflex he shifted aim and sent a short burst into the man's torso. It blossomed out in a mist of sliced bone and flesh as the prefrag bullets punched in and disintegrated, a thousand crystalline buzzsaws of adamantine strength. By the time he shifted back it was too late. Gruederman threw himself backward in a desperate flip, somersaulting and rolling down the short distance to cover. Bullets pecked at his shadow, and then the whole treeline opened up. Magrifle bullets chewed at the stone, and a boulder exploded as a tripod-mounted beamer punched megajoules of energy into its brittle structure. Thunder rolled back from the cliffs.

"Let 'em have it!" Jonah yelled.

Unnecessary, but satisfying. He rolled a half-dozen paces to his right, rose, fired a burst, ducked and rolled again. Hans was shooting from his position over the diggings, single shots. A man screamed and fell from a tree in the valley below, and the beamer fell silent. Over to the left the kzin were popping up for fractional seconds and sending bursts from their captured beamers, using heavy weapons like rifles, inhumanly quick and accurate. Trees below exploded into steam and supersonic splinters. Their screams sounded louder than the noise of battle, daunting in a way that the mechanized death they wielded was not. Hair rose on human spines, a fear that went back to the caves and beyond.

Wonder what Tyra's doing, Jonah thought in a second of calm. *Hope she hasn't got buck fever.*

Spots flicked himself up with a heave of his body. It was just enough to clear head and hands above the scree ahead of him; the aimpoint of the beamer settled on the target he had picked on his last shot, and it exploded with steam. From vegetation, and as he dropped and rolled he could smell flash-cooked monkey as well. He shrieked exultantly:

"Eeeeeerreeieiaiiaaiawiowiue!" The kzinti are upon you! He had a wide arc before him, with a deep narrow ravine full of brush that stretched right down to the river. Already an arc of riverbank forest before him was burning. He looked down at the power readout of the beamer; almost half discharged. A pity, since he liked this weapon. The two strakkakers strapped to his thighs seemed like feeble toys in comparison, although the grips had been modified for kzin hands.

The next shot almost brought disaster. A fragment caught his forehead, and stinging blood covered his eyes as he dropped back into the protection of the rock. With a yowl of impatience he felt at the injury, even as rounds chewed at the tumbled volcanic basalt ahead of him. It was painful enough to wake him to full fury, the area above his brow-ridges cut to the bone and a flap of skin hanging free; his ears rang, and his mouth filled. He swallowed and forced pain and dizziness back. That had almost killed him; many monkeys would die for their presumption, and he would chew their livers. In the meantime he had to get the blood out of his eyes; it was blinding him, and the rank scent of kzin blood dulled his nostrils.

A yowl from Bigs meant that he had caught that smell too. "All's well!" he snarled back. "Look to your front."

There was a length of gauze in his beltpouch. He pushed the flap of skin back into position—he would get a worthy battlescar out of this, but in the meantime it *stung*— and began binding the wound with an X-shaped bandage, anchored by a loop under the base of his jaw and around the rear bulge of his skull. Hurriedly he poured water from his canteen over his brows and eyelashes, snuffling and scrubbing and licking his nose to clear his senses. A sharp scent of eucalyptus almost made him sneeze; some tree damaged in the fight, he supposed.

"Behind you!" a human voice screamed.

It was utterly unexpected, but Spots' reflexes wasted no time on surprise. He dropped sideways.

A bandit lunged through the space he had occupied a moment before, with a vibroblade outstretched before him. It whined into uselessness as the humming wire edge sliced into rock. The knifeman's face had just enough time to begin to show surprise when the kzin's full-armed swing ripped out his throat almost to the neckbone and threw him ten meters through the air. The instinctive full-force effort swung Spots around in a three-quarter turn, his body betraying him in a G field barely a third of the one for which it had evolved. That exposed him to fire from below for a moment—rock spalls stung his shoulders—and left him helpless as the second bandit six meters away raised a strakkaker left-handed. The forty-round clip of liquid-teflon filled bullets would rip the kzin's body open like an internal explosion.

The bandit's head vanished from the shoulders up in a spray of red, gray and pink. The body stood for two seconds with blood fountaining up to where the face would have been, took two stumbling steps forward, and collapsed across Spots' tail. He blinked surprise and looked.

Tyra-human lay prone beside another boulder, slapping another cassette into her rifle. She gave him a brief nod before moving off to a fresh firing position; her face was gray, and she smelled of fatigue poisons and nausea, an acrid scent.

Spots went flat again and readied his beamer, but the savor had gone out of the fight. *Bigs owes a life to Jonah-human. Now I owe a life to Tyra-human. Two lives the honor of the House of Chotrz-Shaa owes to Man. It is too much. How will I know the balance of debt and obligation, unless the Fanged God tells me?* Like most modern kzin, Spots had worked at rejecting religion as unfashionable. The effort wasn't entirely successful. Intellect was one thing; but belief in the Fanged God was built deep into the kzin culture, and a desire to *believe* had been built into their very genes. The Conservators of the Patriarchal Past had a fertile field to sow. Now Spots wished he had listened more closely to the Conservators. It would take a God to figure out this tangle.

Oh, well—there are monkeys down there I can kill, he thought gloomily.

"*Sssisssi!*" Bigs snarled, and forced his clawed hand down again. "We should have pursued," he went on.

"Shut up," Tyra said, working the sprayskin around the depilated patch of singed flesh that ran down the barrel ribs of the big kzin's body. "We're not in any shape to pursue three times our number. Defending gave us an advantage."

Jonah sighed and sipped again at his canteen, looking around the campsite; they had moved into the outer edge of the shaft, in case the bandits tried to sneak a sniper back, and left sensors scattered about outside with Spots to oversee. The kzin seemed depressed; not so Bigs, who was a little manic by his own surly standards. He lifted his beltphone.

"Spots, anything?"

"No. They ran, and continued to run to the limit of the audio sensor's ability to detect the footfalls of their riding beasts." A sigh. "Must we really leave all those bodies?"

"Yes!" Jonah snapped, swallowing at certain memories of his own. *Every once in a while, you remember that they're not humans in fur suits.* "Last thing we want is a posse-mob of outbackers on our trail, understood?" Wunderlanders would *not* react well to the thought of kzin eating even dead bandits.

"Understood." A long, sad sigh.

"Come on in."

Silence crackled between them as they waited; Jonah met Hans's eye, and got a slight nod in return. Tyra finished with Bigs and stepped quickly away, aware that an injured kzin was unlikely to tolerate much contact with a human. *Got brains, that girl*, Jonah thought admiringly. Spots ducked in between the screens and stopped, turning his head inquiringly towards his brother, ears cocking forward and nostrils flaring. Then he rippled his fur in a shrug and squatted against the restraining timbers of the far wall, hands resting on the ground before him.

"We can't stay here," Jonah said abruptly. "There's something you should know: I don't think that those bandits were acting on their own."

It took a few minutes to sketch in Jonah's relations with Buford Early, and Early's campaign of persecution. Silence followed, and he went on:

"We can't lug *that*"—he jerked a thumb over his shoulder at the tnuctipun spyship—"either. Either the bandits will come back with more men, or the real Gendarmerie will show up. The bandits will kill us, the Gendarmerie might—and the government will *certainly* stamp everything Excruciatingly Secret and silence us, one way or another. I'm a pariah, you two are kzin, Fra Nordbo here comes from a suspect family subject to pressure—"

"And I'm a worthless old bushcoot," Hans said cheerfully.

"If we were lucky, they might buy us off," Jonah continued. "If we want to make anything of what we've got, we'd better get out quick and make a sale to the only one who has the resources to make something of this—to Montferrat-Palme. At least we'll have *some* bargaining position with him."

"*That . . . is . . . not . . . all,*" a voice said behind him.

Jonah shot erect, turning before he came down again. Within its sac of fluid, the tnuctipun's eyes had opened. It stayed in its fetal position, hands wrapped about knees. The three eyes blinked vertically, and the mouth moved; the lips seemed almost prehensile, and they were not in synch with the words that he heard. The translator program, then.

"*I . . . will . . . not . . . be . . . buried . . . again.*"

• **CHAPTER SEVENTEEN**

Durvash whimpered to himself, eyes squeezed tightly shut. Agony, agony to speak. Agony to *think*. Last. He was the last. *I failed*. Suicide night had succeeded. The thrint had won. *Egg mother. Womb mother. Father. Siblings. All dead.* The tnuctipun race was dead, and he was the last. The last by three *billion* years. One-celled organisms had evolved to intelligence while he lay within this planet's crust. He was not even sure it was the planet he had lost consciousness on; there was more than enough time for his damaged craft to have drifted through several systems. Time for all the bodies of thrint and tnuctipun and shotovi and zen-gaborni to rot away, and the fabric of their cities to erode to dust and the dust to be ground down under moving continents, and for stars to age and—

Rest, the faithful machines said; they had no souls, no souls that longed for the deep red velvet sleep of death. *Your functions are at less than 45% of optimum and you must rest for the healing to be complete.*

He jerked. *No. I must think.* He was *not* the last tnuctipun! His race had won, not the mouth-beshitting Slavers. Joy brought Durvash tears as painful as despair.

291

He existed; his autodoc and computer existed. They contained the knowledge to clone his cells, to modify the genetic structures to replicate individuals of all three sexes. Genetic records of *thousands* of tnuctipun; that was part of the general autodoc system. His rubbery lips peeled off his serrated teeth in aggression-pleasure. Tnuctipun were pack-hunters of great sociability; group survival was sweet ecstasy.

I will need facilities. Laboratories, tools, time. The current sentients here would be complete fools to allow a rebirth of the tnuctipun species, of tnuctipun culture—and all of *that* was encoded in the memory of his computer as well.

They were not complete fools. Not very bright by tnuctipun standards, but then few races were. They were certainly more acute than thrint—by about a fifth to a third, he judged, from the hour or so of conversation, and to judge from their technology. It was fairly advanced, in a quaint sort of way—the beginnings of an industrial system, interstellar travel and fusion drives.

They were divided, too. Species from species, as was natural: the tnuctipun word for "alien" translated roughly as "food that talks." Also individual from individual, a common characteristic of inferior races—he quickly suppressed memory of his own rivals at home. Durvash knew what to make of that. He had been trained as a clandestine agent, and his proudest accomplishment had been an entire thrint world wiped clean of life by engineering a civil war between thrintun clan elders.

The large carnivore, he decided. Carnivores were easiest to work with, in his opinion—as he was one himself. *He is in a minority of one.* It should be easy to persuade him to use the neural-connector earplug. That would make communication easy, and certain other things, if the biochemistries were similar enough.

Durvash squeezed his eyes shut. No warrior of

tnuctipun had ever been so alone as he. He had lost a universe; there was a universe to win.

If I do not go mad, he thought; although his autodoc would probably not let him do so. He did not know if that was fortunate, or the most terrifying thing of all.

Sleep . . .

The little caravan prepared to depart in the blueish half-light of Beta dawn, with Alpha still a hint on the horizon, blocked by the peaks whose passes they would have to traverse. The mules had become inured to kzin scent—somewhat—and were loaded first, to proceed Tyra's skittish horses who were doubly disturbed by the smell of carnivore and the dead horses from yesterday's battle. Fading woodsmoke and coffee smells mixed with the crisp earthy scent of dew on the bushes, and the cries of birds and gliders cut a sharper undercurrent through the sound of the waterfall. That came into focus again, now that they were leaving it after so many months of labor.

"Done right well by us, this mountain," Hans said reflectively, strapping the packsaddle of his mule. "Wonder if it has a name? Not likely," he decided. "Too small." The little eroded volcanic peak was a midget among the Jotuns, even in the comparatively low hollow.

"Muttiberg," Tyra said, passing by with her saddle over her shoulder. The dog Garm pressed against her leg, casting another apprehensive look back at the two kzin. He had been trying to keep himself between her and them since she rode into camp, despite the flattened ears and tucked tail of intimidation. Kzinti were nightmares to canines, of course. "The locals call it the Mother Mountain—for obvious reasons."

Probably a man named them. This and the hill opposite did look like a woman's breasts, if you squinted and had the right attitude. Muttiberg.

"Let me give you a hand with that," Jonah said; then he was a little surprised at the weight of the saddle. *Strong for a Wunderlander*, he thought; but then, you could tell that from her build, almost like an Earther's.

Bigs lifted the life-capsule possessively. It was lighter than it should be, some application of gravity polarizer technology beyond current capacities, and opaque now as well. The whole assemblage had seemed to *ooze* through the wall of the spaceship, leaving no mark of its passage. For the first time in his life Bigs felt lust as a purely mental state, not just the automatic physical reaction to kzinrette pheromones. It was an oddly cerebral sensation, yet it had the same obsessive quality of excluding all other considerations. The tnuctipun-voice murmured in his ear, and he commanded them not to twitch. Only the slightest subvocalization was necessary to reply, too faint even for Spots's ears to catch.

He fitted the life capsule into one side of the pack saddle; the other was balanced with sacks of gold dust, worthless as dirt now. '*We have a means of converting matter into energy along a beam,*' the voice said. Bigs's mind blossomed with visions of monkey warships flashing into fireballs, galaxies of fire to light the triumphant passage of kzinti dreadnoughts. Planetary surfaces gouted upward, gnawing down to fortresses embedded in the crusts. '*Matter-energy conversion is also available as a power source.*' Fleets crossed between suns in days, weeks. Once or twice, no more, in the history of the Patriarchy a warrior—a Hero—had been adopted into the Riit clan, promoted to the inmost lairs. What reward would be great enough for Chotra-Riit, savior of the kzinti? What glory great enough for the one who brought the Heroic Race domination not merely over the monkeys, but over a galaxy as well? Man was not the only enemy of the Patriarchy. *None* of them could stand against the secrets of the tnuctipun. The Eternal Pride would sweep the whole spiral arm in a conquering rush.

Slaver dripped down from his thin black lips to the fur of his chest. He ignored it, taking the mule's bridle as tenderly as he might have borne up his firstborn son.

". . . and so after Father was forced to leave on that crazy astrological expedition with Riao-Captain, Mutti had more and more trouble with the kzin," Tyra went on.

Jonah leaned his head closer, interest and concern on his face. They were strung out over rocky plateau country, following a faint trail upwards toward the nearest pass through the central Jotuns. The mountains curved away northeastward, this slightly-lower hilly trough between the main ranges heading likewise; directly east and south were the headwaters of the Donau, and the long road down to the fertile lowlands where Munchen lay. Tyra hesitated and went on; Jonah seemed to be that rare thing, a man who knew how to *listen*. Not to mention looking at you without salivating all the time, something that was more subtly flattering than open interest.

"She had not his strength of body. Or," she went on more slowly, "his strength of will—they were very close. So she must yield more to the kzinti, and the replacement for Riao-Captain was less . . . willing to listen, in any case. Things were growing worse all over Wunderland then; the war was going against the ratcats, and they squeezed harder on the human population." She scowled. "Yet Mutti did her best; more than can be said for some others, who were punished less."

"I agree with you," Jonah said. "Your family seems to have gotten a raw deal. Mind you," he went on, "I wasn't here, dealing with the kzin occupation. That twists people's minds, and there's little justice in an angry man—or a frightened one."

She nodded, liking him better for the honesty than she would have for more fulsome support.

"In the meantime," he went on, lowering his voice, "I'm worried about our kzin here and now." He dropped into English, which was a language they shared and the sons of Chotrz-Shaa did not. "They're not acting normal."

Tyra blinked puzzlement. They had been sullen, true. "Kzinti are not supposed to be talkative or gregarious, are they?" she said.

"Tanj, no," Jonah said, taking a moment to fan himself with his hat. This high up the heat was dry rather than humid, but the pale volcanic dirt and scattered rocks threw it back like a molecular-film reflector.

"Bigs is surly even by kzin standards, but now he's downright *euphoric*. Not talking, but look at the way his fur ripples, and the way he holds his tail. Spots *is* talkative—for a kzin. Now he's miserable."

Tyra looked more closely. The smaller kzin was plodding along with back arched, the tip of his tail carelessly dragging in the dirt, even though it must be sore. His nose was dry-looking and there was a grayish tinge to its black, and his fur was matted and tangled, with burrs and twigs he had not bothered to comb out. Bigs's pelt shone, and his head was up, alert, eyes bright.

"It is a bad sign when a kzin neglects his grooming, isn't it?" she murmured.

"Very bad."

She glanced aside at him. "You know them very well. From having fought them so long?"

He shrugged. "I know these two," he said. "You have to be careful you don't anthropomorphize, but offhand I'd say Spots is thoroughly depressed and worried. I don't know if that worries me more than Bigs being so happy, or not."

❖   ❖   ❖

Spots folded his ears. "Must you torture that thing?" he said to Hans, as the old man blew tentatively into his harmonica. "It screams well, but the pain to my ears is greater."

Off curled asleep around the canvass-wrapped tnuctipun module, Bigs's ears twitched in harmony. His hands and feet were twitching as well, hunting in his sleep, and an occasional happy *mreeowrr* trilled from his lips.

Hans shrugged and put it away, picking up his cards. "Don't signify," he said mildly. "You want to bet?"

"Sniff this group of public-transit tokens," Spots snarled, throwing down his hand. "I fold. Count me out of the game." He stalked off into the night, tail lashing.

"Ratcats don't have the patience for poker," Hans observed. "Bids?"

"I fold too," Jonah said. Tyra had dropped out a round before.

"Neither do youngsters," Hans observed, showing his hand; three sevens. He raked in the pot happily. "Could be we'll all be very rich, but I never turn down a krona."

Jonah made a wordless sound of agreement and looked over at the girl. She was sleeping, curled up against her saddle with one hand tucked beneath her cheek. He smiled and drew the blanket up around her shoulders . . .

"*Awake!*" Spots shouted, rushing back into the circle of firelight on all fours.

Jonah leaped. Tyra awoke and stretched out a hand for her rifle in its saddle-scabbard; Garm growled and raised his muzzle.

The kzin kicked his brother in the ribs and danced back from the reflexive snap. "*Awake*. Are you injecting sthondat blood? Get ready!"

He turned to the humans. "A dozen riding beasts approached; their riders dismounted and are coming this way, a half-kilometer. They will be within leaping distance in a few minutes."

Bigs awoke sluggishly, shaking his head and licking at his nose and whiskers. Spots efficiently stripped the beamer from a pack-saddle and tossed it to his brother before freeing his own weapon. Jonah checked his rifle; Tyra and Hans were ready.

"Careful," he said. "These might be the bandits—but they might not. We can't fight our way back to Neu Friborg through a hostile countryside."

Spots snorted. "Who would be pursuing us but the ones we fought, thirsty for blood and revenge?" he said. Bigs was growling, a hand resting on the module. Still, the smaller kzin licked his nose for greater sensitivity and stood stretched upright, sniffing open-mouthed.

"The wind favors us," he said after a moment. "And I do not recognize any individual scents. That does not mean these are not the ones we defeated—I had little time to pay close attention then." He sounded disappointed, thwarted in his longing to lose himself in combat and forget the decisions that had been oppressing him.

"Spread out and we'll see," Jonah said; it made no sense to outline themselves against their campfire. "No, leave the fire. If you put it out, they'd know we'd spotted them."

Not bandits, was his first thought, as he watched through his field glasses. The bandits had been in a mismatch of bits of military gear and outbacker clothes. These were in coarse cotton cloth and badly tanned leather, with wide-brimmed straw hats and blanket-like cloaks. Their weapons were a few ancient, beautifully-tended chemical hunting rifles, and each man carried a long curved knife, heavy enough to be useful chopping brushwood. *Tough looking bunch*, he thought, but not particularly menacing. They stopped a hundred or so yards out from the fire and called, a warning or hail. He could not follow their thick backcountry dialect, but

Hans and Tyra evidently could. They stood and called back, and Jonah relaxed.

"Act casual," Hans said as they all returned to the fire. "These people are deep outback. They've got peculiar ways." He frowned a little. "Don't think they'll like we've got kzin with us."

The men did stiffen and bristle when they saw the silent red-orange forms on the other side of the fire, but they removed their hats and squatted none the less, their hands away from their weapons. One peered across the embers of the fire at Tyra and smiled, nudging the others. That brought a chorus of delighted, crook-toothed grins; the kzinti controlled themselves with a visible effort.

"I passed through their village," Tyra explained.

"What do they want?" Jonah asked.

Now that fear was gone it was a nagging ache to be delayed. They *must* get to Neu Friborg before Early and his cohorts could think up something else. Jonah never doubted for a moment that the bandits had had Early's backing, doubtless through his Nipponjin friends. The ID cards proved that, the forgery was far too good for hill-thieves to have managed.

"Got to handle the formalities first," Hans said. "Go on, light up."

The outbackers were passing around their pouch of tobacco; Jonah clumsily rolled a cigarette and passed it to Tyra, who managed the business far more neatly, even one-handed. She poured cups of coffee and handed them around as Hans filled his pipe, lit it with a burning stick from the fire and passed that likewise; the kzinti were pointedly ignored, crouching back with their eyes shining as red as the coals. Time passed in ritual thanks, in inquires about their health and that of their horses and mules, talk of the dry weather . . .

Tyra leaned forward intently as the real story came

out. "They had a brush with our bandits," she said. "And—oh, Gott, no!"

Hans took up the story, listening intently; Jonah could catch no more than one word in three. "Sent some of their kids up-hill for safety. Ran into an ambush. Couple of men killed; they got the kids back, but they'd been hit with some sort of weapon they don't understand. The kids are alive and breathing, but they won't wake up."

Jonah's skin crawled. He relayed a few questions through the two Wunderlanders. "Neural disrupter," he said, when the villagers had answered. "Didn't know they had one—nasty thing, short-range but effective."

"They want—they want us to do something for them, heal the children," Tyra burst in. "What can we do?"

"Hmmm." Hans broke off to rummage through their medical kit. "Yep. That *might* work." He spoke to the headman of the strangers; they stood. "Wants us to come right away. That'd be better. Take a day or two to get to their settlement, two three days there."

Jonah opened his mouth to object—couldn't they call in to one of the lowland villages and get a doctor in by aircar?—and then shut his mouth again when Tyra looked at him. *Damn. Shame works where guilt wouldn't.*

Bigs felt no such objection; he shot to his feet, sputtering in the Imperative Mode of the Hero's Tongue, with his brother only half an expostulation behind. A dozen outbacker heads turned to the aliens like gun-turrets tracking, hands moving towards rifles and machetes. A sudden chill hit Jonah's stomach as he heard Bigs:

"We *will not* delay."

Even then, Jonah frowned in puzzlement. His command of the Hero's Tongue was excellent if colloquial, and he could have sworn that that had been in *Ultimate* Imperative Mode—which only the Riit, the family of the Patriarch, were entitled to use. Not that there was anything on Wunderland to stop Bigs using any grammatical constructions he pleased, but it was an unnatural thing for the big kzin to do. He was a traditionalist to a fault, that much had been clear for months. Spots stopped in mid-yowl to glance aside at him, confirming Jonah's hunch.

No matter. Both kzin were on the verge of fighting frenzy, and a very nasty little battle could break out at any second with a scream and leap. Garm backed up, bristling and barking hysterically; the kzinti ears twitched, and that was just the extra edge of hysteria that might set them off.

"*Shut* that damned dog up!" he barked. Tyra grabbed its collar and soothed it. "You two, you won't get extra speed by starting a battle now."

"What are the kittens of these feral omnivores to us?" Spots said, all his teeth showing. "You pledged to cooperate in this hunt with us, Jonah-human. And you were the one who said we risk failure with every minute of delay. Is the word of Man good, or is it not?"

A weight of meaning seemed to drop on that last phrase; Spots was watching him intently, not staring at the outbackers the way Bigs did. Jonah had a sudden leaden conviction that more rested on his decision than he could estimate.

"Look . . ." he began. Then an idea struck. "Tyra, these people, they're trustworthy?" An emphatic nod. "You and Hans are the ones with the medical training. You two go to the village; Spots and Bigs and I will take our . . . load on ahead. You can catch up—the outbackers will lend you a horse, surely, Hans."

Bigs' head jerked around to look at him, and his muzzle moved in the half-arcs of emphatic agreement. Spots brushed back his whiskers, as if confirming something to himself.

"That would be according to your oath," he said softly. "I apologize." Jonah was a little surprised; 'sorry' was something kzinti were reluctant to say, especially to other species.

The outbackers followed the exchange with wary eyes. Hans turned to them and spoke, then smiled at Jonah:

"As it turns out, young feller, they don't want our kzin anywhere near their place anyway. Just me and Fra Nordbo here are fine. We'll start right away, if that's all right with you. Sooner begun, sooner done."

Tyra rose. "Will you be all right?" she asked softly.

"We'll manage," Jonah replied.

"I do not have to account to you," Bigs said loftily.

"*Stop using that tense!*" Spots snapped in a hissing whisper, glancing ahead to where Jonah walked beside the lead mule. "Who contacted the Fanged God and promoted you to royalty, Big-son of Chotrz-Shaa?"

"I am self-promoted," Bigs replied softly, but with no particular effort to keep his voice down. "And the Fanged God fights by my side. How else would the two monkeys remove themselves? We will take the northeastern path, abandoning all but the beast necessary to carry the capsule. Alone, we will make better time. There is a kzin settlement at Arhus-on-Donau. We will seek shelter there. We will *build* a means to get off-planet, or buy it—these monkeys will do anything for money."

"You are self-befuddled!" Spots said. "*Fool*. What will Jonah-human say to this?"

"It is what Durvash says that is important," Bigs said, resting his hand on the module. "He becomes clearer all the time."

Spots recoiled. "Now you, oh *patriarchal* warrior, take orders like a slave from that little horror?"

Bigs bristled, suddenly swelling up and hulking over

his smaller sibling in dominance-display. Spots forced himself to match it, letting his claws slide free.

"At least it is a carnivore, you . . . you *submitter-to-omnivores*," Bigs grated. "Your breath stinks of grass!"

Spots's mouth gaped at the horrendous insult. All their lives they had sparred and tussled for dominance, insulting each other in the friendly fashion of non-serious rivals. That was a blood libel.

"Is your oath nothing to you?" he grated.

"Oh, I will allow the monkey to fight me . . . bare-handed," Bigs said, with a sly, horrible amusement in the twitch of his ears and brows. "That fulfills the oath." He paused for effect. "What of *your* blood-obligation to the Patriarchy and the Heroic Race, Spots-Son of Chotrz-Shaa?"

Abruptly, Spots collapsed into a fur-flattened, droop-eared, limp-tailed puddle of misery. "I know," he muttered. "I am ripped in half. If you have forgotten your honor in madness, I have not. We are the last of the line of Chotrz-Shaa. Two lives and the life of our House we owe these monkeys. Your life to Jonah-human. Mine to a female! Yet we owe blood and honor to the Patriarch."

Bigs smirked, and Spots flared into a gape-jawed scream of rage: "*Stop whacking at my tail, fatherless sthondat-sucker!*"

He could see Jonah turning, alarmed at the sound, and he forced calm on himself with an effort greater than he had thought was in him.

"No killing by stealth," he finished, dropping into the Menacing Tense. "Or you die."

Bigs smirked again, and continued in the infuriating inflections of a Patriarch: "You will conspire with a monkey against your own sibling?"

"No. But I will not allow you to kill him."

A sneer, just showing the ends of the dagger incisor-fangs. "He is helpless as a kit at night."

"I will be watching."

"How long can you go without sleep, *brother*? I will feast on his liver yet." Bigs stalked off after the train of mules. As he came level with the last his hand rested on its pannier, and Spots could hear the edge of a whisper.

My tail is cold, he thought in panic. *What can I do? What can I do?*

Three nights later Spots watched desperately as Jonah prepared for sleep, tilting his broad-brimmed hat forward over his eyes; it was a bright night, alive with the shooting stars so common on Wunderland and with Beta Centauri overhead near the moon. The human gave him a puzzled look as he settled in, and then his breathing grew slow and steady, his heartbeat sounded like an ancient Conundrum Priest drum to Spots's straining ears. A heavy drum, regular, soothing. Heavy as his eyelids, so soothing as they dropped across dry and aching eyes, so pleasant. Making the ground soft tike piled cushions, like piled cushions in the palazzo when he was young, and his father was crooning:

"Brave little orange kzin
Brave little spotted kzin,
Turn to the din
And if it makes you smile,
Leap
But if it is nothing at all
Really nothing at all
You may turn-in;
And droop your eyes while
You sleep."

Spots sighed and turned, drifting, content. Then shot half-erect, trembling, his fur laid tension-flat on the bones of face and body, tail out and rigid.

Bigs was halfway from his lair of blankets to Jonah, moving with ghost-lightness. Moonlight and Betalight glinted on the heavy blade of the wtsai in his hand. He caught his brother's eye and shrugged with fur and tail, grinned insolence, flared his nostrils.

I scent that which you do not. Slowly, insultingly, he sauntered back to his blankets, laid himself down. Then he yawned, a pink-and-white, curl-your-tongue yawn of drowsy contentment, stretching every limb separately and grooming a little. He circled, finding exactly the right position, and curled up with tail over nose. One eye remained open for a second, glinting at Spots from beneath the tufted eyebrow.

You were lucky. But I only have to be lucky once.

Spots whimpered, tongue dangling as he panted with envy and despair.

"Are you all right?"

Spots blinked. *What am I doing lying on the ground?* he thought.

The mule had stopped, pulling at the brushes nearby with a dry tearing sound as leathery leaves parted. One limb at a time, the kzin pulled himself up. Heavy, heavy, more heavy than the battle-practice in the old days, when their Sire worked them to exhaustion under kzin-normal gravity in the exercise room of the palace. Something seemed to hold his hands to the dry packed soil, and pains shot up his back as he stood and squinted into the bright daylight. He ran his fingers through the tangled mass of his mane, and hanks and knots of hair came loose, the furnace wind snatched it from him and scattered the long orange hairs on the air, on the dirt, on the scrubby bushes and sparse grass. He stood, dully staring after them.

"Are you all *right*?" Jonah asked again. Then he recoiled hastily from the vicious snap that nearly ripped open his arm. "If that's the way you want it," he said, tight-lipped, and went back to the lead mule.

Bigs's ears smirked as he came by, his hand on the capsule. He never left it, now. "Soon we will camp for the night," he jeered. "Won't it be good to sleep?" More seriously: "It will be for the best, brother."

"I have no brother," Spots rasped, and stumbled forward to take the reins of his mule.

Even the scream hardly woke Spots. His eyes were crusted and blurred even when he opened them. The savage discord of metal on metal jarred him to some semblance of consciousness, and the scent of hot fresh-shed blood. He stumbled erect, mumbling, and stepped forward. The raw-scraped tip of his tail fell across the white ash crust that covered the embers of the fire, and he shot half a dozen meters into the air, screeching.

When he came down, he could see. Bigs's first leap had failed, and Jonah had gotten out of his blankets and erect. Now the two were circling; Jonah had a four-furrowed row of deep scratches across his chest, and the very tip of Bigs's tail was missing. The wtsai gleamed in the kzin's hand, and Jonah had his arm-long cutter-bar whistling in a figure-eight between them. Totally focused, Bigs lunged forward. Density-enhanced steel shrieked against the serrated edges of the bar and Bigs danced back, smooth and fast. There was a ragged notch in the blade of his honor knife, and his snarl grew more shrill. For a moment Spots thought desperately that his brother would walk the narrow path of honor, weapon against weapon.

"Get back," Bigs flung over his shoulder, reaching for the strakkaker at his waist.

The world stood still for Spots. *I owe my life to Jonah-human. I owe my life to the Patriarch. This is my brother. That is my—* There was no more time for thought.

Spots screamed and leaped. *"No!"* he howled. His leap carried him onto the larger kzin's back.

There was nothing wrong with Bigs's reflexes. Even as Spots fastened on to him with all sixteen claws he ducked his head between his shoulders to avoid the killing bite to the back of the neck and threw himself backward, stabbing with reversed wtsai. The blade scored along Spots's massive ribcage, but there was no soft unarmored midsection to a kzin body. He twisted to lock the arm as they rolled, accepting the savage battering and the pain as they rolled across the campfire, fangs probing deeper and deeper through fur ruff and into the huge muscles of Bigs's neck. Groping for the vulnerable spine, to drive a spike into the nerve.

Jonah stepped forward, cutter bar raised to strike in a chop that would have cut through Bigs's torso to the hearts. To the hormone-speeded reflexes of the battling kzinti, the movement might as well have been in slow motion. A full-armed swipe of Bigs's free hand caught him across face and neck and shoulder, sending him spinning limp to the ground in a shower of flesh. In a tuck-and-roll that was a continuation of the same movement Bigs levered his brother off his back and sent him a dozen meters away. They screamed together and met in a flowing curve of both their leaps, mouths open in the killing gape, hands and feet ripping and tearing and stabbing. Rolling over and over in a blurred mass of orange fur, blood, distended eyes, flashing steel and gleaming inch-long fangs.

Spots's grip on his brother's knife-wrist weakened, the claw-grip on his throat choking him until his eyes bulged almost out of their deep-set sockets. Stronger and fresher, the muscles of the short thick arm straining against his were as irresistible as a machine. Pain shot through his hand as his thumb popped out of its socket, and then something cold and very hot at the same time lanced into his body. Gray swam before his eyes as vision narrowed down to the killgrin of his brother's face, then winked out.

Sleep, he told himself. *You fought to the death.*

Victory was cold and pain and nausea, after the first liver-jolting flash of adrenaline. Bigs staggered away, away from the body that lay at his feet with blood bubbling on its chest-fur, blood in mouth and nose and eyes where his teeth had savaged it. He threw away the broken hilt of his wtsai and gave a sobbing shriek of grief and triumph at the risen moon.

"I have killed my brother. *Howl for God!*" His brother, guardian of his back in the tussles of childhood. Last son of Chotrz-Shaa beside himself.

"Not now," the voice whispered in his ears. "You have work to do. Gather the equipment. Bury the bodies. We must move."

Bigs shook his head as if shaking off water, clawing at his own ear. The little implant seemed impossible to dislodge; sometimes these days in evil dreams he felt that it was growing tendrils into his brain from his ear. Pain shot through his head at the thought.

"Nonsense. Now, get to work."

Howling again, Bigs beat fists on the capsule until the mule reared and kicked and nearly escaped. Then he seized the halter and dragged it after him into the night. He must run, like Warlord Chmee, run from his guilt. Had not Chmee broken an oath for ultimate power? He must *run*.

"Stop, you brainless savage! Obey!" The pain again, but Bigs ignored it.

"I did it for the Heroic Race!" he screamed into the night. "None shall command us. No more monkey arrogance. *I did it for you, my brother!*" His grief rose shrill, a huge sound that daunted even the *advokats* pack that had come to prowl at the edge of sight, attracted by the blood. Dragging the mule behind him, Large-Son of Chotrz-Shaa ran into the darkness.

The pain in his head was continuous now. Sometimes he felt as if his brain were being dragged out, and he found himself walking in a circle to the left, head bent to his shoulder. When it lessened, he was conscious of the voice again. It was daylight, but he was uncertain of the day. They were over the pass, and the ground on either side was covered in long grass, with patches of trees on the higher slopes. The cool damp scent from the lowlands spread out below him was like a benediction in his nostrils; there was no sight of Man, not even of his herdbeasts.

"Very well," Durvash said. "We will proceed straight. That pack of scavengers probably finished them off in any case. No time may be spared to go back, in any case."

Bigs mumbled something. He felt he should resent the tone; did the ancient revenant not know he was speaking to a Conquest Hero? Soon to be the greatest of all Conquest Heroes? Yet the emotion was far away, as if muffled behind a thick layer of sherrek fur. Why was his mind wandering so? Great chunks of time seemed to be missing, and sometimes his vision would blur like a badly adjusted holoscreen. It kept the grief at bay, though. With that he began to weep, an *eeeuuureuee* sound.

"My brother fought for me when the older kits pulled my nose," he mumbled to himself. "I grew bigger, but he never quarreled with me." Not enough to really draw blood. "We shared our first kzinrett." An under-the-grass transaction with a warrior needing quick cash to cover a gambling debt. "We—"

"Silence."

"Urr-urrr—" Bigs's throat would not work any more, and he found he had lost interest in speaking.

✧   ✧   ✧

Well, now I know how the implant will work on these kzin, Durvash thought sourly. *Badly.* It had been designed to use on thrint and thrintun slave species, of course, with multiband capacity. Kzinti seemed very resistant to pain-center stimulus, and on a strange species the control of volitional routines was impossibly coarse.

Report, he thought/ordered the autodoc system. Impatiently, he ran through the diagnostic and came to the conclusion. *Prepare to decant me,* he told it. Warnings flashed, but he overrode. The autodoc would be priceless as part of his breeding program, since it was capable of acting as an artificial womb, but he must not run down the base supplies of organic molecules for recombinant synthesis before he was sure of obtaining more. The local biochemistry was unlikely to have all a tnuctipun metabolism required.

Besides, I am hungry and mad to see the sky, to smell fresh air again. If he was to be reborn into this new world, let his fangs and tongue take seizin of it.

"I will emerge," he said to the kzin. It stood apathetic, eyes dull; he ordered the machine to jolt its pleasure centers and relax forebrain restriction, and awareness returned to the big golden eyes. "Where are we?"

"Near . . . hrreeawho, how did we come here so fast? Where is . . . we are near Neu Friborg, I think. We are there, I think."

It lifted the module to the dirt and sank exhausted to the ground. Fluid began to cycle out of Durvash's lungs, and he wrapped his lips against the pain.

• CHAPTER EIGHTEEN

Something was biting his tail.

Spots groaned and tried to open his eyes, but they were gummed together. The biting stopped, and water fell across his face. He heard shouting. Feebly, he scrubbed at his eyes with a wrist, and blinked back to wakefulness. An *advokat* slinked in the middle distance, huge jaws working, matted pelt stinking of carrion.

Jonah-human was looking down at him, from a safe distance, canteen in hand. Matted blood covered one side of his face, and fresh blood glistened on clumsy bandages around his neck and one arm. They glanced aside from each other's eyes, and the human stepped forward and sank down by the kzin's side.

"Got to stop the bleeding," he rasped. "Here, drink."

Spots lapped water from his cupped palm, and then seized the canteen to guzzle with his thin lips wrapped awkwardly around the spout. He coughed and felt tearing pain in his chest; water spurted out of his mouth. Looking down, he could see the bright gleam of steel among the tangled red mass of his flank.

"It is not as bad as it looks," he wheezed, after taking a careful deep breath. "See, the steel must have turned aside and snapped on the ribs—thanks to your cutter bar, which weakened it. My lungs are not pierced, nor my intestines." He licked at his nostrils and sniffed again. "I would smell that."

"Could be stuff inside hanging on by a thread," Jonah said worriedly.

"I will survive while you pursue the oath-breaker," Spots said grimly. Then the voice broke into a howl of woe.

"Not until we get you to help. This *would* happen while Hans and Tyra are away with the medkit . . . that'll be the closest place. You can lean on one of the mules, I can catch them. I think."

My sibling attached him dishonorably, yet he will forego revenge to save my life, Spots thought. *I am ashamed.*

"First," he said aloud, "you'll have to get this out of me."

Jonah blanched as he looked down at the knifeblade. The stub of it moved with every breath.

"We really *should* get under way," Tyra urged, with a sigh.

"Yep. Figure we should."

Hans smiled beatifically, and leaned back in the hammock. His was strung between two orange trees, and a few blossoms had fallen across his grizzled face. He brushed them aside and took another sip of the drink in his hollowed-out pineapple. There was rum in it, and cherries and cream and a few other things—passionfruit, for example—and it helped to make the warmth quite tolerable. So did the tinkling stream which flowed down the narrow valley under the overhanging cliff, and the shade of the palm trees. Hans Shwartz had been a grown man when the kzinti came; he was into his second century now, and even with good medical care your bones

appreciated the warmth after so much hard work. The
air buzzed with bees, scented with flowers.

"Thank you, sweetling," he said, as a girl handed him
a platter of fried chicken; it had fresh bread on the side,
and a little woven bowl of hot sauce for dipping. The
girl smiled at him, teeth and green eyes and blond hair
all bright against her tanned skin. Someone who looked
like her twin sister was cutting open a watermelon for
them. Not far away in a paddock grazed six horses, three
for him and three for Tyra, and they had been turning
down gifts of pigs and sheep and household tools for a
solid day now.

"These are sweet people," Tyra said, as the girl handed
her a plate as well.

"No argument," Hans said, gesturing with a drumstick.
The batter on it was cornmeal, delicately spiced; he bit
into the hot fragrant meat with appreciation. "They need
some help, though. Someone to guide them through
the next few years, getting back into contact with things.
Otherwise they'll be taken advantage of."

"True enough," Tyra said, more somberly. "I was
surprised at you, the way you diagnosed those children
and managed the treatment." Her young eyes were
guileless, but shrewd. "What *did* you do before the
conquest, Freeman Shwartz?"

"This and that, this and that," Hans said, repelling
her curiosity with mild firmness. The youngsters were
all up and about, although they would need further
therapy. Unfortunately, that would cost; it would be some
time before Wunderland could afford planetary health
insurance again.

"And we *should* get going; I'm worried about Jona—
about Freeman Matthieson, alone with those kzin."

Hans suppressed a smile. His tolerant amusement
turned to concern as the headman of the village dashed
up, sweating, his eyes wide.

"Your friend," he gasped out. "Your young friend and one of the accursed ratcats—they are here. They are hurt!"

Hans tossed his plate and drink aside, yelling for his medkit as he landed running down the pathway. Tyra was ahead of him, her long slim legs flashing through the borrowed sarong.

"Finagle, there is a heaven after all," Jonah murmured. The cool cloth sponged at his face and neck as he looked up through matted lashes at Tyra's face. Sheer relief made him limp for long moments, his head lolling in her lap. *A man could get used to this*, he thought.

Then: "Spots!"

"He's all right," Tyra said. "In better shape than you, actually. The locals were a bit leery of having him in the village, but they put up a shelter for him and Hans has been working on him."

"Speak of *der teufel*," Hans said, ducking through the doorway of bamboo sections on string. "Aren't you sitting pretty, young feller," he added. Tyra blushed slightly and set Jonah's head back on the pillow.

"Your furry friend is fine, as far as I can tell," the old man went on. "Growling and muttering about that brother of his."

"Who nearly killed both of us," Jonah said grimly.

He felt at the side of his face; the swellings were gone, and his fingers slid over the slickness of spray-skin. From the slightly distant feel from within, he was on painblockers, but not too heavily.

"He *would* have killed me, if Spots hadn't jumped him." Jonah shook his head. "I'm surprised. Usually, if a kzin swears a formal oath, they'll follow it come core-collapse or memory dump; look at the way Spots stood up for me. I can see Bigs challenging me, but to try and kill me in my sleep—"

"Temptation can do funny things to a mind, human or non," Hans said shrewdly. "Seem to remember one feller who wouldn't believe there was a fuzzball under a rock, on account of temptation."

Jonah flushed, conscious of Tyra's curiosity. "When will I be ready to ride?" he said.

"Not for a week at least," Tyra said firmly.

Hans tugged at his whiskers. "Funny you should ask; Spots said the same thing, more or less." His button blue eyes appraised the younger man. "Neither of you was infected." Wunderland bacteria were not much of a threat to humans; the native biochemistry lacked some elements essential to Terrestrial life, and vice versa. "He's healing real fast, seems to be natural for him. You're dehydrated, and those cuts shouldn't be put under much strain, sprayskin or no. Say three days, minimum."

"One," Jonah said grimly. He held up a hand at Tyra, stopping her before the words left her lips. "It's not just what we—Montferrat—could do with the knowledge. It's what that tnuctipun could do, once it's out of its bottle. I think we badly underestimated it. I believe it's controlling Bigs, somehow. Control, hypnosis. Maybe what the Thrintun do for all I know. That thing is a deadly danger every instant it's free, never mind what the government or the ARM would do with it. I think it would be better if the ARM *does* get it. Maybe they can dispose of it."

Hans nodded. "Can't say as I like it, but you're talking sense," he said.

Slowly, reluctantly, Tyra nodded too. "I might have expected boldness like that from you," she murmured.

"Tanj. It's common sense."

"Which is not common."

Bigs shook his head again, trying to clear the stuffed-wool feeling. It refused to go away, even though he was thinking more clearly again. More calmly, at least. The mule-beast brayed in his ear, then shied violently when he threatened its nose with outstretched claws.

Stupid beast, he thought with a snarl, then exerted all his strength to haul it down again and hold it back; they were both very thirsty, but he could not let it run to the little watercourse ahead. *It is does not even have enough brains to obey through fear.* The ruined manor-house was half a kilometer ahead, and Neu Friborg beyond that. He would rest for the day in the ruins, and help Durvash when he emerged from the autodoc. Then he would pass the town in the dark and walk down the trail to Munchen until he could buy a ride on a vehicle.

"And abandon this stinking, stupid mule-beast," he muttered to himself.

With grim patience he led it down the steep clay bank to the slow-moving creek and moved upstream, throwing himself down to lap. It was the ground-scent that alerted him, since the wind was in his face. That and the clatter of pebbles as feet walked the bank behind him. He was up and turning in a flash, but his feet and hands were further away than they should have been, and he shook his head fretfully again. *Spots. I smell Spots. Stand by me, brother. Bare is a back without brother to guard it.* Spots was dead, he remembered, and forced his fur to bottle out.

Four humans, all armed but scruffy and hungry-looking, their ribs standing out. The leader-beast a taller one with heavy facial pelt and the remains of a swollen belly. Bigs grinned and waited.

"Hey, what's a ratcat doing here outback?" the leader asked. The voice had a haunting familiarity, except that the stuffing in his head got in the way.

"Nice mule," one of the others said, examining the beast. It snapped at him, and he slapped its nose down with an experienced hand. "Hey, good saddle too."

Bigs snarled. "Away from my possessions, monkeys," he said, backing toward the animal and retreating slightly to keep all the humans in his field of vision. They were ambling forward, not seeming to spread out deliberately but edging around behind him all the same. His head swiveled.

"Hey, that's not polite!" the big manbeast said, grinning insolently. "You shouldn't call us monkeys no more, on account of we kick your hairy asses."

Bigs felt fury build within him and his tail stiffen, then inexplicably drain away. *I must dominate them*, he told himself.

"We just poor bush-country men. You got any money? That's a fine strakkaker you got, and a nice beamer. Maybe I recognize the beamer—maybe we had one like it a while ago, before my luck got bad?" The leader's face convulsed. *"Maybe Ed Gruedermann should boot some head, hey?"*

"Get back!" Bigs said. The monkeys continued their slinking, sidling advance.

His hand blurred to the strakkaker, and he pivoted to spray the monkey nearest Durvash, he would turn and cut them all down. The weapon clicked and crackled—there was sand in the muzzle! He crouched to leap, but something very cold flashed across the small of his back. Something huge, like his father's hand, slapped him across the left side of his head, and he was falling. Falling for a very long time. Then he was lying, and he hurt very much, but his head seemed clear.

"Forgive me, brother," he whispered. Soft hands reached down out of time to lift and hold him, and a tongue washed his ears. A voice crooned wordlessly. He closed his eyes, and welcomed the long fall into night.

"Hey, Ed—look at that!"

Ed Gruederman glanced over to where a rifle muzzle

prodded the huge wound on the dead kzin's head, right where his left ear would have been. Silvery threads were lifting out of the blood and grey matter, almost invisibly thin, twisting and questing in the light. He slid his cleaned machete back into the sheath behind his right hip and walked over to the mule.

"Get back from that, you scheissekopf," he called to the man by their victim. *Stupid ratcat, not to think we had a sniper ready.* "That's some kzin shit, it may be catching, you know, like a fungus."

The bandit jumped back and leveled his rifle, firing an entire cassette into the dead carnivore. When it clicked empty the torso had been cut in half, but the tendrils still waved slowly.

"Watch it, fool, we're close to town—you want them to hear us and call the mounted police?" Then: "Yazus Kristus!"

They all crowded around, until he beat them back with his hat. "Gold," he said reverentially, lifting one of the plastic sacks from that side of the packsaddle.

They all recognized it, of course. Nobody could be in their line of work in the Jotuns and not recognize gold dust; for one thing, nothing else was that heavy for its size. They counted the bags, running their hands over them until their leader lashed the tarpaulin back.

"Ten, fifteen thousand krona," one muttered. "Oh, the verguuz and bitches I can buy with this."

"Buy with your share, if Ed Gruedermann can keep your shitty head on your sisterfucking shoulders that long," their leader replied. "Back! There's an assessor's office in Neu Friborg. We'll stop there and get krona and sell the mule, and then head for Munchen or Arhus-on-Donau, the Jotuns is no place for an honest man these days—too many police. Look at them, letting ratcats wander around attacking humans."

That brought grins and laughter. "What's this, boss?"

one asked, lifting the smooth featureless egg that balanced the mule's load.

It shifted in his arms, and he dropped it with a cry of surprise. That turned to horror as it split open, and a spindly-limbed creature rose shakily from the twin halves; it was spider thin, blue-black and rubbery with three crimson eyes and a mouthful of teeth edged like a saw.

"Scheisse!" the bandit screamed. The mobile lips moved, perhaps in the beginning of *wait*.

The motion never had time to complete itself. A dozen rounds tore the little creature to shreds, until Gruedermann shouted the bandits into sense—they were in more danger from each other's weapons than from whatever-it-was. Even then three of them hacked it into unrecognizable bits with their machetes. Their fear turned to terror as the twin halves of the egg began to glow and collapse on themselves.

"We get out of here," Gruedermann said. "The *advokats* will take care of the bodies." There were always a pack of them around a human settlement, waiting for garbage to scavenge, impossible to exterminate. "Come on. Money is waiting."

"Not more than an hour or so," Jonah said, with an odd sense of anticlimax. *And yes*, he thought. *Sadness*. The mangled remains of the tnuctipun were pathetically fragile in the bright light of Alpha Centauri. *To come so far, so long, for this. There Ain't No Justice.*

Tyra shied a stone at a lurking *advokat* that lingered, torn between greed and cowardice. It yelped and ran back a few paces; tears streaked her face.

"Come look at this!" Hans said sharply. He reached down with a stick and turned the dead kzin's head to one side. Not much of the soft tissue was left after the *advokat* pack, but for some reason they had avoided the shattered bone.

Spots began a snarl of anger, then stopped as he saw what was revealed. The others stood beside him, watching the silver tendrils move in their slow weaving. Hans probed with the stick; several of the threads lashed towards it and clung for a moment. A button-sized piece of the same material was embedded in the shattered remains of Bigs's inner ear.

"Stand back," Spots said, unslinging his beamer.

None of the others quarreled with that; they crowded back with the gaping outbackers as the kzin stood on the edge of the creekbank and fanned a low-set beam across the bodies until nothing was left but calcinated ash. The tendrils of the device in his brother's brain shriveled in the heat, and the central button exploded with a small *fumf* of released pressure. Spots kept up the fire until the wet clay was baked to stoneware, then threw the exhausted weapon aside.

"That . . . *thing* explains a good deal," Jonah said; Tyra nodded, reached out an hand and then withdrew it.

"I am owed a debt of vengeance by a race three billion years dead," Spots said, in a voice that might have been of equal age. "How shall I requite it?"

"There's a debt of vengeance only about three hours old," Hans said sharply. "Those tracks are heading for Neu Friborg."

"Let's do it then," Jonah said grimly. "Let's *go*."

"Hey, it's a good mule," Ed Gruedermann said. "But we don't need it any more—we had good luck up in the mountains."

His men were on their best behavior; grinning like idiots with their hats clasped to their chests, and keeping their mouths silent the way he had told them. Gruedermann felt a swelling of pride at their discipline; he'd had to boot plenty of head to get them so well-behaved. A big crowd had gathered around the mule with the unbalanced load as the four of them led it into town. Well, nothing ever happened in little arse-pimple outback towns like this, even if it did have a weekly run down to the lowlands. Fine well-set men like themselves were an event. He caught the eye of a young woman, scowling when she looked away.

"This the assessor's office?" he said. It should be, the best building in the town and the only one of prewar rockmelt construction.

"Ja."

A young girl of ten or so had slid under the mule, examining the girth and then running a hand down the neck. She seemed interested in the bar-code brand; not many of those out in the hills, he guessed. Then she ran up the stairs into the building.

"How long did you say you'd been up in the Jotuns?" a man said, his tone friendly.

The crowd was denser now; Gruederman felt a little nervous, after so long in the bundu, but he kept his smile broad, even when he felt a plucking at his belt. Nothing there for a pickpocket to get, but in a few hours he'd be *rich*. With luck, he might be able to shed the others before he got to Munchen and cashed the assessor's draft. Pickings were slim in the Jotuns these days. From what he heard, Munchen was a wide-open town with plenty of opportunities for a man with a little ready capital and not too many foolish scruples.

A woman in a good suit came down the steps with the little girl and touched a reader to the mule's neck.

"That's the one," she said quietly.

Danger prickled at Gruedermann's spine. He shouted and leaped back, reaching for his machete. It was gone, hands gripped him, the honed point of his own weapon pricked behind his ear. He rolled his eyes wildly. All his men were taken, only one had unslung his weapon and it was wrestled away before he could do more than fire a round into the air. The crowd pushed in with a guttural animal snarl.

"Kill the bandits!" someone shouted.

The snarl rose, then died as the woman on the steps shouted and held up her hands:

"This is a civilized town, under law," she said firmly. "Put them in the pen—tie them, and two of you watch each of them. We'll call the police patrol back, they can't have gone far."

"Take your hands off me!" Gruedermann screamed, as rawhide thongs lashed his wrists behind his back and a hundred hands pushed him through the welded steel bars of the livestock pen. "You can't do this to me!" He spat through the bars, snapping his teeth at an unwary hand and hanging on until a stick broke his nose. "Motherfuckers! Kzinshit eaters!"

He screamed and spat through the strong steel until the square emptied.

"What do we do now, boss?" one of the men asked, from his slumped position on the floor of the cage.

"We fuckin' *die*," Gruedermann shouted, kicking him in the head. His skull bounced back against the metal; it rang, and the bandit fell senseless.

Neu Friborg seemed deserted in the early evening gloaming, as Jonah and his party rode down the rutted main street. He stood in the saddle—painfully, since riding was not something a singleship pilot really had to study much—and craned his neck about. He could hear music, a slow mournful march, coming from the sidestreet ahead, down by the church.

A little ahead of the riders, Spots lifted his head and sniffed. "They are there," he said flatly. "Also a large crowd of monke—of humans. Many armed. They do not smell of fear, most of them; only the ones we hunt."

"Odd," Jonah said.

He swung down from the saddle. *Finagle, but that beast was trying to saw me in half from the crotch up*, he thought. It had been downright embarrassing in front of Tyra, who seemed to have been born in the saddle from the way she managed it. She'd said something, about how a spacer must know more *real* skills than riding, though . . . *quite a woman*.

"Cautious but polite," Jonah said, leading the way. "Remember that." For Spots' benefit; the kzin seemed to be in a fey mood, bloodthirsty as usual but relieved. Perhaps that his brother hadn't broken an oath entirely under his own power, although Jonah suspected the tall kzin had been a willing victim at the start. The temptation was simply too great. *There are times when I think Early is right*, he mused. *But they never last.*

The little laneway opened out into a churchyard, and a field beyond that; the crowd stood in an arc about the outer wall of the graveyard. There, outside the circle of consecrated ground, four men were digging graves. A double file of armed men and women faced them, with Provisional Gendarmerie brassards. Seeing the genuine article, Jonah wondered how he could have been taken in by the bandits, even for a moment. He also decided that the mounted police were decidedly more frightening than the freelance killers had ever been. Beside him, Tyra checked for a moment at the sight of the tall crop-haired blond officer who led the firing party.

Jonah scanned the slab-sided *Herrenmann* face, and reluctantly conceded the family resemblance. *If you subtract all the humor and half the brains*, he decided. Aloud, in a whisper: "Your brother?"

"Ib," she confirmed.

One of the digging men swung his shovel too enthusiastically, and a load of dirt ended up in the middle grave. The man there climbed out and leaned over to swat the culprit with his hat, cursing with imaginative obscenity. Hans shaped a soundless whistle.

"Seems the Provisionals got in before us," he said. "Can't say as I'm sorry."

"Neither am I," Jonah said.

"*I* am," Spots grinned.

The bandits stood in front of the graves they had dug. The rifles of the squad came up and Ib Nordbo's hand swung down with a blunt finality.

Whack. The bodies fell backward, and dust spurted up from the adobe wall of the churchyard behind. A sighing murmur went over the watching townsfolk, and they began to disperse. The Gendarmerie officer cleaved through them like a walking ramrod, marching up to the little party of pursuers.

"So," he said, with a little inclination of his head. "Sister."

"Brother," she replied, standing a little closer to Jonah. Ib's pale brows rose.

"This is most irregular," he said, and turned to Jonah, ignoring the kzin and Hans as an obvious commoner. "You are the owner of the stolen mule and gold?"

"We are," Jonah said with a nod.

"You understand, everything must be impounded pending final adjudication," he said crisply. "Proper reports must be filed with the relevant—why are you laughing?"

"You wouldn't understand," Jonah wheezed. Beside him, Tyra fought hiccups, and Hans's face vanished into a nest of wrinkles. Even Spots flapped his ears, although his teeth still showed a little as he watched the work-crew shovel the dirt in on the dead bandits.

"Ah, life," Jonah said at last; twin red spots of anger stood out on the young policeman's cheeks. "Tanj. And now, we'd like a line to Herrenmann Claude Montferrat-Palme, and transport to Munchen—*if* you please, Herrenmannn Leutnant Nordbo."

"Except for me," Hans said, turning his horse's head. He leaned down to shake hands. "Goin' back. These people, they need me. You know where to reach me— always more fried chicken and rum for visitors!"

Jonah began to laugh again as the old man touched a heel to his horse and the outbackers fell in behind him.

"One happy ending at least," he said.

"Oh, perhaps more," Tyra said.

"Perhaps," Spots murmured.

• CHAPTER NINETEEN

Buford Early's laughter rolled across the broad veranda of the Montferrat-Palme manor. Evening had fallen, purple and dusky across the formal gardens, still with a trace of crimson on the terraced vineyards and coffee fields in the hills beyond. The ARM general leaned back in his chair, puffing at his cigar until it was a red comet in the darkness. The others looked at him silently; Montferrat calm and sardonic as always, Jonah stony-faced, Tyra Nordbo openly hostile. Only Harold Yarthkin and his wife seemed to be amused as well, and they were not so closely involved in this matter. With the human-style food out of the way Spots had joined them, curled in one of the big wicker chairs with saucers of Jersey cream and cognac, still licking his whiskers at the memory of the live zianya that had somehow, miraculously, been found for him.

"Glad you're happy," Harold said sardonically, pouring himself a glass of verguuz and clipping the end off a cigar.

"Why shouldn't I be?" Early said. "An excellent dinner—it always is, here, Herrenmann Montferrat-Palme—"

"Please, Claude."

"—Claude. And fascinating table talk, also as usual. Politics aside, I enjoy the company here more than I have on Earth for a long, long time. But you said you had something to negotiate! It seems to me you've wound this affair up very neatly, and just as I would have wanted. All the evidence buried or gone, the bandits conveniently dead, and nothing of the tnuctipun but rumors. You might," he added to Jonah, "consider writing this up as a holo script. It'd make a good one."

"Not my field," the ex-pilot said with a tight smile.

"You're forgetting something, my dear fellow," Montferrat said with wholehearted enjoyment. "You know the *approximate* location of the tnuctipun spaceship. We know the *exact* location, and as you love to point out, you don't believe in swift direct action. We can get to it before you can—in fact, we just *might* have secured and moved it already. In which case you could look forever, it's a big planet. Treasure-trove law is clearly on our side too, for what that's worth. We could decipher some of those secrets you're so afraid of, and send them off—to We Made It and Jinx, for example. Think of the joy you'd have trying to suppress it *there*."

"No joy at all," Early sighed, taking the cigar out of his mouth and concentrating on the tip. "I don't suppose an appeal to your sense of responsibility for interstellar stability . . . no. You *might* try not to be so gleeful," he went on. "What terms did you have in mind?"

"Well, my young friends here—" Montferrat nodded at Jonah, Tyra and the kzin "—and their rather older friend back in the outback, have all gone to a great deal of trouble and expense. I think they should be compensated. To about the extent of a hundred thousand krona each, after tax."

"Agreed," Early said, sounding slightly surprised. "What's the *real* price?"

"Well, in addition, you might get the blacklisting on Jonah removed—and have him and Fra Nordbo given security clearance for interstellar travel."

Tyra's face lit up with an inner glow at the ARM general's nod.

"And?" he said with heavy patience, sipping at his Cognac.

"And you go home. Or to another star system, but you get out of Alpha Centauri."

Early laughed again, more softly, and set the snifter down. "I hope you don't think I'm the only agent the . . . ARM has?" he said.

Jonah cut in: "No. But you're the smartest—or if you're not, we're hopeless anyway. It's a start."

"It will win me time, which I will use," Montferrat added.

Early sat in silence, puffing occasionally, while the sun set finally; the stars came out, and a quarter moon, undimmed by Beta Centauri. A flash of shooting stars lit up the night, ghostly soft lightning across the hills and the faces of humans and the kzin.

"More time than you might expect," he said. "Bureaucracies tend to get slower as they age, and mine . . ." More silence. "Agreed," he said. "It's time for me to move on, anyway. I'm getting too well known here. Lack of discretion was always my besetting sin. There's still the war—we have to organize the ex-kzin slave worlds we're taking as reparations—and doubtless other work will be found for me. *Ich deinst*, as they say." He looked over at Montferrat. "Checkmate—for now," he said, rising and extending his hand.

"For now," Montferrat agreed. "Harold here to hold the stakes?"

"Agreed; we can settle the details at our leisure." He bowed to the ladies, an archaic gesture he might have picked up on Wunderland. Or not, if he was what they suspected. "And now, I won't put a damper on your victory celebrations."

He strolled like a conqueror out to the waiting aircar, the stub of his cigar a comet against the night as he threw it away and climbed through the gullwing door. The craft lifted and turned north and west, heading for Munchen, an outline covering a moving patch of stars.

"I doubt he's going to accept defeat gracefully," Jonah said, sipping moodily at his coffee. Montferrat had winced a bit when the younger man dumped his cognac into it. "Especially when he discovers the interior of the spaceship melted down into slag when the tnuctipun bastard died."

"The hull alone is a formidable secret; he'll have the satisfaction of putting that in the archives," Montferrat said judiciously. "You know, I could almost pity him."

That brought the heads around, even Spots's. "Why?" Harold demanded, pulling himself out of reverie.

"Because he's so able, and so determined—and his cause is doomed to *inevitable* defeat," Montferrat said. At their blank looks, he waved his cigarillo at the stars.

"*Look* at them, my friends. We can count them, but we cannot really know how many. The number is too huge for our minds to grasp! With the outsider's gift of the hyperdrive, we have access to them all—and the kzinti will too, in their turn, you cannot keep a law of nature secret forever, despite what the ARM thinks."

His voice deepened. "The universe is too *big* to understand; vastly too big to control even by the most subtle and powerful means, even this little corner of it we call Known Space. There is an age of exploration coming—as it was in the Renaissance, or the twenty-first century. Nothing can stop it. Nothing can stop what we—all the sentient species—will do, and venture, and become. *That* is why I pity Buford Early—and why I never despair of our cause, no matter how bleak the situation looks. Tactically we may lose, but strategically, we *cannot*."

Jonah looked thoughtful, and Harold grinned across his basset-hound face. Tyra Nordbo laughed, and leaned forward to put a hand on his arm. The jewels in her tiara glistened amid the artfully-arranged piles of blond hair, and the shimmering silk of her gown clung.

"Thank you for everything," she said.

"Nonsense," he said, watching Jonah's gaze on her, warm and fond. *Bless you, my children*, he thought sardonically. *And if I wasn't a middle-aged eighty and didn't have commitments elsewhere, you wouldn't have a chance, Jonah the Hero.*

"The *stars*," she said. "For both of us."

"Perhaps," Montferrat said. "Someday."

"Someday."

Jonah laughed. "Myself, after the past couple of years, I'm not so sure I'll ever want to leave the confines of Greater Munchen again."

Tyra laughed, but Montferrat had a suspicion the Sol-Belter might mean what he said; he sounded very tired, at a level below the physical.

"May," Jonah added, standing and extending his crooked arm, "I show you the gardens, Fra Nordbo?"

"I would be delighted, sir," she said.

Montferrat watched them go. "A satisfactory conclusion, all things considered," he said. "Very satisfactory indeed."

EPILOGUE:

Harold's Terran Bar was far too noisy and crowded and smelled of tobacco smoke. Spots-Son of Chotrz-Shaa still felt it was appropriate, in memory of his brother. He had taken the same booth for the evening, and the remains of a grouper lay clean-picked on his plate. Glen Rorksbergen and Jersey mingled in yellow and amber delight in a saucer, beside his belt computer.

It will take many years to decode that download, he thought. There had been far more in the tnuctipun spaceship's system than the mere fifty terabytes his belt model could hold, as well. Piecing together the operating code with nothing but fragmentary hints and sheer logic would be a torment.

Still, he had time.

To you, my brother, he thought silently, dipping his muzzle towards the drink. *I dedicate the hunt.*

THE END

PRAISE FOR
LOIS MCMASTER BUJOLD

What the critics say:

The Warrior's Apprentice: "Now here's a fun romp through the spaceways—not so much a space opera as space ballet.... it has all the 'right stuff.' A lot of thought and thoughtfulness stand behind the all-too-human characters. Enjoy this one, and look forward to the next." —Dean Lambe, *SF Reviews*

"The pace is breathless, the characterization thoughtful and emotionally powerful, and the author's narrative technique and command of language compelling. Highly recommended." —*Booklist*

Brothers in Arms: "... she gives it a geniune depth of character, while reveling in the wild turnings of her tale. ... Bujold is as audacious as her favorite hero, and as brilliantly (if sneakily) successful." —*Locus*

"Miles Vorkosigan is such a great character that I'll read anything Lois wants to write about him. ... a book to re-read on cold rainy days." —Robert Coulson, *Comics Buyer's Guide*

Borders of Infinity: "Bujold's series hero Miles Vorkosigan may be a lord by birth and an admiral by rank, but a bone disease that has left him hobbled and in frequent pain has sensitized him to the suffering of outcasts in his very hierarchical era.... Playing off Miles's reserve and cleverness, Bujold draws outrageous and outlandish foils to color her high-minded adventures." —*Publishers Weekly*

Falling Free: "In *Falling Free* Lois McMaster Bujold has written her fourth straight superb novel.... How to break down a talent like Bujold's into analyzable components? Best not to try. Best to say 'Read, or you will be missing something extraordinary.'" —Roland Green, *Chicago Sun-Times*

The Vor Game: "The chronicles of Miles Vorkosigan are far too witty to be literary junk food, but they rouse the kind of craving that makes popcorn magically vanish during a double feature." —Faren Miller, *Locus*

MORE PRAISE FOR
LOIS MCMASTER BUJOLD

What the readers say:

"My copy of *Shards of Honor* is falling apart I've reread it so often.... I'll read whatever you write. You've certainly proved yourself a grand storyteller."
—Liesl Kolbe, Colorado Springs, CO

"I experience the stories of Miles Vorkosigan as almost viscerally uplifting.... But certainly, even the weightiest theme would have less impact than a cinder on snow were it not for a rousing good story, and good story-telling with it. This is the second thing I want to thank you for.... I suppose if you boiled down all I've said to its simplest expression, it would be that I immensely enjoy and admire your work. I submit that, as literature, your work raises the overall level of the science fiction genre, and spiritually, your work cannot avoid positively influencing all who read it."
—Glen Stonebraker, Gaithersburg, MD

" 'The Mountains of Mourning' [in *Borders of Infinity*] was one of the best-crafted, and simply best, works I'd ever read. When I finished it, I immediately turned back to the beginning and read it again, and I can't remember the last time I did that."
—Betsy Bizot, Lisle, IL

"I can only hope that you will continue to write, so that I can continue to read (and of course buy) your books, for they make me laugh and cry and think ... rare indeed."
—Steven Knott, Major, USAF

DAVID WEBER

Honor Harrington (cont.):

Field of Dishonor

Honor goes home to Manticore—and fights for her life on a battlefield she never trained for, in a private war that offers just two choices: death—or a "victory" that can end only in dishonor and the loss of all she loves....

Other novels by DAVID WEBER:

Mutineers' Moon

"...a good story...reminds me of 1950s Heinlein..."
—*BMP Bulletin*

The Armageddon Inheritance

Sequel to *Mutineers' Moon*.

Path of the Fury

"Excellent...a thinking person's Terminator."
—*Kliatt*

Oath of Swords

An epic fantasy.

with STEVE WHITE:

Insurrection
Crusade

Novels set in the world of the Starfire ™ game system.

And don't miss Steve White's solo novels,
The Disinherited and Legacy!

continued